CW00547752

THE HAMPSTEAD POISONINGS

A Mycroft Holmes adventure

THE
HAMPSTEAD
POISONINGS
A Mycroft Holmes Adventure

Glen Petrie

IAN HENRY PUBLICATIONS
PLAYERS PRESS

© Glen Petrie, 1995

ISBN 0 86025 285 X (U.K.)

Library of Congress Cataloging-in-Publication Data

Petrie, Glen.
    The Hampstead poisonings / by Glen Petrie.
    224 p. 22 cm.
    ISBN 0-88734-915-3
    I. Title.
PR6066.E755H28 1995
823'.914--dc20

Printed by
Redwood Books
Kennet House, Kennet Way, Trowbridge, Wiltshire BA14 8RN
for
Ian Henry Publications, Ltd.
20 Park Drive, Romford, Essex RM1 4LH

CHAPTER ONE

"Ah, my dear Mycroft! I do believe Billy has found you a hansom at last." Sherlock Holmes rose from the sofa, went across to the window-bay and, peering round the edge of the blind, looked down at the street below. "Hallo! Unless I am much mistaken, I am about to receive a second visitor."

"At this hour!" Mycroft exclaimed.

He was appalled by the thought of the effect on one's chances of a night's sleep caused by the mental stimulation aroused by a visitor calling after eight o'clock.

For his own part, he would not have disrupted his own invariable evening routine by undertaking the rigours of a journey from Pall Mall to 221B Baker Street, had he not been requested to do so by Sir James Swarthmoor, the Cabinet Secretary. Sir James had asked him to convey the Prime Minister's gratitude to Sherlock for the discreet way in which he had resolved the painful matter of the Dundas Separation Case.

Sherlock beckoned to Mycroft to join him in the window-bay. Mycroft dragged himself out of the embrace of his brother's Holland armchair, and stumbled across to the window. The weight of his footfall caused the gasogene on the table in the centre of the room to rattle inside its wire mesh frame.

"It would seem you attract people whose habits are as intemperate as your own," he remarked, stepping over the Stradivarius which lay, with its E string snapped, on the rug by the sofa.

Sherlock stepped aside to allow him to look down into the street. Below, there was the stationary hansom, its lights dimly illuminating a narrow area of pavement through drifting layers of fog. Mrs Hudson's bootboy, Billy, had left the cabby up in his seat, and was running down the area steps.

Under the lamp nearby, stood a tall, slender young man. His top-coat was draped over his shoulders, his scarf hung loose like a stole, and his face, as good-looking and aquiline as Sherlock's own, was tilted upwards in the direction of the other first-floor front window.

Sherlock examined Mycroft's face. "He is unsure whether or not to ring the bell," he observed. "He judges from the presence of the stationary cab that I may already have a visitor...You will, my dear Mycroft, have perceived that he is a lawyer only recently called to the bar. He is wearing recently-tailored *sub-fusc,* and his neck-tie is freshly tied. Now, who but a member of the bar, if he did not bathe and put on fresh clothes for the evening, would nonetheless change his neckwear?"

Mycroft grunted. He let the blind fall back into place. "It is a relief to me, my dear boy," he said, "to find that your over-indulgence in tobacco and your taste for modern German music of the passionate, neurasthenic sort, have not entirely blunted your powers of observation."

He turned, took up a pair of opera glasses from where they stood on the table, and handed them to Sherlock. "Though you do not appear to have noticed that our young friend has, also recently, married - and not entirely happily, I would suggest. Look carefully, my dear Sherlock." He pointed downwards with one plump finger. Sherlock raised the glasses to his eyes.

"There is a protuberance inside the stall of his glove on the third finger of his left hand," said Sherlock. "It is, however, a signet ring, not a wedding band. He does not wish to follow the Papist custom of wearing a wedding band for the remainder of his days. On the other hand, he is newly enough arrived at the honourable estate of matrimony to wish to advertise the fact..." He paused, lowering the glasses.

"Capital!" said Mycroft. "So far," he added.

"He has made his way on foot?" Sherlock sounded a questioning note. "But - since he is carrying neither wig-case nor bag - he has come from his own hearthside..."

Mycroft grunted encouragement.

"...which," Sherlock continued, "from the state of his dress one may deduce cannot be far from here. The uppers of his boots are mired, yet the pavements hereabouts are as dry as the fog permits. They were mired, therefore, before he set out from home this evening. A truly devoted young wife would never permit her new husband to go out to pay an evening call in mired boots."

He left the window and went across to the door.

"...Ah! Come in, Billy!"

"Sorry for bein' so long, Mr Holmes, sir," the boy said to Mycroft, as he entered. "Had to go all round by North Audley Street 'fore I found a cab!"

Mycroft dredged a sixpence from his fob pocket and spun it across to Billy who caught it neatly.

"Now go down and answer the front-door bell," Sherlock ordered him. "And save the excellent Mrs Hudson a journey."

"What front-door bell?" Billy protested. The doorbell sounded from the depths of the kitchen. Billy gazed at Sherlock in wonder.

"Go! Go!" Sherlock waved his hand impatiently. "Or Mrs Hudson will be there before you."

He slumped back onto the sofa and crossed his legs.

"The poor fellow comes on a fool's errand, of course," he remarked. "The Lauriston Gardens business is likely to occupy me to the exclusion of all else for at least the next week or two. If he had only come a fortnight ago, it would have been an entirely different matter. I was in a torment of ennui; swear I would have welcomed the opportunity to assist a dowager countess find her lost lap-dog. As it was..." He glanced defiantly at his brother. "...a seven-percent solution was the only remedy!"

Mycroft knew when he was being deliberately provoked. He ignored the challenge by remarking, "You omitted, my dear Sherlock, to point out that our visitor is a member of the Middle Temple - an oversight, I am sure."

"Forgive me, but am I known to one of you two gentlemen?" the newcomer asked, hesitating in the doorway.

"By no means, my dear sir," Sherlock replied. "Neither by repute nor any other way. Pray do come into the warmth."

He waved the young man in without himself rising from the sofa. "I am Sherlock Holmes. This is my brother, Mycroft Holmes. We deduced from your appearance that you have been called to the bar. It is my brother's whim that you should also be a member of the Middle Temple."

"I am indeed a member of Mr Forrest Fulton's chambers in the Middle Temple, sir," the young man addressed himself to Mycroft. "My name is Marshall Hall, sir - Edward Marshall Hall."

"Your boots give you away, sir," said Mycroft with a perfunctory wave of a flipper-like hand.

Marshall Hall glanced down at the articles mentioned.

Mycroft, having completed his mission, was anxious to return to the warmth and security of his own rooms at 73A Pall Mall, particularly since the fog was closing in. He was about to take his leave when Sherlock called to Billy on the landing, "Billy! Be so good as to invite Mr Mycroft's jarvey to get down and wait in the kitchen. I'm sure Mrs Hudson will have no objection to his taking a jug of beer and some bread and cheese."

"Very good, sir!" Billy called, and thumped down the stairs.

The comfortable vision of a light supper by his own fireside, consisting of buttered muffins and a lightly poached egg followed by a pot of tea and several slices of Mrs Turner's rich fruit cake, began to drift further and further from Mycroft's reach, like a ship sailing from the quay. He sighed heavily and subsided with a heavy creaking into Sherlock's cane armchair beside the copper coal-scuttle in the hearth and the Persian slipper tobacco-pouch hanging on the wall.

"The welts of your boots are scuffed, d'you see?" he explained 'o the increasingly bewildered Marshall Hall. "And there are drops of dried mud on the uppers. They indicate that you have trodden heavily for a man so lightly built - probably down steps on which water has gathered under gravel. The quickest way from the Middle Temple to the new Law Courts or the Old Bailey is down a flight of gravelled steps facing the river, is it not?"

"Remarkable!" exclaimed Marshall Hall.

"Not in the least," Sherlock interposed dismissively. "Boots are the greatest betrayers in the world - they tell all. Do sit down by the fire, Mr Marshall Hall, so far as my brother will permit you."

Marshall Hall, somewhat diffidently, took one of the upright chairs at the table.

"I hope you will forgive me intruding on you at this hour," he said. "But I am much vexed in my mind. It is a matter of some delicacy, and I did not know to whom I should turn..."

"Our discretion is a matter on which you may make yourself entirely comfortable," Sherlock told him. "As a lawyer, you will know that it is the essence of any professional consultancy. My brother, here, is a strongbox - a depository of the nation's secrets."

"Thank you, gentlemen," said Marshall Hall.

He sighed, and his face sank into a solemn, handsome melancholy.

"Yesterday morning, against my better judgement, I accepted a brief - a brief to defend a lady against a charge of murder...

Sherlock lay back, the back of his head Sunk into the cushions, his eyes fixed staring up at the tobacco-stained ceiling.

"Mr Holmes?" Marshall Hall asked anxiously, seeking permission to continue.

"Pray do go on," Sherlock reassured him.

"The fee was marked at fifty-five guineas," Marshall Hall went on. "I need hardly point out to you that it is an extraordinarily generous remuneration for one called to the bar as recently as myself."

"Who is to lead you in the defence?" asked Sherlock.

"I am to lead," Marshall Hall replied.

If Sherlock was surprised at this information, he did not reveal it.

"Have you been informed who is to prosecute?" he asked. "Sir Richard Webster, by any chance?"

"Yes, Mr Holmes." The young man was taken by surprise.

"Poison is the lethal weapon normally employed by ladies, Sherlock explained. "And it is the practice for the Attorney General to prosecute in cases of poisoning... I presume the victim was your client's husband. Mycroft, my dear chap..." He had raised his head to call to Mycroft who was showing every sign of settling down to doze in front of the blazing fire. "...poison is the routine instrument by which ladies of the middle classes free themselves from the restrictions and more distasteful obligations of a wretched marriage. Ask any medical practitioner; the estimable Dr Watson will tell you there have been at least twenty cases in which he has suppressed his suspicions in signing a death-certificate, so that some unfortunate female who has endured years of servitude and humiliation at the hands of a brute of a husband my enjoy a new-found liberty."

"It is not the case in this instance," said Marshall Hall. "The prosecution will present it as *un crime passionel*, I'm afraid. The lady is accused of procuring the death by poison of the gentleman who employed her as his cook-housekeeper..."

"And his mistress, I presume," Sherlock remarked.

"I'm afraid so," Marshall Hall agreed.

"There's no avoiding the bedroom in these cases," sighed Sherlock, closing his eyes. After a moment's pause, he asked suddenly. "Who are the lady's instructing solicitors? The gentlemen who are offering you such generous terms to defend a domestic servant?"

"It is the oddest thing," Marshall Hall explained. "Their clerk, a fellow by the name of Josiah Hartz, came to me in the robing room at the Bailey, last night. The courts had risen; to all intents and purposes we were alone. It was most irregular. He said that his employers were one of the oldest and most respected law firms in Lincoln's Inn Fields. Yet neither myself, the fellows in chambers, nor our own clerk, have any recollection of them..."

"Their names, Mr Marshall Hall?" Sherlock gently chided him.

"Marcus, Bullfinger, Stote, and Marcus," Marshall Hall replied.

"The man, Hartz, said that one of the senior partners, Mr Augustine Bullfinger, had been present when I was appearing before Mr Justice Stonor at Marylebone, on behalf of the plaintiff in *Wallaby versus Westminster City Corporation.* He told me that Mr Augustine Bullfinger had 'liked the cut of my jib'..." He broke off.

"I have to admit that the name Bullfinger means nothing to me," said Sherlock. He glanced over the back of the sofa. "You appear, however," he continued. "to have aroused the interest of my brother."

In an attempt to pass the time agreeably, Mycroft had closed his eyes and imagined himself sunk deep into the seclusion of his deep, high-winged, porter's chair in the holy calm and silence of the Diogenes Club's smoking-room. At the names of Marcus, Bullfinger, Stote and Marcus, he had been shot into full wakefulness. He squeezed his corpulence round between the creaking arms of Sherlock's armchair, opened the coal-scuttle which his brother used as a humidor, and extracted from it a Trichinopoly cigar. He held it under his nostrils for a moment; his face expressed his disfavour, but he knew he would find nothing better at 221B Baker Street. He removed a pair of small, folding, gold scissors from his waistcoat pocket, and snipped off the end. Gasping with the effort of shifting himself in the confined space of the chair, he said at last,

"A very fortunate day for you, so it would seem, Mr Marshall Hall!" Stooping as far as his stomach permitted, he helped himself to the coal-tongs and lit his cigar from a live coal. Tossing the coal back into the fire, he settled back once more and drew deeply on his cigar several times. "One might go so far as to say, a *most* fortunate day for a young advocate like yourself - with his way to make. Marcus, Bullfinger, Stote and Marcus are indeed a very old-established firm. They advise and act on behalf of a small handful of clients; but those clients are drawn from amongst the highest personages in the land - the very highest, my dear sir..." He paused and drew on his cigar once more. "You would be entirely justified in asking yourself, who is there of significance who is taking an interest in the defence of your cook-housekeeper client - and why?"

Sherlock uttered a brief, sharp laugh. "My brother invariably favours the inductive approach in solving a conundrum," he said. "Raise a hypothesis and mould the facts to suit it. I daresay it suits the world of Government and Diplomacy. I favour the deductive method - that is, proceeding from the raw data. Therefore, the facts contained in your brief if you please, my dear fellow; the dry facts."

CHAPTER TWO

"My client, Mrs Diana Tuttle," Marshall Hall began, "is a twenty-eight-year-old widow. Her husband, a poor curate, died four years ago of a consumption contracted while working as a missionary among the destitutes of Limehouse and Shadwell. Her husband left her penniless. The Reverend Mr Tuttle had been in Orders only a little longer than they had been married. The trustees of the Clergy Widows and Orphans Benevolent Society, to whom she applied for assistance, took the view that she had to pay the penalty for her husband having taken her to wife before he was in a position properly to provide for her.

"However, the chairman of the Limehouse Mission which had employed Mr Tuttle - Dr. Thomas Simkins, Rector of Christchurch, Hampstead - took a more liberal view. Through his good offices, Mrs Tuttle obtained employment in his parish - indeed, scarcely more than a stone's throw from the church - as cook housekeeper in the home of Captain Septimus Meadowthorpe, lately of the Second Lancers..."

"Captain Meadowthorpe, I take it, being the victim of the alleged poisoning," said Sherlock.

"Quite so," Marshall Hall agreed.

Sherlock had pressed together the tips of his forefingers which he now pointed at the young barrister. "Do you know, Mr Marshall Hall? It is just such a female as your client who most resents finding herself in the position of a servant. A duchess will empty a bucket of slops without giving the matter a moment's thought. A governess would prefer to throw herself into the river. I make this point only because it might occur to the jury! But pray do continue. This Captain Meadowthorpe, lately of the Second Lancers: was he a man of substance?"

Substantial enough to keep his carriage," Marshall Hall replied. "His house, I am informed, is one of the old two-storey Queen Anne dwellings up on Squire's Mount, with a view over Hampstead Heath. Besides Mrs Tuttle, the establishment consisted of a house-parlourmaid, a kitchenmaid, and a coachman-gardener. There were others, of course, who came by the day.

"Captain Meadowthorpe, I must tell you, was one of the handful of survivors of the massacre of Lord Chelmsford's column by the Zulus at Isandhlwana; he managed to find his way to Rorke's Drift, and took part in the famous action there. Because of the wounds he sustained, he was compelled to retire from active service. It was then he married and established a home..."

"Forgive my interrupting once again," said Sherlock. "As I recall, those officers and senior non-commissioned officers who survived the action at Rorke's Drift were awarded the Victoria Cross by Her Majesty. I do not recall a Meadowthorpe among their number."

"That is more than I know, Mr Holmes," replied Marshall Hall. Sherlock glanced across to Mycroft who returned the glance.

"Captain Meadowthorpe's marriage was of short duration," Marshall Hall continued. "I believe the couple had been together six months or so when the Captain retained Mrs Tuttle's services. Shortly after she had settled into her new situation, Captain and Mrs Meadowthorpe travelled on holiday, to Italy. In Italy - in the city of Florence to be exact - Mrs Meadowthorpe, overcome by the noonday heat, insisted on drinking water from a public fountain. As a result, she contracted a slow fever which she was unable entirely to shake off. When it had diminished somewhat, the Captain brought her home. But she never entirely recovered; a few weeks later the fever returned with all its virulence, and the poor young lady passed away."

"Florence," asked Sherlock. "You are certain that the public fountain from which the unfortunate young lady drank was in Florence?"

"So I have been informed," Marshall Hall confirmed.

Sherlock raised his eyebrows slightly in Mycroft's direction. Mycroft returned an almost imperceptible nod.

"Continue, if you please, Mr Marshall Hall," said Sherlock.

Marshall Hall cleared his throat. "Some months after the death of his wife," he went on, "Captain Meadowthorpe and my client entered into a relationship... of an intimate nature..."

Sherlock took advantage of the young man's natural reticence to interrupt yet again. "Which lasted, of course, until the brave Captain found a more suitable young woman for a lifetime's companionship?"

"That is exactly what seems to have occurred, Mr Holmes," Marshall Hall told him.

"You see, Mycroft?" Sherlock called delightedly over the scroll back of the sofa. "And who was this new candidate for the Captain's affections, Mr Marshall Hall?"

"She is a lady closely related to Captain Meadowthorpe's deceased wife. Indeed, I am led to believe they had been regarded as sisters, even though they were not related by blood," Marshall Hall replied. "The Captain entered into an engagement to marry the daughter of the late Mrs Meadowthorpe's legal guardian and, prior to her marriage, trustee to her property.

Marshall Hall did not wait for permission before pressing on with his narrative: "Only a week or two after this engagement had been announced, Captain Meadowthorpe fell ill of a wasting sickness. For the following five or six weeks he suffered irregular bouts of nausea, vomiting and fever. Late one evening, he was visited by one of these attacks - a more severe attack than usual. He begged Mrs Tuttle to go in person to fetch his regular medical adviser, a Dr John Bickleigh of Downshire Hill, below Hampstead. The quickest way from the house on Squire's Mount to Dr Bickleigh's home is, it would appear, to take a footpath across the Lower Heath. It is no great distance: a ten minute walk, perhaps a quarter of an hour when encumbered by a woman's skirts; but a lonely one, according to my client, through scrub and woodland, well away from any street lighting.

"My client says that when she was hurrying down the footpath, she was waylaid by a pair of ruffians of the labouring sort. They did her no great physical injury, merely snatched at her waist and tried to force her to grant them a kiss. By the time she returned to Squire's Mount with Dr Bickleigh," Marshall Hall went on, "Captain Meadowthorpe was a dying man. To my client's utter astonishment, the Captain, who had not spoken a harsh word to her previously, pointed his hand at her and accused her of having poisoned him. She says she can only suppose that he had fallen into a delirium as a result of her involuntary delay in fetching the doctor."

"Will anybody support the assertion that there had never been a harsh word between Meadowthorpe and your client?" asked Sherlock.

"Mrs Tuttle has said that it is her belief the servants will testify to that effect," Marshall Hall replied.

Sherlock shook his head slightly. "It would only demonstrate the proper reticence of two well bred gentlefolk when within the hearing of members of the lower orders," he said.

"I suppose you are right, sir," Marshall Hall told him with a hint of embarrassment.

"Of course I"m right!" replied Sherlock. He laughed abruptly. "I suppose that the medical man..."

"Dr Bickleigh," Marshall Hall reminded him.

"Quite so... Withheld the death certificate as a result of this accusation against your client?"

"Yes sir. Dr Bickleigh had the deceased's body removed immediately to the North London Hospital for Consumptive Diseases at Mount Vernon. He performed an autopsy there in the presence of two assistant registrars. That is when the evidence was discovered of Captain Meadowthorpe having died from arsenical poisoning. Dr Bickleigh informed the local constabulary. A search of Captain Meadowthorpe's residence was undertaken the same night... No warrant was required," he added. "My client was happy to assist the police in every way she could."

He paused before continuing. "A medicine bottle was discovered in my client's room; it contained a compound of arsenic suspended in chloral..."

He paused again. Sherlock waited.

"It had been hidden," Marshall Hall said, "behind the clock on the mantlepiece."

"Behind the clock on the mantlepiece," Sherlock echoed. His narrow lips twisted into a sardonic smile.

"My client was formally charged with procuring Captain Meadowthorpe's death by poison, and cautioned." Marshall Hall sighed. "She is now held in Millbank Prison awaiting her appearance before the next Middlesex Sessions."

Sherlock drew in breath sharply, then sighed. "We may take it that the gravamen of the case for the Crown will be the suggestion that the gallant Captain's intimacy with your client was no more than an anodyne resorted to in order to ease the pain of his recent bereavement," he declared. "Whereas, it will be proposed your client was moved either by mercenary considerations - her perceived need of a wealthy protector - or, worse still from the jury's point of view, by sensual passions incompatible with any proper sense of female decency."

"There are also the terms of the settlement which was to have accompanied Captain Meadowthorpe's betrothal," said Marshall Hall. "As well as the usual clause that, upon signature, in the case of his decease, his bride and their issue should be his beneficiaries, there was a clause insisting on the dismissal of my client from his service as soon as was practicable."

"A very natural stipulation on the part of the future bride's parent," Sherlock commented.

"It was, according to my client, entirely unnecessary," said Marshall Hall. "She had given Captain Meadowthorpe her notice as soon as she had heard of his intention to wed Miss Manyon..."

"Miss Manyon, you say?" asked Mycroft in a sudden, high pitched voice. "Also of Hampstead?"

"Yes," Marshall Hall started from his seat. He had long since been persuaded of Mycroft's lack of interest in the case. "Of the Vale of Health, Hampstead Heath."

"The young woman is not, by any chance, related to Mr Villiers Manyon?" Mycroft asked.

"Why yes, sir," he replied. "The gentleman is her father."

"The proprietor of the Lakeside Spa Hotel and Sporting Rooms in the Vale of Health, Hampstead?"

"So I believe," Marshall Hall agreed.

"Villiers Manyon is no gentleman!" Mycroft shook his head till his jowls rolled. "To say he is an adventurer would be an offence against truth. He is a proprietor of a gambling-hell; a brothel keeper, sir, albeit of the most discreet and, alas, fashionable kind." He turned to Sherlock. "Manyon ran the establishment in North Street known as the Sheol Sporting Club, you'll recall, under the very shadow of the Palace of Westminster. He closed it and removed to Hampstead when the editor of the *Pall Mall Gazette* threatened to expose it as a market in female flesh. Hampstead is outside the jurisdiction of the Westminster watch-committee but not so distant as to inconvenience Manyon's wealthy and noble patrons."

Sherlock remained motionless for a short time, his finger against his lips as if enjoining silence.

"Mr Marshall Hall," he said suddenly. "You have no reason to regard your client as a complete fool - except, perhaps, in her choice of protector?"

"By no means," Marshall Hall replied.

"You would not suppose her to be so foolish, having murdered her lover, as to hide the poison bottle behind a clock on her mantle-piece?" asked Sherlock. "And to leave it there after her lover's medical adviser had taken away the corpse in order to perform an autopsy? She had all the time in the world to throw it away, to bury it in the garden, or even, when she knew the police to have been sent for, simply to have concealed it inside her petticoats."

He shook his head and pointed his finger at Marshall Hall. "When your client returned with the doctor... where was the Captain? On his bed? On the sofa? On the floor? Where?"

"I believe Dr Bickleigh and my client found him lying at the foot of the back stairs," replied Marshall Hall. "He had suffered a violent attack while trying to summon assistance from the servants."

"The backstairs lead to the servants' quarters?" asked Sherlock.

"Upstairs to the housekeeper's room and maids' bedroom, and downstairs to the back kitchen quarters, I presume," Marshall Hall replied.

"You presume?" Sherlock snapped. "You did not think to apprise yourself of such details?"

"No, sir," Marshall Hall replied. "I took them to be matters for the police."

"For the police! Oh, my dear young fellow!" Sherlock laughed. "The police are your adversaries - they are interested solely in obtaining a conviction!... This violent attack, you mentioned. May we assume it had all the properties peculiar to arsenical poisoning? I mean, of course, *inter alia*, paroxysms of vomiting?"

"Mrs Tuttle has informed me that Captain Meadowthorpe had been vomiting," replied Marshall Hall.

"And did the Hampstead constabulary examine the servants' staircase for traces of vomit?" Sherlock asked. "Either up toward the housekeeper's and servants' rooms...?"

He pointed his finger toward the ceiling. "Or..." swivelling his finger to point at the carpet, "... down to the kitchen quarters?"

"Not so as I have been informed," Marshall Hall replied.

Sherlock nodded. "If they have not done so," he said, "it is most remiss of them - a point which you might use to advantage."

He paused again for a moment's reflection. "Do you suppose," he asked, "there is anybody who might support your client's statement that she gave notice of her intention to leave Captain Meadowthorpe's employ as soon as she heard of his intended alliance with this Miss Manyon?"

"Mrs Tuttle did say that she believed the housemaid was outside the door..."

"As is the way of housemaids," Sherlock interrupted.

Mycroft took his cigar from his lips. "My dear Sherlock!" he exclaimed, billowing blue cigar smoke. "Sir Richard Webster, or any Treasury junior, if it comes to that, will make nonsense of testimony of that sort, given by an ignorant young servant girl..."

"Such a girl's evidence may be of value to the accused's defence even if it doesn't stand up in court," replied Sherlock. "It may be the piece of the puzzle which enables one to read the whole picture."

He drew himself to his feet, picked up his pipe from the table and rolled its long yellowed stem in his fingers. "Mr Marshall Hall," he said, "you came here because you believed that you had taken on a losing case. The possibility had occurred to you that the instructing solicitors had come to you rather than to a more eminent member of the bar precisely because they take it to be a losing case..."

He closed one eye and stared with the other into the empty bowl of the pipe. "You are a young man at the beginning of his career. You have your name to make and a wife to support. Whether you win or lose, the fact that you are to defend a handsome young woman against a prosecution led by the Attorney General will ensure that your name is reported in all the popular newspapers. Unfortunately, however, since meeting your client and speaking with her, you have become convinced of her innocence..." .

"Yes, sir," Marshall Hall nodded.

Sherlock dredged in the bowl of the pipe with his little finger, and extracted a fragment of dottle which he let fall on the carpet. He paused before saying, "I regret, Mr Marshall Hall that I cannot be of assistance to you, the more so because of the points of considerable interest in the case: the extraordinary wish of an officer and gentleman, for instance, a hero of Isandhlwana and Rorke's Drift to ally himself not once but twice to the family of a moral degenerate. I am sorry, my dear sir. Two days ago, it would have been another matter, but the worthy Chief Inspector Gregson has sought my assistance in a case which also has features of remarkable interest. I make it a point never to engage in two cases simultaneously."

He leant over the back of Mycroft's chair, and filled his pipe with tobacco from the Persian slipper which hung under the mantlepiece.

"I trust I have suggested to you certain lines of inquiry which you might profitably pursue," he added.

Marshall Hall appeared stunned by these sudden tokens of dismissal. Mycroft, all too well acquainted with his brother's abrupt manner, heaved himself out of the armchair. He pulled his waistcoat down over the roundness of his stomach and adjusted his watch-chain.

"I have a cab waiting outside," he told Marshall Hall. "I am returning to Pall Mall. I would be glad of your company if you should be travelling in that direction."

"It is most kind of you, sir," Marshall Hall told him. "I'm going only as far as Upper Seymour Street. It is scarcely worth your trouble..."

Mycroft glanced out of the window. "The fog is closing in," he said. "My driver will have to procure the services of a linkman when we reach Portman Square. You may get down there conveniently... would you do me the favour of waiting downstairs for a moment, while I exchange a few words with my brother?"

"Of course." Marshall Hall picked up his coat and put it on.

When he had left, Mycroft put on his own coat, dragging it up over his shoulders. "Your intemperate appetite for music of the frenetic sort..." he thrust his stick in the direction of the violin lying on the floor, "...is sapping your intellect."

Sherlock put his pipe down on the mantlepiece. He went over and picked up the violin.

"Before you came this evening," he remarked, glancing about for the bow. "I was taking advantage of Watson's absence to master Paganini's *Capriccio No. 17 in E flat*. It is regarded by masters of the instrument to be one of the most taxing pieces in the repertoire. Not one to be undertaken by somebody whose intellect or delicacy of mind is in decay. Do you wish me to play it to you?"

"Marcus, Bullfinger, Stote and Marcus rarely concern themselves with criminal cases," observed Mycroft, ignoring the offer of a recital, "unless they are of the matrimonial sort - and then only if people of the highest rank or distinction are involved. They shun publicity precisely because they are legal advisers to men of the highest eminence. You will recall my telling you of the potential scandal over a certain Royal personage's relationship with an actress which threatened to become public knowledge some twenty years ago. It was the firm of Marcus, Bullfinger, Stote and Marcus who saw to it that the affair was consigned to oblivion and the actress to the farthest shores of the United States of America. There was the case of the Bishop of Armagh and the corporal-major of the Blues; Marcus, Bullfinger, Stote and Marcus, acting on instructions from Lambeth Palace, nipped that in the bud before anybody from the newspapers heard a word about it. There was the Mordaunt Divorce Case in which Sir Charles Mordaunt threatened to cite the Prince of Wales as co-respondent; it was Marcus, Bullfinger, Stote and Marcus who, before the matter went before the court, arranged for Lady Mordaunt to be committed to a lunatic asylum on the signatures of two of the most reputable medical men in the land. There was the case of Signor Ricoletti, Chancellor at the Royal Italian Legation, which you resolved at my request; your fee was paid by the firm of

Marcus, Bullfinger, Stote and Marcus. And if you care to examine the cheque with regard to the Dundas Separation Case which I presented to you earlier this evening, I think you will find that the signature representing the payees is that of Mordecai Stote.

"How do you suppose such a firm comes to involve itself in a common case of domestic poisoning?" asked Mycroft. "And why should it retain a young, inexperienced member of the bar to plead?"

"You would hardly expect me, my dear Mycroft, to inform our young friend that he had been retained in order to let his client go hang, eh?" asked Sherlock.

He returned to the sofa, reclined on it once more, and proceeded to obscure the room with the noxious blue fug from his pipe.

"Such is the situation, of course," he added. "One may assume that Marcus, Bullfinger *et cetera* have been retained by men of some position who wish to prevent the public probing into Villiers Manyon's part in this affair which an experienced defender and a protracted trial might provoke... I'm deuced sorry Gregson got to me first - I am indeed! It may well prove to be the prettiest little case imaginable, make no mistake about it!"

Mycroft picked up his gloves and stick. "That is precisely why I'm of a mind to assist young Marshall Hall myself," he announced.

Sherlock looked at him in astonishment. Then he burst out laughing. "My dear old chap!" he exclaimed. "Stay in your own element, I beg you. The Chancelleries of the Great Powers are your arena. You have no insight into the criminal psyche!"

"I daresay it differs little from that of those we please to call statesmen," Mycroft replied coldly. "Besides, I have no intention of standing idly by while a mockery is made of our English Justice!"

He planted his hat on his head and tapped it in place with the silver knob of his stick.

CHAPTER THREE

Even as Mycroft plumped down in the waiting hansom cab, forcing his young companion to twist against the cracked leather side of the vehicle to make way for him, he had begun to have misgivings. His days followed the strictest regimen. He was aware that his brain was regarded by Her Majesty's Government - whether of the Liberal or Conservative persuasion - to be of inestimable value. It was his patriotic duty, therefore, to ensure that he followed a rule of life no less strict than that of a religious, in order that his intellect remained unclouded by emotional indulgence, and protected from unnecessary wear and tear. Rarely did he permit himself a temporary lapse from this rule, and then only at the urgent behest of his friend and immediate superior, Sir James Alexander, the Cabinet Secretary. There had been the Dorking Gap Affair, for instance; there had been the episode in south Purbeck, four or five years ago; there had been the sorry business regarding the Sultana of Ruwenora which had necessitated him voyaging to the Pacific, the memory of which still caused him to shudder; and there had been his crowning triumph, his intervention in the unfortunate and very foolish affair in Florence of the Countess Kilgarden and the Papal Nuncio to the Court of Savoy which, had it ever been allowed to become public knowledge, would certainly have destroyed Anglo-Italian relations at a particularly delicate moment in European diplomacy.

But such cases had been of critical national importance; now, perhaps in a moment of wholly untypical vanity, perhaps in a moment of equally untypical Quixotry, he was threatening to disturb both his routine and his peace of mind by intervening in a case of common, domestic criminality. Why? he asked himself; whatever had possessed him to speak as he had spoken to Sherlock?

As they reached the corner of Portman Square and Seymour Street, the fog closed in around them as impenetrable and palpable as the blanket to which it was so often compared. The cab ground to a halt against the pavement. Marshall Hall managed to push himself forward out of his cramped position to open the wooden apron over their knees. He climbed out and dropped down on to the pavement; the fog wreathed around him. He raised his hat. Then, as an afterthought, he said, "Do you know, sir? The man Hartz suggested that it was you I should apply to, rather than your brother."

"Did he, by Jove!" Mycroft exclaimed. "Sounds a damn'd

impudent fellow if you ask me."

He eased himself to the centre of the seat.

"Your brother's address is well known in the Inns, of course," said Marshall Hall. "But I did not know where to apply to you. So it was a stroke of fortune for me that you should have been calling on your brother tonight, d'you see?"

He returned his hat to his head and disappeared almost immediately into the fog.

Mycroft rapped on the ceiling of the cab with the knob of his stick. The cab lurched forward. It proceeded out of Portman Square at a snail's pace. There were occasional disembodied shouts, and sounds of bronchial coughing isolated in the damp, drifting obscurity. Naphthalene flares glowed like globular jack o' lanterns, hissing and spluttering in the damp and casting strange shadows against the shifting banks of fog. After some minutes, he called up to the driver, "Do you know exactly where we are, my good fellow?"

"Not exactly, so to speak, sir," the man called down. "I think we jest a-crossed over Grosvenor Street. If I'm right, we'll be entering Berkeley Square any moment now."

"Very well," called Mycroft. "Put me down at the corner of Bruton Street, if you can."

Princess Sophie Trubetskoy, a friend of many years' standing, had her London rooms only a few yards off Berkeley Square. He had begun to think of them as a secure haven on such a night as this.

The hansom drew up against the pavement. Mycroft opened the apron once more and stepped down. "Buy yourself a good dinner, and take yourself home," he told the cabby. "It's no weather for man or beast." He reached up and gave the fellow a whole guinea piece.

"Why, God bless Your Honour!" thecabby called after him.

Mycroft set off down Bruton Street, counting the doorways as he went past. There was no need; the light from the double front door of the mansions where Princess Trubetskoy had her home shone like a welcoming beacon down the steps into the fog.

"'d evening, Mr Holmes!" the porter called from his tiny office. "Not a night to be out, eh, sir?"

"Not in the least," Mycroft called back.

He took in a supply of breath and mounted the broad, curved stairs to the first floor. It was several minutes before the Princess's old nurse answered his knock. The eiderdown-like garment she had wrapped about her, and the shawl over it, made her look like some peasant Easter egg. Her grey hair straggled loose on either side of her dumpling face.

"*Bozhe moy!*" she exclaimed angrily. She held her clenched fist to her forehead as she came up behind the footman. "*Gospodin Gholmes! Moya lyubimitsa pomolit'syet... na Blazhenya Dyeva!*" she went on, signing herself three times with the Cross.

Mycroft and the old woman had known each other for as long as he and the Princess had been friends. He ignored her scolding.

"Go to her, my dear," he told her in halting Russian. "The mist... I cannot find my way home. She is a Christian: she will not turn me away."

She gave him a look as if she were considering arguing the point. Then her face cracked into a broad smile. "You are a wicked one, *Gospodin Gholmes!*" she told him.

She shuffled away down the vestibule, her eiderdown sweeping the tiled floor behind her.

"*Sofya Sergeyevna!*" she called. "*Golubushka!*" Then, in a mock-scandalised tone, "*Shto ty podurnayesh', Golubushka! Vot Meestr Gholmes!... Bozhe moy!*"

Princess Sophie Trubetskoy emerged from a passage leading away from the vestibule. She was in her night-clothes; she had thrown on a cream silk shawl, but Mycroft could see that under it her lawn nightdress was untied at the throat so that it had slipped off her shoulders on to her arms.

"*Nyanya! Bezmolviye!*" she exclaimed to the nurse.

She came running down the vestibule, reaching out her hands to Mycroft.

"Mr Holmes! You will pay no attention to what Nanny says - no attention in the world!" she said.

She had scarcely altered since Mycroft had first met her, that warm Sunday afternoon in Pall Mall, ten years ago. Her slight form, her disorganised mass of dark brown curls, her luminously blue eyes set above high, slavic cheekbones, with the hint of a steppe dweller's Mongolian slant - he had thought her then, and he still thought her, despite the tiny crow's feet which had formed about her eyes and the corners of her firm little mouth, the loveliest woman he had ever set eyes on, the more so because she was also the least flirtatious. She smiled with genuine affection, raised herself on her toes and kissed him on the cheek, not with the formal three-fold kiss, but once, with lips slightly parted, the salute reserved for old, intimate friends.

He stepped through the door, giving hat, stick, and gloves to the footman. Then he took off his coat. Princess Sophie took his hands.

"Nanny is getting old and a little simple," she said in her slightly too precise English. "I bear with her as others must bear with us when we grow old."

"You will never grow old, Princess," he told her.

She laughed. "Be careful, my dear! Or you may wake up one morning to find yourself a courtier, and that would never do!"

She released on of his hands and led him by the other across the marble floor of the vestibule to the drawing room. At the moment he was about to follow her in, he saw emerging from the same passage from which the Princess had come, the unmistakeable figure of Cyril, her London-born black attendant, tiptoeing barefoot, the skirts of a short striped nightshirt dangling about his black knees, from his mistress's quarters. Without turning his head, as if by not doing so he would remain invisible, the fellow disappeared through the door leading to the servants' quarters.

There had been a time when Mycroft was scandalised by Princess Sophie's disregard of accepted notions of feminine virtue. But her *gout pour les hommes* did not exclude a capacity for warm and affectionate friendship of a more conventional sort, and this had made him tolerant. Moreover, there was no gainsaying that Cyril was an amusing rogue with an independent air which, for all his dusky appearance, women seemed to find attractive.

Princess Sophie drew him to the fireside. She called to the old nurse to send her maid, and to take herself off to bed.

"I was making my way home from my brother's diggings in Baker Street," Mycroft explained, "when the fog became impenetrable. I managed to find my way here, to throw myself on your mercy."

"You were quite right," Princess Sophie assured him. "Sit down close to the fire. You are damp all over, even out of your coat! You shall have tea - out of a pot, of course! - and muffins - always the muffins with butter, even if they do make you fatter and fatter."

"I should have left my brother's place two hours ago," Mycroft told her. "I was on the point of leaving, when a young lawyer arrived seeking our advice regarding a client of his who is charged with poisoning her lover."

"Oh, my dear Mr Holmes!" laughed the Princess. "I would not have thought you would be interested in such a thing!"

"Sherlock insisted I should stay."

He stopped as the Princess's maid came in, a pretty French-woman of the same age as her mistress. Princess Sophie told her to fetch a pot of Assam tea, a dish of muffins, and a saucer of butter.

"We shall toast the muffins for ourselves, at the fire," she added.

Princess Sophie settled down among the cushions on the sofa facing Mycroft across the hearth. Flamelight flickered on her face. Like a child, she tucked her small bare feet under her, and spread her nightdress about her knees.

"And is this case - of the lady poisoner - an interesting one?" she asked brightly.

"My brother and I are far from convinced that the lady is a poisoner," Mycroft replied. "But I fear there may be a conspiracy afoot to hang her with as little fuss as our judicial system affords."

"And does the Great Detective think the same?" she asked.

"My brother is presently assisting the Scotland Yard detective police on a case," said Mycroft. "I fear he hasn't time to involve him-self in this one."

"But you will - you must!" exclaimed the Princess. She herself had spent the first years of her life sharing the imprisonment of her father, Prince Sergey Trubetskoy, in Siberia. "Tell me all about it."

She drew up her knees to clasp them and to rest her chin on them like a child listening intently to a bedtime story. When he had told her as much as he had learnt of the case, she lowered her knees once more, and again tucked her feet under her.

"I have heard of your Mr Villiers Manyon," she told him. "And your wicked Lakeside Spa Hotel on Hampstead Heath. Eddy Barnaby has told me about it. Gentlemen take their *demi-mondaines* up there to play at *baccarat* and *chemin-de-fer* just like at Bad Homburg... But I expect it is extremely tedious really."

"Tedious, I daresay," Mycroft told her. "But not in the least like Bad Homburg."

"Do you mean it is... oh what is the word?"

The drawing-room door opened, and the maid, Jeannine, entered, followed by a second maid pushing a silver tea-trolley.

"In French, perhaps *louche*?..." Princess Sophie suggested. "You have brought the toasting fork, Jeannine?"

Jeannine gave a little shrug. "But of course, *Altesse*," she replied. "Shall I pour the tea, *Altesse*?"

"No, no. Mr Holmes and I shall manage very well for ourselves,"

Princess Sophie replied. Then suddenly she asked, "*Qu'est-ce que c'est en Anglais, une maison louche?*"

Before Mycroft could think of an English equivalent fit for the ears of a lady, "A 'ouse of disrepute," the maid translated, with only a tightening of the mouth to mark her further disapproval.

"I suppose," said Mycroft, "the whole business may have resulted from 'the pangs of despised love' on the widow Tuttle's part."

Princess Sophie sniffed contemptuously. "It would only need another woman to speak to her to learn whether that were so or not!" she told him.

She looked across at him. Their eyes met. "But you knew that already, didn't you, Mr Holmes?" she said with only the faintest hint of accusation.

She glanced across to the two maids. "You may go now," she dismissed them. "You will see that a fire is lit in the guest-room for Mr Holmes, and the bed warmed. Then you may retire for the night."

The maids curtsied and left.

As the door closed behind them, she went on, "You wish me to go to Millbank Prison to speak to this Mrs Tuttle?"

"It was not in my mind when I came here," Mycroft protested. "Besides, I could not ask you to do such a thing!"

"*You* would not be able to find out what you wish to know," Princess Sophie said scornfully. "You do not have a woman's apprehensions."

"There are other considerations which would make it a mistake for me to go to Millbank," Mycroft replied. "A man in my position would not be permitted to converse with her except in the presence of the instructing solicitor..."

"Which," Princess Sophie interrupted him, "if the suspicion held by you and your brother is correct, would scarcely serve the purpose?"

"Exactly so," Mycroft agreed.

Princess Sophie stared for a moment into the fire. She pursed her lips. "So you believe," she said, "and your brother suspects, that this poor lady's own lawyers want to see her hanged?"

"I would not go so far as to say that," Mycroft replied hastily. "Marcus, Bullfinger, Stote and Marcus is a firm of the highest possible reputation. If our surmise is correct, their aim would be to ensure that the matter is dealt with as expeditiously as possible, and with the minimum fuss."

"But if the price of that is Mrs Tuttle's life...?" asked the Princess.

Mycroft did not reply.

"Would it be easy for me to obtain permission to visit the unfortunate lady?" asked the Princess.

"Millbank Prison is no place for a personage of your rank and breeding to visit, Princess,"

"*O moy lyubymiyi droog!*" she laughed. "Do you think I am not familiar with such places? I?"

Mycroft nodded, indicating his mistake. She reached across the intervening space to take his hand.

"Would it be easy?" she repeated.

"If we provided you with some plausible reason, some philanthropic motive," he suggested. "Your conversation with Mrs Tuttle would be observed, of course. A prison matron or some such would remain in attendance. But she would be a person of the respectable lower orders who would regard somebody like yourself, Princess, with a decent awe. She might even regard the idea of eavesdropping on you with some abhorrence."

"Then it is settled," said the Princess, releasing his hand. "I shall visit poor Mrs Tuttle the day after tomorrow, if it can be arranged. And you shall dine here with me, the same evening, to hear how well I have succeeded."

She removed the lid from the silver dish on the trolley, picked up one of the muffins and impaled it on the toasting fork.

"Is there anything else you wish me to discover for you? she asked. "As well as whether Mrs Tuttle poisoned her lover out of jealousy?"

"My brother seemed to regard certain material details to be of significance," Mycroft told her. "Such as the place and position in which Mrs Tuttle found Captain Meadowthorpe lying when she returned from fetching the doctor."

Princess Sophie reached out the muffin to the flames in the hearth.

"Anything else?" she asked. There was a note in her voice which suggested amusement.

He refused to be put off. "I think we should know whether Mrs Tuttle's bedroom - where the poison is said to have been found - was in fact up the backstairs in the servants' quarters."

"It is the celebrated Mr Sherlock Holmes who should be

employed on this case," remarked Princess Sophie.

"I would have agreed with you entirely, only a short time ago," Mycroft replied. "But even as we sit here discussing the case..."

He broke off, a look of anxiety on his face. "You must turn the muffin, Princess, to toast the other side. One must not hold it to the flame so long on one side that the interior is toasted. It must remain soft in order that the butter may melt through the surface and soak into it..."

As she drew in the toasting-fork and did as he instructed, he continued, "More and more I find myself becoming convinced that there is something deeper here and more malevolent than the rude criminality which attracts my brother's best attention."

CHAPTER FOUR

Sophie stepped down from her carriage into a bitter west wind smelling of salt mud and decayed pitch. Jeannine got down after her and signified her disapproval with a loud sigh. They were only five minutes drive along the river bank from Westminster Abbey and the Houses of Parliament, but the new embankment and the broad road it carried had ended abruptly in a wasteland of rotting timbers - the skeletons of long-disused river vessels - and beachcombers' tarred shacks. From the crest of the muddy strand, a neglected meadow trampled and rutted with dust-cart tracks stretched to the high, sightless walls of the Millbank Penitentiary.

"Ah! *Quel atrocité!*" Jeannine exclaimed, staring upwards at the top of the prison wall with its frieze of black iron spikes.

She was holding Sophie's black sable muff in one hand. Sophie took it from her as the groom led them up a cinder-track across the churned-up waste. A sharp breeze off the river forced her to hold her veil down over her small chin. There were heaps of refuse and still-smoking clinker. Small gangs of dirty, ragged children sifted the rubbish, their coats tied with knotted pieces of string about their waists. Some were barefoot, some had broken shoes tied to their feet. They looked up as Sophie and Jeannine went by, their eyes glittering with the predatory hunger of vermin.

Sophie and Jeannine followed the groom under the wall and round a corner. The door to the Governor's lodge was set in the thickness of the wall, at the top of four steep steps; it was of black oak studded with black iron nails. The groom went up and pulled at the bell. There was a jangling within which sounded deeper and deeper into the interior as if from vault to ever more obscure vault. A small judas-window rattled open; a pock-marked face peered round the bars.

"What's your business?" the voice demanded.

Sophie mounted the steps behind her groom. She drew a letter with the Home Office seal from her muff and gave it to him. A moment later, there was the rattle of bolts and the creak of the lock being drawn back. The door swung open.

"You may return to the carriage," Sophie said.

The groom inclined his head, touching the rim of his top hat as he passed her on the step.

"Enter, ladies, if you please," the gaoler said, his gloved hand touching the polished peak of his cap in salute.

He stood stiffly to attention in his dark blue, black buttoned and bemedalled topcoat. He carried a heavy blackthorn stick under his arm. From the broad leather belt about his waist was suspended a weight of enormous keys. Sophie stepped up past him, through the massive thickness of the doorway, and into the passage beyond. It was a dark tunnel with tiled walls still damp from a recent washing-down; above her head, roof-tiles shone like dark satin, while all about there was a smell of carbolic and ammonia.

The gaoler locked the outside door behind Sophie and Jeannine with a heavy thud and much rattling of bolts. Jeannine sighed again. He showed them into a small office to one side of the passage. Except for the tiny, heavily barred window which was set just under the ceiling so that it afforded no view of the outside world, and the damp cold of the stone walls, it might have been the place of business of a lawyer or accountant of the more old-fashioned sort. There was the usual wainscotted partition behind which, on a dais, two clerks were perched up on their stools, scratching away in their ledgers - differing only from businessmen's or solicitors' clerks in the grey of their jackets and trousers, and their grey caps, marked with the stencilled arrowheads.

The gaoler told Sophie, his hand to the peak of his cap again, "The Governor will be about his duties, but I'll send word immediately that you're here."

As he went out, the silence enveloped her. From somewhere close by there was the sound of a woman sobbing. The pen-nibs of the convict-clerks scratched and scratched at the ledgers. Occasionally the two men darted quick glances at Sophie, but only for a split second.

She was kept waiting for a quarter of an hour, during which the clerks' pens scratched, the sobbing occasionally resolved into a wailing, and Jeannine, standing beside her, sighed more and more frequently. Then the monotony was broken by the echoing click of a woman's pattens on stone from the passage, and the whisper of skirts. A pretty, fresh-faced girl of about fifteen or sixteen stepped up into the office. She had thrown on a shawl in some haste; under it, she was dressed for indoors, with a muslin pinafore over her simple afternoon dress; her plaited hair was uncovered.

She bobbed a curtsey to Sophie. "Please forgive my Papa and me for leaving you in this awful place, Your Highness," she said in the breathless tone of one who had been preparing the speech at least for a few seconds. "As soon as he heard you had arrived, Papa sent to tell me to fetch you in - he's about his duties, you know?"

She had just enough breath left for a nervous little giggle. Sophie rose from her seat. Holding out her muff for Jeannine to take, she clasped the girl's lace-mittened hand.

"My dear child, you must address me as 'Princess', *tout court*," she smiled. "I fear being a princess in my country is nothing like so grand as being a princess in yours... So you are Miss Bradfield?"

She released the girl's hand.

"Yes, if you please. Cecily Bradfield," the girl replied. "I'm an only child. My poor Mama died before she could have any more children - I can't even remember her. So I keep house for Papa!"

In the yard at the end of the tunnel, female prisoners in their clean but hideously unbecoming garb were talking to visitors under the eyes and ears of the wardresses. From closer, the noise of the woman's dry, harsh sobbing was trapped between the scrubbed walls.

"Forgive my curiosity, Miss Bradfield," Sophie said as she followed the girl down the passageway. "But who is that woman? Why is she so distressed?"

The girl shrugged. "It's one of the convicts who has gone a bit loopy," she replied. "Papa keeps the Silent System here, you know?"

She stopped at a low door let into the curve of the wall and, taking a key from the battered leather purse she had hung over her sleeve, opened it.

"Welcome to our home, Princess," she said, standing aside to admit Sophie and Jeannine.

Sophie entered a comfortably furnished hallway, for which the outside had left her unprepared. The floors were carpeted and the walls were panelled and hung with watercolour studies of gentle English countryside. The velour-curtained windows were opaque, showing only the misty shape of the bars on the outsides. The girl closed the door behind her, excluding instantly the noise of the sobbing. The smell of carbolic and ammonia was exchanged equally suddenly for the scent of beeswax. A maid, some ten years older than her mistress, came out of a door on the opposite side of the hallway. She was in afternoon black with white lace streamers. Only the small lozenge patch of hodden grey stitched to her leg-of-mutton sleeves betrayed her true situation.

"Fetch the tea-things to the parlour, Hilda," the girl ordered.

There was a precocious harshness in her tone. The maid bobbed and said, "Yes, m'm." Her lips were thin and sullen; above her sunken cheeks were the etched lines and weary shadows of a garret seamstress.

"May my maid go with her?" asked Sophie.

The girl was clearly unused to lady visitors who brought their attendants with them. She looked doubtfully at Jeannine.

"I'm sure Jeannine will not object to taking a cup of tea with your staff," Sophie told her.

She glanced at Jeannine.

"*Comme dit Mademoiselle la Princesse,*" Jeannine replied sourly.

She followed the parlourmaid out of the room with the hauteur of an aristo stepping down to the waiting tumbrel.

"Hilda and Cook and the kitchenmaid are convicts, of course," the girl explained. "But they were recommended to Papa for their genteelness and their good behaviour."

"What is this 'Silent System' you mentioned?" Sophie asked.

Papa keeps the female prisoners strictly apart," the girl replied, "so they may not speak to one another."

"They are never allowed to speak to one another?" asked Sophie.

"Never. That way, Papa says, they cannot influence one another in the ways of wickedness. I'm sure he's right," the girl said. "Let me take you into the parlour, if you please."

"Do they never speak at all?" asked Sophie, following the girl.

"Oh yes! They may speak to one of the wardresses if they need anything - really necessary, you know? And to the Chaplain: they may speak to the Chaplain once a week, if they so desire."

They passed the foot of a flight of stairs, and mounted two carpeted steps into a small, comfortably furnished room where a fire was burning handsomely in the hearth. There were china ornaments on the velvet-hung mantlepiece, and velvet tassled curtains and pelmets over the opaque glass of the windows. At the far side, three steps led down to where a faded tapestry hung from heavy wooden runners to screen off another door.

"Some of the women do go a bit loopy because of having to keep silence," the girl explained. "Papa says women of their sort have to go loopy; it's only then they begin to understand how sinful they have been. Please do be seated. I'm sure Papa won't keep you long."

Sophie sat down on the upright chair at one end of the walnut table in the centre of the room. On the opposite wall, occupying most of the space beside the door through which they had entered, hung a large oleograph reproduction of Christ standing in a prison cell, his head lit by a ray of light from the high, barred window. At his feet crouched a woman in the drab grey flax apron of a convict, her head bent low to kiss the Saviour's feet.

The girl's limited conversational resources were becoming depleted. She had begun commenting on the weather, twisting the muslin flounce of her pinafore-apron around her forefinger as she did so. The small room was too close for such a blazing fire; Sophie wished she could remove her paletot without causing offence.

There came the grinding of a heavy lock turning in the door behind the faded tapestry. Daylight lit the edges, bringing with it a welcome gust of fresh air.

"Here is Papa!" exclaimed the girl delightedly.

She ran and clutched the tapestry in her arms to hold it back from the door. The Governor stepped up into the parlour.

"Milady!" he announced. "I hope you will forgive me for not being here to greet you on your arrival."

The girl released the tapestry as a turnkey closed the door from the outside, and locked it again. General Bradfield gave his cane and gloves to his daughter.

"Your duties, General," Sophie agreed. "I understand perfectly."

"You are indulgent, Milady. And soft-hearted too, I may make so bold as to say..."

Something suggested to Sophie that he did not mean it entirely as a compliment.

His bulk seemed to fill the room. Already she had begun to imagine to herself how a female prisoner might feel at his bearing down on her. He was wearing a dark blue coat with black braiding and buttons which suggested military uniform without actually being such; it had been tailored to flatter his considerable girth. His face was florid; no more so than that of dear Mr Mycroft Holmes, but without Mr Holmes's expansiveness and gentleness of spirit.

"The Princess says you should address her simply as 'Princess'," his daughter announced. She took his hat from him and dropped his gloves into it. She had placed his cane against the alcove wall by the chimney breast. She put down his hat and gloves on a stool beside it. "She says that being a princess in her country isn't the same as being a princess here." She smoothed down the apron of her pinafore.

"Does she, indeed, madam?" General Bradfield replied.

His daughter giggled up at him. She, at least, was not overawed by him.

"Miss Bradfield is perfectly correct, General," Sophie told him. "And, may I say?, she has been entertaining me most charmingly."

"You are most kind, Princess," said General Bradfield.

"I have ordered Hilda to bring a tray of tea for the Princess, Papa," said the girl.

"Quite right, madam." said General Bradfield. "You will forgive my child's forwardness, I trust," he continued to Sophie. "She is motherless, you know. And as she is one's sole domestic companion, one becomes indulgent..."

"There is nothing whatever to forgive," Sophie told him.

General Bradfield cleared his throat, indicating that the exchange of pleasantries was over. He drew the envelope embossed with the Home Office crest from his pocket.

"The Under-Secretary, Mr Dykes-Robinson, writes to say that you are to be permitted to speak to the prisoner, Tuttle..."

He removed the paper from the envelope and unfolded it. "He writes here that your attention has been drawn to the woman Tuttle's situation because you knew of her late husband's Christian work among those of your fellow-countrymen who had settled here in London."

"That is so, General," Sophie confirmed. "The Reverend Mr Tuttle's name is not unknown in St Petersburg."

For a moment she was afraid he would recognize it for the nonsense it was.

"It is gratifying, is it not," General Bradfield asked, "to know that news of a simple man's good deeds may travel the length of Europe? Do you not agree, Cecily?"

"Oh yes, Papa!" his daughter replied.

"One can only believe that it was the act of a merciful Providence that he should have been removed to a better place before he could witness his wife's shame."

General Bradfield cleared his throat again, as if temporarily affected by the thought.

"Perhaps," suggested Sophie, "the poor woman would have known no shame had her husband not been removed 'to a better place'?"

"Your opinion does you credit, Princess," General Bradfield assured her, with a wave of an empurpled finger. "But, as I have sought to impress on my motherless child here, my semi-orphan as I sometimes think of her, character will out in the end, whatever the circumstances in which one finds oneself. I do not suggest that Tuttle is guilty of the appalling crime of which is accused - that is for a jury to decide. But there can be no doubt that her misfortune results from her behaving as no decent woman should behave..."

Sophie made a point of never engaging in argument with somebody whose ideas were not open to modification.

"It is for the sake of her husband's memory," she cut short General Bradfield's homily, "that I felt the urge..." She pressed thumb and forefinger under her breast, in the region of her heart, "...to see if there was anything I might do ameliorate..."

There was a knock like a muffled thud on the door behind the tapestry.

"I ordered the woman Tuttle to be brought over from her cell, Princess," General Bradfield explained. "I appreciate that somebody of your rank and sensibilities has put herself to sufficient inconvenience already, without my having to inflict on her the discomfort of speaking with the woman in one of our interviewing cells... Your coming here is a great kindness, Princess. Admirable, quite admirable - is it not, Cecily? I'm sure the hardest heart would be softened by your example."

"Oh yes, Papa!" his daughter agreed.

General Bradfield went over to the tapestry. He paused, holding it. "I have to insist on two points, however, prison regulations being, I fear, as immutable as the laws of the Medes and Persians. Tuttle must sit there, at the opposite end of the table to yourself, and the prison-matron who accompanies her will remain with you, chiefly for your own protection. You will find it no different from the presence of a servant during a dinner conversation, I daresay, eh?"

Which was approximately what Mr Holmes had suggested to her. She managed to smile agreement at General Bradfield. The latter lifted the edge of the tapestry and rapped on the door. Once again it was unlocked from the outside. Again there was the rush of fresh air into the room. Gruff male voices barked down in the yard outside. A lean woman of uncertain age, her crabbed face framed in a stiff, dark blue bonnet, and wearing a navy-blue bodice buttoned in military style over the top of her stiffly starched apron, came up the steps. Behind her came a second, smaller and younger woman wearing the mob cap, apron, and hodden grey gown of prison uniform. Her auburn hair was in a fringe just visible under the frontlet of her cap, and bound in a bun on the nape of her neck. The unfashionable freckles on her face, and her small snub nose, would have made her what the French call *jolie laide* and the English, 'fetching' - but for the premature ageing about her eyes and mouth and the weary shadows above her cheeks. She stood looking dully at General Bradfield.

"Mrs Tuttle," said the General. She stared dully at him.

"Make your curtsey to the Governor, Tuttle!" the hard faced prison-matron whispered loudly.

Mrs Tuttle did so.

"This is Princess Trub..."

"Trubetskoy," Sophie helped him.

"...who has come all the way from Russia to visit you in your misfortune," General Bradfield continued.

"From Bruton Street, General," Sophie corrected him, but too gently for him to pay any attention.

"Not on account of any merit of your own, you understand," General Bradfield persisted. "But because of the charitable acts of the late Reverend Mr Tuttle toward certain poor compatriots of hers..."

"Compatriots, sir?" asked Mrs Tuttle, as if she could not quite collect her thoughts. "Russians?" she asked.

"Please do be seated, Mrs Tuttle," Sophie intervened hastily, indicating the chair at the opposite side of the table.

Mrs Tuttle looked towards her.

"Immigrants!" General Bradfield barked at her. "Your husband's ministry at St Saviour's Wharf..."

Sophie waved her hand at the chair.

Mrs Tuttle slumped down on it. "Danskers," she ventured. "Chinamen and poor Lascars, as I recall..." She shook her head vaguely.

There came a scratch at the inner door. Cecily ran to open it. The maid, Hilda, came in; she put the tea-tray with its silver pot and cream jug, and a silver dish of ratafee biscuits, beside Sophie.

"This is most kind of you and Miss Bradfield," said Sophie. She paused. "General? Would you indulge me in one thing?"

"What would that be, Princess?" asked General Bradfield.

"There is only one cup and one plate. Surely.." she smiled sweetly at him, "...Mrs Tuttle may be permitted to take a cup of tea with me?"

"By no means, dear Princess!" he told her with a deprecatory smile at her such as one might offer a child whose offence is mitigated by the innocence of its intention. "Though it does you the greatest credit in the world, we cannot allow your womanly softness of heart to run away with us. Regulations, my dear, affect all of us - and prisoners take refreshment only at the times prescribed."

Sophie nodded. "You are kind, General," she told him, "to be so patient with a foreigner like myself."

She stared directly across at Mrs Tuttle, willing her to meet her gaze. "Mrs Tuttle," she said, "I don't believe you are able at such a terrible time for you as this to know who your true friends are."

She nodded slightly, urging her to agree with her. At last Mrs Tuttle looked directly at her.

"Friends who wish to help you so far as it is possible," said Sophie.

Mrs Tuttle nodded. Sophie relaxed a little.

"Your husband helped so many poor people!" she went on. "I'm sure you couldn't remember all of them. But they remember him."

Mrs Tuttle nodded again. Her lips stretched slightly in what might just have been a smile. Sophie turned to General Bradfield.

"Dear General," she appealed to him. "I should like to speak to Mrs Tuttle about women's matters."

"Of course, dear Princess," he replied, to her relief.

As he took his leave, he remarked that as well as the matron who was present in the room, there were turnkeys stationed outside the yard door and in the passage; the Princess only had to call out should she need any assistance. Sophie took Cecily's hand as she was about to follow her father.

"You are a good girl," she said. "I can see that your Papa is rightly proud of you."

Standing aside at the inside door to let Cecily go through before him, General Bradfield smiled at Sophie with a warmth whose genuineness shone through his unctuous pomposity. Perhaps, she thought, his daughter would be the saving of him, but she doubted it.

Now she and Mrs Tuttle were left alone, except for the grim visaged matron, who sat on a stool by the tapestry, staring at the opposite wall as if she were dead inside her skull.

"The night your employer died," said Sophie. "Captain...?"

"Captain Meadowthorpe?" asked Mrs Tuttle.

"It must have been a terrible experience," Sophie suggested. "Horrible!"

Mrs Tuttle turned her face away. "I have spoken about it to the police - many times," she replied. "And to Mr Bullfinger."

She sighed. Then she stared up at the pelmet draped about the mantlepiece above the fire. "I am tired of speaking about it," she said.

"Have you discussed it with Mr Marshall Hall?" asked Sophie. "Or any of your other friends?"

"I have no other friends," Mrs Tuttle replied.

Sophie poured a cup of tea. "You have, my dear," she said. "More than you know. And I hope you will count me one of them."

"I don't wish to talk about it," said Mrs Tuttle.

"It is very hard to speak to people when you know that they do not really believe what you are saying," Sophie told her.

She pushed the cup of tea toward her. There was no reaction from the matron.

"If you talk about it to me," she went on, "I shall believe you. That is why I have come here... Besides, it is one thing to tell police and lawyers, and quite another to speak to friends. To the police, one tells facts. With a friend, one shares - how do you call it? - *la crainte*?"

Mrs Tuttle thought for a moment. "The mood?" she suggested. "One's apprehensions?"

"One's apprehensions!" Sophie agreed. "*Exactement*! So trust me, my dear - and drink up the tea."

She did not expect Mrs Tuttle to start talking immediately; she was content to wait in silence for a minute or two. Mrs Tuttle took several sips from the cup. Then she lifted up her face.

Sophie saw that her eyes were filled with tears. She nodded.

CHAPTER FIVE

"Perhaps I did kill him! It's the question I keep asking myself all the time!" She stared across the table at Sophie as if Sophie might be able to relieve her of the burden. Sophie noticed the unhealthy pallor of her skin behind the freckles. Kept in solitude, away from the light, she would have nothing to distract her from morbid reflection.

"I had a dear sister," Sophie told her in a matter-of-fact voice. "She took poison and died - she was driven to it by an evil man. Like you with your Captain, I had to stand by helplessly, and like you, I asked myself... Oh, so many times!"

She waited before continuing: "Nor must you reproach yourself with what the poor man accused you of when you brought the doctor to him. People don't know what they are saying when they are delirious."

"You have been told about that?" asked Mrs Tuttle.

"Yes."

"And you have still come here to be kind to me?"

But for the lines etched in by care and distress, with her freckled face and small, retroussé nose, Mrs Tuttle would have looked like a wondering child.

"You see me here," Sophie replied. "And I will tell you this my dear: you have friends who believe you did everything you could to bring the doctor to your Captain's side as quickly as possible, that dreadful night."

"Nobody knows how often I tried to persuade Captain Meadowthorpe to send for Dr Bickleigh during those weeks he was ill," Mrs Tuttle replied. "But he wouldn't hear of it. He said it was all stuff and nonsense - that it was something he had caught when he was in Africa during the Zulu War. He said doctors in England knew nothing of such things and only made matters worse. But that - last - night, he begged me to to myself to fetch Dr Bickleigh."

"Please... do continue, if you wish," Sophie urged her.

Mrs Tuttle nodded. "That was how I could tell how ill he really was," she went on. "When he implored me to go myself, and not just send one of the servants. He was taken ill almost immediately after dinner. At first he thought it was something he had eaten which had disagreed with him. But below stairs we had eaten the same food as he, and none of us had been taken sick. I helped him to his couch in the study; he said he did not want to go to bed. I tried to make him comfortable, but he just lay there groaning and perspiring terribly - that is when he wasn't... vomiting..."

She looked across at Sophie. She shook her head. "There's no call for me to go burdening Your Highness with all this," she said.

"Mrs Tuttle, my dear," said Sophie, "I came in the hope that you might be prevailed upon to confide in me. Please go on."

"He asked me what time it was," Mrs Tuttle continued. "I told him that it was very nearly half-past eight. I wondered why, when he was in such a state, he should want to know the time. It was then he said he wished me to fetch Dr Bickleigh and I realised he'd wanted to know the time because he hadn't wished to disturb the doctor at his dinner. Captain Meadowthorpe wasn't always so considerate; usually he was wilful like a little boy, but then most men are, aren't they? That's why we love them, I suppose."

"I suppose so," Sophie replied to encourage her to go on.

"I told him I'd send Flett - he was Captain Meadowthorpe's coachman. But Captain Meadowthorpe told me most pressingly he wanted me to go. He said that he trusted me beyond any ordinary servant, and that if I took the path across the Lower Heath, I would reach Downshire Hill and Dr Bickleigh's address in no time at all."

"Do you mean that Captain Meadowthorpe told you, a young woman, to cross this heath unaccompanied and in the dark?" asked Sophie, genuinely shocked.

"Please, Your Highness!" Mrs Tuttle begged. "I wouldn't want you to think the worse of him for it. I knew the path as well as my own hand; I went down it in daylight almost every day, round the lower pond to the shops in South End Road. The brickworkers' cottages are at the bottom end of the ponds. They use the track to go across to the brickfields, and their women use it every day to take them their midday meal; so it's almost a road really, although it isn't lit. I didn't stop even to put on a hat and coat. I just wrapped my shawl round me and ran out. I was about halfway along the path across the Lower Heath - there's a piggery at the end of South End Road, the better class of people down there are always complaining about the smell, and I could smell it quite distinctly, so I wasn't very far from the bottom of the Heath - when two huge burly men stepped out of the undergrowth in front of me. It was just as if they had been lying in ambush waiting for me, like old-fashioned footpads. I'm not very big, as you can see - almost any man is bigger than me."

Sophie nodded, encouraging her.

"And these stood right up against me, blocking my path. I asked them what they wanted, but they just laughed. They smelt far worse than any piggery. When they began clutch at me, it was as if I was being dragged down into freshly dug earth - you know how sometimes there's a smell of decay about freshly dug earth when it's clay? I felt as if they were going to bury me alive, as if the mud was going to get into my throat and suffocate me..."

"Did they - harm you?" Sophie asked. When Mrs Tuttle did not reply, she added, "I mean - force you?"

Mrs Tuttle shook her head. She glanced back over her shoulder at the matron, who was staring impassively in front of her. She leaned forward.

"They put their hands into my dress," she said in a lower voice. "I remember telling myself that for Captain Meadowthorpe's sake I must endure all - that I must not faint or become incapacitated - because when they were done with me I must go on to Downshire Hill to fetch Dr Bickleigh. They made me kiss them, and they pawed my linen with their filthy hands. Then they stopped quite suddenly... They vanished into the darkness as silently as they had appeared."

"Perhaps they were too drunk to have their will of you?"

Mrs Tuttle stared across the table at her. She shook her head again. "They smelt vile," she said. "But of wet, stinking loam, not of strong drink. I know the smell of strong drink; I can recall it from the days when I helped my late husband at the mission on St Saviour's Wharf... Anyway, when I managed to reach Dr Bickleigh's house, I was in such a state that both he and Mrs Bickleigh thought it was I who was in need of medical attention. At first, I couldn't find the words to explain why I had come... I fear I was a little hysterical."

She laughed abruptly. "The Devil got my tongue! That's what they say, isn't it?"

"Mrs Tuttle! Collect yourself, please!" Sophie said. "I'm sure you have more you wish to tell me."

The matron had turned her head and was watching Mrs Tuttle keenly.

"If I hadn't let the Devil get my tongue, I expect Dr Bickleigh would have been in time to have saved Captain Meadowthorpe," said Mrs Tuttle. "That's why Captain Meadowthorpe accused me of killing him."

"Captain Meadowthorpe could not have known how brave and loyal you were," said Sophie.

Mrs Tuttle was clenching her fingers so tightly that her knuckles looked as if they might burst through the skin.

"Drink your tea," Sophie said quietly, pointing to the cup.

"He would not have died had I managed to keep my head," said Mrs Tuttle.

Sophie kept her finger pointing to the cup. The matron was staring in front of her once more. Sophie nodded. Mrs Tuttle picked up the cup and drank from it. She held it in both hands; she was shaking so much she could not have held it steady otherwise.

She put the cup down. "If it had not been for Mr Manyon, we would not have been in time to see Captain Meadowthorpe alive," she said. "By chance, Mr Manyon was calling on Dr Bickleigh that night, so we were able to return to Squire's Mount in his carriage."

"Do you mean Mr Villiers Manyon?" asked Sophie.

"I see you have heard of him," Mrs Tuttle said sharply. "I suppose everybody has."

"Did Mr Manyon go in with you and Dr Bickleigh when he put you down?" Sophie asked.

"He excused himself," Mrs Tuttle replied. "He said there was a party of distinguished guests arriving at the Lakeside Hotel, and as proprietor, his presence would be expected."

"So you and Dr Bickleigh were by yourselves when you returned to Captain Meadowthorpe's side?"

Mrs Tuttle nodded.

"In the study?" Now Sophie would have to put the question Mr Holmes particularly wished her to ask. She hoped she wasn't beginning to sound like an investigator.

"He was still in the study?" she pressed. "He had not tried to go upstairs to bed?"

Mrs Tuttle had her hand over her face. Her distress was so evident, Sophie was afraid that the matron would insist on putting an end to the proceedings.

"It may help you to tell me," she urged across the table.

"Nothing will help me now," Mrs Tuttle replied from behind her hand.

"Mrs Tuttle! If you please!" She must not sound too urgent, Sophie told herself.

To her relief, Mrs Tuttle lowered her hand.

"I think he had tried to fetch assistance," Mrs Tuttle replied, her voice hoarse. "He was lying at the top of the stairs leading down to the kitchen."

"The stairs leading down to the kitchen - which is also the foot of the back staircase up to your room and the servants' quarters." Sophie was careful to make it sound like a statement, but she looked full into Mrs Tuttle's eyes.

Mrs Tuttle nodded.

"And then the Captain started to accuse you?"

"Yes," croaked Mrs Tuttle.

"I expect Dr Bickleigh was surprised, was he not?" asked Sophie.

"He was distressed and embarrassed. At first he said just what you have said, Your Highness," Mrs Tuttle replied. "That Captain Meadowthorpe was delirious... I don't think he was delirious." Her voice cracked. "I think he knew perfectly well what he was saying."

"Mrs Tuttle!" Sophie exclaimed.

"I knew whether Captain Meadowthorpe was fully conscious or not," Mrs Tuttle told her with a hoarse defiance. "I know he meant what he said. I don't know why he said it."

"Did he say why he was lying where you found him?" asked Sophie.

Mrs Tuttle shook her head.

"You called for a servant, I expect," said Sophie.

"Annie came - Annie Gibbs, the general-housemaid," Mrs Tuttle replied. "She called Flett to help carry Captain Meadowthorpe back to the study while she mopped up... the mess. Annie was always a good girl."

There was silence between them for a moment. Sophie did not wish to press Mrs Tuttle too far. Then she asked, "Mrs Tuttle. How did the poison bottle come to be behind the clock in your room?"

Mrs Tuttle stared back as if she had suddenly been accused.

"The police put it there, I expect," she said. "Save themselves the trouble of looking for a real murderer, don't you see?

For the first time she smiled, but it wasn't a pleasant smile.

Sophie could think of policemen in other lands, including her own, who would do such a thing. But not English policemen. She shook her head.

"You think our policemen are so good, don't you, Your Highness?" sneered Mrs Tuttle. "A little stupid perhaps, but honest as daylight. If you lived down in Whitechapel in Shadwell or the Jago, you'd soon hear a different story, I can tell you!"

Sophie could see that the matron's interest had been aroused.

"Come now, Mrs Tuttle," she said.

"Well, I never put it behind the clock," said Mrs Tuttle defiantly. "And I'll take my oath on it, it wasn't anybody else in the house. Captain Meadowthorpe was a good master to the servants; after Mrs Meadowthorpe died they knew they'd never find a more comfortable and agreeable situation."

"I expect that was partly your doing as housekeeper," Sophie suggested gently. Before Mrs Tuttle had an opportunity to say anything further to arouse the hostility of the matron, she went on, "Tell me, had the Captain been deeply affected by the death of his wife?"

"From what I saw," Mrs Tuttle replied, "you could say Mrs Meadowthorpe's death came as a blessed relief."

"Because of the sickness she contracted in Italy?" asked Sophie.

"Not only that, but she had a wicked tongue in her head. And she was no beauty, either."

It was just as well, thought Sophie, that Mrs Tuttle would never be called upon to give evidence on her own behalf - she would surely condemn herself within minutes.

"I suppose Captain Meadowthorpe married her for her fortune."

"I doubt it," Mrs Tuttle replied. "She had been Mr Manyon's ward, and Mr Manyon was always coming to Captain Meadowthorpe to borrow money. Do you know? Mr Manyon made Captain Meadowthorpe settle a fortune on his real daughter, Parthenope, before he'd let him become engaged to marry her!"

Sophie noted the outrage in her voice. "You must have been deeply injured by that engagement," she said.

"Oh, I knew he was never going to marry me!" Mrs Tuttle exclaimed sharply. "He had always made that quite clear!" She paused for a moment. "Of course, I never really believed him," she said in a softer tone of voice. "One doesn't, does one? I mean, one clings on to a sweet dream... There's one thing I'm absolutely certain about!"

"What is that, Mrs Tuttle?" asked Sophie.

"He didn't want to marry Parthenope Manyon! Oh, she's a pretty enough little thing in her doll-like way..."

The intensity in her voice alarmed Sophie. She had learnt enough; it was time to bring the interview to an end. "Calm yourself, Mrs Tuttle," she urged.

"We were lovers!" Mrs Tuttle went on. "Who was in a better

position than myself to have known if there had been any lessening of his passion! Miss Manyon is nothing if not her father's creature - a creature without a will of her own!"

In her excitement, she had half risen to her feet. She was leaning across the table. Strands of her auburn hair had fallen from under her cap and were plastered to her cheek where the heat from the fire was causing her to perspire.

"He didn't love her," she tried to shout. The words came out as a series of croaks. "Any more than he loved his wife!"

The matron was on her feet. She had her hands on Mrs Tuttle's shoulders to push her down on to the chair.

"We don't want you making a spectacle of yourself, Tuttle," she said sharply "Her Highness come here out of the kindness of her heart. Not to hear ravings like you was a poor demented - which you ain't."

"You know who Captain Meadowthorpe was really going to marry, don't you?" Mrs Tuttle tried to shout. "Mr Villiers Manyon! That's who!"

She struggled to stand up again. The door behind the tapestry opened letting another welcome gust of cold air from the yard into the overheated room. A navy-blue uniformed turnkey came up the steps.

"Begging your pardon, ma'am," he said to Sophie, before grasping Mrs Tuttle by the upper arm.

Sophie rose from her chair. "I'm sure there is no need..." she began.

But Mrs Tuttle had begun to laugh noisily.

"It was Mr Villiers Manyon he was going to marry!" her voice cracked. She tried to twist out of the turnkey's grip. She went on laughing though the sound of it was more like wheezing. Sophie did not hear the door opening behind her, but she felt the draught whipping past her, and her own perspiration turning chill on her face. A second turnkey rushed past her. The matron had stood aside. There were two uniformed men now holding Mrs Tuttle, who was writhing, but to little effect. Her cap had slipped from her head and was dangling from its ribbon about her neck. The locks of her violently loosened hair were shaken about her face so that she looked like a Romantic painter's vision of the Medusa. The wardress came forward again. She put her hand on Mrs Tuttle's face, pushing it back to speak into it.

"You be good, my girl!" she said. "It'll be the best for you - take my word!"

Sophie was sickened by the spectacle but knew there was nothing she could say which would not make matters worse. The matron uttered a sudden scream of pain. Mrs Tuttle had craned her head forward and bitten her in the wrist.

"Perhaps I may be permitted to escort you to your carriage, Princess?

General Bradfield had come in unnoticed, and was standing behind Sophie.

"Bread and water for you, madam!" the matron exclaimed.

As the turnkeys and the matron lifted Mrs Tuttle bodily down into the yard, Sophie took the Governor's proffered arm.

"Thank you, General," she said, as amiably as she could.

She ignored the expression of disapproval on his florid features, which was intended to inform her that he had known she had come to cause trouble but had been too courteous to remark on the fact.

She crossed the wasteland back to her carriage. Sophie looked neither to the left nor to the right. It was not until the groom had lowered the step and had supported her with his arm into the carriage, that she allowed herself to look back across the desert of sparse grass, trampled mud, and refuse heaps in front of the prison. On the farther side, another carriage was parked, an enclosed four-wheeler, black as a hearse. She shuddered so violently that Jeannine, who had climbed into the carriage and was taking her place opposite, leaned over and took her by the wrist.

"*Altesse? Vous êtes bien?*" she asked.

"*Parfaitement, merci, Jeannine,*" Sophie replied. Jeannine released her arm, and she sank back into the cushions. "*Tout est bien,*" she added.

But it wasn't. However much she told herself that it was the chill off the Thames which had gripped her, it was the sense of watchful malignancy which she carried back with her to her apartments in Bruton Street, and which would not leave her until she had bowed and blessed herself before the icon of the Vladimir Mother of God which hung in the corner of her bedchamber.

CHAPTER SIX

"So the damned fool let himself fall into Villiers Manyon's clutches, and Manyon was renting him for every penny he could squeeze out of him," Mycroft pronounced.

"Now wait a minute, Holmes, m'dear chap!" protested Sophie's old friend and sometime companion, Colonel Edwin Barnaby. "It don't answer! It don't answer in the least!"

Cyril, Sophie's black servant who seemed to have elevated himself to the rôle of her butler, leaned over Mycroft's shoulder and placed the humidor beside his brandy glass. Mycroft devoted his entire attention to its contents.

"I am not positing a theory, Barnaby," he replied in a note of abstraction. "I'm stating a fact... My dear Princess! *Vegueras legitimas*! Your taste in cigars is quite admirable!" He picked one out and rolled it carefully between his fingers before placing it under his nostrils.

Cyril brought a chased-silver casket from the sideboard. Sophie, who had never conformed to the notion that, when presiding at her own table, she should leave gentlemen-friends of long standing to take tobacco without her, selected a liquorice black cigarette. She lit it from a taper, then impaled it on a long jewelled pin with which she put it to her lips. Cyril took the taper round for Colonel Barnaby to light his cigar.

"Your mistress said that you're a black scoundrel without a vestige of Christian manners," Mycroft told him.

Cyril picked up the splint and carried it round to Colonel Barnaby.

Sophie lowered her cigarette. "Mr Holmes," she asked, "are you going to offer us your view of how Captain Meadowthorpe came to be poisoned?"

"My dear Princess," Mycroft replied in a tone of mild rebuke, "you are assuming that I have a view, as you put it. You should be aware, by now, of my reluctamce to entertain hypotheses."

Sophie smiled indulgently. She reached across the table and placed her small hand over his pudgy fingers. "Not even to amuse us over our brandy, my dear?" she coaxed him. "Not after all I have told you about my visit to your dreadful Millbank?"

"Least of all while we are drinking your excellent Armagnac, Princess," he replied. "In the words of the mediæval schoolman whom I regard as the greatest of masters, '*in mero, merum in multi licatio coniectarum cammutatum est.*' You will find it in the fifth book of Occam's *Defensorium contra errores* of 1339." He glanced at Colonel Barnaby uncomprehending features. "'In unwatered wine,'" he translated, "'simple fact is converted into a multiplicity of theories.'"

"Had Greek thrashed into me at school," said the Colonel. "Deuced if I can remember a word of it!"

"If you was to ask me..." Cyril repeated, moving round the table.

"Nobody has the slightest intention of asking you anything, you rogue," Mycroft told him.

"Just if you was to ask me," Cyril persisted.

Mycroft was pleased with himself both at having had the opportunity to quote William of Occam and, as he imagined, at putting down Cyril. He made the mistake of sitting back comfortably in his chair and putting his cigar in his mouth. Cyril seized the opportunity.

"This captain you was talking about - this 'unhappy deceased' as you might put it - I'd say as he p'isoned hisself."

"And why do you think he would have done that?" asked Sophie indulgently.

"Mr Holmes said as this Manyon fellow might have been renting him," Cyril suggested. "Some people'd say that was a reason for him topping hisself. Or p'raps he might not have meant to top hisself at all. I mean, p'raps he gone and done it accidental-like..."

Mycroft removed his cigar from his mouth. Cyril caught his eye. Mycroft nodded. "Go on, man!" he said.

"He could've been like that king in the olden days," Cyril continued, "what took p'ison a little at a time so as in the end his body got so used to it like, nobody could kill him by p'isoning him."

"Mithradates, King of Pontus?" said Mycroft. "Very good. But why do you suppose Captain Meadowthorpe thought anybody would have wished to poison him?"

Cyril gave a tolerable impression of somebody exercising his intellect to the limit. "Supposing this Manyon fellow had married his adopted daughter or whatever she was, to the Captain for the Captain's money. Only the Captain had escaped his clutches 'cause of the young lady snuffing it. Manyon then has another bite of the cherry, as you might say - with his real daughter this time. He makes the Captain leave all his worldly goods to her, don't he? - even before the wedding! But the Captain, he's saying to hisself, soon as I've married the girl, Mr Manyon's going to have a go at p'isoning me!"

Mycroft snorted. Princess Sophie laughed, "*Imbécile!*"

Colonel Barnaby tugged at his whiskers as if he would pull them out at the roots. "If Manyon mawwied off his adopted daughter, ward, what have you, so as to help himself to Meadowthorpe's fortune... well, it was deuced silly of him! Deuced silly - that's all I can say!"

"Do you mean to say you were acquainted with this Meadowthorpe fellow?" Mycroft demanded. "My dear Barnaby! Why ever didn't you say so before?"

"I did try!" Barnaby protested. "Only you all have so many deuced clever ideas, I didn't weally have a chance, don't you know?

"Why do you say it was silly, Eddy?" Sophie asked gently.

"Bounder never had a ha'penny to his name!" Colonel Barnaby replied. "If he ever had a fortune he'd lost it to cardsharps, women or on the gee-gees, long before his regiment embarked for Natal."

"Did you know Meadowthorpe personally?" asked Sophie.

"Not personally, exactly," Colonel Barnaby replied. "By weputation, don't you know? I mean, the fellow was a sponge of the first water. He'd left his marker unpaid in evewy cavalwy mess in the kingdom. Tradesmen's bills are one thing: Meadowthorpe welshed on his own bookmaker! And then there was poor little Lady Viola Stanfield's emewald tiara. The night the 2nd Lancers were embarking, they found he'd snitched it and hocked it to uncle; needed to waise the wind a bit before he left, I suppose. Most awful fuss. The Light Cavalwy had to waise a subscription to wedeem it."

He drew on his cigar several times to rekindle it. "I'd say," he continued, "that it's a deuced sight more likely Meadowthorpe was blackmailing Villiers Manyon than the other way round, eh?"

Mycroft cleared his throat. "Can you be entirely sure he had not restored his fortunes to some extent - passage of time, and all that?" he asked. "After all, he had become a hero of Isandhlwana and Rorke's Drift."

"Hero!" Colonel Barnaby exclaimed his voice becoming shrill. "The blackguard was cashiered, don't you know? Bwoken! For cowardice in the face of the enemy! He was sent home in utter disgwace; if there'd been a single spark of decency in him, he'd have put a pistol to his head instead of waiting four years or more to poison himself!"

"What had he done?" asked Sophie.

Colonel Barnaby shook his head. "Sowwy, Pwincess. Too distasteful for a lady's ears, don't you know?" He glanced at Mycroft.

"It might be of help if we were to know," Mycroft said.

"Tell us, if you please, Eddy," Sophie said.

"Very well. On your heads be it," Colonel Barnaby replied.

He reached for the silver coaster, drew it to him, replenished his brandy glass, then drew once more on his cigar. He lay back in his chair, rolling the cigar between his fingers "Dawn of Isandhlwana," he began, "General Hamilton-Browne sent Meadowthorpe out of the main camp with a detachment of Russell's Mounted Infantwy to weconnoitre the Zulu position on the Nqutu Plateau five miles away fwom Base Camp. Three days later he turned up, like the pwoverbial bad penny, on foot at Worke's Dwift with a flesh wound in his wight shoulder. Claimed he'd weceived the wound as he was returning to the main column to weport that the Zulu impi had moved off the Nqutu Plateau. He said that he'd been ambushed by natives, knocked fwom his mount and concussed, and by the time he'd come-to it was nightfall. He had staggered up the slope of Isandhlwana - or so he said - to find in the light of the burning waggons that the entire column had been massacred.

"Well, Surgeon-Major Reynolds was vewwy suspicious - so he said at the court-martial. Meadowthorpe's wound had been inflicted by a Colt point forty-five wevolver At point blank wange; Reynolds could tell from the scorch marks on Meadowthorpe's tunic. And while it pwevented Meadowthorpe fwom taking part in the action at Worke's Dwift, the bullet had avoided touching bone and sinew in a way which was wonderful to behold. Also, according to the gallant Surgeon-Major's evidence, there was no sign of bruising on Meadowthorpe's skull - and if a fellow is concussed by a fall fwom his mount, it follows he's going to have suffered a bruise, don't you know? Deuced good thing in a way, of course! If Meadowthorpe hadn't been wounded, being the ranking officer at Worke's Dwift, they'd have had to let him take command, haw, haw, haw! Good as handing the Cape Colony to the natives, what?

"Anyway, the second morning of the siege of the Mission, when the Taffies thought they were finished, and the last of 'em were pwepawing to die at the wamparts like the bwave fellows they were, they found Meadowthorpe was gone. Mind you, with five thousand bloodthirsty savages on the kopje above 'em, they weren't going to spend much time looking for him. Only, you'll recall, that morning, the Zulus didn't attack. They came off the kopje, saluted our gallant lads with a bit of heathen singing and dancing, and marched back to their kraals. So there were the Taffies, left standing with Zulu bodies piled all awound the Mission high as the wamparts. They found Meadowthorpe lying among 'em, half suffocated to death under a heap of 'em. Birthday-naked, he was; he'd smeared himself with burnt cork and boot-dubbin. He was holding an assegai and a zebwa-skin shield. The Zulus always withdwew for the night, don't you know? So under cover of darkness, he'd cwawled out of the hospital building, and hidden himself under the bodies, so as to escape the fighting the next day. Do you know how the Taffs spotted him? He was the only black man there who had fallen with his back turned to our fellows.

"Chard and Bromhead placed him under awwest pwetty damned sharpish. Didn't want any of the Kaffir iwwegulars to see how a Bwitish officer had disgwaced himself. Sent him stwaight to General Clifford's headquarters, escorted by a couple of Boer twoopers. Sir Henwy Clifford had him court-martialled and dismissed the service. The last thing Meadowthorpe did before wetuning to civilian life was to bowwow his fare back to Southampton fwom his defending officer - Castle Line, first class state-room, starboard side, don't you know?"

Colonel Barnaby relit his cigar again, and drew on it. Sophie removed the remainder of her cigarette from the pin she was using as a holder, and stubbed it in the small crystal ashtray beside her place.

"And the next we hear of Captain Meadowthorpe - or ex-Captain Meadowthorpe, should we call him?" she asked, "is his owning a fine old house in a modish quarter up on Hampstead. Perhaps..." She took a second cigarette from the silver-chased box, impaled it on the jewelled pin and waited for Cyril to light it for her. "...Eddy is right. Perhaps Meadowthorpe, being himself *detrimental, soumettait ce detrimental*, Villiers Manyon, *a chantage.*"

"One villain blackmailing another," Mycroft echoed her. He grunted as he considered the possibility. "You say, Princess, that Mrs Tuttle believes Manyon to have visited Meadowthorpe in order to sponge off him. But Mrs Tuttle had only Meadowthorpe's word for that - not what one might call a gilt edge affirmation, what? On the other hand, Manyon appears to be in a strong enough position *vis-à-vis* Meadowthorpe to insist on Meadowthorpe not merely marrying his daughter, but on his settling his fortune on her."

"Despite what Mrs Tuttle said," suggested Sophie, "let us suppose Meadowthorpe was genuinely attracted to little Parthenope Manyon."

"And this Meadowthorpe bloke, 'cause he's gone all spoony over the Manyon girl, settles all his money on her," Cyril intervened.

"So her Pa finds a way to destroy his inconvenience, his little daughter remains at home under his protection, and all the *chantage* he had had to pay to Meadowthorpe now comes back to him - *voila!*"

"Bravo!" Colonel Barnaby clasped his hands. "What do you say to that, eh, Holmes? Deuced clever our Pwincess, what?"

"Admirable," Mycroft replied.

He waved his cigar in the air, leaving a trail of blue smoke to drift above the table. "There is one question to which you omitted to address yourself, Princess. Who was the servant whom Manyon placed in the household on Squire's Mount - a creature who had the opportunity to administer doses of poison gradually, day by day, week by week, under Mrs Tuttle's very eyes."

He surveyed the ash on the end of his cigar, debating whether to leave it where it was as a compliment to the quality of the smoke, or whether to tap it into the ashtray. He decided on the latter. "The maid who was on duty the night of Meadowthorpe's death. She would have had an opportunity of placing the poison behind the clock in the housekeeper's room. What was her name?"

"Annie Gibbs," Sophie replied.

"Ah yes!" he went on. "A name one would remember because it is so delightfully unmemorable; junior domestics always have such undistinguished names, don't you think? Now, this Annie Gibbs..." He turned to Colonel Barnaby. "...she could be our man, in a manner of speaking. What do you say, Barnaby? Who could have had a better opportunity?"

Colonel Barnaby stared at him. "Damn it!" he declared. "Deuced if a fellow can tell if you're serious or not!"

Mycroft laughed and shook his head. "I suppose it is not quite impossible that this Annie Gibbs should have committed the crime - not quite impossible," he declared. "In any case, I daresay it might prove interesting to speak with her. But tell me, Barnaby. You are a man of the world. Would you know how to dispense poison in order to kill a man by degrees? Would you know the dosages required? I mean, as in this case, the proportion of arsenic to chloral? Or the proper intervals to observe between doses? Not to mention finding - or making - opportunities to administer them. We are talking here about a substantial household but not, I think, a grand one. I do not suppose this girl, Annie Gibbs, is one of your half-educated house-parlourmaids from the lettered artisan class. More probably she is the sort you find in so many houses of the newly prosperous *bourgeoisie*: some poor illiterate slavey put into bombazine and streamers for afternoon and evening when her more menial work is done..."

He drew on his cigar only to find that it had gone out. He reached for the taper, but before applying it, continued, "Which is not to say that she could not cast light on the comings and goings on Squire's Mount, if we can trace her. For I daresay she will have found herself another situation by this time."

He relit his cigar and puffed satisfactorily. "But there are other doors into this strange affair which might yield entry if we were to try the latch," he continued. There is the odd business of Mrs Tuttle going to Dr Bickleigh's house to find Villiers Manyon there. A man in Manyon's position who, although *un detrimental*, rubs shoulders with the high and mighty, doesn't call on a medical adviser; he sends his carriage to fetch him..." He puffed on his cigar thoughtfully.

"Unless, of course, there is a connection other than the obvious, I mean the professional one... And there is the question of the bell in the study."

"What bell in the study?" asked Colonel Barnaby.

"Why," asked Mycroft, "should Meadowthorpe have gone all the way to the servants' staircase to seek assistance when he could perfectly well have rung for help from the study?"

"Unless," Cyril intervened, "he weren't looking for help at all."

Mycroft looked at him and nodded. "One other thing," he said. "You have told us, Princess, that Mrs Tuttle is wearing prison garb, and that she is being held under the rules of the Silent System."

"That is so," Sophie agreed.

"The rules governing a prisoner held on remand, awaiting trial, state that she should be allowed to wear her own dress, that she should speak whenever she wishes, to whomsoever she wishes subject, of course, to the good order of the prison, and that her diet may consist of what she can afford or what her friends choose to send to her." Mycroft paused to ensure his cigar was alight. "According to the law, a prisoner awaiting trial is to be presumed innocent, within the limits imposed by her necessary confinement. Certainly she should not be subjected to the humiliation of wearing prison garb or the restrictions which are applied to a convicted felon. Why do you suppose General Bradfield is not observing the usual procedures in Mrs Tuttle's case? Why do you suppose Messrs Marcus, Bullfinger, Stote and Marcus have not protested on her behalf?"

He returned to smoking his cigar. Sophie shook her head.

Colonel Barnaby broke the silence. "Deuced wum thing, eh?" he said. "Dashed if a fellow can make it out!"

"I had a pal once," said Cyril. "Chrissie Yallop her name was. Did business back of the Haymarket. She got herself arrested for helping her gusset-cove play the badger game. He's doing a niner on the Moor. She went mad after six weeks silence-and-solitary in Brixton. She always were a talker were Chrissie Yallop; only she don't need nobody to listen to her now, just yacks on even when there ain't nobody with her."

Mycroft said nothing.

It was Sophie who asked finally, "Do you suppose they wish to drive the poor creature insane?"

Mycroft continued smoking for a moment. "Were Mrs Tuttle to decline into a state in which she was deemed unfit to plead," he said, "there would be no testing of evidence by the court, no calling of witnesses, no examination or cross-examination. It would be as if she had pleaded guilty. I daresay she would be removed to an asylum where, in this modern age, she would be treated humanely. As far as the outside world is concerned, it would be as if she were entombed."

"Oh, I say, Holmes!" Colonel Barnaby protested. "You ain't suggesting that the Governor of Millbank and the lady's own solicitors are combining to dwive her insane!"

Mycroft shrugged his shoulders.

"Do you know?" said Sophie, "I believe we should pay a call on Dolly Murray. You are acquainted with Dolly Murray, aren't you, Eddy?"

"Lord Adolphus? I should say so!" Colonel Barnaby replied. "The vewy best sort of fellow, old Dolly. We wode together, don't you know? to Kandahar, with Lord Bobs's welief column."

"His place is on Hampstead Heath, isn't it?" asked Sophie.

"Kenwood," Colonel Barnaby told her. "It's his elder bwother's place weally - Lord Mansfield's, you know - but Dolly and Lady Dolly have the wun of it. Mansfield can't bwing himself to leave Scotland. Damned if I know why; deuced wet and windy place, Scotland - except in the gwouse season, of course!"

Understanding dawned on him. "Deuce take it, Pwincess! I see what you're dwivin' at! Lord Dolly'll know what goes on wound Hampstead and the Heath. He owns half of it!"

"If Dolly himself doesn't know," said Sophie, "his people will. Servants always know everything. Mr Holmes! We shall take you up to Highgate to meet Dolly Murray," she added decisively. "I shall have Brown call for you with the carriage, on Sunday morning."

Highgate was a drive of no more than six miles from Pall Mall, but Mycroft regarded anything east of Temple Bar or north of Regent's Park as undiscovered country from whose bourn travellers might quite easily not return.

"I attend Divine Service at St James's, Piccadilly, on a Sunday morning," he hastened to tell her. "It is my invariable practice."

"I shall instruct Brown to wait outside Number 73A for you to return," Sophie told him. "I expect he will welcome the opportunity o read his newspaper."

She reached across the table to take his hand in hers. "Dear friend," she said. "It was you who set me on this chase. But you aren't going to leave it to me, are you?"

"By no means, Princess," Mycroft told her, though he could not, at that juncture, see any need to move beyond the purlieus of Westminster.

As he was leaving, that night, to return to Pall Mall, Sophie came with him to the door of the apartments. She waved the footman away who had given Mycroft his hat, coat and stick.

"I do not think it was my imagination, my dear," she told him, "but I am sure that I was being watched when I went to visit Mrs Tuttle."

And she told him about the closed black carriage which had been waiting on the other side of the wasteland meadow.

"It is unlikely to have been officials of our government or police," Mycroft told her. "The Home Office had given permission for your visit. In any case, there were enough people in Millbank itself to keep an eye on you, had they so wished. It is possible, I suppose, the carriage belonged to another visitor to some poor unfortunate."

He caught her eye. "Hmm!" he grunted, as if trying to convince himself as much as her.

CHAPTER SEVEN

"Oh, my dears! Don't mention the name Manyon in Dolly's hearing, whatever you do!"

"Why ever not, Lady Dolly?" asked Colonel Barnaby.

He had ridden up to Kenwood House, behind Princess Sophie's carriage. Surreptitiously he was trying to pick fragments of mud which had dried on his scarlet cavalry cloak.

"Because he'll carry on for hours, my dear!" Lady Adolphus Murray replied. "Sophie, my darling, it is wonderful to see you. Such a lovely surprise. Do you know? One of your Royals has been making inquiries about leasing Kenwood for his eldest son - the Grand Duke Michael, I believe. He was here for dinner a couple of months ago - such a handsome young man! Did you speak with him?"

"I missed him, I'm afraid," Sophie replied. "I was staying with my mother in Nice at the time."

"He was quite smitten with the view from the North Lodge bank," said Lady Adolphus. "He said the silver birches made him feel so much at home. He had so many silver birches across the north meadow... Mind you, if the Grand Duke knew what that oick Manyon is up to, he might not be so smitten with the place. We didn't tell him, of course... Do you think, Mr Holmes, that it counts as *lèse-majesté* to call an acquaintance of Bertie Wales an oick?"

She laughed her tinkly laugh. "Mind you," she went on without waiting for a reply, "Tum-tum does tend to allow the most extraordinary people into his set. Tommy Lipton, for example. I mean, Dolly would prefer to die rather than have a grocer at his table... Talking of table, your party will stay for dinner, of course, won't they, darling Sophie? One dines at half-past three on a Sunday. It's very old-fashioned, I know; but it's convenient for the servants, and one does have to be so careful with the lower orders, these days..."

"Lady Dolly," asked Mycroft, "why do you say that the Grand Duke Michael might not wish to lease Kenwood if he were to find out what Villiers Manyon is up to?"

"The best way of explaining is to show you, Mr Holmes," Lady Dolly replied. "Keep your things, and we'll go out by the terrace... And Eddy, dear, do stop worrying about that mud, for goodness' sake! Dolly lets the dogs put mud everywhere, so one really isn't going to notice a little bit more."

She patted her chignon into place under her wide-brimmed hat, drew her shawl about her, and offered her arm to Sophie.

"What's that Her Ladyship is saying about me, hey?" Lord Adolphus Murray appeared round a marble archway.

"Lady Dolly is saying she's deuced cwoss with you, Dolly old chap," Colonel Barnaby told him, "because you let your dogs put their muddy paws on evewything."

"Eddy!" Lord Adolphus shouted. "My dear fellow! What a surprise!" He clapped him on the shoulder. "And Sofya Sergeyevna, my very favourite princess!" He stooped his great height to bestow a whiskery kiss on Sophie's cheek. "How are you my dear?"

Sophie introduced Mycroft to him.

"You know, Dolly!" said Lady Dolly. "You've heard of Sherlock Holmes, the famous detective? Well, this Mr Holmes is his brother."

Mycroft forced back the scowl which began to form across his features. Fortunately, Lord Adolphus said immediately, "Mr Mycroft Holmes's name is familiar to me." He grasped Mycroft's hand with a manly sincerity which caused Mycroft to wince. "I have heard so much about you from Lord Derby and my old friend Jack Swarthmoor - the Ruwenora business, and the - who was it, now?... Ah, yes, I remember, that unfortunate matter when King Victor Emmanuel was still at the Pitti... Over Lady Kilgarden, wasn't it?. They say that was a marvellous job, you did, Mr Holmes!"

Mycroft felt a modest blush rising to his cheeks. "You are very kind, Lord Adolphus," he mumbled.

"About to take a stroll across the park, eh?" asked Lord Adolphus. "We've a splendid arboretum over there, across the lake. And over there..," he swept his arm round, "...we've as fine standing timber as you could wish. Interested in trees, are you, Mr Holmes?"

Mycroft could not have told a beech tree from a blackthorn, but he was saved embarrassment because, like his wife, Lord Adolphus did not stay for an answer. A page-boy had opened the terrace door, letting daylight and a stream of cold fresh air into the vestibule. Three dalmatians came bounding out of one of the passages, one of them pushing Mycroft out of its way so that he thought he would be toppled like a ninepin, before bounding out on to the broad gravel of the terrace.

"Felix! Marmaduke! Bella!" shouted Lord Adolphus. "Heel!"

The dogs paid not the least attention. Lord Adolphus selected a stick from the tallboy by the door. Mycroft groaned inwardly as the human party followed the dogs into the open air. As they set off down the steps from the terrace onto the sweeping meadow which led to the lake, there was something about the way Lord Adolphus was brandishing his stick and breathing in the air which suggested to Mycroft that it was not a stroll they were setting out on, but a country hike.

There was no help for it, of course. Of necessity, he followed the others down the long grass slope. At the bottom, instead of standing meditatively to observe the tranquil, lily spattered water, they turned and followed the shore to the end, then, crossing a low brick bridge over the stream which fed into the lake, they passed through a curtain of trees. Before them, to Mycroft's appalled gaze, another prairie-like open meadow, punctuated by small copses of silver birch-trees fluttering their leaves in the sharp breeze, stretched away to darkly ominous woodland. Worse still, Mycroft observed to himself, the path across the meadow was uphill all the way.

The possibility that their hosts would deem it sufficient for them simply to behold the second meadow was rudely snatched away. The dogs galloped ahead to make themselves the kings and queen of boundless space; Lord Adolphus strode after them, ineffectually ordering them to come back. Without so much as looking back at Mycroft, Princess Sophie and Lady Dolly gathered up their skirts, slung them over their arms, and set off upwards, arm in arm, chatting to each other with that intense but agreeable exclusivity which, in his opinion, indicated that women were the closest freemasonry on earth. Colonel Barnaby loped behind them on his long, bandy, cavalryman's legs as if walking came to him as naturally as riding.

The way became much steeper at the far end of the meadow where the roots of two gigantic sentinel beeches erupted through the bare sandy soil for a hundred yards about their bases. Mycroft toiled upwards after the rest, heaving himself forward on his stick and gasping for breath. At the top, Princess Sophie turned round at last. She regarded him with not the least compassion. "Oh, do come on, Mr Holmes!" she called. To Lady Dolly, she remarked, "He is such a - how do you say it?... I know! - slow-coach!" And then, to make matters worse, she laughed.

Both women stood between the two giant trees staring back at the view of the house across the meadow and the parkland, as if it would occupy their attention as long as it took Mycroft to drag himself up to join them. They were joined there by Colonel Barnaby, and it was Lord Adolphus, ever the attentive host, who slithered back down to join him, sending fragments of gravel bouncing down the dry earth.

"Expect it's having to spend all your days chained to a desk in Whitehall, eh, Holmes?" he announced. "Wouldn't change places with you - don't mind telling you!" He put his hand in the small of Mycroft's back and pushed him upwards.

Mycroft was allowed no time to catch his breath at the top. They passed through an ornamental gate out of the Kenwood demesne and into the woodland beyond. As they followed the track under the trees, Lord Adolphus remarked, "It'll be downhill on the way back."

It was to excuse their climbing another steep incline which brought them out of the woodlands onto a meadow plateau.

"My brother, Lord Mansfield," he explained to Mycroft, "has the standing timber as far as the Battery Heights over there. Beyond it's 'appy 'ampstead - common land still, except that our neighbour, Mr Villiers Manyon, has acquired the rights to the sand-soil for his brick making down on the East Park Estate."

Mycroft recovered his breath remarkably quickly. "Manyon, you say?" he asked. "Brick making?"

Lord Adolphus pointed with his stick. "Down there, Holmes. You can't see the brickfields from here, thank the Lord. But those are his people's cottages, over there."

He waved his stick to indicate over the treetops and scrubland stretching away for a mile and a half to where a straggle of poor cottages formed the ragged skirts of a mass of crooked tiles and chimney pots spreading as far as the eye could see: thousands and ten thousands of chimneys, each contributing a thread of seacoal smoke to be absorbed into a grey pall of fog which hung over all like a vast, limitless roof. Rearing above them like the hulls and upper works of beached vessels were the familiar shapes of St Paul's Cathedral and Westminster Abbey, the towers and spires of City churches, and the pinnacled Gothic pile of St Pancras Station Hotel.

"Ain't surprising they say a hundred thousand Londoners came up here for the Bank Holiday, eh?" Lord Adolphus observed. "First breath of fresh air the poor things had ever known, eh, what? Damned noisy, of course, but innocent fun."

"A dashed sight more innocent than the activities of that place!" remarked Lady Dolly.

Immediately below, as if dug into a hollow in the hillside, was a cluster of tall houses built in the recently fashionable 'Bavarian' style. Dominating them all was a monstrous, castellated edifice with wrought-iron balconies at every window, surmounted by a clap-board, crenellated tower on the top of which a Union flag flapped and snapped from its pole in the breeze.

"Marmaduke! Bella! Felix!" Lady Dolly called. "Oh, Dolly, do bring them in! They never do anything they're told!"

The dalmatians had run halfway down the slope; they were frisking about in the long grass.

"Manyon's establishment?" Mycroft asked.

"The Vale of Health Lakeside Spa Hotel and Sporting Rooms," Lord Adolphus nodded.

"So he's made a reputable business of the venture?" Mycroft asked.

"It don't mean he's given up his true avocation," Lord Adolphus replied.

"Dolly!" Lady Dolly warned.

"Oh, it's all perfectly legal and above board, of course." Lord Adolphus paid no more attention to her than to the dogs. "You can see the fashionable equipages every night, coming up East Heath Lane from Town. Nothing like that, after nightfall!"

He waved his stick in the direction of the small lake at the foot of the building. There were a handful of rowing boats on the water being propelled by men in pea-green or grey coats with velvet collars and cuffs; many wore their bowler hats perched dashingly on the backs of their heads. They were engaged in playing at naval manœuvres with one another. As they swung their craft about to ram or to evade being rammed, their fair passengers sat crammed in the sterns, wide-brimmed hats firmly secured with angora wool scarves tied under chins, and petticoats under vividly dyed matinée coats, drawn tight about their legs to avoid the splash from the oars, shopgirl voices squealing excitement across the water. The lake was overlooked by a long verandah with a black wrought-iron balustrade which ran the length of the hotel. A scattering of portly, middle-aged men, accompanied by full-blown beauties in taffeta and satin gowns with extravagantly ruched apron fronts and bushes, were standing along the rail shouting encouragement to the oarsmen below. Several of the women were smoking small cigars.

"After dark," said Lady Dolly, "it's *le plus haut ton*, I do assure you. 'Fine and genty' as they say among Dolly's people."

"How 'fine and genty', Lady Dolly?" asked Mycroft.

"Finer than it would be discreet to say, Mr Holmes," Lady Dolly replied.

"Fine enough to provide Manyon with the means to acquire the brick fields and the East Park Estate," said Lord Adolphus. "And to donate half a thou' to Parson Simkins to replace the lead on the church roof. Gusset-keeper turned respectable entrepreneur, eh? They say prayers of thanksgiving for him at Matins on a Sunday!"

"Dolly!" Lady Dolly protested again.

"It's no secret, my dear," Lord Adolphus replied. "He began by buying the new villas down there in the Vale from John Culverhouse, who the speculator who built the damn' things. Then, after Culverhouse died, he acquired the sandpits over on West Heath and the East Park brickfields from the estate. I recommended my brother to buy 'em, but he don't take any interest in his properties south of the Border any more. The claygate pits down there beyond the Vale, mixed with best Heath sand, make the finest brick in the south of England. Manyon's planning to build more of those damn' stucco and brick monstrosities all along the Hampstead-Highgate parish boundary line. It'll split the Kenwood property off from the Heath, and be a damned eyesore from both sides, deuce take the fellow!"

"Dolly, you really shouldn't...!" Lady Dolly intervened.

But Lord Adolphus had discovered an audience, albeit of only one, who manifested every sign of being interested in what he had to say. "And now the villain has just acquired the East Park Road and Sir Thomas Wilson's viaduct over Top Pond - must have knocked Manyon back a pretty penny, don't you know? And you can imagine what that will mean, can't you?"

"I fear not, Lord Adolphus," Mycroft replied. The mere idea of him knowing anything about a region so remote from Pall Mall was absurd. On the other hand, his curiosity was increasing by the moment. "Perhaps you would be good enough to show me?"

"Mr Holmes!" Lady Dolly protested. "You are encouraging Lord Dolly!"

She sounded as she had discovered that one of her friends had thrust a viper into her bosom. Lord Adolphus brandished his stick in the direction of an entrance into the undergrowth of the woods - a descending track on the slope below that which had brought them from the top gate to the Battery Meadow.

"Bella! Felix! Marmaduke!" he called to the dogs.

As if appreciating that their master was calling them to a more interesting spot, they bounded up the slope and thrust into the bushes ahead of him. Princess Sophie called out in genuine concern, "Mr Holmes! You mustn't over-fatigue yourself!"

Lord Adolphus halted in a glade of ancient gnarled oaks, in the very heart of the wood. A few paces behind him, Mycroft had been on the point of taking a swipe at one of the dogs who had persisted in gambolling around his legs. He lowered his stick just in time to avoid Lord Adolphus catching sight of what he was about to do.

"He means to have 'em all down," Lord Adolphus waved at the oaks. "They've been standing here since King Alfred's days, but that don't mean a thing to his sort. He's going to build hideous red brick and stucco villas: for neighbours, we'll have every publican and grocer who has the means to buy a house up here!"

Mycroft followed him, slithering down a steep earthy bank to a broad track deeply rutted with cart wheels. Lord Adolphus pointed his stick both up and down the track.

"Cut his way through, d'you see? Destroyed some of the oldest standing timber in the kingdom for his damned brick-carts!"

He marched off down the track at a brisk pace, Mycroft lumbering after him. They reached the margin of the trees; in front of them stretched the gravel road of a red brick viaduct high above a small, kidney-shaped lake covered in lily-pads. All sense of fatigue had fallen from Mycroft; he strode across the viaduct with the jaunty step of a *boulevardier*. At the far side, he halted and leaned on his stick, to survey the landscape stretching before him. To the right of the cart track, mud terraces formed a steep valley, at the bottom of which stood pyramids of freshly baked bricks and stands of timber covered in tarpaulin. At the far end of the deepest of the terraces stood a long, tin-roofed shack with an enormously squat, soot-blackened stone chimney. About it, on the plateau of beaten earth constituting its yard, lay heaps of coke and stout, iron-bound wooden vats. Mycroft recognised it to be the oven-house for baking bricks. Narrow, steep plank walkways bridged the banks of the terraces; they were caked and ridged with mud where wheelbarrows had been laboriously trundled up and down. The whole scene was deserted in a Sabbath calm, every heap and vat covered, every barrow and cart tilted up on its shafts.

Lord Adolphus came up behind him. "What do you see, Holmes?" he asked.

"It's not what I see, Lord Adolphus," Mycroft replied. "It's what I smell."

"Vile, ain't it?" Lord Adolphus agreed. "When the wind's in the wrong direction we can smell it over in the house." He pointed his stick at the iron-bound vats below the muddy terraces. "Deuced rum thing, don't you know? Smells exactly like the plague pits round Peshawar when Eddy Barnaby and I were there."

Mycroft turned away from the viaduct parapet. Without waiting to see if is host was accompanying him, he stepped out on to one of the plank walkways and started descending into the dank, earthy valley with complete confidence despite the steepness of the incline. Lord Adolphus followed him, stepping more gingerly down the muddy planks. Mycroft stopped on the first terrace-ledge to let him catch up with him.

"Villiers Manyon can't have received a penny yield on his investment as yet," he remarked.

"Not a penny," Lord Adolphus agreed.

"Yet the acquisition of all this must have required a very pretty capital outlay," suggested Mycroft.

"I know nothing of such things," Lord Adolphus replied, on his dignity. "But I daresay you're right. My agent tells me he holds the freehold on the hotel, and on the adjacent properties."

"There will be a mortgage, I imagine," said Mycroft, almost to himself. "And some very well-bred clients who would regard it as a sporting wager to act as his guarantors..."

"What are you driving at, Holmes?" demanded Lord Adolphus.

"The Marlborough house set?" asked Mycroft. "His Royal Highness, even?"

"That is not for me to say," replied Lord Adolphus stiffly. As if unable to maintain his discretion, he blurted out, "Sir William Gordon Cumming, and the whole damn' *baccarat* crowd, I'll tell you that!"

The bitterness in his voice took Mycroft by surprise. Lord Adolphus's lips were clamped so tight they had turned pale.

"There'll be a percentage rake-off on every marker," said Mycroft. "He has his rents - and a spot of renting on the side, I daresay. But it ain't enough - nothing like enough to have acquired and to exploit all this!"

The dogs, which had been exploring the undergrowth in the woods, had tired of their futile pursuit of squirrels. They came bounding across the viaduct, their paws thudding into the sandy ground, their tails lashing. They jumped down one of the plank walkways and slithered down to the bottom. Lord Adolphus shouted to them to come back, but gravity and their own inclination prevented them. Instead, they scampered away along the valley floor, heading straight for the oven house. They went directly to one of the iron-bound wooden tubs, cocked their legs or squatted against it, danced about it and leaped at it, scraping the sides with their claws as if determined to tear their way through to its contents.

"Deuce take it!" exclaimed Lord Adolphus, now thoroughly out of sorts. "They'll stink to high heaven, and there'll be the devil to pay!"

As if to confirm his worst expectations, Lady Dolly came running across the viaduct.

"For goodness' sake, Dolly!" she called. "What ever are you two up to down there? Call them off, this minute!"

Lord Adolphus passed Mycroft and slithered to the bottom of the walkway. Mycroft followed him and at the bottom overtook him again. He positively strode between the brick heaps, thrusting his stick before him, until he reached the tub which the dogs were attempting to break into. Without a moment's hesitation, he beat them off with his stick, and they retreated to sit watching him with a cowed look from a few yard off. Clamping his stick under his arm, and employing ah his strength, he threw the heavy wooden lid from off the top of the tub on to the ground.

"Mr Holmes! What are you doing?" Princess Sophie called from the end of the viaduct above.

Lord Adolphus came up and looked into the tub. "My dear man!" he exclaimed, then coughed and buried his face in his sleeve.

Mycroft looked up to the Princess, where she was standing on the cart track with Lady Dolly and Colonel Barnaby. "If you would be so kind as to join us, Princess!" he called up. His voice echoed across the deserted terraces.

Lady Dolly looked at Sophie in amazement. "What on earth possesses your friend Mr Holmes to suggest such a thing?"

"He has discovered something, Lady Dolly," Colonel Barnaby said. "He needs our Pwincess to help him."

"Eddy is right, you know," Sophie replied. "It can't be helped..."

She raised her arm for Colonel Barnaby to take. He did so, and led her carefully down the muddy planks to the bottom. As she approached the open tub, she wrinkled her nose and pulled a dreadful face. "Ah!" she exclaimed. "*C'est exécrable!*"

She drew a small lace handkerchief from inside the cuff of her glove and applied it to her nostrils. Mycroft did not appear to be in the least put out by the stench which so disturbed the others. Dipping the end of his stick into the grey, claggy contents of the tub, he held it out to Princess Sophie .

"Mr Holmes!" she protested, turning her face away from him and coughing as if she was about to retch.

"Oh, I say!" Lord Adolphus exclaimed, raising his face from his coat sleeve. "Holmes!"

"Claygate," said Mycroft, lowering the end of his stick. "You recall, Princess, what Mrs Tuttle said when she was describing the men who assaulted her that night, on the Lower Heath?" he wiped his stick on the rough grass. "She said that they 'smelt worse than any piggery' when they were close upon her. Do you remember?"

Sophie looked at him. She nodded. "'It was as if I was buried in freshly dug earth... clay...,'" she quoted. "And then she said something about 'a sour smell of decay.'"

Mycroft nodded approvingly. "There," he pointed with his stick, "is Squire's Mount - under Christchurch spire over there. And down there, at the bottom of Lower Heath, is the entrance to Downshire Hill and the home of Dr Bickleigh. From here, you may follow the path taken by Mrs Tuttle on her mission of mercy that fateful night."

"Mission of mercy, Holmes?" asked Lord Adolphus. "I take it you are referring to the dreadful killing of Captain Meadowthorpe."

"I am referring to the presumed killing of Septimus Meadowthorpe," Mycroft replied.

"The view taken by people of the better sort hereabouts is that the least said about the sorry affair, the better," said Lord Adolphus.

"A view shared by Villiers Manyon, I'm sure," said Mycroft.

Lord Adolphus was on the point of assisting Princess Sophie up the first level of the mud terraces. He stopped and turned about. "My dear Holmes," he said quite severely, "I have not spoken about the business up on Squire's Mount in front of Lady Murray, and I would be greatly obliged if you would follow my example."

He returned to assisting Princess Sophie up the incline. "The culprit has been apprehended he announced, "justice will be done upon her, and there's an end to it, eh?"

Sophie glanced back over her shoulder and pulled a grimace at Mycroft as if to say, "Now you have been told!"

"I'm sure you are absolutely right, Lord Adolphus," said Mycroft. "I shall not breath a word, I assure you."

CHAPTER EIGHT

"What ever did you say to poor Dolly," asked Princess Sophie, "to put him in a bad temper?" They were driving out on to the summit of Whitestone Hill from under the dark trees which lined the Spaniards. They could see in the long shadowed sunlight of late winter, below the vertiginous slope of a huge sand quarry, the roof-tops of the Vale of Health through the forked branches of the trees, and beyond, the bare heath stretching down to the towers, spires, and smoking chimneys of London and Westminster.

"I had to go to a great deal of trouble," Sophie continued, "to speak to Lady Dolly out of his hearing about Meadowthorpe's housemaid, Annie Gibbs..."

She leaned forward and prodded him with a gloved finger on which sparkled one of the famous Trubetskoy diamonds.

"Are you paying attention to me, Mr Holmes?" she demanded.

Mycroft turned his head from observing the scene. "It was my response to something Lord Adolphus told me as we were walking down to the brickfields. Lord Adolphus mentioned the *baccarat* set..."

"The *baccarat* set?" asked Sophie. "What is that?"

"Who are they?"" he corrected her. "The playing of *baccarat*, like roulette, is illegal in this country. Villiers Manyon was expelled from his North Street premises in Westminster not because he traded in young female flesh - which he did - but because he was running a gaming house. Many of the highest in the land are addicted to *baccarat*: H.R.H. of course; Lord Hartington; the Duchess of Manchester. They have all followed Manyon to the Vale of Health, out of reach of the Westminster vestry committees and the watchful eyes of scribblers for the evening press. It was the name of one of H.R.H.'s most devoted familiars and partner at the tables which appeared to effect the alteration in Lord Adolphus - Lieutenant-Colonel Sir William Gordon Cumming."

"Ah!" exclaimed Sophie. "His name would be quite enough to explain *son mauvais humeur!*"

Mycroft was sitting with his back to the horses drawing the Princess's brougham. Sophie glanced above his head at the tiny trap through which she communicated with her coachman. Mycroft raised his stick over his shoulder and with it, slid it shut.

"Dolly called him out, you know?" Sophie said. "It happened - oh! - two years ago or so. I will tell you only because I know you to be utterly discreet..."

They had begun the descent down Heath Street into Hampstead, the brakes of the carriage screeching on the rims of the wheels. Through the windows they could see the raw brick and stucco of the new suburban houses, and the unsuitably classical terracotta urns and statues in the small gardens.

"...Dolly and Lady Dolly were guests at Partingdale Croft at the same time as the Prince of Wales and Sir William. It was for the Newmarket race meetings. One evening, Sir William and Lady Dolly encountered one another in the Long Gallery upstairs - they had just been changing for dinner, you know? Sir William thought they were alone together; he made a certain, very unwelcome proposition to her. Now Lady Dolly - I can tell you for certain - has not so much as looked at another man since she met Lord Dolly on the hunting field when she was fourteen. She was very angry, but because the Prince of Wales was in the house, she did not want to cause a disturbance. So she told him not to be silly, and tried to walk away. But Sir William grabbed hold of her and said to her - I will tell you his precise words - 'My dear little girl, don't you know? All the young wives have tried me!'" Neither she nor Sir William, of course, knew that Lord Dolly was taking a nap before dinner in one of those big, old, high-backed armchairs, and that he was only a few feet away. He called Sir William out. According to Lady Dolly, Sir William just laughed in his face. He told Lord Dolly that his position as equerry to His Royal Highness forbade him from giving him satisfaction."

Mycroft sat back in his seat. He breathed heavily as he always did when he was giving due consideration to some matter of importance. "Sir William Gordon Cumming," he said, "figures somewhere in the background to the story of Regina versus Tuttle... Oh, yes!" he nodded to Sophie. "You see, Sir William is Lieutenant-Colonel of the Blues...Colonel Barnaby will confirm what I'm telling you..." He pointed out of the window to where Barnaby was riding beside the carriage. "Sir William was, therefore, senior cavalry officer in the late wars in Natal Province."

"So he was Captain Meadowthorpe's commander in South Africa?" Sophie exclaimed. "And must have known about Captain Meadowthorpe's cowardice."

"He must have been responsible for formally disgracing Meadowthorpe and sending him home," Mycroft told her.

"And Lord Dolly says that this Sir William is an acquaintance of

Mr Villiers Manyon?"

"Exactly so, Princess."

"And Mr Manyon was to be Captain Meadowthorpe's father-in-law..?"

"Twice over, in a manner of speaking," Mycroft confirmed.

"*C'est incroyable!*" Sophie exclaimed as if to herself.

"What is unbelievable?" asked Mycroft.

"Let us suppose Mr Manyon requires the services of a scoundrel," Sophie suggested. "One with the manners and appearance of a gentleman - yes? Let us suppose he says so in Sir William's hearing, at the table or *dans une cachette privée*. And Sir William replies, 'Mr Manyon, I know the very chap for you - *ochen' raspushchenyi*, a most wicked fellow! - whom I kicked out of his regiment, a Captain Meadowthorpe of the something Lancers.'"

Mycroft considered the Princess's idea.

"Are we to believe," he asked, "that this cashiered officer is of such value to Manyon that it is worth his going to the expense of setting nim up with a gentleman's household on Squire's Mount? Not to mention marrying him to his adopted daughter?"

Sophie waited until she was certain he was finished.

"While Lord Dolly, Eddy and you were smoking your cigars after dinner," she said. "I prevailed upon Lady Dolly to take me down to the kitchens. There were two downstairs maids who said that they knew Annie Gibbs. They said she was the daughter of a pig-keeper down at the bottom..." She waved her fingers at the carriage window. "They said that after Meadowthorpe's death, she found a new situation straight away. Do you want me to tell you where?"

Mycroft looked directly at her again. "At the Lakeside Spa Hotel."

"Clever boy!" said Sophie.

"But that," Mycroft told her, "need only mean that Manyon is the most important single employer of domestic staff here in Hampstead. There is, however, one more thing we have discovered on this afternoon's jaunt. And that is of the utmost importance to the case."

"What is that?" asked Sophie.

"The two men who prevented Mrs Tuttle from reaching Downshire Hill in time to save Meadowthorpe were employees of Villiers Manyon, from the East Heath brickfields." He suddenly lifted his stick and rapped with the knob on the carriage roof. "Pull up!" he called. "Pull up immediately, if you please!"

As the brakes squealed and the horses clattered to a standstill, Sophie had to clutch at the strap to prevent herself from losing her seat. "What is it?" she demanded.

"I see no purpose in fatiguing ourselves with making two journeys so far out of Town," Mycroft informed her, "when we may make do with one."

"What do you mean?" she asked.

The groom had already jumped down from his seat beside the coachman.

"Where are we?" she called through the window.

"Haverstock Hill, ma'am," the groom replied.

Colonel Barnaby rode up level with the window.

"Eddy, my dear," Sophie called, "it is Mr Holmes's whim we should stop here, on this Haverstock Hill!"

The carriage swayed as Mycroft rose to step down onto the road. The groom assisted him.

"You do not propose to speak to the servant, Annie Gibbs?" asked Sophie.

"No, Princess," he replied, as the groom helped her down to join him. "It is Sunday. Such persons, humble though they may be, are frequently of a Sabbatarian disposition. Nobody, however, would deny the propriety of employing a Sabbath afternoon in paying our respects to the mortal remains of Villiers Manyon's ward, the unfortunate Mrs Septimus Meadowthorpe... This is our way, I believe!"

Pointing the direction with his stick, he led Sophie and Colonel Barnaby across the street and up Baker's Row, a steep, narrow incline between the windowless backs of high buildings. "*Charmant!*" exclaimed Sophie as she picked her way between the ruts of dried ordure left by the nightsoil men's handcarts.

At the upper end of the alley they stepped out on to the cobbles of Church Row, a broad roadway with graceful eighteenth century town houses on either side, and, blocking off the far end, the elegant porch and spire of St John's parish church visible between the yews and cypresses of its churchyard. To their right, the last rays of sunlight touched the ragged tops of the ancient trees on the flank of Hollybush Hill.

"Oh, I say, Holmes old chap!" Barnaby protested. "You ain't taking us to church, are you?"

"I fear not," Mycroft replied.

Sophie stopped. She stared up at the church spire, its tip

glistening in the last of the sunlight. Her attitude had changed. "It is so very peaceful here," she said wistfully.

Mycroft took her arm. "I wish I could say I had brought you here because of its peacefulness," he told her.

At the end of the row of houses, behind one large, ancient and spreading yew-tree, a graveyard additional to that around the church spread up the hillside. There was an air of neglect about it, the quaintly lettered stone memorials and broken columns being half-concealed in the dank long grass and elder shoots. It was secluded from view by the low branches of the sycamores, yews and elders which grew all about it.

Mycroft led them through the decayed wooden lych-gate and up the overgrown path to a plot near the farthest corner. There, under the gnarled, arthritic branches on a solitary oak, the encroaching briars had been cut back and the grass scythed. At the far end of a shallow grass mound stood a plain black marble headstone, raw in its newness and its unsuitedness in such antique surroundings. The inscription read,

HELENA née BEWICK 1856-1879
Dearly beloved wife to
Septimus Athelney Meadowthorpe, lately Captn. 2nd Lancers,
whose anguish at her loss is equalled only
by his faith that in Death
she had been received into the arms of ONE
whose love for her exceeds even his own.
'So wise so young, they say, do ne'er live long.'

Mycroft stood for a moment uncovered, head lowered. Beside him, Sophie bowed to touch the grass with her finger-tips. She blessed herself. Colonel Barnaby stooped with the stiffness caused by cavalry corsets, picked a fallen twig with its bedraggled leaves still hanging on it, from the low mound and threw it away into the undergrowth.

Mycroft raised his head after a decent interval of silence, and replaced his hat. "We need have no further doubt as to the innocence of Mr Marshall Hall's unfortunate client," he announced "At least with regard to felonious killing."

"Can you tell from this," Sophie asked, pointing to the headstone.

"Yes, my dear," he replied. "Not perhaps so as to convince a jury. But to my own satisfaction. My suspicions were aroused regarding the fate of this particular young lady from the very start - when my brother and I were informed that she was taken ill as a result of drinking water from a public fountain in Florence. Had it been in any other Italian city, it might have been plausible. But the public fountains of Florence emit the purest water to be found in the South; it comes straight down from the Tuscan Hills, do you see?" He jabbed the ferule of his stick at the marble headstone. "And that confirms my suspicions."

"How - confirms?" asked Sophie.

"Deuced if I can see it!" Barnaby exclaimed. "Bad taste, eh? Something like that?"

"You are well-read in our National Bard, Princess," said Mycroft. "I expect you're more familiar with the poetry of Shakespeare than either Villiers Manyon or the late Sir Septimus Athelney Meadowthorpe." He pointed his stick at the epitaph "I daresay Helena Meadowthorpe's principal mourners - I mean Villiers Manyon and her husband - had no idea of the context from which these words were taken.

"They were taken from *King Richard the Third*, Act Three, Scene One," he told her. "The words of a wicked guardian intent on killing his ward..." He paused momentarily "...for his inheritance! And they were supplied by somebody whose conscience was burdened with a knowledge he dared not share by any other means save this epitaph."

"Deuce take it, Holmes!" said Barnaby. "What knowledge?"

"I think Mr Holmes means the knowledge that it was Villiers Manyon who poisoned Mrs Meadowthorpe - his own ward," replied Sophie.

A rook cawed bleakly over the hillside. The last rays of the sun had disappeared.

"Why should he have wanted to do a thing like that?" asked Barnaby.

"That I shall find out," said Mycroft. "I shall certainly be paying my respects to Dr Bickleigh in the near future. But first I shall find out the answer to that question. It should not prove difficult as these things go."

Sophie shuddered. She raised her arm for Barnaby to take. "Let us drive back to London," she said.

CHAPTER NINE

"'Morning, sir. And it's going to be a nice one 'less I'm much mistook."

Aggie rattled back the guest-room curtains. Edward Marshall Hall forced himself to open his eyes. The echo of his wife's taunting still haunted his brain - it was quite remarkable how heavily he had slept despite all the wretchedness of what, last night, had been too one-sided to be called a quarrel.

Aggie went out onto the landing to fetch in his hot water. A mist-filtered sunlight fell in bars across the vivid crimson rosebuds which flecked the buttery yellow of the wallpaper. The wallpaper was Ethel's choice, like everything else in the house. He had let her have her way in that, only to be led by her from room to room while she sneered at how common it all looked and told him how she had chosen to show his father what a fool he had been to allow his son to marry a tradesman's daughter. That had been the dreadful moment when he had realised she might not be altogether sane.

He wished he could wash the self-pity from his mind, if only to clear it for today's business. This morning, at half-past ten, he was to appear at the new Law Courts in the Strand, on behalf of the plaintiff in *Wainwright versus Krebs*; a suit brought under the recent Industrial Injuries Compensation Act, it was likely to command a considerable amount of attention.

"Is your mistress awake yet?" he asked Aggie as she returned with the hot-water jug.

"Not yet, sir," the girl replied, opening the jug lid with the edge of her apron and pouring the hot water into the basin. "Leastways, she ain't rung."

Her real name was Ellen. Ethel had decided it sounded too like her own name so she had rechristened her after one of the housemaids in her parent's home. She was sixteen, neat, clean and capable. Marshall Hall sometimes thought how restful it would be to be married to her instead of to Ethel.

Over breakfast, he glanced through the pages of *The Times*. He found he could not concentrate on the dancing columns of dense print; all the time he was listening for any indication of Ethel rising, and praying that he might escape from the house without attracting her attention. If only he could be successful enough to afford a manservant and membership of a good West End club, he could seal himself off as so many gentlemen did, from the pains and penalties of a disastrous marriage.

He laid his napkin beside his plate and folded *The Times*. He rose from the table and crossed the hall to his study. There, he gathered up his brief on *Wainwright versus Krebs* and tied it in its ribbon before thrusting it into his portfolio. With some bitterness he recalled how much more acute his advocacy would be if did not have to suffer the mental fatigue resulting from Ethel's interminable diatribes.

As always, Aggie was waiting for him in the hall, holding his hat, gloves and cane. She was swathed in a coarse blue apron; Ethel would never stand for so much as a hint of dirt on the maids' uniform-dress. One day, he thought, he would succumb to the temptation to kiss Aggie; the result would be disastrous since they depended on Ethel's settlement until he managed to make his way properly.

"Thank you, Aggie," he told her gravely as she opened the front door for him.

Then the voice called from the landing rail above, as piercing as it was unexpected: "Don't hurry home tonight, will you, Edward? You know how I prefer my own company!"

He breathed the morning air. Sunlight and a spring warmth was struggling through the hanging vapour. Before she closed the door behind him, Aggie gave him a smile of warm, honest encouragement. But over the girl's shoulder came Ethel's voice: "I don't mind if you never come back."

A lean angular figure stepped out from the area railing. "Ah, Mr Marshall Hall! Good morning, sir." He raised a pea-green bowler hat two inches above his thin sandy hair. "And a very good morning it is going to be, if I may make so bold."

"Mr Hartz?" said Marshall Hall.

"Of Marcus, Bullfinger, Stote and Marcus, sir. Very good of you to remember me. We have a closed carriage, only a step round the corner, in Bryanston Street."

He indicated the direction with a thrust of his hat brim. "Mr Bullfinger - that is Mr Augustine Bullfinger - takes a carriage from his house in St John's Wood every morning, to Lincoln's Inn Fields. A small detour, sir, and he has the pleasure of being able to offer you a lift to Mr Forrest Fulton's chambers in Fountain Court. Irregular, I know, to confer during a carriage ride. But Mr Bullfinger hopes that you shall not find it inconvenient... This way, if you please, sir."

Marshall Hall followed him out into Portman Square. Although the man Hartz did not appear to be hurrying unduly as he loped round the garden in the square's centre, Marshall Hall found that he very nearly had to break into a run to keep up with him.

"I fear Mr Bullfinger may find that I'm unable to devote the attention to Mrs Tuttle's case which it merits," he managed to say without betraying too much shortness of breath.

"Mr Bullfinger is fully cognizant of the fact that you are appearing in *Wainwright versus Krebs* this morning," Hartz assured him. "The eyes of the legal profession are on *Wainwright versus Krebs*. And you, sir, are a young gentleman who is on his way - that is what you are, sir, if I may make so bold. Which is why Marcus, Bullfinger, Stote and Marcus is gratified that you should have accepted our instructions on behalf of poor Mrs Tuttle... This way, if you please, sir. Another few paces, that is all."

He led him into Portman Street. A newly varnished growler was standing at the corner of Bryanston Street. He smiled reassuringly as he opened the door for Marshall Hall to climb inside. The latter was greeted with a pungent fume of cigar smoke for which he was unprepared at so early an hour. Mr Augustine Bullfinger, a man of huge girth, sat occupying two thirds of one of the seats. His polished top hat was pulled down to his eyebrows, a voluminous, fringed woollen shawl was drawn about him over his expensively tailored black overcoat.

"Good of you, Mr Marshall Hall" he said. "Much obleeged to you." He forced his words through a wheeze of bronchial phlegm, then coughed and cleared his throat. With the hand holding a cigar he indicated a dark, sallow cheeked gentleman wearing a gold *pince-nez*, a black homburg hat, and a coat with Persian lamb collar and cuffs, who was sitting in the corner of the seat opposite. The gentleman drew the skirt of his coat up on to his knee to let Marshall Hall take his place beside him.

"Dr Moldwyn Pugh," croaked Mr Bullfinger. "Mr Marshall Hall is one of the most promising of our younger practitioners at the bar."

Dr Moldwyn Pugh passed the chased-silver knob of his stick from one hand to the other. He offered his gloved fingers to Marshall Hall. His face was as gaunt as a death's-head; even through the soft kid of his gloves his fingers felt as brittle as old bones.

"Glad to make your acquaintance, young sir," he said in a West Wales accent which had in its softness an air of menace. "You have undertaken to defend our young client, as I hear."

About the thin mouth there was no hint of even the most formal of smiles, while any expression in the sunken eyes was lost behind the lenses of his *pince-nez*.

Hartz climbed in after Marshall Hall. He squeezed his lean frame in beside Mr Bullfinger's ample bulk, leaned out and closed the carriage door.

"Snug," croaked Mr Bullfinger. "We are very snug, eh, Mr Marshall Hall, what d'ye say? Do us the honours, Mr Hartz, if ye'll be so kind."

Mr Hartz rapped on the carriage roof with the handle of his cane walking-stick. "Middle Temple, if you please!" he called up.

Marshall Hall did not feel in the least snug as the carriage lurched forward. Mr Bullfinger's kneecap was pressed painfully against his own knee joint. Mr Bullfinger drew on his cigar and plunged the enclosed space with smoke. "I am sure you are asking yourself, my dear young sir," he pronounced, "why we should have sought your kind indulgence so early in the day." He coughed. "Particularly when your mind must be preoccupied with a case, a most interesting case, in hand. You have a right to ask, sir - and you shall have your answer." Mr Bullfinger leaned forward, sending a stab of pain shooting up Marshall Hall's leg from his kneecap. "Yesterday after-noon, despite it being the Lord's Day and the inconvenience both to himself and his daughter, General Bradfield was good enough to permit Dr Moldwyn Pugh to examine Mrs Tuttle - even to the extent of escorting us to the poor lady's cell in person and remaining with us during the examination. Now what do you say to that, sir?"

Marshall Hall felt a clammy sense of apprehension come over him. Inexperienced as he was in criminal practice at the bar, he knew well enough that what was about to be proposed was a means by which his client might at the same time plead guilty and save herself from the noose.

Mr Bullfinger drew on his cigar again with an expression of profound self-satisfaction. Marshall Hall stared out of the window; he felt like a prisoner himself. They were passing down Oxford Street. Early though it still was, lines of cabs had drawn up in front of the various emporia, and were discharging cargoes of mothers in broad-brimmed feathered hats and sealskin coats, and daughters in high-buttoned boots, tam-o'-shanters, and sailor collars. He felt a dreadful resentment at their fresh, cheerful expressions.

"I fear we may have lost you, Mr Marshall Hall," observed Mr

Bullfinger.

"Not at all," Marshall Hall replied. "You are about to tell me that Mrs Tuttle finds herself to be in an interesting condition."

Mr Bullfinger wheezed a dreadful bronchial laugh. "Interesting indeed, young man! But not quite as you suppose, eh, doctor?"

Dr Moldwyn Pugh gave the slightest inclination of the head. Mr Bullfinger's knee pressed even more acutely against Marshall Hall's kneecap.

"We seek Counsel's advice, Mr Marshall Hall," Mr Bullfinger said. "As to whether it would be more advisable to submit that our client is unfit to plead due to the state of her mind, or whether we should have her plead guilty but insane."

Marshall Hall was taken by surprise. "I saw no sign of insanity about her!" he exclaimed. "She told her story to me in the clearest, most lucid, manner."

"Such is often the case with dangerous lunatics," observed Dr Moldwyn Pugh in a gentle voice. "One recalls the case of Mr Dadd the painter, who stabbed a loving father with a penknife..."

"It will save her from the noose, Mr Marshall Hall, sir," Hartz intervened.

"But we have not exhausted other lines of defence!" exclaimed Marshall Hall. "There are still inquiries to be pursued! There's no need to proceed to so extreme a contrivance!"

"Contrivance, sir?" asked Mr Bullfinger. There is no question of 'contrivance' as you put it! The plain fact is, the woman is unfit to plead! Dr Moldwyn Pugh has so diagnosed - and let me tell you, young man, he is as distinguished an alienist as he is a physician. He has travelled from Paris where he practises at the Salpetrière Hospital, at our most urgent request."

Marshall Hall glanced at the gaunt figure beside him. Dr Moldwyn Pugh was staring into vacancy as if deliberately distancing himself from Mr Bullfinger's commendation.

"Would it not have been appropriate to inform me of this consultation before it took place?" asked Marshall Hall.

"It is a medical matter, Mr Hall. Not one of jurisprudence," said Dr Moldwyn Pugh.

"May I ask how you arrived at your conclusion with regard to my client, Doctor?" asked Marshall Hall.

"*Our* client." Mr Bullfinger drew on his cigar once more.

"Did you employ hypnotism?" asked Marshall Hall, struggling to keep his voice clear through the smoke. "I believe that is the preferred method under Dr Charcot at the Salpetrière!"

"There was no need for hypnotism, sir," Dr Moldwyn Pugh replied, "to perceive that your unhappy client is in no condition to plead before judge and jury. I have no wish to confuse you by using the language of Psychopathology; in plain English, your client is mad. For her own sake as much for others', she needs to be put in a place of secure confinement."

Mr Bullfinger leaned forward again, drawing his shawl about him as he did so. "You need not fear for your fee, Mr Marshall Hall," he wheezed. "It shall be paid in full, according to our agreement. Mrs Tuttle's benefactors have assured us of that."

"I am thinking of Mrs Tuttle's interests" Marshall Hall replied.

"Then we are in concert, are we not?" said Dr Moldwyn Pugh in the gentlest of whispers.

For the first time, a smile played about his death's-head features.

CHAPTER TEN

The first time he heard the low, rumbling sound, Mycroft thought that it was one of his audience snoring. He had been summoned from the Treasury to the Foreign Office to give a group of the new professional diplomats the benefit of his advice on the developing situation in the Rhineland following the accession of the widowed Grand Duchess Jolande to the throne of Pfalzel-Buckelburg. As always when he attempted to warn members of the Foreign Office against the expansionist policies of the new Imperial Germany, his views were greeted with an amusement amounting to contempt.

The rumbling sound came again. This time, he established its source, under his waistcoat. It was reminding him that it was lunch-time, and that in the Cock Tavern on the opposite side of Whitehall, lamb chops would already be sizzling on the grills. It signalled, he decided, a happy coming together of interests between himself and his signally unenthusiastic audience.

He was stepping into the enclosed forecourt of the Foreign Office, when he saw Sir James Swarthmoor standing on the steps opposite talking earnestly with three other gentlemen, their silk hats tipped forward over their brows. He looked to salute his old friend and superior, but the latter appeared too engrossed in what he was relating to the others to be disturbed, so Mycroft walked on. He was already in the passage leading out on to King Charles Street when Sir James called after him, "Holmes, my dear fellow! Hold your horses, eh?"

Mycroft turned and waited as Sir James came hurrying along the steps to join him. "I presume you are on your way to take lunch at the Cock Tavern?"

"That is so."

"Will you permit yourself to be my guest?"

"Very well," Mycroft replied. "I'm much obliged to you."

The dining room of the Cock Tavern had once been the kitchen of a spacious town house of the time of Good King Charles's golden reign. The entrance, almost opposite the Treasury Building, was down a flight of basement steps. Below, on the stone flags, surrounded by whitewashed walls with a ceiling of black wooden beams, were four rows of heavy tables with high backed oaken settles on either side. The settles with their rough-hewed wings provided a certain privacy for those dining at each table. That it was a fashionable eating place for those who lacked time to go to their clubs, for all the clumsy modesty of the furniture and the plain but hearty plates of chops, beef puddings, and potatoes carried by the waiters, was indicated by the silk hats and silk-lined overcoats suspended from the hooks at the ends of those settles which were occupied.

The head waiter led Sir James and Mycroft to an empty table. Sir James ordered a mutton chop for himself and, without asking him, a steak and kidney pudding for Mycroft, together with a bottle of Château Margaux 1870. When they had been served, and Mycroft had tasted the wine, Sir James asked, indicating Mycroft's glass, "I trust it's to your satisfaction."

"Perfectly, thank you, Sir James," Mycroft replied. He put it down. "And now," he said, "may I be permitted to know what do you wish to put to me while indulging me in one of my favourite dishes and one of my very favourite wines?"

He impaled a large segment of suet and cured beef on his fork, dripping gravy down his chin, and conveyed it to his mouth. He dabbed his chin with his napkin. With his mouth still half-full, he added, "We are not here, I think, to discuss the German question."

"There you are mistaken," Sir James replied. "Let me put it this way. Your rôle as unofficial Cassandra to HMG is far too important for you to intervene in a paid house-keeper's *crime passionel*. Even your brother does not concern himself with crime below stairs. In any case, this affair in which you have begun to take an interest is now the concern of the courts - of a jury of twelve honest men."

"Indeed," Mycroft agreed. He impaled a further quantity of steak, kidney, and potato on to his fork. Holding it above his plate, he added, "It would be, if it was ever allowed to go before a jury."

"I have no idea what you mean," said Sir James.

Mycroft replaced the food on his plate. "Ensuring there should be no wilful perversion of the rules of evidence is not the least of Her Majesty's great matters of state," he pronounced.

Sir James looked genuinely taken aback. "I hope you are not suggesting there is conspiracy to pervert the course of justice here?"

"That is precisely what I am suggesting, Sir James."

Sir James shrugged. "Such things don't happen in England," he said. "Not in the nineteenth century."

"I put it to you, Sir James, that you were not, just now, standing on the Foreign Office steps by chance," Mycroft told him. "No, no, Sir James, you should know better than to try pulling the wool over my eyes. You have not retained my services these last few years in order that I might so easily be deceived. You have been 'put up to this'. And if you, my dear old friend, *have* been 'put up' to distract me from my purpose," Mycroft continued, "it must have been by somebody occupying a position of eminence!"

He avoided searching Sir James's face. He had said as much as he wished to say; now he occupied himself with mopping up gravy with the food on his fork and lifting it to his mouth. Even when his companion emitted a sigh he continued to concentrate on his eating. He laid down his knife and fork, and wiped his mouth with his napkin. He reached for the wine bottle which was still one third full, and lifted it from its coaster. "You permit me?" he asked.

Sir James nodded perfunctorily. "Certainly," he said.

But before Mycroft could pour the wine into their glasses, he leaned forward over the table.

"If I may employ one of your own favourite expressions, Holmes," he said, "there are deep waters here. Deeper than you are aware of!" He looked across at Mycroft's face.

"I doubt it," said Mycroft.

He finished pouring the wine and returned the bottle to the coaster. He too leaned over the table as far as his girth permitted. "Let me suggest," he said softly, "that one is dealing here with the game of *baccarat*? - and one of its most elevated *aficionados*?"

Sir James hesitated momentarily, as if unsure whether to pursue the matter. "How do you arrive at this hypothesis?" he asked.

"Hypothesis?" Mycroft protested, raising his voice so that Sir James had to put his finger to his lips. "There are two pieces of evidence which, if taken as complementary, must lead one to such a conclusion. Firstly, we have the fact that when Villiers Manyon's North Street establishment was closed by the Westminster vestry, he was able to acquire almost overnight the Vale of Health Lakeside Spa Hotel safely beyond the reach of the London watch committees. Secondly, there is the strange fact that no sooner was the unfortunate Mrs Tuttle apprehended for the murder of her somewhat disreputable employer, than an anonymous benefactor retained the services on her behalf of Marcus, Bullfinger, Stote and Marcus: a firm better known for pursuing cases in Chancery and Admiralty and Probate than in the criminal courts. And I may add..." Here he deliberately allowed a note of anger to creep into his voice "...a firm so distinguished for its thoroughness has shown a wonderful negligence in preparing its client's defence. One may be forgiven for supposing it has no very wholehearted desire to win a verdict in her favour."

"I see you have indeed embarked on a course which you may discover to be fraught with peril," said Sir James, lowering his voice still further. Then, unable to contain himself, he exclaimed, "Deuce take it, man! Haven't the Mordaunt Case and the Aylesford scandal been enough without dragging the reputation of our Royal Family further through the mire? What do you think Dilke and his republican friends will make of a case of murder - of domestic murder - touching the heir to the throne?"

"Forgive me, Sir James," Mycroft replied. "But do we have something here beyond a royal predilection for a rather childish game of chance?" Mycroft asked.

Sir James stared directly at him. "Holmes, I beg you! Leave well alone!" he pleaded. He glanced about him as if expecting eaves-droppers to appear at the end of the table. "Parthenope Manyon," he said in the lowest of possible voices, so that Mycroft had to strain to hear him. "What do you know of her?"

"That she is Villiers Manyon's younger daughter," Mycroft replied, "that she was Meadowthorpe's intended bride and is the inheritrix of his entire fortune."

He stared back at Sir James as the truth dawned on him. "Dear God!" he whispered. "You don't mean...?"

Sir James nodded. "Parthenope Manyon," he whispered back, "has been one of His Royal Highness's *petites amities* for the last ten months. It has been a well-kept secret. Even the Jersey Lily knows nothing of it - and she is reputed to know everything."

"I grow old, Sir James - senile before my time." Mycroft clutched his forehead.

"You need not blame yourself," Sir James assured him. "Simply take my advice, and leave well alone."

"Leave well alone," Mycroft exclaimed. "Don't you realise that unless we arrive at the actual truth of this matter, the mire will be made deeper through which the Prince of Wales's reputation may be dragged... How could I have been so blind!"

Lowering his open hand from his head. He whispered, "There is more than human weakness at work here," he said. "There is a purposed wickedness which cannot - must not be allowed - to run its intended course!" He looked directly into his companion's eyes. "Believe me, Sir James," he said earnestly.

CHAPTER ELEVEN

The liveried attendant had come up from the porter's desk; he was signalling from the doorway of the smoking-room to attract Mycroft's attention. The rules of the Diogenes Club respecting its members' right to absolute silence were observed more strictly than the laws of the Medes and Persians. The matter was therefore of some urgency.

Mycroft stirred himself from the deep of his black leather porter's chair, his habitual place of meditation and repose between a quarter to five and twenty to eight. He knocked back the last of his brandy and seltzer, replaced the glass noiselessly onto the rattan coaster by the arm of his chair, and pulled his bulk with an effort to his feet. Clasping his half-smoked Havana *veguera* between his lips, he crossed the heavily piled carpet to the door, and followed the attendant down the marbled staircase to the vestibule.

He did not feel the least resentment toward the attendant; he was, he decided, growing a deal more tolerant and good-natured with the advance of years - he was approaching his thirty-fifth birthday. In any case, he had known from the moment he had settled down with his brandy and cigar that he would not be allowed to drift into that seemingly disembodied tranquillity in which his intellectual processes moved most freely and directly to a conclusion.

On leaving the Cock Tavern that afternoon, he had paused only until Sir James Swarthmoor had disappeared round the bend in the railings of Downing Street before calling up one of the cabs which were parked along the pavement awaiting the convenience of lesser servants of the Crown, and had instructed the driver to take him to Somerset House. What he had discovered there, among the boxes containing dried and cracked parchments, was sufficient for him to return to the cab and order the driver to take him back to Whitehall and the Home Office. There, with all the considerable authority he could command, he asked to be allowed to speak with the Home Secretary in person. Sir William Vernon Harcourt came out on to the landing to greet him.

"Holmes, m'dear fellow! Just caught me!... How are ye, my dear chap?... Come in! Come in!... That's all right, George - close the door behind ye, if ye'll be so good... Now, Holmes! What can I do for ye? That was sterling work ye did for us over that Irish Land League business - put Parnell out of countenance for once, eh what?... So what is it now?"

"A much simpler matter, Sir William," Mycroft assured him. He hoped he had got to him in time. "Your authorization, if you will. For an exhumation."

"An exhumation?" asked Sir William with a look of amusement. "Turned grave robber, have ye, Holmes? Or is it resurrectionist?"

"I need your peremptory authorization for the exhumation from the churchyard of St John's Church-in-Hampstead of the body of the late Mrs Septimus Meadowthorpe," Mycroft told him. "Her medical adviser signed her death certificate in the belief that she had contracted a disease by drinking impure water. I have reason to suppose that she was murdered by poison for gain, and that the beneficiary of the crime is still at liberty and enjoying the fruits of his crime."

"Well!" said Sir William. He looked sternly at Mycroft. Mycroft knew that he was too late. Sir William pointed a finger in the general direction of Mycroft's watch-chain. "Somethin' to do with the Tuttle case, is it?" he asked.

"Something to do with preventing a serious miscarriage of justice, Sir William," Mycroft replied boldly. He had nothing to lose.

"Deuced awkward, ye know!" said Sir William. "I mean, havin' to tell a fellow who has 'done the state some service' that he's makin' a damn' fool of himself! Attractive woman, Mrs Tuttle? Pretty little horse-breaker, is she, Holmes?"

"She is accounted pretty by some," Mycroft replied. "I myself have never set eyes on her... Sir William, I do not for a moment deny that I seek to prevent an injustice being done to Mrs Tuttle. But I have reason to suppose that the implications of the case may reach well beyond the fate of one unfortunate female."

"I'll be frank with you, m'dear Holmes," snapped Sir William Vernon Harcourt. "That is precisely why I shall certainly not issue an exhumation certificate - and why I beg you, for your own sake, to keep your mind on the Treasury, sir, and foreign affairs! The cobbler should keep to his last, don't 'e know, what?"

As he stepped out onto the pavement of Whitehall, Mycroft's first idea had been to hail a cab and to drive straight round to Bruton Street and Princess Sophie's apartments. He was not accustomed to being abruptly dismissed by Ministers of the Crown, even those of the highest rank - and certainly not without being granted the opportunity of justifying his stated opinion. Almost immediately, however, he had thought better of it; he would call on the Princess, but only after several hours of meditative silence in the Diogenes had provided the antidote to the fevered restlessness of the day's activities.

There had, of course, been no such antidote; he had been jarred by his encounter with Sir William Vernon Harcourt, sufficiently for him to be reconciled to his being disturbed.

As he turned the stairs, he saw the young man waiting below by the porter's desk, holding his hat and gloves in his hand. He recognized immediately the lean, handsome, chiselled features.

"Mr Marshall Hall!" he greeted him.

"Mr Holmes, I beg you to forgive me this intrusion on your quiet. Your fellows..." he indicated the porter and his silver-buttoned acolytes behind the desk. "...were most reluctant to disturb you."

Mycroft nodded. The club servants had only to make two such mistakes of judgement to forfeit both position and character.

"I had to seek advice from someone, sir," Marshall Hall continued. "I did not know to whom I should turn."

"But you did, my dear boy!" Mycroft contradicted him with unexpected magnanimity, "you came here to me!" And he put his hand on the younger man's shoulder. The faces of the servants shone with relief. "It would never do to talk here, however," he added. "It would not answer at all. My own place is only a short walk across the street; we shall find it as convenient as you would wish... Austen?" he called before Marshall Hall could demur. "My hat and coat, if you please."

They crossed the busy thoroughfare. Mycroft, as was his invariable practice, brought the traffic to a standstill - brewers' drays, delivery vans, carriages, and at least one omnibus - to allow himself and Marshall Hall to pass, raising his stick high into the air as if he were Moses dividing the Red Sea. He unlocked the front door of 73a with his passkey and, glancing up and down the pavement, pushed his companion before him into the narrow hallway. Closing the door after him, he thrust his stick into the Japanese vase kept by Mrs Turner for the purpose, and indicated that Marshall Hall should do the same.

The comfortable figure of his landlady appeared through the door beyond the stairs. On perceiving that Mycroft had brought a gentleman in with him, her hand went straight to the thick, gipsy-black tresses under her cap, to ensure they were pinned to best advantage.

"Begging your pardon, Mr Holmes," she said. "There is a matter I must speak to you about..."

"Not just now, Mrs Turner," Mycroft interrupted her.

He started up the stairs, beckoning Marshall Hall to follow him.

"It's about a gentleman, Mr Holmes, sir!" Mrs Turner called up to him. "I thought as I'd better inform you straight away."

Mycroft gripped the banister. It had been a most fatiguing day, and it wasn't over yet. "You have let the second floor rooms?" he suggested. "To a Third Secretary from the Montenegrin Legation...? Last year," he explained to the bewildered Marshall Hall, "Mrs Turner let the rooms above mine to a Mr Melas, a Greek gentleman, an interpreter who worked *inter alia* for the Royal Greek Legation here. On feast days and high holidays he smashed plates."

"He did not!" Mrs Turner replied indignantly. "He was a nice, scholarly gentleman; quiet as you like."

"Even quiet Greeks smash plates, my dear woman," Mycroft informed her. "It is their national pastime, don't you know?" To Marshall Hall, he continued, "In fact, he did exactly what I am doing now: involved himself in an affair which wasn't his business. It proved his undoing, I fear!"

"Mr Holmes will have his little joke, sir," Mrs Turner told the astonished Marshall Hall.

"A pot of tea, if you will be so kind," Mycroft told her. "And a dish of hot buttered muffins."

"But your dinner, sir," Mrs Turner told him reproachfully.

"Mr Marshall Hall will not be dining here," Mycroft replied. "He will require muffins - toasted and well buttered."

"Please!" Marshall Hall intervened. To Mrs Turner, he said, "Do not trouble yourself on my account."

"Stuff and nonsense, my boy!" Mycroft told him. "You need hot buttered muffins. There is nothing to equal them - they are restorative to the over-fatigued body and sedative to the overwrought mind."

In the study, Marshall Hall removed his coat while Mycroft tidied copies of *The Times*, the *Morning Post* and the *Pall Mall Gazette* littering the well-worn, comfortable armchairs on either side of the fire. Mycroft leaned forward and poked the coals into a blaze.

"So you have come to me straight from *Wainwright versus Krebs*, I daresay," he observed. "Interesting case. I make a point of committing to memory the calendar of the Supreme Court of Judicature. One never knows how useful it may prove to be. I hope your concern over Mrs Tuttle's predicament didn't distract you from putting across your client's case in Queen's Bench Seven. You see, my dear young sir, I believe I know what it is you have come to tell me."

With a wag of his finger, he indicated that Marshall Hall should remain silent. "Your instructing solicitor has put it to you that Mrs

Tuttle should plead guilty but insane in accordance with the McNaghton Rules. Or that, after consulting with certain medical men, testimony should be put before the jury at her trial of her unfitness to plead on grounds of insanity."

"That is the position exactly," exclaimed Marshall Hall. "How did you find out?"

"I did not 'find out'," replied Mycroft. "I deduced." He planted his hands over his stomach.

"A dear friend of mine - a lady of the highest rank, and of a most charitable disposition - has visited Mrs Tuttle in Millbank. I do not know whether you have observed what she observed - I mean, that your unfortunate client, far from being treated as a prisoner awaiting trial is entitled to be treated, has been deprived of clothes becoming a gentlewoman of her station, is compelled to wear prison garb, and is being subjected to the full rigours of the Silent System."

"I had noticed her garments," Marshall Hall said. "I assumed that... well, there was some reason..."

"My friend sought to alleviate her condition," Mycroft interrupted him. "By sending food, delicacies, books, and other small comforts to which prisoners on remand, even those facing a capital charge, are entitled. The Governor of Millbank forbade them absolutely."

"I did not know that," said Marshall Hall. "And Mr Bullfinger made no objection to Mrs Tuttle being held under such conditions?"

Mycroft smiled indulgently. He drummed his fingers on his waistcoat. "The deprivation of human intercourse enforced under the Silent System, and the punitive degradation applied to those subjected to it," he continued, "have been known to upset the mental balance of the most hardened criminal. It is impossible to imagine the effect it must have on a genteelly brought up clergyman's widow, however wayward her recent behaviour. But this, sir, is the point I wish to emphasize: one cannot for a moment suppose that a firm with a reputation for thoroughness in their clients' interest as is enjoyed by Marcus, Bullfinger, Stote and Marcus, remains unaware of the hard condition which has been laid upon her. One is ineluctably drawn to the conclusion that they are party to the injuries which are being done to her. From that, it is but a step to the realization that they are party, equally, to the result which those injuries are intended to produce - I mean, a wilfully wrought disturbance of her balance of mind."

Marshall Hall gasped in astonishment: "But it is iniquitous! Mr Holmes, if this is not a fancy...!"

"I am never fanciful," Mycroft assured him. "It is not in my nature."

"Then I shall most certainly speak to General Bradfield," said Marshall Hall. "And, if I get no satisfaction from him, I shall go straight to the Home Office..."

Mycroft admonished him to be silent with a flipper-like movement of his hand. Mrs Turner entered with the tea tray; she was followed by Maisie, the small general maid whose starveling appearance belied both her voracious appetite and her mistress's generous indulgence of it. Maisie placed the cake stand beside Mycroft's chair.

"Thank you, Mrs Turner," said Mycroft. He lifted the cover from the dish and the room filled with the scent of toasted, buttered muffins. "Excellently done!" he exclaimed. "I am sure that you need to refuel your vigour, Mr Marshall Hall, after an exhausting day pleading in the new Law Courts... Thank you, Mrs Turner," he repeated pointedly.

He waited until she had withdrawn, with Maisie like a lean, small sloop in her wake. He poured out the tea and handed a cup to Marshall Hall.

"My first view, when you spoke to us the other night in my brother's apartment in Baker Street was that it was intended you should lose the case... In a word, that your client should be hanged."

He held out the muffin dish, refusing to continue until Marshall Hall had, with some reluctance, taken one.

"I have since perceived that, for once, I was mistaken." He examined the muffin dish with an expert eye, then took a muffin in either hand. Without waiting to finish his mouthful, he said, "It would have been too blunt an instrument for the sort of mind with which I believe we are dealing here. Tidier by far would be for Mrs Tuttle's case, to all intents and purposes, not to come to trial at all."

Marshall Hall sat with the muffin on the small plate on his lap. "Mr Holmes," he said, "that is exactly what I came to inform you - that Mr Augustine Bullfinger had decided that no evidence should be placed before a jury save that regarding Mrs Tuttle's state of mind."

Mycroft took a bite out of his second muffin.

"May I ask, sir," Marshall Hall persisted, "if this lady of your acquaintance is of the opinion that Mrs Tuttle is in her right mind?"

Mycroft pointed to his plate. "Eat your muffin," he said. "The lady was of the opinion that your client's account of herself was both clear and precise - admirably so, in fact."

He decided against adding that Princess Sophie had thought Mrs Tuttle to be on the verge of mental collapse. "Mrs Tuttle was, however, in a state of considerable distress at her condition."

Marshall Hall nodded his understanding. "I believe there was an attempt to offer me a financial inducement, this morning," he said, "to follow the course recommended me by Mr Augustine Bullfinger." He related now Mr Bullfinger had given him a lift in his carriage.

"There was nothing of which I could complain to the Law Society or to the Lord Chancellor's office, you understand. It was merely made clear to me that I would not be the material loser if the case never came to trial in the fullest sense."

Mycroft took another bite of one of his muffins. "As things stand, your client would appear to be completely innocent of the crime of which she stands accused," he said with his mouth full.

"Is there more you should tell me?" asked Marshall Hall.

"Not at this juncture," Mycroft replied. He finished his muffins. "You shall not go into the court unarmed. Have no fear of that."

He drew a large bandanna handkerchief from his sleeve and wiped his fingers. "I would urge you, however, to say nothing of this conversation - either of its substance or of the conclusions which we may have reached to anybody, least of all to your instructing solicitors. You must try to win your client's confidence while, at the same time, not giving Messrs Marcus, Bullfinger, Stote and Marcus the least intimation that you do not propose to follow their suggestions when the case comes up for trial. My continuing interest in your client's fate is conditional upon that, you understand?"

He flapped the bandanna in the air, then replaced it in his sleeve. More gently, he continued, "I wish I could give you concrete reasons why you should do as I say. But there are things which, for the moment, it is better you should not know - which it is personally safer for you not to know or guess at. There is, however, one thing which you must discover..."

He leaned forward in his chair. "It is the name or names of those who have retained the services of Marcus, Bullfinger, Stote and Marcus on Mrs Tuttle's behalf - and, of course, through them, your own. I can tell you who has not, even though he is the man most likely to benefit from your client's condemnation. An apparently fair and open trial by jury of your client, followed by her execution, would suit Mr Villiers Manyon very well. But I am entirely certain that a firm such as Marcus, Bullfinger, Stote and Marcus would never involve themselves with such a fellow as Manyon is. In any case, while allowing Mrs Tuttle to appear to be guilty, they wish to preserve her life, while it would suit Manyon to see her executed. Now let us suppose, your clerk at Fountain Court were to entertain their chief clerk to a dinner of mutton chops and a pint of claret - that is how these things are usually accomplished in the legal world, I believe - it is just possible we might find out who is behind this conspiracy to deny your client the chance to demonstrate her innocence. We would then be in a tolerable way to know what is afoot here."

When he was alone, Mycroft looked at the plate beside his late visitor's chair, and at the muffin with the single bite taken out of it. He picked it up and finished it. Wiping the crumbs from his lips, he took his hat and coat and descended the stairs once more. He met Mrs Turner on her way up.

She held out a small, embossed pasteboard card. On it, under the tiny embossed and gilded coat of arms, and inscribed in gold copperplate, with the legend,

Lieut. Col. SIR WILLIAM GORDON-CUMMING Bart.

"Said as he wanted a word with you, sir, 'as a matter of urgency'," Mrs Turner told him. "Very smart, well-spoken gentleman, he was. An important sort of gentleman, if you ask me."

"I daresay, I daresay" Mycroft replied. The possibility that Septimus Meadowthorpe's old commander in Southern Africa might wish to provide him with information about his late and disgraced subordinate entered his head. But he entertained the idea only for the briefest of moments. Sir William Gordon Cumming was also a courtier, a sportsman, a bosom companion to the Prince of Wales. It was infinitely more probable that he would wish to obstruct rather than advance any investigation into Meadowthorpe's death. Mycroft wondered what he should do if Sir William were to deliver a direct command from His Royal Highness that he was to desist from his investigation. What then would be his duty as a loyal subject?

He squeezed past Mrs Turner, and continued down to the front door. He took his stick from the vase.

"You're never going out again, sir!" she exclaimed. "Not at this hour!"

"I fear I am," Mycroft replied.

"But this is the time you usually come in for your dinner, sir."

"Extreme circumstances demand extreme measures," he announced.

CHAPTER TWELVE

The cab deposited Mycroft at the corner of South End Road and Downshire Hill. To his right, behind the sooty brick pumping station, and bathed in the western twilight, stretched the heathland scrub scarred by the brickfield terraces; it was fringed with shabby, low-roofed cottages with broken, sack-filled windows, surrounded by dirt paths on which ragged children played amongst the starveling hens which sought to peck and scratch an existence from the grit. Fires burned on the plateaux formed by the clay pits, their orange flames reflected in the oily water of the ponds. Over all, hung the damp dung smell of decay.

To his left rose the graceful wisteria-clad villas built at the beginning of the century, rising among the trees, one above another, to Hampstead High Street and beyond.

"Hey, fellow!" Mycroft held up a gold sovereign to the driver. He rapped the ferule of his stick on the brass bar round the man's seat. "Wait for me here, and you shall have earned yourself another before this night is through, d'ye hear me?"

Clutching his whip against his cheek, the jarvey tilted his mittenned hand toward the last of the sunlight to examine the coin. "God bless you, sir!" he called down.

"Go and refresh yourself, if you will," Mycroft told him, pointing to the Freemasons' Arms which stood at the corner of Downshire Hill like a frontier post between the squalor of the brickfields and the prosperous homes and gardens that rose behind it.

Mycroft set off up the hill. A small knot of women was standing by the back wall of the public house, under the gas lamp which was flickering in the half-light. Several were clutching bottled beer, others, chipped and stained enamel jugs. There was a sound of women's laughter and singing from the public bar. A young woman, a ragged straw hat pulled down over her matted brown hair and a half sack about her arms and shoulders by way of a shawl, sauntered over.

"Give us somefink for a 'alf pint, mister," she asked.

Mycroft looked at her tattered, filthy appearance and pinched little face. Her skin was wizened about her mouth where most of her teeth were missing. It would have been impossible to estimate her age.

He took his purse from his pocket. She eyed it with the intensity of a cat eyeing a saucer of milk which its owner was about to place on the floor.

"You are from the cottages...?" He pointed with his stick in the direction of South End Road.

"Yer?" the young woman replied inquiringly. "We all is. What of it?"

The others were watching.

"Then it is possible you are acquainted with a girl called Annie Gibbs?" he asked.

Pertness was transformed instantly to an acute wariness. "What's it to you, mister?" the young woman asked. She glanced back at the others. "Wants to know about Annie!" she said. "Annie Gibbs."

She came up close to Mycroft while the others watched as eagerly as rats. "What you want to know 'bout Annie for, mister, eh?" she demanded. Starveling though she was, with scabby sores about her mouth, she was challenging him. Mycroft opened his purse. He took a calculated risk.

"Just to speak with her," he said. "But not at the Lakeside Spa Hotel."

"You ain't going to speak wiv Annie," the girl replied. "Ain't nobody goin' to speak wiv Annie. Annie done herself in, see?"

By the shrillness of his tone Mycroft betrayed the fact that he had been taken by surprise. "How, 'done herself in'?" he asked.

The girls watching the encounter were pretending to hide their faces behind their hands.

"She drownded herself," said the first girl.

"Where?" asked Mycroft. "When?"

"The men fished her out of the ponds, yesterday morning like..." the girl began.

Another girl came forward, a ragged, barefoot mite clutching an enamel jug, who looked as if she were ten or eleven years old.

"They found her in the rushes, like that there Moses in the Bible!" she announced, staring fixedly at Mycroft's purse which was at her eye-level. "On'y Annie Gibbs were dead as a door nail."

"Perhaps she had an accident," Mycroft suggested. "Perhaps she fell into the water."

"Hah!" exclaimed the mite still staring at the purse.

"Why do you say that?" Mycroft asked.

"Anyone can tell that!" scorned the mite. "She weren't wearin' any coat when the men hooked her out, was she? An' she hadn't taken off her cap an' apron. She were werry proper were Annie Gibbs! She'd never have gone walking out in her cap an' apron..."

"Shouldn't 'ave taken a sittiation at the Lakeside Hotel if you asks me," interrupted the first girl. "Weren't the sort, if you knows what I means."

Mycroft placed his stick under his arm and unbuttoned his purse. Both girls watched avidly. The smaller one wiped one hand on her ragged skirt.

"Did any of you know Annie Gibbs well enough to speak to?"

"Yerse!" said the smaller girl immediately.

"You fibber! You never did!" said the first girl. To Mycroft, she said, "Annie weren't the sort to speak to the likes of us."

"Out of which pond was she pulled, yesterday morning?" he asked.

"'ighgate," said the first girl. "Highgate Pond."

"But Highgate Ponds are on the farther side of the Heath!" he exclaimed.

"She were the bashful sort, were Annie Gibbs," said the girl. "Wouldn't say boo to a bleedin' goose - begging your pardon! She'd never want to put nobody to trouble if you knows what I mean."

Mycroft gave half-a-crown to each of the two girls. The expressions of astonishment on their faces, and the rarely concealed gasps from those looking on, were enough to tell him that sixpence would have been regarded as more than generous.

As he went up Downshire Hill between the steeply-banked gardens on either side of the road, he pondered the news that before she died Annie Gibbs had crossed the full width of the Heath on a rainy night without putting on hat or coat. Surely, he thought, the removal of her cap and apron before she went out, even on such a desperate errand, would come as second nature to a young woman who regarded herself as a social step up the ladder from the labouring girls loitering outside the public house... The news disturbed him sufficiently to make him light up a cigar then and there, in the street.

He was more than halfway up Downshire Hill, past the elegant white portico of the church of St John, when he saw the brass plate set in the wall on the opposite pavement, John Bickleigh MD, BCh, FRS. He was standing by the doors of a stable yard, firmly locked for the night. The object of his journey so far out of London's West End was probably at home. He rang the bell at the garden door and let himself in. He mounted the steps of the terraced garden to the front door. A fresh-faced young general maid was waiting for him on the step. He asked to speak to Dr Bickleigh.

"Beg pardon, sir." The girl bobbed and took the card. "The Doctor bain't at home."

She was a country girl by her accent and healthy appearance, and the blue stuff gown under her pinafore-apron smelt of camphor.

Mycroft was not in a mood to take 'no' for an answer. He waved his stick in the general direction of the stable doors.

"He is not pursuing his professional avocation," he remarked.

The young servant gawped in bewilderment at him.

"He is not out visiting, a patient, my dear," he told her.

The girl clutched and unclutched her apron. "Dunno, sir," she whispered.

"Milly?" a voice called sharply from an adjacent room. "'oo is it, Milly?"

"A gentleman, ma'am! To see the Doctor, if you please, ma'am!" the maid replied.

"Well, tell him the Doctor is not at 'ome, then!" called the woman.

"He has been told, madam!" Mycroft called. "But he insists on seeing Dr Bickleigh, if he may."

"Drat the gel!" came the woman's voice, despite Mycroft's explanation.

Preceded by a rustle of silk flounces, its owner came out into the hallway - a full-figured woman with steel-grey hair tied in a bun under an old-fashioned muslin mob.

"Beg pardon, ma'am!" the maid whispered. "Didn't mean..."

But Mycroft hadn't the patience to let her tell her mistress what she didn't mean. "My fault, madam - entirely," he told her, raising his silk hat. "A case of what 'commercials' call, I am led to believe, the foot in the door. I have made a long journey to speak with the Doctor, your brother."

He managed to make it sound as if he had travelled from the wilder shores of the Limpopo.

"Ay do not think ay 'ave the honour of your acquaintance, sir - do ay?" the woman asked with some surprise.

"No, madam," Mycroft smiled. "Nor does your brother. You are not wearing a wedding ring under that charming lace - Brugeois, is it not? But you are clearly mistress of the house. Therefore, I take it you must be sister and brother."

"You are observant!" the woman simpered. "I am indeed Miss Bickleigh."

"And I am Tennerby," Mycroft told her. "Joshua Tennerby, barrister-at-law, of the Outer Temple. Deuced inconvenient, my appearing on your doorstep in the evening like this, I daresay. But necessary."

"The Doctor truly ain't at home, Mr Tennerby," Miss Bickleigh told him. "Ain't just a figure of speech, don't you know. Ay'm sorry you should 'ave been put to the trouble..."

Mycroft was suddenly inspired. He waved his stick in the direction of the fading twilight over the Heath.

"My business with your brother, ma'am," he announced, "concerns the brickfields and Mr Villiers Manyon's proposed building development on the East Park. There are many people of the better sort - people of quality, like yourselves, you understand - who are much distressed by Mr Manyon's proposals ..."

"Distressed is not too strong a word for it, Mr Tennerby, ay do assure you!" Miss Bickleigh exclaimed.

She noticed the little maid who was still standing just behind her. "Stop wool-gatherin', gel!" she exclaimed. "Downstairs with you! Ay expects Cook 'as plenty of work for you to do!"

As the maid retreated, she explained. "Ay was just about to say 'ow anxious we all are about that dreadful Mr Manyon's plans for the 'eath. Couldn't speak in front of the gel, of course. Ay mean, one mustn't discuss one's neighbours in front of the domestics, must one? But Dr Bickleigh says as 'e ain't seen so much illness about as there's been since that Mr Manyon acquired the brickfields - and it's all on account of people worryin' 'emselves out of their 'ealth, don't you know? Actually, ay'm surprised you ain't 'eard of the meetin' up at the 'ollybush Assembly Rooms, 'ollybush Place - that's where you'll faind may brother. Sir John Thwaite 'as called a meetin' of the 'ampstead vestrymen to discuss ways of stoppin' Mr Manyon. All the local nabobs, as may brother is pleased to call 'em, will be there: they're all his patients, of course."

"Hollybush Place, eh?" said Mycroft.

He raised his hat again. "Most sorry to have disturbed you, Miss Bickleigh. I'm greatly obliged to you."

He left her with her mouth opened to continue talking at him, and set off down the garden steps to the street. There was the sound of a mechanical piano playing in the public bar of the Freemasons' Arms, and women's voices singing in accompaniment - or shouting raucously. The knot of women who had been standing outside now had their backs to the street, and were standing on tiptoe attempting to watch the activities inside through the luridly lit windows, their apron strings swinging and jigging against the backs of their patched skirts as they skipped up and down in time to the music.

He reached the waiting cab. The driver had been watching out for him from the doorway of the public house. He emerged, wiping the beer from his mouth with the back of his hand.

"Hollybush Place, if you please," Mycroft told him.

The man looked doubtful. With the end of his whip, he pushed the weatherstained brim of his bowler hat to the back of his head.

"Up 'ill all the way, sir," he said. "No h'objection to carryin' you," he added, looking straight at Mycroft's ample belly. "But you'll be as quick walking, sir. An' that's the truth."

The idea of further physical exertion appalled Mycroft. "My dear man!" he exclaimed. "Never heard such nonsense! Whip up your nag, and let's be on our way!"

The jarvey pulled a blanket off the horse's back and removed its nosebag. Mycroft had his foot on the stirrup and was about to climb aboard when he turned and called, "Tell me, were there many men in the public bar over there?"

"Funny you should ask me that, sir," the jarvey replied "All women, it were, savin' one or two old uns. Been a long time since I were the h'objick of so much attention, as you might say!" And he laughed as he heaved himself up on to his seat.

The cab could only go as far as the top of Hampstead High Street. Mycroft got down outside the new Police station with its clock-tower, and paid off the driver; he would have to find another vehicle to take him home, he decided. Beyond leading further up the hill to the summit of Mount Vernon, twisting alleyways with flights of steps wound round the tall brick backs of dwelling places. There were gas-lamps along the street and outside the police station, but above the entries to the darkened lanes and alleys there was a more ominous glow against the steep slate roofs - that of torchlight. A weatherbeaten wooden sign-post pointed upwards: it read, *Hollybush Place*. Mycroft followed its direction, up into the blackness of the alley. As he ascended, he heard from above the surge of voices in a crowd. There were two policemen at the foot of the first flight of steps, with bull's-eye lanterns at their belts.

"The Hollybush Assembly Room?" asked Mycroft, pointing upwards.

"Aye, sir," one of the policemen touched his helmet in salute. "But I wouldn't go up there, if I were you."

"There is a meeting there, I believe," said Mycroft.

"So there is, sir," said the policeman. "And a meeting outside it, too - eh, PC Hawkshawe?" He turned to his companion.

"All the way down 'ollybush Place," Hawkshawe confirmed. "Jam-packed it is!"

"I wouldn't be wrong if I was to say as you wasn't a vestryman, would I, sir?" said the first policeman. "An' it is a meetin' of the vestry. Gentleman of the press, are you, sir?"

"Most certainly not!" Mycroft exclaimed. "I have business - urgent business with Dr Bickleigh."

"Ah!" said the first policeman, glancing at his companion.

"Medical matter, would it be, sir?" asked PC Hawkshawe.

"That is the usual reason why one seeks out a medical man at this time of night," Mycroft replied.

"Best take the gentleman up, Hawkshawe," said the first officer.

"It's the working men from down on the East Heath brickfields," Hawkshawe explained to Mycroft as they mounted the steps. The vestry is meeting to try to stop the building on the East Park Estate 'cause of it spoiling the view from the heights. And the men's afraid they'll all be turned off if the building's stopped. You can see both's point of view if you thinks about it," he added judiciously.

Mycroft was too out of breath, toiling up the damp steps, to express an opinion. In fact he wasn't entirely sure he wasn't going to die from the combination of mental and physical fatigue at the end of a peculiarly wearying day, and the thinness of the air at such a height. They were drawing closer to the baying of the crowd, and already there was an orange glow of flamelight on the high uprearing walls ahead of them. There was a sudden roar from the street some distance above their heads.

"Stop to catch your breath, sir," PC Hawkshawe suggested solicitously. "That'll be one of the vestrymen a-trying to leave the Assembly Room, I daresay. There'll be no real trouble, long as they remains in the Assembly Room. I mean, this ain't Paris, or one o' them sort of heathen places. You'll find the men quite reasonable when they knows you want to bring the doctor to a sick bed and that."

They mounted a few more steps and rounded a corner. A narrow court gave on to a steep lane with a kennel gobbling and bubbling fiercely between the paving stones. Men were crowded on either side of the kennel, against the brick walls and the sills of the shuttered windows. Torches blazed, tattered bannerets of naphthalene fluttering in the draughts which blew down the narrow defiles; the wind blew the smell of burning pitch and tallow into Mycroft's face.

PC Hawkshawe asked him, "D'you mind telling us your name, sir? I find it always helps if you can give a pertikiler name to a gentleman on these occasions, like."

"Tennerby," Mycroft replied.

"Mr Tennerby," PC Hawkshawe repeated. "Roberts?" he shouted.

Faces turned to look down the steps; they glowed in the torchlight as they peered through the oily wreaths of smoke - the lowering, pithecanthropoid brows over haggard, sunken eyes, and grit stained, jutting jaws of the poorest sort of labouring men. A burly fellow, evidently better fed than his fellows, with a decent cloth cap on his head, moleskin jacket, and a clean red bandanna about his throat, came pushing his way to the top of the steps where they gave on to the lane: one of the new Union men, Mycroft decided, a professional agitator.

"What d'you want?" the man shouted down, his voice echoing from wall to wall.

''Gentleman here!" Constable Hawkshawe shouted back. "Mr Tennerby! Come to fetch Dr Bickleigh to a sick bed. Says as Dr Bickleigh's up in the vestry meeting. Says as it's urgent."

"Urgent, eh?" the man Roberts called down.

He stared insolently down at Mycroft. "How urgent, eh, Mr - er - Tennerby?" he called. "Urgent enough for a nice clean gentleman like yersel' to come up here amongst all us rough workin' lads, eh?"

There was laughter from behind him.

Mycroft resisted the temptation to suggest that the fellow had never done an honest day's toil in his life. Another man came from the ruck to the top of the steps. He was holding up a torch to enable Roberts to see Mycroft the better; gigantic shadows danced against the walls, and flame dripped hissing onto the steps.

"There is no need for you to come with me, constable," Mycroft told Hawkshawe. He mounted several of the steps.

"You could say that it is a matter of life and death," he said in an even voice to Roberts.

"Matter of life and death, eh?" Roberts laughed, taking the torch from the man at his shoulder, and holding it out over the steps in order to search Mycroft's face. "If we lets you fetch Dr Bickleigh -

an' I do say if, mark you - you can tell him from us that he ought to be ashamed of hisself, seeking to do honest fellows out of employment!"

"Aye! Aye!" voices bayed up and down the lane behind him.

"Now that is a matter of life and death, eh, lads?" Roberts appealed to the men around him.

"Aye!" the voices shouted their agreement. "Life and death for our women and little ones!"

The heat from the torches beat against Mycroft's cheeks. This was how a French nobleman must have felt, he thought, confronted with a Jacobin mob. He would have liked to reach for the rail - he felt half suffocated with the warmth and the reek of pitch.

"Let me pass, if you please," he said, and mounted the steps.

For a moment, he thought the man Roberts would block his way. He felt a drop of burning naphthalene fall past his neck. It hissed in a tiny puddle beside his boot.

"Dr Bickleigh don't care about them as can't pay for 'im an' 'is physic!" somebody shouted from the crowd.

Roberts smiled into his face. "What d'you say to that, eh, Mr Tennerby?" he demanded.

"I say," Mycroft replied as coolly as shortness of breath permitted, "that I wish to walk on the Queen's highway, and that you are obstructing my path. Now - if you please..."

Pointing his stick in front of him, he advanced up the steps. Roberts hesitated for a moment, then stood aside. "Let the gentleman pass!" he roared up the street.

As Mycroft made his way up the dank, crowded lane, the men squeezed back to make way for him. Hollybush Place was bright with torchlight. All round the square the small, elegant Georgian houses were firmly shuttered against the crowd which filled it. Here and there, up on front doorsteps, between the area railings and under lamplit fanlights stood a policeman or two, including one in the braided peaked cap and black ribbon frogging of an inspector. They appeared content to remain observing the activity of the crowd from their positions of vantage.

At the end of the square, built on a stone platform over the steep hillside, whitewashed, with lancet windows like a chapel, stood the Assembly Room, the object of the crowd's attention. Mycroft pushed his way towards it, saying, "If you will allow me!" as he went. Ahead of him went the call, "Bobs says as the nob's to be let through!... The nob's been sent to fetch Dr Bickleigh - matter of life and death!" For the most part, men stepped aside to let him pass. There were one or two, however, who protested, "'e's after our jobs, like the rest of 'em!" and "'e wouldn't do you no favours!" He was approaching the steps leading up to the double doors of the Assembly Room, when a ball of wet mud hurtled past his shoulder to splatter against one of the doors with such force that fragments of it stung his face. A moment later something struck his hat a heavy blow, tilting it over his forehead so that he had to catch it to prevent it falling from his head. He attempted to brush the dirt from the black silk surface with his glove. As he did so, he glanced across at the doorstep where the police inspector was standing with two of his men. They were studiedly ignoring his predicament.

He planted his hat back on his head, boldly mounted the steps, and rapped on the double doors of the Assembly Room with the knob of his stick. He had to rap several times, with increasing authority, before there was a scuffling noise within, and a man's voice called, "Who are you? What do you want?"

"My name is Tennerby," Mycroft replied. "Myles Tennerby of Judge's Walk. I have a most urgent summons for Dr Bickleigh... In his professional capacity," he added.

There was further scuffling inside, and muttering. A second, more authoritative voice called, "You see how things are with us, Mr Tennerby. The police say they cannot be answerable for our safety if we step outside."

"I shall be answerable for Dr Bickleigh's safety," replied Mycroft.

"How do we know you are who you say you are?" demanded the second voice.

"Good God, man!" Mycroft exclaimed. "Do I sound as if I'm one of this rabble?"

There was the sound of voices conferring inside. Then came a rattle of bars, bolts, and chains. One of the doors opened just sufficiently to allow a man to pass through. A plump, round, smooth pink face appeared. It had lank grey wisps of grey hair under the rim of its hat, like the straggle of a monk's overgrown tonsure. Its owner was a head shorter than Mycroft; his form, under his unbuttoned overcoat and white comforter, was round, to match his face.

"Mr Tennerby?" he asked apprehensively.

"If you like, Dr Bickleigh," Mycroft replied.

"What do you want with me, sir?" asked the doctor, his voice filled with anxiety.

"Does Mr Villiers Manyon know that you are here, Dr Bickleigh?" Mycroft asked. "Or, to put it another way: do your friends up here know that Mr Villiers Manyon and you are on calling terms?"

"Sir, I beg of you!"

Mycroft thought that he had rarely seen a man so frightened.

"What do you want with me?" Dr Bickleigh asked, almost pleading.

"I wish to consult you regarding one of your patients."

"Which patient, sir?" Dr Bickleigh's voice fell to a whisper. "You know that my professional oath binds me to...."

"Mrs Meadowthorpe," Mycroft replied without waiting to hear about the doctor's obligations under the Hippocratic Oath. "Mrs Helena Meadowthorpe. "

"Mrs Meadowthorpe has been dead these four years!" Dr Bickleigh said in a hoarse whisper.

"Precisely so," Mycroft told him. "And the drowned girl, Annie Gibbs were you called to certify her death also? Shall we go?"

Dr Bickleigh joined him out on the step. There was a rattle of bolts and bars as the doors were locked behind him. Mycroft held out his visiting-card between his fingers. Dr Bickleigh snatched it and slipped it into his fob pocket without so much as a glance at it.

"This way, Doctor," Mycroft said.

He raised his stick as he was in the habit of doing when he wished to halt the traffic on Pall Mall of an evening, when he wished to cross from the Diogenes Club to 73A. At the same moment, a mud pat flew dripping past his ear, and slapped across Dr Bickleigh's cheek. A voice very close by shrieked, "Rob us of our livelihood, would you, you black 'earted villain!"

Hands snatched at Mycroft's raised stick, wrenching it from his grasp. Another voice shouted, "'e were a-strikin' at me, the double-dyed villain!"

Men were all round him, hemming him in. He saw the streaming, ragged banners of torch flames in the wind, over their shoulders. Then he saw that some of them were in uniform, and that Dr Bickleigh was being hurried away from him by a knot of four policemen. He felt his wrists gripped together as in a vice. His hat had fallen forward again over his eyes, but not before he had seen the manacles snapped shut over his shirt-cuffs.

"What the deuce!" he shouted.

A policeman was holding his stick. A man in a soft hat and serviceable tweed cape, with military moustache and whiskers - the man who had put the manacles on him - said to the policeman, "You hold on to that, my boy. Material evidence, that is."

To Mycroft, he said, "You come along, Mr Holmes, like a good gentleman, eh?"

Mycroft saw Dr Bickleigh staring back at him from between the policemen who were hustling him away.

"What is the charge, Inspector?" asked Mycroft.

"Chief Inspector, sir. Chief Inspector Wilmot, K Division, Scotland Yard. It could be, making an affray and forcibly resisting arrest..."

He gently pushed Mycroft through the grinning mob. "But if you don't cause any further trouble, sir," he went on, "we'll reduce it to behaviour likely to cause a breach of the peace, eh?"

CHAPTER THIRTEEN

Mycroft heaved himself up from the hard, lumpy straw pallet; he had wrapped his coat about it in the hope of containing any animal life which had made its home under the stained, discoloured ticking. He threw the rough blanket with its faint vomitory smell off his knees.

"'morning, Mr Holmes, sir," the desk sergeant-cum-gaoler announced cheerfully. "Your friends is come for you - and it's half-past five a.m."

He was carrying a wooden tray by its clumsy, unpainted handles. On it, under a cloth, was a silver coffee pot and a dish with a silver cover. The aroma of freshly made coffee filled the narrow cell.

"No need to ask how you slept, sir," he remarked as he put the tray down on a stool and removed the cloth. "Like a babe, you did! Didn't even wake when we brought in the drunks!"

He turned up the gas-flame in its wire cage, the blackened wires of which were encrusted with the charred remains of dead insects. Mycroft looked up at the small, barred window above his head. The patch of sky was a thin, watery grey; the sun had not yet come up. He rubbed his wrists. When he had lain down on the pallet, the previous night, he had been sure he would not sleep a wink; he had decided that he would spend the night preparing his case against wrongful arrest and imprisonment, and honing a few well chosen apophthegms regarding the police station breakfast he felt sure would be placed before him. The fatigue of an all-too active day had overcome the shock of finding himself a prisoner in a barbarous land so far from the domestic comforts of Pall Mall; he had not so much slipped as plunged into unconsciousness.

There was a prolonged groan from a neighbouring cell - a dawning pang of alcoholic remorse.

"Your friends have a carriage waiting, sir," said the sergeant. "Only the servant what brought your breakfast 'cross from the French Bakehouse - black fellow, black as a lump of best coal, says as his mistress says as you ain't to hurry yourself on her account."

Mycroft lifted the cover from the dish. There were three freshly-baked *brioches*, a saucer of white, farm butter, and a glass saucer of tawny orange marmalade.

"We ain't supposed to let you have a knife," said the sergeant. "'cause of how you might do an injury to yourself. Only, in your case, sir - I don't think it's likely."

"Not until I've spoken to Sir Philip Doughty about this outrage, you may be sure of that!" Mycroft replied.

He split one of the warm *brioches*; with the vapour released from its white interior, the aroma of fresh baked bread mingled with the smell of coffee. He filled the small loaf with butter and marmalade, and sat down on the edge of the pallet.

"You must do what you think best, I'm sure, sir," said the sergeant. "I'll leave the door open. If you'll just be so good as to sign your name at the desk when you leave, sir..."

When he had finished the third and last *brioche* and, having ensured that nobody was spying on him, had licked his fingers to pick the last crumbs from his plate, Mycroft plucked his coat from the pallet and slung it over his arm, and took his hat and gloves from the shelf above. Walking down the single line of cells to the steps leading up to the vestibule, he heard more sounds of groaning and hoarse muttering of oaths from inside.

Having ascended the steps, he signed his name in the ledger the sergeant pushed across the rough wooden counter to him. From the stained panel of the wall beside him, pen-and-ink drawings of wanted men and women leered at him. They looked less like genuine human beings than caricature illustrations of underworld characters in a six-penny edition of Charles Dickens; he wondered if policemen finally came to see everybody as potentially criminal grotesques.

"May I have my stick, if you please," he asked, as the sergeant rolled his blotter over his signature.

He could see it through the open door behind the sergeant. It was standing propped against the wainscot of the inner office beside a low, wicker bassinet. There were labels tied round both the handle of the bassinet and under the silver knob of the stick, so that they looked as if they were in a railway-station luggage office.

"Sorry, sir," said the sergeant with his impenetrably good humoured politeness. "They say as it's material evidence. You'll have it back after your case has come up, I daresay. Unless you've committed a pertikilerly horrible murder with it, sir - in which case, it'll be placed in the Black Museum down in the Yard!"

He laughed. Mycroft placed his hat firmly on his head and rapped it into place. He took his purse from the inside pocket of his frock-coat, and placed half-a-crown on the counter.

"For your widows and orphans fund," he said, and left, drawing on his gloves as he stepped into the fresh morning air.

He felt uncomfortable - slightly naked - without his stick, though there were few enough people about at that hour to see him. The lamps were still lit down Haverstock Hill, competing on equal terms with the early daylight.

There was a milkman's pony-cart; the milkman himself in his striped apron was holding his pony's bridle; two young women in men's coarse shirts with the sleeves rolled to the elbows, with heavy yokes and milk pails across their shoulders, were filling the jugs left on doorsteps. A postman with deep canvas and leather bags hung against either hip was plodding in their wake. Maids, their hair under their mobs still tousled from sleep, were out polishing doorknobs, or sitting cleaning upstairs windows, their skirts bulging over the sills.

The smell of a cheap cheroot drifted on the otherwise unpolluted air. A voice was singing thoughtfully to itself from round the corner of the police station, the pavement at the bottom of Hollybush Lane: "All dem darkies am a singin', Singin' to de ole banjo. All de bells in Heaven am ringin' To hear dem darkies singin' so. Chicken in de basket, Chicken in de pot, Oh, all dem darkies am such a happy lot!"

"You took your time coming up here, you rascal!" Mycroft grumbled without bothering to look round the corner. "Thanks to you and your mistress, I've spent the most damnably uncomfortable night of my life," he lied.

"Didn't get back from the h-Opera till half-past three, did we?" said Cyril. He came grinning round the corner. He was wearing footman's livery with silk stockings under his pea-green caped ulster. Mycroft could not help noticing for the first time how well-shaped the fellow's legs were.

He noticed also the object he was clutching in his hand; if it hadn't been for the black ribbon tied around the narrow plaited queue, he might have taken it for a limp, woolly, white dead animal.

"Aren't you supposed to be wearing your wig?" he asked with a certain sadistic satisfaction.

Cyril stared at it and pulled a face. "Not if I can help it!" Then he retaliated: "The Princess is waiting in Minerva Court, 'cross the street there - out of sight. 'spect it's 'cause Her Highness don't want to be seen h-associating with the criminal classes."

"Why, you scoundrel!" Mycroft began.

But without his stick, he felt powerless. Even crossing the road, though there was no traffic approaching from any direction, he felt as vulnerable as a turtle without its shell.

A lane between high brick walls brought them into a square, in which Princess Sophie's closed landau, two glossy-coated chestnut geldings in the shafts, was not in the least out of place. Her coachman was up in his seat, wrapped to his armpits in a tartan rug, his head nodding on to his chest as he dozed. A few yards away, a kitchen-maid who had been scrubbing the area steps behind a kitchen railing had come up to the gate to join a baker's boy in gawping at the spectacle, wiping raw hands on her hessian apron as she did so. She squawked, "Ooh lawks a mercy! It's a 'eathing - a black 'eathing!"

She let go her apron and clamped her hand to her mouth. She turned and fled down the area steps; but, halfway down, curiosity got the better of her, and her eyes under the limp cotton flounce of her mob peered across the pavement level.

The baker's boy with his shallow wicker basket on his arm was made of sterner stuff. As Cyril approached he said loudly enough for the maid to hear, "Tried soap an' water, 'ave yer, Snowball?"

Without so much as a glance and without breaking step, Cyril brought his foot down smartly on the boy's toe. As he went to the carriage door to open it for Mycroft the boy's cries of pain and the sound of his hopping about on one foot echoed behind them.

"Good morning, Brown!" Mycroft called up to the coachman.

The coachman jerked awake. He blinked. "'mornin', Mr Holmes, sir," he replied. Mycroft, his coat still slung over his arm, mounted the carriage step.

"Well!" said Princess Sophie. "What have you been up to, Mr Holmes? They say you were causing a riot in the street!"

She was lying back in the cushions, wrapped in her white furs, diamond earrings gleaming in the light from the carriage window. She leaned forward to him in one graceful movement, and reached out, diamonds glittering green crystal and blue water round the wrist of her white satin glove. "My poor dear friend!" she said, holding his large hand in her own small one, her blue forget-me-not eyes smiling sympathetically into his. "I think, my dear, as they say in my country, somebody has been stuffing you into their overshoe."

"Do you mean I was ambushed?" Mycroft asked.

She nodded. "Something of the sort." Then she exclaimed, looking down at the red, raised weal on his wrist, "Oh, my dear!"

Cyril swung himself up on the step beside him. "They put the darbies on him!" he remarked with something like awed respect.

"*Bozne moy*!" whispered Sophie. "They chained you?"

"Not when I was actually in the lock-up," said Mycroft. "Only when they were taking me there."

"But why?" she asked, releasing his hand.

"As a warning, I daresay," he replied. "They do not wish me to speak with Dr Bickleigh. They arrested me on this absurd charge by way of advising me I should not try communicating with Dr Bickleigh a second time."

"You had better get in," said Sophie, "both of you. We'd better not stay here a moment longer."

"Get inside, man!" Mycroft pushed Cyril up on to the step in his hurry to have him inside before anybody remarked on the peculiarity of a black footman riding with his mistress.

He was about to heave himself into the carriage when, glancing up the pavement, he saw the ponderously burly figure of a constable approaching at a trot. Under his arm was Mycroft's stick, with the police station label still tied to the knob. "Mr Holmes, sir!" he called.

Mycroft stepped back on to the pavement. "What is it now, constable," he asked.

"Just returning of your property, sir, if you don't mind," the policeman gasped.

He paused to catch his breath. He touched the rim of his helmet with two fingers. "Happy to tell you the charge against you is to be dropped, sir," he said. "We just had word from Chief Inspector Wilmot at the Yard, sir."

"So quickly?" asked Mycroft, taking the stick.

He removed the small gold scissors which he used for clipping cigars from his waistcoat pocket, and snipped the label from the stick.

"You surprise me," he said as the label fluttered to the pavement.

He watched the policeman go, then climbed up into the carriage. Cyril closed the door. He fell into the seat opposite Princess Sophie.

As the carriage turned in the narrow square, he said, "I made a very foolish mistake yesterday afternoon. I called at Somerset House, and what I found there made me drive straight to the Home Office to see Sir William Vernon Harcourt in person. I asked him to issue a certificate for the exhumation of Helena Meadowthorpe's body. Sir William refused; instead, he appears to have instructed Scotland Yard's K Division that I should be followed and even put under restraint. I came up here last night to speak to Dr Bickleigh. Chief Inspector Wilmot was lying in wait for me. I tell you this - they'd sooner have me clapped in irons and thrown into some foul dungeon than let me discover what really happened up on Squire's Mount!"

"Why?" asked Sophie.

A darkness fell over them as they passed under the arch leading from the square out on to Haverstock Hill.

"Because, my dear, the Prince of Wales has been taking an interest in Parthenope Manyon, the young woman Meadowthorpe was intending to marry when he died.

"La, la, la!" whispered Sophie.

"I fear His Royal Highness's interest is not the rarest mark of distinction among pretty young women of a certain class," continued Mycroft. "This particular choice was however a trifle unfortunate in its timing, and I fear there are members both of Court and Government who may consider the interest of the Nation best served by concealing Truth and permitting a gross miscarriage of Justice..."

"May I ask what you found at this - Somerset? - House," she asked, "to send you to the Home Secretary?"

"Somerset House is the Registrar General's office," Mycroft replied. "I discovered there that Helena Meadowthorpe, née Bewick, had been, at least while she remained unmarried, a wealthy young woman. As is usual in the case of an infant, the property she inherited under her parents' wills had been settled on her in trust. While she remained an infant in the eyes of the law, her legal guardian, Villiers Manyon (and who knows what means he employed to persuade her parents to place her into his care?), enjoyed the fruits, that is the income, of her estate. When Helena came of age, this lucrative source of income dried up so far as Manyon was concerned. Her property remained in trust, but the income was hers, to dispose of as she wished - until she married. When she did marry her entire and very substantial property passed into the hands of her husband..."

"So this man, Meadowthorpe," Sophie exclaimed, "this officer broken for cowardice in the face of the enemy, was granted all his wife's estate and property! What strange laws you have in this country! I assure you, my dear, I shall never marry here!"

"Bear with me, Princess," said Mycroft. "Helena Meadowthorpe died. Eighteen months later, Meadowthorpe engaged to marry Manyon's true daughter, Parthenope. This time a will was drawn up signed by Meadowthorpe bequeathing in the event of his death his entire estate to his future wife."

"So this Parthenope Manyon has now inherited all Mr Meadowthorpe's fortune!" exclaimed Sophie. "And it includes, of course, everything he obtained from his late wife."

"Exactly so," Mycroft confirmed. "And Parthenope Manyon is only just nineteen years old."

"So it is her father, Villiers Manyon, who controls all this wealth?" asked Sophie.

Mycroft nodded. There was a sudden warmth as the low sunlight shining across the meadows of Chalk Farm caught their faces. Sophie turned her head to it.

"Poor lady!" she said softly.

"Of whom are you thinking, Princess?" asked Mycroft.

"Helena," she replied. "Alone, defenceless, caught between two villains.

"There is something else I unearthed, yesterday afternoon," said Mycroft. "The trustees to Helena Bewick's fortune were Villiers Manyon himself, of course; the other was Dr John Bickleigh."

Sophie turned her head again to look at Mycroft.

"So, when Meadowthorpe was taken ill, that fatal night," Mycroft continued, "and Mrs Tuttle went to fetch Dr Bickleigh, she was way-laid on the Heath, on an obscure and rarely used path, by two brick-field labourers, employees of Villiers Manyon. Abused and distressed, she arrived at Dr Bickleigh's house to find there Villiers Manyon - on that night of all nights! And it was he who drove them back up to Squire's Mount!... Not only that. It was Villiers Manyon who had provided the platform on which this drama was played out; he was the original purchaser of Squire's Mount; it was he who installed Meadowthorpe there, at no little expense."

He sighed and sat back against the velvet upholstery of the carriage. "And we have lost our one possible material witness!"

"The house-parlourmaid?" asked Sophie. "Annie Gibbs?"

Mycroft nodded. "I spoke to a couple of labouring girls last night, on the corner of South End Road. They told me that Annie Gibbs had been found drowned in one of the Highgate Ponds."

He explained how her dress - the fact that she had been in working cap and apron, without a coat, had led people to believe that she must have run away quite suddenly from the Lakeside Hotel, crossed the Heath in a disturbed and distressed state, and drowned herself. When he had finished, Sophie murmured, "*Bozhe moy*! This is a fearful business!"

"I'm afraid," said Mycroft, "we may not yet have plumbed the depths of it."

CHAPTER FOURTEEN

Mycroft had Princess Sophie put him down outside 221B Baker Street. As Mrs Hudson showed him into his brother's study, Sherlock gave him the briefest of glances over the top of *The Times*. Mycroft noticed with some disapproval that Sherlock was reading the front page: governments might topple, Grand Dukes might be blown to pieces by Nihilist bombs, but Sherlock's invariable breakfast reading was the Agony Column on the front page.

"So your Russian princess has brought you back from Hampstead, I perceive," said Sherlock from behind the paper. "Where, if I am not much mistaken, you spent the night in police custody... Ha!" he exclaimed. "I see from Watson's honest face that he regards that as a circumstance deserving of my full attention." He lowered the paper, folded it, and placed it beside him. "The marmalade, Watson. There's a good fellow." He reached for a slice of toast.

Mycroft sat down at the table and looked at Dr Watson. "It required no great powers of perception on my brother's part, I do assure you, Doctor. Don't delude yourself into supposing his faculties to be more acute than they actually are," he explained. "He heard the carriage drawing up beneath the window; he knows very well that the two-horse landau is only used by ladies of rank and title who can afford such an equipage. He has noticed that I have mud on my boot and that it is claygate; a child could deduce from it that I have come either from the vicinity of Dorking in Surrey or, more likely, from Hampstead. He has noticed, moreover, what is perfectly obvious - that I have spent the night in my clothes, though not in my coat or overcoat. Where else would a man be compelled to sleep in his clothes yet be warm enough to remove his outer garments but in a police cell?"

"Watson knows my methods - I keep no secrets from him," said Sherlock, taking a bite out of his toast and marmalade. "In any case," he added, "nothing of this explains why the no-doubt honest constabulary of Hampstead should regard you as such a dangerous fellow they must needs bang you up - that is the cant phrase among the criminal classes, I believe - for the night."

Mrs Hudson entered the room unbidden and placed a fresh pot of coffee before Mycroft. While he drank several cups, he related what had happened since his last visit to Baker Street.

"Fascinating!" exclaimed Sherlock when Mycroft had done. "You make me quite envious!...Oh dear! I see it is already late, and I promised Gregson that I would join him at Audley Court by half-past eleven."

He had risen from the table while he was speaking. Removing his dressing-gown as he did so, he went through into his bedroom. "The criminal type," he called back through the half-open door, "bears a resemblance to the maiden Ariadne at least in this: that he leaves a thread by which his pursuer may trace him through the darkness of his labyrinthine contrivances. The problem for the pursuer is to find the thread's end to start with. In this case, my dear Mycroft, I would suggest it is to be found in the death by drowning of the poor house-maid - Annie Gibbs. Shall we say, Manyon suspects at the time of Meadowthorpe's final sickness she may have observed more than is compatible with his own safety? She is the humblest of creatures, of no significance in the world. He takes her into his establishment. She is a shy little thing; she could never be happy in such a place. So, in Manyon's eyes, she becomes more dangerous still..."

He reappeared framed in the doorway, adjusting his collar. "As the proprietor of a certain type of *Hades*, I daresay it would not have been the first time he had, without a qualm of conscience, disposed of a child of the labouring class."

"I say, Holmes!" exclaimed Dr Watson. "If you are right, the man must be a monster of iniquity!"

"It's a sorry world, Watson," Sherlock replied with equanimity. "You have been my colleague long enough to have discovered that."

"But you say he is a friend..." Dr Watson paused. "...of a certain Royal Personage?"

"Not a friend, Doctor," Mycroft explained. "Nor yet an acquaintance save in the most literal sense. He provides a service - in the case of H.R.H., a suitably discreet venue for the playing of a certain game at cards. The excellent Mrs Turner's grocer provides me with a service. I have no familiarity with either his vices or virtues save in his capacity as a grocer."

"On the other hand, Mr Holmes," Dr Watson replied, "I do not suppose you have struck up an acquaintance with your grocer's daughter."

"*Touché*, my dear Mycroft!" Sherlock smiled.

He reached behind the door for his necktie and started to tie it, his prominent jaw thrust toward the chandelier. "And so far as you are concerned, my dear fellow, that is the crux of the matter. That is why you are being obstructed in your pursuit of justice for Mrs Tuttle. That is why you spent the night in a police tank."

He released his tie half-tied and, gripping the back of one of the chairs, stared intently into Mycroft's face. "That is what removes this pretty little conundrum from the realm of common criminality into that of affairs of state from my realm to yours," he said. "Tell me, when Sir James Swarthmoor invited you to lunch in order to warn you off the case, what had you been up to at the Foreign Office?"

"I had been addressing certain gentlemen there on the dangers of a Prussian expansionist policy directed toward the Western European Powers..."

"Has it not struck you as strange," Sherlock asked, "that just at the time when the situation in the Rhineland becomes critical - to employ a chemist's metaphor - and you are called on to brief staff at the Foreign Office, you find yourself engaged in activities which are unlikely to find favour in the highest circles? Do you suppose it might be possible that the Tuttle Case has been trailed before you to draw your attention away from events in the Rhineland - so that in the eyes of Royalty and the Government, one of its shrewdest and most valued counsellors might be compromised?"

Mycroft felt Sherlock's hand on his shoulder. His eyes were smarting with fatigue.

"I know you don't approve of my methods of deduction," Sherlock continued. "But I suggest most earnestly that you find out exactly who it was who set our young friend from the Middle Temple to seek our, and more particularly your assistance."

Mycroft knew who had been responsible. Mr Marshall Hall had told him, that foggy night as he put him down from his cab in Portman Square. It had been Josiah Hartz, clerk to Marcus, Bullfinger, Stote and Marcus, who would use every means to protect the interests and good name of the Prince of Wales, but not to the extent of interfering with the drawing up of Her Majesty's Government's foreign policy. Was it possible that Josiah Hartz had two masters?

"And now," Sherlock was saying as he finished buttoning up his top-coat, "I must send Billy out for a hansom immediately. I shall be going over the river, over Waterloo Bridge."

He brushed his silk hat on his sleeve. "It will be the easiest thing in the world, my dear Mycroft, to put you down in Pall Mall. You look quite done in."

CHAPTER FIFTEEN

'Extreme situations call for extreme measures'. Mycroft's first act on his return to 73A Pall Mall was to ask Mrs Turner to sent the boy round to fetch his barber from Jermyn Street; he had always found submission to a professionally wielded razor and an application of hot towels efficacious after a restless or uneasy night. His second act - since the interval between a breakfast taken at first light and lunch consumed at the usual hour would prove excessive - was to call for a light collation of poached eggs on smoked haddock.

Refreshed outwardly and inwardly, with smooth cheeks and clean linen, he came downstairs, gloves in hand, to set off albeit somewhat late for his desk at the Treasury. Maisie was standing in the narrow hallway giving his hat a final rub up with her sleeve. Mycroft had just taken it from her, when there was the grind of a boot on the step behind the closed outer door, and the thin clatter of the bell below in the kitchen. Maisie was on the point of giving him his stick out of the Japanese vase. She hesitated. Mycroft took the stick from her.

"Open it, my dear," he told her.

But he planted his hat firmly on his head as she was fumbling with the lock, to make it clear to whomsoever was calling that he was pressed for time.

The gentleman on the step was at least six foot four, with high coloured cheeks under a faint, boyish down of blond stubble. He stared bullishly at Mycroft, his gaze high over the top of Maisie's blue cotton mob. Maisie bobbed and said, "If you please, sir?"

The gentleman ignored her. "You are Holmes, I suppose," he announced, his voice reverberating round the confined space of the hall and stairs.

"And you are Sir William Gordon Cumming."

The cavalryman was clearly evidenced by the splay of the legs in tight riding breeches and boots, and the luxuriance of the gingery moustache which spilled down on either side of the thick but firmly set mouth. The habit of command over soldiers and tradesmen alike was clear from the truculent expression, and the affected thrust of an already prominent jaw. Sir William, Mycroft decided, had classified him as a tradesman.

"We have not been introduced as far as I can recall," Sir William announced. The inference was that he would not have recalled it, even if they had.

Maisie retreated, to watch from the corner of the basement stairs.

"You came asking for me, yesterday evening," Mycroft said. "I did not suppose you would return so soon, and at such an hour."

"Had to come at this hour, damn it, man!" Sir William replied. "You'd have been out gaddin' otherwise, eh?"

"No, sir," Mycroft told him. "You have returned here at your own convenience."

Before he could remove it out of his reach, Mycroft touched the sleeve of his short-frocked riding coat with his bare forefinger, and lifted it to one nostril and then the other.

"Last night, after you had been here," he said, "you returned to your club, the Traveller's, to dress; you then went out of Town to the Vale of Health Lakeside Spa Hotel and Sporting Rooms, where you spent a night at cards and other diversion. It amused you when morning came, to borrow a suit of riding clothes, and to drive down from Hampstead in a dog-cart with a woman who had been your companion at play, to take her out on the Row to instruct her in horsewomanship as if she were a lady. You have just now dismissed her, and it suits you very well to call here on your way back to the Traveller's. And now, sir, perhaps you would be good enough to state your business. As you see, I am on my way out. I am expected at the Treasury immediately."

"You followed me, sir! You spied on me!" roared Sir William, his face turning a rich purple so that his stubble appeared even more blond. He grasped his stick halfway down its length as if he was about to use it as a club.

"I would not engage in so unnecessary an activity," Mycroft replied, "even if I wished to study your nocturnal habits - which I certainly do not. You proclaim them clearly enough to anybody with only half the powers of observation and deduction which I possess. You are a most distinguished member of your club, and it is well enough known that you make it your home when you are alone in Town. But you did not pass the night there. You shaved last night but not this morning. The clothes you are wearing are clearly not your own; I daresay you counted yourself fortunate to find somebody at the Lakeside Spa Hotel who approximated to your size, but, for someone who prides himself on his appearance it is still only an approximation. I might have guessed from common gossip that Manyon's establishment was your place of resort. I do not, however, indulge in guesswork unless there is strong supportive evidence - which, in your case, there is. You drove back into Town in a dog-cart or governess's carriage: there is a distinctive fleck of mud on the upper right-hand sleeve of your coat, but not on the left. It was thrown up while driving a vehicle - there are no similar markings on your boots or breeches, as there would have been if you were in the saddle. The fleck is almost horizontal, therefore the vehicle was sprung low off the ground, and the splash was incurred when you were driving down a steep hill - Haverstock Hill, I daresay. The dirt is on your right sleeve - a driver sits on the extreme right edge, thus incurring the risk of being muddied only when he has a passenger beside him. You have incurred another tell-tale mark. There are grains of powder on your left sleeve above the cuff of a colour which is known by those who use it for the adornment of their faces as blush. It bears traces of the scent *patchouli* - a scent, I hazard, you would not expect your mother or sisters to wear. If you were assisting an inexperienced *equestrienne* into the saddle - a side saddle - she would mount from the horse's left flank, and you would be facing her, assisting her with your left arm. For powder which had been transferred from her cheek to her glove to be so impressed on to your sleeve, she must have relied heavily on the support of your arm."

"Let me tell you," Sir William Gordon Cumming laid the knob of his stick on Mycroft's arm, "...you are too observant for your own good, sir!"

Mycroft took the knob gently between his fingers and removed it from his sleeve.

Sir William looked as if he was wondering whether to replace his stick on Mycroft's arm. Instead, he contented himself with exploding, "There are several gentlemen of my acquaintance who say so - gentlemen of rank, sir! They say your brother knows his place. You should learn from him!"

"I don't imagine you came here to discuss the more regrettable aspects of my character, Sir William," Mycroft replied. "Would you be so good as to inform me precisely why you are here? You were the commanding officer in Southern Africa of the late if unlamented Septimus Athelney Meadowthorpe, I believe. Is it him you wish to speak to me about?"

"Certainly not!" roared Sir William, so loudly that passers by across the street turned their heads. "Wouldn't sully m'lips with the man's name. Deuce take it, I'd have paid, myself, for the defence of the spirited little filly who poisoned him!"

"But you haven't?" asked Mycroft quickly. "Paid for Mrs Tuttle's defence, I mean."

"No, sir. There was no need."

"Who has?" asked Mycroft.

Sir William stared at him. "An acquaintance of mine..." He recollected himself in the nick of time. "Nothin' whatever to do with you, sir!" he roared.

He put his hand into his pocket and drew out a broad, cream-coloured envelope. He handed it to Mycroft. "Commanded to give it to you in person," he said.

With an amazement only equalled by his sense of dread, Mycroft read the legend inscribed on the front in a clerkly copperplate:

M. W. HOLMES, ESQ., M.A., D.LITT.

He turned it over to find the gold coronet, ostrich feather plumes, and the motto, *Ich dien*, embossed in the apex of the sealed lip.

"I'm commanded to stay for your reply," announced Sir William, impatiently tapping the knob of his stick in the palm of his hand.

Mycroft drew out the stiff, gold-edged card. He noted the same crest and motto as the envelope, and the signature scrawled below the formal copperplate and above an almost illegible post-scriptum - that of Sir Henry Ponsonby, Personal and Private Secretary to Her Royal Highness Alexandra, Princess of Wales.

Sir Henry was commanded to convey Her Royal Highness's sincere wish that Mr M. W. Holmes should attend upon Her Royal Highness at Sandringham House, for ten days, commencing Monday of the following week. There were instructions as to the time he should take the special train which would carry him with other guests from the Great Eastern Railway terminus at Liverpool Street, via Cambridge and Ely and the Hunstanton and West Norfolk Railway the hundred and five miles to Wolferton, two miles from Sandringham... Ten days enforced rustication, thought Mycroft: in exile on those bleak, grey Norfolk flats - the nearest England afforded to Siberia. It was, of course, a royal command, with no possibility of evasion.

"Why...?" he began. He prevented himself from expressing his horrified bewilderment further.

"H.R.H. asked Lord Granville, the other night, what he knew about some tin-pot Rhineland principality," Sir William replied. "A friend of Baron von Goeben, some ghastly Prussian nobleman - Colonel-General Graf von Varzin, or some such nonsense - who's been sent over here to offer H.R.H. the honorary colonelship of the

Seventh Uhlans, suggested the fellow to ask about it was a Whitehall wallah - namely yourself. Pussy Granville agreed: said he'd asked you to point it out on the map, and you'd put your finger straight on it like some damn' schoolmaster."

"You will convey my profoundest sense of gratitude to Sir Henry Ponsonby, won't you, Sir William?" he asked.

Sir William Gordon Cumming smiled for the first time. It was not pleasant. "I suppose I shall see you at Sandringham, next week."

Mycroft inclined his head. Sir William stepped down from the pavement and set off in the direction of St James's, swinging his stick with the jaunty air of one who has put behind him a distasteful task. Mycroft remained in the hallway, the front door still open deciphering the semi-literate, crabbed scrawl on the card below the signature.

'Grand *battus* Wed & Fri,' he read. 'Shooting excellent. Pheasants and woodcock splendid this season. Compliments. Wales.'

He slipped the card into his frock-coat pocket. He stepped down on to the pavement in a leaden daze. He told himself that he had always tried to avoid rushing to conclusions: that he had no reason to suppose that this sudden, last-minute invitation to be a house-guest at Sandringham was anything more than a Royal Personage's impulse to seek information from, and to favour, somebody who had done the state some service in the past. In fact, if brother Sherlock's surmise were correct, he should positively welcome the opportunity of being allowed to express his views on the threat to British interests building up along the Rhine. On the other hand, a ten day's exile in Norfolk would be as effective way as any of handicapping his investigations into the Tuttle case.

What of Sir William's remark that a Colonel-General von Varzin, a friend of the German Ambassador who was visiting London, had recommended him to the Prince of Wales's attention. How could that be squared with Sherlock's theory that the Tuttle case was being exploited to distract him from events proceeding in the Rhineland?

To add to his general malaise, he loathed shooting as he detested all blood sports; when dining one evening at Hughenden Manor he had described hunting, to Lord Beaconsfield's unfeigned delight, as 'the unspeakable in full pursuit of the uneatable' - only to hear of it being repeated at every fashionable dinner-table as the latest epigram of a young Dublin æsthete lately down from Oxford. Like himself, Lord Beaconsfield had found peculiarly revolting the provision of thousands of game-birds for the Prince of Wales's battus, so that they would fly over their royal master in such numbers that even he, a notoriously bad shot, could not miss them all.

Mycroft had set out for Whitehall at last and, still fathoms deep in thought, was crossing Horse Guards Parade, when a cheery voice called, "Mycroft Holmes! It is Mycroft Holmes, isn't it?"

Mycroft had to look twice before he recognised the speaker. "Freddie Colton, by Jove!" he exclaimed.

The face was still as open and honest as it had been a full dozen years before, when its owner had been Second Secretary at the British Legation in Florence - too honest for a diplomat's. Now, however, it bore the lines of maturity and responsibility, if not of gravitas. Sir Frederick Colton was at present British Minister to the Rhineland Grand Duchy of Pfalzel-Buckelburg.

"Gone native, I see!" said Mycroft.

He waved his stick to take in Sir Frederick's appearance - his Bavarian jacket, knickerbockers, and Alpine hat with an eagle's feather stuck in the brim.

"Goin' to wear them about Town for a couple of days," Sir Frederick replied. "They'll become just the thing - you wait and see, dear old chap!"

Mycroft was going to say that he wouldn't be seen dead wearing anything like that. Then he thought of the following week, trudging across the flat wet fields near the Wash, wearing Norfolk jacket and plus-fours.

"So what has brought you from Pfalzel-Buckelburg?" he asked.

"Consultation - 'summoned home for consultation', is what we call it," Sir Frederick replied. "Getting told what and what not to do by Pussy Granville or whoever, and the Permanent Secretary; that is what it actually is... Do you have such a thing as a decent cigar, old chap? Haven't had a chance to toddle round to Oxford Street yet."

Mycroft pulled out his cigar case. "Are you at liberty to tell me what this consultation is about?" he asked.

"The changing situation resultin' from the accession of the new Grand Duchess," said Sir Frederick. "Somebody seems to have put it into Pussy Granville's head that there may be a threat to the independent status of the Grand Duchy. Pussy's a sound enough fellow where the Froggies are concerned - he speaks Frog like a *Normalien*. When it comes to the old *Platte Deutsch*, he's a bit wanting... When I was with him, just now, he was tryin' to find Mainz on the map. Didn't know the Rhine from the Danube; he was stabbing his finger somewhere between Innsbruck and Vienna. "His expression changed. "Princess Trubetskoy - she's a friend of the Grand Duchess Jolande, isn't she?" he asked.

"They were acquainted when the Princess was living in Nice, I believe," Mycroft replied.

"Is the young Princess in Town?" Sir Frederick asked eagerly.

Mycroft had not forgotten the *petite amitie* enjoyed between Princess Sophie and Freddie Colton; it had been ten or eleven years ago, before Mycroft had met her - and, with the exception of the devoted and long suffering Edwin Barnaby, her *petites amities* were like the sparrow of which the Venerable Bede wrote, which flew in from the cold night into the firelight only to flutter for a brief while before disappearing once more into the night.

"I am dining with her tomorrow night, at Bruton Street."

"Are you, by God?" said Sir Frederick. Then he said after a brief pause, "Wouldn't mind renewin' an old friendship, eh? Is she in good health - and looks, what?"

Mycroft flicked a stone chip across the sandy gravel with the end of his stick. "The Princess has the secret of eternal youth," he said.

Between Freddie Colton and Princess Sophie, he might well learn something for himself of value to take to Sandringham.

"If you care to accompany me, my dear Freddie, I'm sure Princess Sophie will be delighted."

Sir Frederick beamed. "Are you sure, old chap?" he asked.

"Quite sure," Mycroft told him. "Fetch me at eight o'clock from 73A Pall Mall. Only for Heaven's sake change out of those appallin' togs you're wearin'. You look like one of those dreadful *Heldentenors* in *Der Freischutz,* or some other frightful German tosh."

CHAPTER SIXTEEN

That same night, at his regular hour of a quarter to eight, Mycroft crossed Pall Mall to his lodgings after spending almost three hours in the silence of the Diogenes Club. He was on the point of going upstairs to his rooms, when Mrs Turner appeared.

"There's a young female, Mr Holmes. Been waiting for you these past two hours."

"What sort of 'young female' is she?" Mycroft asked.

"Just a housemaid, sir. She's been sent down from Hampstead by her master to return something to you, you left there last night. I said I'd take it for you, but she said she'd been told to give it to you personally. She walked all the way here - four or five miles, it is."

The girl herself had appeared at the top of the basement stairs. She was wearing a well-worn boy's coat over her stuff gown and pinafore apron. The square toes of her boots were scuffed. She held out a small, untidily wrapped package in Mycroft's direction.

"Dr Bickleigh's girl, aren't you?" Mycroft asked. "Milly?"

"If you please, sir," the maid executed a rough curtsey.

"I fear your mistress has put you to a great deal of unnecessary trouble," Mycroft told her. "I left nothing."

"'tweren't the mistress what sent me," said Milly in a hoarse whisper. "'twere the doctor hisself. An' he said most pertikilar I were to give un to you, personal like."

Mycroft took the package. He cut the string with his gold cigar scissors, and removed the brown wrapper. Inside was a battered silver-plated cigarette-case, a valueless piece of trumpery. He opened it: behind the half-dozen or so cigarettes secured by an elastic ribbon was a piece of paper tightly folded. He snapped the case shut and slipped it into his pocket beside the crested invitation card.

"Foolish of me," he said. "Milly? Tell your master I'm beholden to him - exceedingly."

He took out his purse and handed a half-sovereign to Mrs Turner.

"Be so good as to send round to the livery stables behind Charles Street," he told her, "and have one of Maguire's men bring round a pony and trap. We cannot have this young woman return on foot all the way to Hampstead at this time of night."

He put a half-crown into Milly's hand, and turned to go upstairs. He looked over his shoulder and said, "Milly, your master was relatively well acquainted with Mr Meadowthorpe. Did you yourself happen to know anybody of the household on Squire's Mount - any of the junior maids, Annie Gibbs, for instance?"

"Yes, sir," the girl replied, with a look both apprehensive and questioning. "Annie an' me was pals," she whispered so hoarsely that he had to make an effort to hear her. "We walked out together on our afternoons off, like... My mistress said as it were all right, Annie bein' such a respectable girl."

Mycroft nodded. He paused for a moment, patting his full lips with his fingers. "I expect Annie confided in you something of what she had seen on the night of Captain Meadowthorpe's death," he suggested. "It was she who found him, was it not?"

"Yes, sir," Milly whispered.

"She must have been deeply shocked to have found him like that - taken by a sudden attack and fallen downstairs..."

"Yes, sir," Milly agreed in her same hoarse whisper. "The poor gentleman had been sick on the stairs, so Annie said, an' 'e slipped."

"Mr Holmes!" Mrs Turner exclaimed. "You shouldn't encourage the child in such talk!"

"Indeed not!" Mycroft responded. "You are a good girl, Milly. And because I know you to be a good girl, I shall not mention a word of what you have said to me to your master or mistress." And he smiled benevolently upon her.

"Thank 'ee, sir," the girl whispered.

She, for her part, looked bewildered and tearful. But Mycroft ignored her evident distress. He proceeded up to his study; without bothering to remove his coat, he took the cigarette-case from his pocket and drew the tightly screwed paper from behind the cigarettes. Tossing the case and its contents into the wastepaper basket, he turned up one of the gas-mantles above the fireplace and unfolded the paper.

Dear Mr Holmes, he read, *Pardon if you will this irregular and hasty scrawl. You informed me last night that you wished to ask me questions relating to the late Mrs Septimus Meadowthorpe. As a gentleman, I'm sure you will appreciate the delicacy of my position regarding that unhappy lady. You will be aware, I am sure, that the ethics of my calling lay upon me certain restraints.*

I have heard something of your interest in the unhappy events which occurred at the Meadowthorpe home on Squires Mount and I have given the matter my profoundest consideration. Thus I have come to the conclusion that there is one piece of information which overrides the discretion imposed on me by my professional oath.

Shortly after Mrs Meadowthorpe's unhappy decease, Mrs Tuttle came to me begging to be allowed to speak to me in confidence. You may imagine my surprise when she told me that she was afraid Captain Meadowthorpe might have procured the death of his late wife by poison. According to Mrs Tuttle, the gardener had remarked that one of the small palm-trees in the conservatory had outgrown its pot, and had announced his intention of replanting it the following morning in a larger container. She reported the matter to her employer. That same evening, or so she informed me, she was walking up from the kitchen garden below the house, when she caught sight of Captain Meadowthorpe in the conservatory. He was removing from the earth surrounding the palm-tree a small bottle containing a dark, purplish liquid. He slipped it hastily in the pocket of his smoking-jacket, and then replaced the earth tidily about the tree. She would not have felt impelled to come to me, she said, but that the symptoms shown by Mrs Meadowthorpe had been painfully similar to those she had heard of when working beside her husband in a darker and more dreadful world than that of Hampstead, and that the bottle had borne a clear resemblance both in size and colour to those she had seen used in the extermination of vermin.

I assured Mrs Tuttle that she must have been mistaken, and that to repeat such suspicions could bring the most dreadful trouble on her head. While I did not wish to make matters worse for the woman by discussing the matter with her employer, I did think it proper to mention the matter to Mr Villiers Manyon. Fortunately for Mrs Tuttle, Mr Manyon showed some amusement at what I told him, and remarked that her opinion of Captain Meadowthorpe was in process of undergoing a remarkable alteration. As things turned out, this seemed to be no more than the truth; and however I might have deplored the improper liaison between Mrs Tuttle and her employer, it succeeded in putting her extraordinary statement to me from my mind. Until, that is, following the death of the Captain, the police found a bottle answering exactly to the description given me by Mrs Tuttle. It was then I reminded that the cock-and-bull story she had given to me had been nothing more nor less than a dastardly scheme to prepare the ground, as it were, for her own slaying of an employer who was showing her, however reprehensibly, nothing but favour.

As for her motives in abusing so foully Captain Meadowthorpe's good name, or for procuring his death - they are not for me to deduce. My concern is for yourself, Mr Holmes. You are, I am sure, acting solely out of a spirit of kindness toward one whom you see as a poor defenceless female. But you are misguided, sir! Mrs Tuttle is of the sisterhood of Messalina or Lucrezia Borgia! Believe me, sir, she is no proper object of the attentions of a knight-errant, but rather, a suitable subject for the Judgement! I beg you, therefore, to desist from inquiries which may only cause you trouble and perhaps distress.

I have thought it best for both our sakes to communicate with you discreetly, and I assure you that in so doing I am acting solely out of concern for one - namely yourself, sir, who is, I am given to understand, worthy only of the most profound respect.

I am, sir, and hope to remain your humble and obedient servant,
John Wentworth Bickleigh

Mycroft smiled to himself. He folded the letter once, smoothing the paper against the surface of the mantlepiece with the edge of his hand. He had no doubt whatever that his 'humble and obedient servant' had been responsible for the message on Helena Meadowthorpe's headstone. And this missive, and the manner of its delivery, was redolent of a confusion of anxiety and guilt which was unlikely to stand up to the examination in court even of a young tyro like Mr Edward Marshall Hall.

CHAPTER SEVENTEEN

"Goodnight, Marshall," Mr Forrest Fulton called into Marshall Hall's room. "And congratulations on the Wainwright verdict. You did a first rate job - couldn't have done better myself. Mastered your brief; that's the secret in makin' out a good case, eh, my boy?"

"Thank you, sir. Kind of you to say so," Marshall Hall replied.

"Don't you go burnin' the midnight oil over that damn' Tuttle case," Mr Forrest Fulton added. "You need a good rest after a day on your feet before the Queen's Bench. And there's no law worth speakin' of in domestic crime - least of all when it's a capital offence. Get you home - the best place for a man on a foul night like this is his own hearth. Good night to you!"

"Goodnight, sir!" Marshall Hall called after him. It depends entirely with whom the man shares his hearth, he thought.

He glanced at the senior clerk of chambers who was in the room with him. Burns knew that he had spent several nights recently at Fountain Court in the pretence of studying briefs until dawn.

He was holding his purse in his hand, but waited until he heard the outer door close behind Mr Forrest Fulton, and the latter's foot-steps on the gravel outside, before letting three half-sovereigns fall into his hand. "That should be sufficient, I think," he said, giving them to Burns.

"Quite, sir. Thank 'ee, sir." Burns dropped them into his own small, well-worn purse, snapped it shut and dropped it into his waist-coat pocket. It was understood that there would be no question of there being any change.

"How much, would you say, sir, should I let Mr Hartz know what we suspect about what his firm's up to?" he asked. "It's my experience in dealings like this, you have to let a little go to get any-thing back. Like a return on investment, if you catch my drift, sir."

Marshall Hall squeezed his lips between his finger and thumb. He breathed in deeply through his nose and held his breath for a moment before releasing it. He removed his fingers from his lips. "If you were to drop a hint," he suggested, "that I, as Mrs Tuttle's counsel, might be inclined toward following the course recommended by Mr Bullfinger if I had reason to believe that it would protect the reputation and standing of a Royal Personage, not to mention the maternal sensibilities of that very great lady, his mother... That might serve the turn, don't you think?"

Burns nodded emphatically. "Very likely, sir, if I may say so. Most likely!"

He picked up his bowler hat and umbrella. "Best be making my way across to Lincoln's Inn Fields," he declared. "Don't want Mr Hartz to think I ain't keeping our appointment!"

There was a thin rain falling as he made his way up Chancery Lane to Carey Street, but not enough to make him go to the bother of unfastening his tightly furled umbrella (he was firmly of the belief that an untidily furled umbrella was a sure token of weakness of character, and it was difficult to refurl an umbrella properly on arrival in an eating-house or after climbing on board an omnibus). Above him, the fantastical turrets and iron bannerets of the new Law Courts clawed at the torn night sky. At his feet, the lamplight was reflected in black, oily puddles. There were few people about: one or two clerks were hurrying home; a couple of porters in aprons and scrubbing-women huddled in shawls scurried past on their way to work.

A biting wind slapped him on the face as he reached the end of Serle Street, forcing him to clutch at the brim of his hat as he turned out into Lincoln's Inn Fields. It drove the drizzle into his face, so that he did not recognize Josiah Hartz where he stood waiting against the railings in front of the premises of Marcus, Bullfinger, Stote and Marcus, with his collar turned up to conceal his sallow face and lupine features.

"Evenin', Mr Burns! I must confess, I half didn't expect you to turn up, the weather bein' so inclement."

Josiah Hartz was half a head taller than he, and even in the fitful light over the pavement there was an unhealthy opacity about his pallid stare. It was a stupid fancy, Burns told himself, but he was unable to suppress entirely the idea that the brain behind such eyes was diseased.

"I keep the appointments I make," he replied.

"Of course you do, dear fellow," said Hartz.

"Do you travel home south of the river, Mr Hartz," Burns asked.

"Camberwell, Mr Burns. And yourself?"

"Lavender Hill. So it won't put either of us out of our way if we go to Finnegan's Dining Rooms in Clement's Lane."

"Not in the least. A capital notion, Mr Burns."

It was very strange, Burns thought to himself as they set off the length of Lincoln's Inn Fields, that though he knew no ill of Josiah Hartz whatever, he was reminded, even as Hartz put his hand reassuringly on his shoulder, of Chaucer's 'smyler with the knyf under the cloke'. He felt slightly ashamed of himself; it was, after all, he himself whose intentions were devious, who meant to trick Hartz into providing him with information.

"Unseasonably chilly, ain't it, Mr Burns?" said Josiah Hartz. "The wind drives right through you."

They took a table in Finnegan's in comfortable proximity to the fire. When one of the waiters in straw boater and ribbons had taken their order, and opened a bottle of Château Cantemerle '79 so that they might refresh themselves while their food was prepared, Hartz remarked, "Surprisin' fact that my gentlemen and yours ain't done more business together, Mr Burns."

Burns charged their glasses.

"Mind you," Hartz continued, "yours is a newly established chambers, ain't it? Even newer than Fountain Court. And I don't mind tellin' you, Mr Burns - though only in the strictest confidence - it's the opinion of Mr Bullfinger - Mr Augustine Bullfinger, that is - that your Mr Marshall Hall is every bit as good a trial lawyer as Mr Forrest Fulton, QC. And that, my dear sir, is a fact!... Your health, Mr Burns!" He raised his glass.

Burns knew that he ought to dispute the point. He had been Mr Forrest Fulton's clerk even before the latter had been called to the South East Circuit and Sussex Sessions, ten years previously. All he did, however, was to raise his glass in response to Hartz's toast: "Yours, Mr Hartz!"

Josiah Hartz drank, and sat back in his seat. He smiled. "I couldn't help but observe, t'other mornin'," he said, "that Mr Marshall Hall weren't too happy - weren't happy at all - at Mr Augustine Bullfinger's suggestin' Mrs Tuttle should plead insanity."

He lifted his glass a second time, indicating that Burns should join him in a bumper. As he drank down his first glass of claret, Burns wished he were on his usual omnibus going home to his wife and his own cosy hearthside.

Hartz reached across the table, took the bottle, and recharged both their glasses. "Your health, sir!" he said, raising his glass again.

Was he going to repeat the toast every time he lifted his glass to his lips, Burns wondered. He noticed for the first time how Hartz's sandy hair formed a sharp-pointed widow's peak on his freckled forehead - like the headdress worn by Bloody Mary in the illustrations to his well-thumbed copy of Harrison Ainsworth's *Tower of London*, which he had read and reread since childhood.

He raised his own glass again, in reply.

"It was a disturbin' notion to put to a young barrister with his name to make," Josiah Hartz went on, "when he hadn't scarcely had the time to digest his breakfast. But there's no doubt that it would be wonderfully convenient for all parties concerned if Mrs Tuttle did so plead."

"Has Mrs Tuttle lost her wits, Mr Hartz?" Burns asked. "I mean, as a medical man might see it?"

"Medical men have seen it, Mr Burns," Hartz replied. "And will put their names to it. A gentleman learned in the law like Mr Augustine Bullfinger wouldn't suggest such a thing if it weren't the case. Though perhaps," he added thoughtfully, "you might say losin' her wits rather than lost her wits. In the process of losin' her wits."

He smacked his lips and refilled his glass. "It's always the problem in the legal profession," he continued, "especially, I'd say, in the pleadin' profession. I refer, of course, to a conflict of interests - in this particular case, between Justice and the interest of the client. I daresay Mr Marshall Hall is of the opinion our client is entirely innocent of the terrible charge laid upon her. He wishes to clear her name as much as he wishes to make his own. But, Mr Burns, let us examine what are Mrs Tuttle's true interests. Do they lie in putting a mind already perilously unhinged through the awful ordeal of trial on a capital charge? When what she really needs is the care and attention of experienced medical gentlemen? Why not place her where she will receive the very best of care, without all the stress and strain of a public hearing of her case? What is your opinion, sir?"

But before Burns had any opportunity of organizing his thoughts, Josiah Hartz had raised his glass yet again. "Your very good health, Mr Burns."

Burns raised his glass in reply. He must try to keep his head clear, he told himself. He was not a total abstainer - he had never objected to sharing a glass or two of claret or port with colleagues when there was cause for celebration. But he was not accustomed to drinking at the pace Josiah Hartz was forcing on him.

"I would say, Mr Hartz, that I was in no position to give an opinion unless I were made cognizant of all the facts," he replied.

"Indeed, Mr Burns? And what do you suppose those facts might turn out to be?" Josiah Hartz's lids fell like hoods, half-covering his pupils.

"Let me put it this way, Mr Hartz," Burns replied. "On the one hand, we have the interests of Justice herself. On the other, those of our client, whatever they may be. But there are others whose interests may be involved. What of them? And I'm not speakin' of Mr Marshall Hall's interest in making his way in his profession."

"You are shrewd, Mr Burns - very shrewd, if I may say so! Your very good health indeed, sir! It's a pleasure to take a glass of wine with you..." He leaned forward. "You are thinkin' of the gentleman we may call our paymaster, are you not?" he suggested. "You are consamed - and I daresay Mr Marshall Hall is consamed - lest our paymaster has an interest in this case not entirely altruistic, not entirely in mutuality and compatibility with that of our client... Oh dear, oh dear! No good tryin' to pull the wool over your eyes - eh, Mr Burns?"

The way he said it filled Burns with unease, so that he wished even more that he was on his way home to a wife who, though she had never been as enticingly pretty as some of the young women one saw these days waiting behind shop-counters, operating telephones, and typewriting, had always been wonderfully comfortable.

Josiah Hartz was watching, watching, watching from under snake-like lids. The way he lifted his glass indicated that Burns should do the same. Perhaps, thought Burns, he should take a short cut... cut, he thought... cut the Gordian knot. One of the waiters in straw boater and ribbons, laid knife, fork, and napkin before them. That was good, at any rate. Food was good. Steak and kidney pudding would soak up some of the wine in his stomach and modify its deleterious effect (he must still be reasonably sober if he could conjure up a phrase like 'modify its deleterious effect').

To the waiter, Josiah Hartz said, "I do believe Mr Burns here wishes to order another bottle of your excellent..." He peered at the label on the near-empty bottle. "...Château Cantemerle '79."

Burns was thinking how there was no way he could prevent a second bottle arriving at their table, when Josiah Hartz told him, "I'm greatly obleeged to find myself in the hands of a connoisseur of French wines such as yourself, Mr Burns. I fear I am a complete ignoramus with regard to French wines. Now your German wines - that is another matter entirely, my dear sir. I mean your Hocks, your Moselles, Piesporters, Niersteiners and so forth."

Fearful lest he lose time thread of his own thoughts, Burns said, "When I spoke of other people who might be interested in the case of

Mrs Tuttle..."

"Ah yes, Mr Burns!" Josiah Hartz exclaimed. "You are quite right to return us to our muttons, as the French put it."

"I was thinkin'," he said, "of the interests of some people not directly involved with the case, as you might say - not directly, but obliquely. Because of the late Captain Meadowthorpe bein' related to Mr Villiers Manyon in a manner of speakin'."

He found himself drinking the wine in his glass in an attempt to clear his throat. Mr Hartz was nodding his head at him through the tobacco smoke drifting from neighbouring tables. He was just like a heathen idol, or one of those Chinese mandarin dolls who nod their wooden heads like *perpetuum mobiles* or whatever you call them.

"Dear, oh dear!" he heard Josiah Hartz say. "We are barkin' up the wrong tree, and no mistake! Your Mr Marshall Hall thinks that because Mr Villiers Manyon was Captain Meadowthorpe deceased's father-in-law - well, almost 'is father-in-law - and because of the discreet nature of 'is trade - I mean, the Lakeside Spa Hotel and Sportin' Rooms - he would like to see the whole matter swept away under the carpet. In a word, Mr Burns, your Mr Marshall Hall thinks as Marcus, Bullfinger, Stote and Marcus is actin' on the instructions of Mr Villiers Manyon!... Is that it, eh?...eh!"

He broke off as two waiters arrived at the table. One drew the cork from the second bottle of claret. The other placed steaming platefuls of steak and kidney pudding, carrots, and boiled potatoes before them. Josiah Hartz rubbed his hands together, squeaking his palms moistly as though he were washing them. "Excellently done, Mr Burns!" he exclaimed. "Good wine, good food, and the best of company! Nothin' to equal it, I say! So once again - the very best of health to you, sir!"

He raised his glass, holding it up until Burns followed his example.

"To the founder of the feast?" he suggested. "To our absent host, Mr Marshall Hall, eh, Mr Burns?"

He watched Burns drink, then lowered his own glass and attacked his steak and kidney pudding with a will. "Mr Bullfinger would not be gratified to know Mr Marshall Hall holds the notion that our firm is retained by Mr Villiers Manyon," he continued, his expression turning to one of reproach. "Mr Augustine Bullfinger - let alone old Mr Bullfinger! We are very particular about our clients; you should know that, Mr Burns, with your experience of the legal profession."

Burns was touched to the quick. "It was never Mr Marshall Hall's opinion that your employers were retained by Mr Villiers Manyon," he replied. "Nor mine neither."

"Glad to hear you say that, Mr Burns," Josiah Hartz told him. "Most gratified... Whose interests was you referrin' to, exactly?"

"One or several of Mr Villiers Manyon's clientele - frequenters of the Lakeside Spa Hotel," Burns told him. "Members of the nobility - the highest nobility - afraid for their reputations."

He was finding it hard to concentrate, what with the wine fumes confusing his brain and the tobacco smoke in his eyes and nose.

"I wonder - just wonder, mind you - what would make Mr Marshall Hall think of somethin' so very peculiar," said Josiah Hartz.

He chewed a piece of beefsteak with a relish which suggested that his last remark was peripheral to his real preoccupation, his enjoyment of an excellent repast.

"I suppose," said Burns, "it ain't - 'asn't, that is - escaped Mr Marshall Hall's notice that our client is being held under the Silent System, contrary to all regular practice."

"Indeed!" said Josiah Hartz, as if it was news to him.

"Yes, indeed," Burns continued. His mouth was becoming dry with the effect of the drink and smoke. "Mr Marshall Hall is of the opinion the Silent System is - er - oppressive enough to turn the wits of a genteel young woman..."

"Is he so?" asked Josiah Hartz.

"With no other cause to be looked for," Burns concluded.

Josiah Hartz smiled. He filled their glasses from the newly opened bottle. "Would you say that was Mr Marshall Hall's own, unaided opinion?" he asked. "Or might it be that of Mr Mycroft Holmes?... Your health, my very good sir!"

"It don't make no difference whose opinion it might be," Burns replied angrily. "The fact is that it is a thing so irregular, to keep a prisoner on remand under the Silent System, that the Governor of Millbank wouldn't have done it except on the very highest authority."

Only, he did not say 'authority' but 'autorithy'. Josiah Hartz did not appear to notice the slip.

"Oh, Mr Burns!" he said in a sympathetic tone. "Why should Mr Marshall Hall - or Mr Mycroft Holmes - suppose any exalted personage would worry theirselves over *Regina versus Tuttle*?"

Burns had to struggle to think of an answer. He heard himself reply in a dry croak, "Nellie Clifden... The Princess de Sagan... The

Mordaunt Divorce... Lady Aylesford... "

"Oh dear! Oh dear!" Josiah Hartz sat back and laughed. "Mr Burns, I believe you are a wag!" He pointed at him in mock accusation. "I truly do, sir!"

Again his expression changed to one of severity. "So Mr Marshall Hall seriously supposes 'is paymaster to be none other than His Royal Highness, Albert Edward, Prince of Wales! And which of Captain Meadowthorpe's ladies does Mr Marshall Hall think His Royal Highness inclined towards, eh? 'cause it has to be a question of the ladies, God bless 'em! I mean, don't it?"

"I didn't say anything about 'is Royal 'ighness!" Burns objected angrily. He was shocked at the suggestion.

"Very well, then," said Josiah Hartz. "His Royal Nibs's friends. He thinks it must be one or two of His Royal Nibs's friends, eh?"

He did not stay for an answer, but continued eating, finally wiping the gravy from his plate with a potato. Then he lifted his glass, but this time he did not invite Burns to join him in a bumper.

"What you're tellin' me," he said, "is that friends of the Prince of Wales is retainin' the services of Marcus, Bullfinger, Stote and Marcus, to see that the case against Mrs Tuttle never comes before a jury. 'cause they're afeared of what come out about their little - what do you call 'em? - peccadilloes? - under cross examination."

Burns couldn't recall having said any such thing. But now Josiah Hartz was saying it, it seemed perfectly possible.

"If it is," he replied, "it's no more 'n what your firm did over the Mordaunt Divorce Case." His mouth was so furred he could hardly utter the words. He wondered how he would ever manage to make his way back to Lavender Hill.

"Lady Mordaunt was mad as a March hare from the beginning," Josiah Hartz replied. "Six of the most eminent medical gentlemen in the land put their names to her certificate of committal."

He squeezed up his napkin, clutching it in his fist like some newly slain animal in the talons of a predatory beast. "I'll tell you, Mr Burns, since you been so good as to treat me to an excellent dinner. It ain't His Royal Nibs nor any of his Marlborough House friends. I don't deny our firm nas advised some of 'em from time to time. The firm of Marcus, Bullfinger, Stote and Marcus is privileged to serve the very 'ighest in the land."

He looked across the table at Burns. For all his fuddled brain, Burns could see that he was boasting. It was scarcely possible, he thought; but surely somewhere in the midst of all this, Josiah Hartz was telling him what he had come to find out. He was too fuddled to understand what it was exactly, but he was sure it was there somewhere - as long as he could remember what was being said.

Josiah Hartz pushed aside his empty plate and leaned forward over the table. Dropping his voice to a whisper, he went on, "But not this time, Mr Burns. They would none of 'em 'ave given a toss about the Tuttle case - if you'll pardon the expression. Not, that is, till they found that Mr Mycroft Holmes was stickin' his nose into it. Everybody knows - everybody of consequence, that is - that Mr Mycroft Holmes is a devilish clever fellow. It's 'is interference has set off all the flutterin' and flappin' around the Marlborough House dovecotes. And I daresay the fact Mr Mycroft Holmes ain't like his brother - I mean he ain't interested in criminality as such - ain't one to scan the pages of the *Police Gazette*, as you might say - is what's causin' the nobs a bit of worry, eh, Mr Burns?"

"Then who retains...?"

But Josiah Hartz was already smiling and shaking his head. "Thanks to your excellent wine," said he said, "not to mention your shrewd questionin' - you should be a barrister yourself, Mr Burns, you should indeed! - I've told you too much already. Time we went home, eh?"

Burns paid the reckoning - or, at least, he spilled coins from his purse on to the table, and fumblingly took up the change the waiter was pleased to leave in their place.

"The omnibus you require stops on the Embankment, does it not, Mr Burns?" asked Josiah Hartz, hooking Burns's umbrella onto its owner's arm.

"Yes...yes, indeed," Burns replied.

"Then we step in the same direction," said Josiah Hartz.

Burns wondered whether he would be able to travel home without violently disgracing himself in the omnibus. They stepped out into the fresh air. The rain had stopped, but there was still a cold wind. Perhaps, thought Burns, it would refresh and sober him. He wished it would; his head was spinning unpleasantly.

"I fear I am somewhat...in... in... inebriated," he told Hartz.

"Oh, my dear fellow!" Hartz replied, and gently took him by the arm. "Allow me to see you to the omnibus halt."

Burns felt him guiding him down the pavement. Below, at the end of the street, were the lamps along the Embankment. He could smell the raw mud along the edge of the river.

"I... I must apologize for inconveniencin' you, Mr Hartz," he said. "I fear I make a poor host."

"No inconvenience in the world, dear chap, I assure you!" Josiah Hartz replied.

They walked on a little way in silence. "So Mr Marshall Hall thinks that it was friends of His Royal Highness the Prince of Wales retained us to look after our mutual client," said Josiah Hartz. "Wonders will never cease!"

Burns thought to point out that he had never so much as suggested any such thing, but his condition was such that he could not trust himself to speak.

"You'll be able to put 'is mind at rest on that score, won't you?" said Hartz. "Mind you, there's no denyin' Diana Tuttle is an 'andsome woman when she's in her looks. They do say as 'is Royal Nibs 'as an eye for a good lookin' female - skivvy or duchess, they're all the same to 'im, they say!"

If he had not felt so ill, Burns would have taken objection to the familiar way Josiah Hartz spoke, both of the Heir Apparent and of their employers' client.

Hartz guided him across the wide road to the pavement opposite, and the parapet above the dark expanse of the river. A barge was sailing silently down river, dipping in the choppy water under its bulging, wind-filled spankers. Lanterns hung over bows and stem scattered fragments of light across the lapping waves.

"Thank you, Mr Hartz. Most kind of you - very!" Burns mumbled. He wanted to be left alone, immediately. "The Clapham omnibus - it'll drive past here," he added.

"If you're feeling well enough, old chap," Josiah Hartz said solicitously.

"The fresh air," Burns lied. "Feel better, you know."

Hartz thanked him effusively for his evening's entertainment, shook his hand with an unnecessarily firm grip, and left him. Burns had just enough time to watch him making his way down towards Blackfriars Bridge before he staggered onto the stone platform of a flight of water steps, and was violently sick behind the parapet wall.

He remained there for several minutes afterwards, leaning against the wall, shivering. He could not understand how anybody would ever drink too much for pleasure; he was sure he would never be caught out like that again. Across the wind-ruffled water loomed the giant, unlit shadow of Goding's Brewery with its tall, pylon-like smoke stack pointing up to the broken, cloud racked sky. To Burns, it looked like the spire on a Temple of Evil. The sweet, yeasty smell drifting from it - a horrible incense drowning the smell of the river. It drove him into a paroxysm of empty retching.

He knew he would never manage the long omnibus ride back to Lavender Hill, and the quarter of an hour's walk to his small terrace house. He would have to return to Fountain Court; it was only a minute or two's climb from the Embankment, and he had the passkey. He would have to make himself as comfortable as he could in the tank where the parchments and pens and papers and all the impedimenta of counsels' chambers were stored. Amy, his wife, would be dreadfully angry at him - worry always made her angry - and he had no idea how he would explain his unshaven and rumpled appearance to Mr Forrest Fulton in the morning. But there was no help for it.

When cold and discomfort finally drove him off the water-steps back on to the pavement, he set off in the direction of Blackfriars Bridge. He crossed the street, thankful that the only traffic consisted of one or two cabs some distance off, and reached the foot of Middle Temple Lane at the edge of Temple Gardens, a matter of yards, merely, from the entry to Fountain Court. He was about to mount the steps up to the lane when he saw a four-wheeler parked against the kerb of the unlit street behind the gardens. Its curbside door was open; at it, standing talking to whoever was seated inside, his hat held obsequiously in his hand, his face dimly lit by the low flame of the carriage lamp, was Josiah Hartz. Burns shrank back into the obscurity of the wet laurels hedging the gardens. He could hear nothing of what was being said, but Hartz was nodding then speaking as if in answer to questioning. This continued for some minutes. For all his discomfort, once having hid himself in the bushes, Burns dared not move for fear of being noticed. At last Hartz appeared to have finished reporting what he had to report. In the dim light from the carriage lamp, Burns saw him smile, not the supercilious smile he had seen on his face in Finnegan's Dining Rooms, but one of pleasure - pleasure at being praised. An arm reached from the open door, draped in the full sleeve of a black, deeply caped top coat, and put something into Hartz's palm. Hartz glanced at it momentarily. Clenching his hand, he backed, bowing several times, from the carriage step. He reached for the carriage door and closed it, bowing twice more, and waiting for the cabman to whip up his horse and move off up the darkened street in Burns's direction before finally covering his head. Burns backed as far as he could into the laurel branches, the wet leaves soaking his cheeks and drenching his collar as he did so. As the carriage passed in front of him, turning onto the Embankment, the light from the gaslamp at the head of the steps leading up to Middle Temple Lane shone into its interior. The face of the passenger was turned to him. Burns was appalled. It could have been a trick of the light, or the effect of his own diseased state, but it seemed to him the face of a heavy-jowled, square-jawed giant, set on a giant's massive, black caped shoulders, with staring eyes so utterly devoid of expression that they were blanks - pure albumen, devoid of pupils - and cruel with the insensate cruelty of a brute beast.

From the bushes, Burns watched the carriage drive away into the night without its dreadful occupant apparently having noticed him standing there in the wet darkness. He stepped out cautiously onto the kerb, just in time to see the figure of Josiah Hartz hastening round the farther corner in the direction of Blackfriars Bridge.

CHAPTER EIGHTEEN

"Mr Holmes! Mr Holmes, sir!"

The knocking at the door and Mrs Turner's insistent cry echoed for ages across the landscape of his dreaming before he followed its thread back to its point of origin - his bedroom. The hectic activity of the previous seventy two hours was bound to have had the most damaging effect on his mental and bodily constitution if he were not permitted a full eight or nine hours of deep, uninterrupted slumber in the enclosing warmth of his own bed; yet here was Mrs Turner's voice like an obstetrician's forceps, determined to drag him into wakefulness before his time. Forcing his gummy eyelids open, he saw that the light from St James's Square which crept round the curtains was still only the dimmest grey.

"What is it, Mrs Turner!" He croaked out his irritation like a pond-life castrato.

"Two men at the door, Mr Holmes," she called. "They say they've got to speak to you. One of them's the young gentleman you brought up here, two nights ago."

"Mr Marshall Hall? Whatever does he want at this hour of the morning?"

"Don't know, Mr Holmes. But they say it's important."

Mycroft struggled into a sitting position, leaned forward with some difficulty, and dragged his dressing-gown from off the rail at the foot of the bed.

"What's the time?" he called.

"Just six o'clock, sir."

"Be so good as to show them upstairs... And, Mrs Turner? Is Maisie about yet?" He had no idea what time the maid got up.

"Yes, sir. She's just gone down, sir."

"Tell her to lay and light the fire in the study, if you'd be so kind."

He got out of bed, and wrapped the dressing-gown about his girth. There was no hot water with which to shave, so he contented himself with bringing himself to full wakefulness by sluicing his face with cold water. Glancing at his morning face in the mirror, he was sure that anybody who saw him could tell he had been deprived of sleep from the bags drooping under his eyes.

He went through to the study. Maisie was crouched at the fire-place laying coals on the kindling wood. Marshall Hall, his normally smooth, lean face gritted with a dark stubble, was standing at the window looking down onto Pall Mall. With him was a small crumpled, balding man with an untidy, weeping moustache, who was clutching his bowler hat to the stomach of his ill-fitting, ankle-length coat. Both men looked weary; the small crumpled man looked ill.

Marshall Hall introduced his companion as the principal clerk to his chambers, Mr Burns.

"Ah!" Mycroft exclaimed without bothering to greet Burns. "So you took my advice, I suppose... You entertained the chief clerk to Marcus, Bullfinger, Stote and Marcus, to a supper?" He turned to Burns.

"Y...yes, Mr Holmes." Burns half nodded, half bowed uncertainly. He clutched at his bowler as if he were afraid Mycroft might snatch it from him. He was still shivering.

"I thought you should be informed of what transpired as quickly as possible," Marshall Hall explained.

"Quite right! Quite right!" Mycroft replied. "So... er... Mr Burns, here, came straight to you after he had bid his guest good-night, and you decided to call on me immediately?"

Marshall Hall smiled wanly. "You will nave to forgive us our appearance, Mr Holmes," he said. "We have neither of us been home last night."

"Take off your coats," said Mycroft. "Pray sit down. Maisie will soon have a good fire lit..."

Maisie was in the act of applying a match to the corners of an old newspaper under the kindling.

"...Maisie is a capital incendiary," he continued. "She was instructed by one of those revolutionary incendiaries of the Paris Commune - I am sure of it!"

Maisie who had understood not a syllable of what he said, still sniggered as she sat back to watch the flames take hold. Mycroft notice that the heels of her boy's boots were worn to the welts on the outside. He must remember to give her some money to buy a new pair before he went down to Norfolk.

"I am sure these gentlemen are in great need of breakfast, child," he told her. "They say that sleep is a great comfort to the hungry; I'm sure that sustenance is a comfort to the sleepless..."

Before either Marshall Hall or Burns could object, he continued, "You will please ask your mistress to provide us with scrambled eggs, bacon, devilled kidneys... Oh! and a piece or two of that excellent

Finnan haddock, if she has any, with a poached egg or two on top."

Marshall Hall knew better than to persist in declining breakfast. Burns, on the other hand, protested his lack of appetite.

"Nonsense, man!" Mycroft told him. "If ever I saw anyone in need of nourishment, it's you!"

As Maisie scrambled to her feet, wiping her hands on her over-apron, Mycroft told Burns severely,

"I suggest a small glass of Armagnac for your constitution's sake. Maisie's fire is all very well, but it will take time to give off any heat. And you, my dear fellow, look as if you could do with some more immediate warmth."

Burns was appalled by the idea. "No, sir! I could not, if you please!" he cried. "Greatly obliged to you, truly... but...!"

"As you wish, Mr Burns," Mycroft told him scornfully.

He waited until Maisie had carried her ash-pail out of the room and downstairs before settling in his chair by the hearth. "Very well," he said. "What have you to tell me?"

"Mr Burns entertained Mr Hartz - clerk to Marcus, Bullfinger, Stote, and Marcus - to supper last night, as you surmised," Marshall Hall replied. "The man Hartz..." He pronounced the name with no attempt to conceal his distaste, "...appears to have deliberately set out to make Mr Burns ill."

"And did you not expect that, Mr Burns?" asked Mycroft. "A man of your age and experience? Did you not consider practising the same on Mr Hartz?"

"Certainly not, Mr Holmes!" Burns exclaimed. "I 'ave never been a drinkin' man!"

"Which is why, I daresay, Mr Hartz succeeded in making you thoroughly and unpleasantly inebriated," Mycroft said, quite kindly.

"Not to the extent that Mr Burns could not remember all that had transpired between them," Marshall Hall intervened hastily. "He was able to report to me at Fountain Court exactly what had occurred."

"What do you consider to be the salient feature of Mr Hartz's conversation with you?" Mycroft asked Burns.

"Well - he kept on sayin' that you, sir, believed that his employers, and therefore Mr Marshall Hall here, was retained by..." He broke off, as if what he had to tell would defy Mycroft's credulity.

"Please continue," Mycroft said.

"His Royal Highness the Prince of Wales. Or at least friends of

His Royal Highness. Just about the very last thing he 'ad to say to me before we parted, was to tell you and Mr Marshall Hall as it wasn't the case. In fact, he went so far as to say that there 'adn't been any interest in Society in the case of Mrs Tuttle till it became known that you, sir, was - forgive me for usin' his expression, sir - pokin' your nose into the matter."

Mycroft adopted an attitude of intense concentration, his hands held palm to palm before his face, his fingertips touching his lip. After a minute or two had passed, he lowered his hands again. "Tell me, Mr Burns. What did you - under the influence of too much... claret, I presume - reveal to Hartz?" he asked.

"I said that Mr Marshall Hall had realized that Mrs Tuttle was being held in Millbank under the Silent System - and that we weren't happy about it. Not happy at all."

"I have sent a formal note to Mr Augustine Bullfinger," Marshall Hall intervened, "expressing my concern over the treatment of our client in Millbank, and stating my opinion that a protest should be despatched immediately to General Bradfield together with a copy to Sir William Vernon Harcourt at the Home Office."

"What was Mr Hartz's response to your comment on Mrs Tuttle's treatment, Mr Burns?" asked Mycroft.

"I'd say he was sarcastical. He said, 'Indeed!' several times, as if he was pretendin' he knew nothin' about it, but it wasn't of any particular consequence anyway - if you take my meanin', sir."

"I do, Mr Burns," Mycroft replied. "He wished to draw you into saying more... Did you?"

"I drew 'is attention to Captain Meadowthorpe deceased's connection with Mr Villiers Manyon of the Lakeside Spa Hotel and Sportin' Rooms. I said as I thought there might be certain noble and distinguished patrons of Mr Villiers Manyon who might 'ave an interest in keeping certain personal matters, sort of, well - confidential. I didn't say anything more than that."

But he wriggled uneasily, suspecting that that had been too much. He worked his fingers round the rim of the hat which he still held on his lap.

"And he assured you," said Mycroft, "that there had been despondency amongst members of Society only when it became known that I had involved myself in the case? He was emphatic on that point?"

"Most emphatic, sir."

"So! I wonder how he came by that knowledge? Your Mr Hartz seems a wonderfully well-informed solicitor's clerk. Mind you, it is a breed renowned for keeping its ear close to the ground. Even so, Mr Hartz appears to have a remarkably prompt intelligence into the affairs of his betters. Unless, of course.... No! We must not go before our horse to market!" He turned to Marshall Hall. "What do you make of it, Mr Marshall Hall?"

Marshall Hall had become conscious of the stubble on his cheek; he was rubbing it with his forefinger, against the grain of his beard. He dropped his hand quickly. "Methinks the man Hartz doth protest too much?" he suggested.

"Far too much," Mycroft agreed. "To the point at which we may be quite sure that he wishes us to believe that he is out to deceive us - when, in fact, he is telling us the simple truth."

"The truth!" Marshall Hall exclaimed.

"Oh yes," said Mycroft. "We are not dealing with fools."

"How has he come to know of your involvement in Mrs Tuttle's case?" asked Marshall Hall. "And of the response to it of certain members of Society?"

"I would say that it was anticipation," Mycroft replied. "Wouldn't you?"

"Anticipation?" Marshall Hall asked.

"That he had prior knowledge that I was to become involved, and, therefore, of the effect my involvement would have on certain persons. The person who has retained the services of Marcus, Bullfinger, Stote, and Marcus, intended from the beginning that I should become involved in order to create that effect."

Mycroft paused to allow Marshall Hall to give his proposition due consideration. "Think, man!" he said. "Think back for a moment! Who first put it into your mind that you should search out my brother and, more particularly, myself, eh?"

Marshall Hall closed his eyes. He scraped the stubble on his jaw with his thumb. "Josiah Hartz," he said softly. "Hartz suggests I should seek you out."

It was Burns who broke the silence which had fallen over the little group by the now-blazing fire.

"May I ask a question of you, Mr Holmes?"

"Of course, my dear fellow."

"Mrs Tuttle was bein' held under the Silent System before Mr Marshall Hall called on you, wasn't she?"

"There can be no doubt of that," replied Mycroft. "My friend, Princess Trubetskoy, visited her the following day, and found that the conditions laid upon the poor creature were already taking their toll."

"I don't mean to go into matters which ain't my consarn, sir," said Burns. "But the Governor of Millbank ain't goin' to take a decision like that - to keep a prisoner on remand under the Silent System - on his own account. Seeing as it's against all custom, and custom being the very basis of our English law, as Mr Marshall Hall will tell you. Even before you'd set the cat among the pigeons, somebody had persuaded General Bradfield to do it - somebody of importance."

"Very good, Mr Burns! Very good, indeed!" Mycroft replied. "It's little wonder Hartz felt that he had to ply you with drink. He must have felt he'd met his match!"

"Thank you, sir," said Burns.

But Mycroft's tone had been grave. "The point you so excellently made has been on my mind, too," he said. "There is an answer that occurs to me. But it fills me with apprehension... Ah!"

He raised his hand, indicating that the conversation should cease for the moment. From the landing came the chink and clatter of trays.

"Breakfast," Mycroft intoned solemnly.

He heaved himself from his fireside chair and went to open the door. Mrs Turner, still in her quilted wrapper and curl-papers, and Maisie processed in. They laid the breakfast on the table in the centre of the room. Mycroft indicated that his guests should take their places around it; he lifted the lids from each of the serving dishes, saying "excellent!" as he did so. Burns made a feeble attempt to protest that he had no appetite.

"Nonsense, man!" Mycroft told him. "There's only one cure for a voided stomach - ballast!"

He heaped thickly scrambled egg, rashers of bacon, and a small pile of kidneys on to a plate, and put it down before Burns's place.

As soon as the food and coffee was served, and Mrs Turner and Maisie had withdrawn, Mycroft said, "We may take it that anyone permitted to retain the services of so august and old-established - and discreet - a firm as Marcus, Bullfinger, Stote and Marcus..." He paused to excavate the small mountain of egg on his plate with a piece of thickly buttered toast, and to carry it without mishap to his mouth. When he had swallowed enough to be able to speak, he continued, "...must also be of sufficient standing and sufficiently well-connected to persuade General Bradfield to treat Mrs Tuttle with unnecessary and most irregular harshness. His aim is to create such a climate of fear; fear lest the examination and cross examination of evidence at Mrs Tuttle's forthcoming trial reveal aspects of the shadow-side of some of our greatest personages that, out of a misprized sense of loyalty, some of our principal legislators and even jurists will feel it necessary to collude in subverting the very system of Legality and Justice they are sworn to uphold."

He perilously lifted egg heaped on toast, this time with a half-rasher of bacon laid on top, to his mouth. With his mouth still full, he continued, "We may suppose that whoever this client of Marcus, Bullfinger, Stote and Marcus may be, he had already used some instrument to persuade General Bradfield into the action he took - personal acquaintance would seem the most probable explanation..."

He broke off to dab at his lips with his napkin.

"But to what purpose?" asked Marshall Hall. "To what end?"

Mycroft dropped his napkin back on to his knees. "To put himself in the position of being able to reveal the frailties of certain great personages, thus provoking scandal, and then to compound it by demonstrating the odious, undignified and, I fear, sordid contrivances by which our governors sought to conceal them from public knowledge. There is nothing upon which we English so pride ourselves, justly, as the incorruptibility of our elected leaders, those gentlemen of broad estates and property who so devotedly, and with no thought of profit and self-interest, guide the destinies of our Nation; as the purity and even handedness of our system of Justice, the model and pattern for the rest of the Globe. The odium into which the very thought of the deliberate corrupting of our great institutions of State would plunge some of our greatest figures would cause political upheaval and crisis worse than any of us would wish to contemplate. We may be sure that our man would ensure it was set off at the moment when it best suits his purposes - or those of the potentates or powers he represents."

"But this is more dreadful than I could ever have imagined!" Marshall Hall exclaimed. "It strikes at the very heart of civilized polity!"

"Why do you suppose the poet Dante consigned barretry - the corruption by bribery and nepotism of civic institutions - to the lowest circle of Hell: lower even than parricide, incest or blasphemy?" asked Mycroft. "If not because it strikes at the heart of all decent human association...?" He placed his napkin on the table beside his plate, and, pushing back his chair, stood up. "Pray excuse me for a moment," he said.

He went to the bookcase occupying an entire wall of the room, from floor to ceiling. He mounted the small, stepped platform he used to reach the top shelves. "I should have thought of this before," he said. "But the reaches even of the most acute intellects are limited."

He drew down a heavy but recently bound volume.

"Mr Burns believes that he may have seen our man," said Marshall Hall.

"Indeed?" asked Mycroft, too preoccupied with turning pages to pay any attention. "I keep a small store of directories," he went on. "Not obsessively as does my brother; the recent volumes of *Hansard*, *Crockford*, of course, the *Peerage*, the *Land Register*, and the *Army and Navy Lists*... Ah, yes. Here we are: Cecil Montresor Bradfield, CBE, Major General, retired..."

"Mr Hartz and I parted, last night, on the Embankment," Burns explained. "Mr Hartz was under the impression I was goin' to take the omnibus across Waterloo Bridge. He said as he was goin' to Blackfriars. Only, I decided to return to the Middle Temple, and Fountain Court..."

"Quite, quite!" said Mycroft impatiently. "A moment, if you please!... Served in India as subaltern in the first battalion, Duke of Rutland's Light Infantry. Captain in the same regiment in the Russian War: Yeni-Bazaar, Balaclava - wounded at Vorontsov Road. Gazetted Major, November '55, and appointed aide-de-camp to General Cathcart, etc., etc,... Gazetted Major-General, '67; but never commanded in the field, it seems. Appointed Military Attaché to the Royal Italian Government at the Palazzo Pitti the same year, and to the Royal Government of Prussia at Potsdam, '70... Withdrew from Active List, '77, to become Governor, Lincoln House of Correction; appointed Governor, Millbank Prison, '79. Publications include *A Vindication of the 7th Earl of Cardigan*, by a Veteran of the Crimean Campaigns, 1867; and *With Crown Prince Friedrich from Gravelotte to Versailles: an eye-witness account of the German-French War*, 1873... An account, I daresay, conspicuous for its adulation of Prussian discipline and military expertise when compared to the hedonism and decadence of the French..."

He broke off quite suddenly. "By George!" he exclaimed. "Of course! the very instrument which I suggested - personal acquantance

- was used on General Bradfield to persuade him to take steps to unhinge poor Mrs Tuttle's mind!"

He did not return the volume to its place, but laid it on top of the books on the shelf nearest to hand. As he did so, he said, "Mr Burns, if you please! This man you mentioned - where did you see him?"

Mycroft climbed down from the little platform.

"Mr Hartz didn't expect me to go back to the Middle Temple," Burns began, "so I'm just about to go up the steps to the lane above Temple Gardens, when I see this four-wheeler parked in the shadow behind the Gardens, and Mr Hartz on the pavement by the bushes, talkin' to whoever's inside it. I didn't want him to see I was goin' back to Fountain Court, so I dodged back into the bushes and stayed there till they was done. As it was goin', the cab drove right past where I was..."

"And you had a good view of its passenger?" Mycroft demanded. "Can you describe him to me exactly?"

"I had a prime view, Mr Holmes," Burns replied. "There's a lamp at the foot of the steps leadin' up to Middle Temple Lane. It shone right through the inside of the cab as it drove past me - and seein' as it's a sharpish bend there, leadin' down on to the Embankment, the driver had to pull in his horse..." He paused.

"Go on!" Mycroft exclaimed.

"I don't quite know how to explain it, sir," Burns told him. "He was the strangest lookin' gentleman I've ever seen - and I've seen the greatest gentlemen called to the bar, sir, and the worst felons ever brought to the dock."

"How - strange?" demanded Mycroft. "Be specific, man!"

"He was a big gentleman. He had the broadest shoulders I've seen on anyone," said Burns. "And a head like a giant's - huge, with a square jaw like a pugilist, one of them bare-knuckle pugilists who take on all comers at fairgrounds. But it was his eyes was the thing, Mr Holmes. He looked straight at me - I don't think as he saw me, mind; I was standin' well back in the bushes, out of the light. I tell you, I've never seen eyes like them - and I never wish to again. They were like the eyes of some beast you've never heard of: they looked blank as if they had no pupils, but they was staring like a beast's. I know it's hard to believe, sir. But that is what I saw."

"Yes," said Mycroft. "That is indeed what you saw!"

Burns and Marshall Hall watched him as he returned to his place and took his seat once more. He looked gravely from one to the other. "I must tell you," he said at last, "that the man who has retained the services of Marcus, Bullfinger, Stote, and Marcus - and therefore yours, Mr Marshall Hall - is one of the most influential, most dangerous men in Europe, and certainly the most evil."

After a long pause, Marshall Hall sighed wearily. "I suppose from the first, I suspected that I was being drawn out of my depth. I should never have taken on Mrs Tuttle's defence in the first place. Not in the knowledge that the Attorney General would be prosecuting the case. And now, after what you tell me... Well! It isn't too late for me to return the brief."

"By no means!" excalimed Mycroft. "The good name of English Justice depends on you defending Mrs Tuttle. With my assistance you will be peculiarly well-equipped to do so. To allow the poor woman's defence to collapse at this juncture would be to bring about precisely that eventuality which Hartz's Imperial German masters would exploit to advantage - a deliberate misprision of justice in an attempt to cover up the peccadilloes of one who stands next in line to the Throne."

He leaned forward across the hearth, and laid his hand on Marshall Hall's knee. "There is still a little time left," he said. "You shall be provided with all the evidence you require to secure your client's acquittal - you may depend upon it. In the meantime, you have only one duty - and I pray you perform it with all the vigour at your command."

"And what is that, Mr Holmes?"

"To ensure that your unfortunate client - who has been the unsuspecting instrument of wicked men from the beginning - is in a fit state to plead her innocence before a jury of twelve honest Englishmen. What d'you say, sir?"

CHAPTER NINETEEN

"Do you mean to tell us that Carl Philip Emmanuel Guttmann is paying for Mrs Tuttle's defence?" Sophie asked.

"Thank you, Cyril," Mycroft said as Cyril placed the brandy decanter on the coaster in front of him. He helped himself to a glass. "I would not go so far as that," he replied. "That would be travelling too deeply into the realms of conjecture."

He broke off to glance acutely at both Sophie and Sir Frederick. "We may be certain that the man Hartz is Guttmann's creature," he announced as if he had come to a decision. "And Guttmann, as we know is the Prince von Bismarck's confidential agent and *eminence grise*. What we cannot tell at this juncture, is whether Guttmann is acting on instructions from the Berlin Chancellory, or independently."

He turned to Sir Frederick. "Guttmann is a human beast, lacking reason or compassion. His father was *Kapellmeister* of the Pomeranian Grenadiers, a cold, martinet disciplinarian who passed on to him skill in the practice of music with none of its moral virtues; to listen to Carl Philip Emmanuel Guttmann play a prelude, let us say, by Bach is to experience in microcosm the vast and chilly loneliness of a Universe abandoned by its Divine Creator. His mother, the housekeeper-matron of a military school for orphans at Sans Souci, was cast in the same cold martinet-mould as his father. He is one of those unfortunate beings who, from the moment of his conception neither experienced nor was instructed in the human virtues of kindliness, affection, or empathetic understanding. He knows one duty and one loyalty - to the King and Chancellor of Prussia. In their service, there is no baseness, no wickedness, no seduction so vile he will not practice it. Murder, blackmail, the breaching of that sanctuary of the family home through the corruption of domestic servants - these are the instruments of this appalling trade. In the furtherance of that trade, he gathers about him creatures useful to him, lacking his power of intelligence, but whose childhood was as deprived of instruction in the heart's affections as his own." He pushed the brandy to Sir Frederick. "These days, Guttmann acts less as the Imperial German Chancellor's agent," he continued, "than as a creator of opportunities which the Chancellory in Berlin can exploit while washing its hands of any direct responsibility for them: the Ems telegram, for instance which provided the *casus belli* by which the Prussians could inflict on France the most humiliating defeat suffered by a Great Power in modern times; or the Bulgarian atrocities, which allowed Prince von Bismarck to assume the role of supreme arbiter in the Balkans."

He sat back in his chair, examined the end of his cigar, then relit it. "Guttmann, acting on information supplied to him by Hartz's information, hopes to find himself in the position to cause our Royal Family maximum embarrassment just at the moment his master, von Bismarck, wishes to make his move in the Rhineland. I am quite convinced that Hartz was acting on Guttmann's instructions when he suggested to young Marshall Hall that he should seek the assistance of myself or my brother. He foresaw the nervous flutter that would cause in the dovecotes of Windsor and Whitehall. He knew that if anything would provoke the powers-that-be into circumventing the due process of English Justice, it would be the thought of Mycroft Holmes truffling for the truth in the Hampstead undergrowth."

"So," said Sophie, "that is the plan! To make a scandal out of the Prince of Wales's *affaire* with the brothel-keeper's daughter while Bismarck makes himself master of Grand Duchess Jolande and her Rhineland state... A cigarette, if you please, Cyril."

Cyril offered her the small silver casket, and she took a cigarette. Sir Frederick watched with some surprise as she impaled it on her jewelled pin before turning to Cyril for him to light it for her. Clearly, thought Mycroft, her behaviour had been less *outrée* at the time their relationship had been fonder.

"What a pretty thing this business is, to be sure!" she added.

"I don't believe that His Royal Highness's *petit amitie* with Miss Manyon," said Mycroft, "foolish though it may have been, is to be the direct cause of the scandal Guttmann intends. That is to be His Royal Highness's supposed rôle in perverting of the justice which the great and honourable lady, his mother, swore at her coronation to uphold. Now that could provoke a constitutional crisis, do you see? which would most certainly distract Her Majesty's Government's attention from any developing situation in the Rhineland."

"So that's why you've been spreadin' doom and gloom round the Foreign Office!" exclaimed Sir Frederick. "You put 'Pussy' Granville in no end of a funk! I've had to spend the whole afternoon tryin' to persuade His Lordship there's not the remotest chance of Berlin bullyin' the Grand Duchess into an alliance with the Prussians."

"I'm relieved to hear it," said Mycroft.

"You're never suggesting that Guttmann arranged the whole business on Squire's Mount, surely, my dear?" asked Sophie.

"No. I'm suggesting that he is expert in spotting human weakness and in exploiting an existing situation that weakness has brought about. The Prince has indulged in follies which would scarcely have provoked comment had he been any other *habitué* of clubland. Unfortunately His Royal Highness, in the words of our national bard,

> ...*is subject to his birth,*
> *And may not, as unvalued persons do,*
> *Carve for himself.*

I daresay he was attracted to Villiers Manyon's establishment at first because of his indulgence in a particularly childish card game. When that establishment was removed to the leafy seclusion of Hampstead's Vale of Health, the Prince found it an ideal spot in which to indulge his other weakness. It was most unfortunate that his eye should have lighted on Parthenope Manyon; the fact that she was affianced to Meadowthorpe - a publicly acceptable if *complaisant* attachment - may have added to her charms. Nor do we need look to the chief clerk of Marcus, Bullfinger, Stote and Marcus to realise who it was who passed on to Berlin the news of His Royal Highness's latest peccadillo. Baron von Goeben, the Imperial German Ambassador, is a regular patron of Villiers Manyon's establishment - an *habitué* of the *baccarat* table. It would have been he who transmitted to Berlin the news of the potential embarrassment of the Prince resulting from the death of Meadowthorpe and the indictment against Mrs Tuttle.

"As for the actual case itself - the deaths of Helena Meadowthorpe and Meadowthorpe himself were no more than sordid murders for gain. We may be sure that Manyon set up Meadowthorpe in Squire's Mount as the agent through whom he intended to secure his ward's estate. I daresay he tried the less hazardous tactic of having her committed as a lunatic, but Bickleigh, poor creature though he is, would have shied off so violent an abuse of his Hippocratic Oath.

"I was convinced of the fact that Dr Bickleigh, too, is one of Manyon's agents by his presence the other night at the meeting at the Hollybush Assembly Rooms. I'd take my oath on his having been there as a spy. But he is a weak, shilly-shallying creature bridled by Providence with a sense of goodness - or respectability - which he cannot entirely shake off.

"Helena Meadowthorpe dies at Meadowthorpe's hand, but Mrs Tuttle, not yet hopelessly infatuated with her employer, confides in Dr Bickleigh her suspicion that he poisoned his wife. Bickleigh goes straight to the true author, if not perpetrator, of the crime, Villiers

Manyon. It is probable that what happens next is the result of Bickleigh's moral ambivalence. The physical elimination of Mrs Tuttle might well prove too much for the doctor's suspicions and sensibilities. There must perforce be an interlude between Meadowthorpe's bereavement and his marriage to Manyon's daughter, Parthenope, with all its concomitant financial arrangements.

"Meadowthorpe is a handsome and plausible fellow. Who can tell how far Mrs Tuttle feels impelled to voice her fears to Dr Bickleigh because she is attracted to her employer, and is afraid of the possible consequences of that attraction? - the tingling of *Odi et Amo* in a woman's heart did not die with the Romans. This conflict of emotions has no doubt exacerbated by her admitted dislike for her late mistress and her sympathy with Meadowthorpe in his relations with her.

"In any case, Meadowthorpe ensures her silence by seducing her into his bed - the marriage bed, I daresay... I hope you will forgive the coarseness, dear Princess - it is germane to my exposition. But the seduction is only a means by which Mrs Tuttle's silence may be more firmly ensured. And here I must cause to congratulate our friend, here, on his perspicacity..."

He turned to look up at Cyril. "Before ever the thought had occurred even to me," he said, "Cyril suggested that the wretched Meadowthorpe had emulated Mithradates, King of Pontus - that he had been taking poison himself..."

He removed a cigar from the silver humidor beside him, and handed it to Cyril. "I'm sure Sir Frederick Colton will not object to your joining us, my lad," he said.

Cyril's look of mild surprise at Mycroft's gesture of affability was as nothing compared to Sir Frederick's at the sight of Sophie's black servant sitting at table with them, and lighting a cigar.

Sophie explained, "Cyril is a dear and valued colleague of ours in these matters, Freddy," she said, placing her hand on Cyril's sleeve and thus adding to Sir Frederick's astonishment.

"There is a difference, of course," Mycroft went on. "Mithradates took poison with the aim of becoming inviolable to poisoning. Once he had become engaged to Parthenope Manyon, Meadowthorpe poisoned himself - with Manyon's connivance, we may be sure - with a view to casting suspicion on Mrs Tuttle both for his own sickness and for the death of his wife... He made, however, a fatal mistake. On the night of his death he took a dose of poison, then sent Mrs Tuttle to fetch Dr Bickleigh. When she was gone he went up the back staircase - leading to the servants' bedroom quarters - went into Mrs Tuttle's room, and placed the incriminating bottle on the mantlepiece behind her clock. He was returning down the stairs when he was seized with a paroxysm of vomiting. He vomited down the steps, and on descending further slipped and fell to the floor. He may have been aware that he had taken an overdose, but it is unlikely that he actually knew he was dying; the fact that he accused Mrs Tuttle of murdering him need only have been a figure of speech.

"What we do know is that Mrs Tuttle was hindered from reaching Bickleigh by two of Manyon's employees, and that Manyon was with Bickleigh when finally she reached Downshire Hill."

"Do you mean," Sophie asked, "that Manyon knew that on that particular night Meadowthorpe would take a dose of the poison sufficient to kill him?"

"I would say," Mycroft replied carefully, "that there is a *prima facie* case to answer. Would you not agree?" But he did not wait for an answer. "The problem, with regard to defending Mrs Tuttle is that the evidence of Meadowthorpe suffering, an attack on the servants' stairs and slipping on his own vomit lies in the testimony of a dead woman. We cannot call on Dr Bickleigh's housemaid to give evidence as to what Annie Gibbs told her: such hearsay evidence would never be admitted in court. I fear that Villiers Manyon can say with Good Queen Bess, 'Much is suspected of me; nothing proved can be'."

He sighed heavily. "And I am summoned into Norfolk to prevent me from pursuing the investigation."

⋕⋕⋕

Sir Frederick and Mycroft stepped into Bruton Street and the night.

"Does the Princess make a habit of permitting her negro such liberties in her presence?" Sir Frederick asked with a barely detectable edge of jealousy in the note of surprise.

Mycroft entertained the idea for a moment of explaining Cyril's devotion to his mistress; he even thought of confessing his own liking for the rascal.

He replied judiciously, "Russian tradition, don't you know? Your Russkies take the same attitude towards household servants as the plantation aristocracy in the southern states of America with their niggers. Tend to regard 'em as members of the family, and allow 'em liberties we'd only allow to our old nannies and gamekeepers, what?"

He was rather pleased with his display of tact. There was the sound of hooves and carriage wheels from the direction of Berkeley

Square, but no cab appeared, and the sound died away. It seemed that they would have to walk.

"Somethin' which puzzles me about what you were saying," Sir Frederick remarked as they set off toward the lights of New Bond Street. "I can see why HRH and his advisers should want to keep you a safe distance from the Tuttle case. But you did say that it was a friend of the German Ambassador who had recommended you to HRH as an authority to be consulted over the Rhineland question. Bit fishy, ain't it? I mean, you're the last person whose advice they'd want Her Majesty's Government to take, ain't you?"

"It is more fishy than that," Mycroft replied. "Had it been von Goeben himself, I might have understood it; he shares HRH's taste in childish card games, pretty, witty young actresses, and the slaughter of game. HRH was guest at his hunting-lodge last year. But this friend of von Goeben's, the fellow Cumming says has been sent to offer HRH the Honorary Colonelship of the Seventh Uhlans. This Colonel-General the Graf von Varzin?..."

He looked at Sir Frederick, under the gaslight. Sir Frederick shook his head. "Never heard of the fellow," he said.

"Neither have I," Mycroft told him. "It was the name 'Varzin' which aroused my suspicions..."

"The forest on Prince von Bismarck's East Prussian estates, by Jove! Keeps it for the upkeep of game," Sir Frederick commented.

"Exactly!" said Mycroft. "A 'von' attached to an uninhabited wilderness. I made enquiries at the War Department: they were able to tell me that there was no von Varzin gazetted in the *Imperial German Army List* of 1879 - two years ago. And there is no such title recorded in the Prussian *Almanach*. So we have here a newly minted Count of the Kingdom of Prussia, a Colonel-General of Uhlans, who seems to have sprung from the skull of the Prince von Bismarck with the same alacrity as Pallas Athene from the head of Zeus... And he appears in London at the same time as Guttmann is sighted..."

"'Ere! Sir! 'Scuse me, sir!"

A small girl in a battered, wide-brimmed straw hat, her clothes hidden under the filthy apron about her waist, and an ancient, knitted shawl pinned across her chest, had tugged at Mycroft's coat. Mycroft looked at the basket on her arm, and the bunch of violets clutched in her hand; they looked as if they had been strangled rather than wilted. A pair of small, bare feet, black rather than grimy, were visible under her apron fringe.

"You should not be out alone at this hour," Mycroft told her. "Not at your age."

He felt in his waistcoat pocket for a coin.

"Me Ma won't be back from the public," said the girl in a wheezy voice. "Ain't closin' yet. An' then she 'as to 'ave 'er little sleep on the pavement."

Mycroft held out a sixpence.

"What's 'at for?" The girl stared up at him, her eyes shining like a rodent's in the lamplight from the end of the street.

"Your flowers," Mycroft suggested.

"Garn!" said the child. "Piss off! You don't want 'em! They're all dead!" She threw them down into the gutter. "You Mr 'olmes?" she demanded.

"And if I am?" asked Mycroft.

"Mr Mycock 'olmes, or somefink?" she demanded.

"I am Mycroft Holmes. What do you want with me?"

"The black geezer said..," the girl began.

"Cyril said...?" Mycroft prompted.

"Yer! Shirrul said as I was to keep watch acrorst from 'is 'ouse. Said as I was to tell you if I sees anyfing..." She took a deep breath. "...Per...kew...lee...ar!" she announced. "An' I did!" she added at the end of her breath.

"You did?" asked Mycroft.

"Yer! There were a cab. One of 'em closed ones - waited all the time you was in there, it did. Jest over... there!" She jabbed her finger towards the corner. "It 'ad its curtings drawn," she said.

"You did not see the person sitting inside it?" Mycroft asked.

She shook her head vehemently. Then she said proudly, "An' 'e didn't see me!"

"What about the cabbie?" asked Mycroft.

"'E didn't see me neither! 'cause I were standin' in that doorway, where it's dark."

"You were there all evening?" Mycroft asked.

She nodded. "Were in there till they gone. I see-ed you frew the painted winder, comin' downstairs. So I reckons 'im in the cab did, an' all, 'cause it drives orf straight 'way, 'fore you comes out."

She took another deep breath, as if she was about to utter the most important part of the information she had in store. "Shirrul said as you'd give me a 'ole shillun if I done what 'e tell me," she announced. An' I 'ave!"

Mycroft replaced the sixpence he normally kept for beggars back in his waistcoat pocket. He drew out his purse and took from it a half crown. "What is your name, child?" he asked.

She stared fixedly at the coin then, tearing her gaze from it, she glanced quickly up and down the street. Still holding up the coin, he withdrew his hand beyond her reach. Her gaze returned to the coin. She stood on one leg, and scratched her ankle with the toes of her other foot.

"Ver-woniker," she replied at last.

"Very well, Veronica." He lowered his hand to give her the coin.

She stared at him warily. "What's I got ter do for that?" she asked. "'cause I'm a good girl, I am," she added.

"I'm sure you are, Veronica," Mycroft told her gently. "This a reward for what you have done already - and very well done."

Still staring up at him she pulled the coin from between his fingers. Without saying a word of thanks she walked off up the street towards Berkeley Square, pulling the handle of her flower-basket up her sleeve as she went.

"Now do you see what a useful fellow the negro is?" Mycroft asked Sir Frederick, as they turned into New Bond Street. "He can call on a hundred spies such as that one. And unsavoury as they may be, they are more observant and immeasurably more quick-witted than any policeman I have yet encountered."

They bade one another goodnight when they reached Piccadilly. Sir Frederick was due to return to Pfalzel-Buckelburg the next day.

"What a business!" he said to Mycroft. "You are sure you yourself will be safe?"

"All will be well, and all manner of things will be well," Mycroft replied, "including myself. Provided young Marshall Hall ensures that Mrs Tuttle clearly states her intention of pleading not guilty at her arraignment before the Grand Jury."

But as he continued alone on his way under the moonlit turrets of St James's Palace, he felt less sanguine. It might have been the desolation of the streets and the long tapering shadows thrown by the moonlight which awoke in his imagination those childish dream-fears he so prided himself on keeping firmly under control. As he thought of the royal invitation to Sandringham House, signal honour though it was, the lines from a nursery poem sounded insistently in his head,

'Will you walk into my parlour?' said the spider to the fly.
'Tis the prettiest little parlour that ever you did spy...'

CHAPTER TWENTY

Before venturing forth to catch the special train for Sandringham, Mycroft took the precaution of eating a modest breakfast: porridge, kippers, lambs' kidneys in a cream sauce, several slices of cold ham, rounded off with toast and marmalade. Accustomed though he was to the corridors of power and to having his advice sought by statesmen, the thought of being the house-guest of royalty made him feel as nervous as a new boy at school. There was moreover the sense of danger which he trailed with him like the after-mood of a nightmare. Thus affected, a plentiful intake of food was a necessary sedative.

Once arrived at the Great Eastern's Liverpool Street terminus his cab-driver had no difficulty in spotting where he should be put down. A dun-coloured carpet had been laid stretching from the edge of the pavement, up the steps, and through the right hand door of the ticket-hall. There was a scarlet rope to hold back an ever-growing crowd of onlookers, paper boys, flower girls, carters and railway passengers, who were gathering to watch the arrival of the *illustrissimi* and society beauties who were to be the Prince of Wales's guests, and to display their knowledge of the fashionable world by shouting out their names as they descended from their shining barouches.

Mycroft's humble four-wheeler had to take its place in the line of carriages. He lowered his window and leaned forward discreetly. Ahead of him, a small squad of porters in clean uniforms and polished brass buttons were removing the luggage from the roofs of the carriages. His fellow guests, in a widely spread file, were trailing up the carpet to the station entrance like pilgrims to a cathedral. He leaned his head out further to see if there were any with whom he had a more or less nodding acquaintance. Amongst the attenuated column of nodding feathers, of lace flounces spilling through the vents of velvet-trimmed promenade coats like whites of egg broken in boiling, and of polished silk hats, he recognized Sir Allen Young, gentleman explorer of the North-West Passage and of the more remote Pacific islands. 'Alleno' Young was a bachelor like himself; unlike him, however, he had the reputation of a *roué*, a destroyer of maidens' reputations. In fact, Mycroft was surprised that he should have made one in a mixed house party at Sandringham. He was a friend of the Prince of Wales, no doubt of that. It was reported that on one occasion he had loosed a stag in the High Street, Harrow-on-the-Hill, and that he and the Prince had hunted it down the Harrow and

Edgware Roads to a kill on the concourse of Paddington Station before the horrified gaze of waiting passengers. But Mycroft had good reason to feel grateful toward 'Alleno' Young. During the unfortunate business of the Sultana of the Ruwenora Islands and Rear Admiral Sir Loxley Jones - a matter which would have proved disastrous for British interests in the Pacific had Mycroft not been dispatched to the Sultana's court in the nick of time - it had been 'Alleno' Young who, in his private yacht and under the muzzles of the guns of a French flotilla, had lifted him off the coral reef on which he had been marooned on the orders of the Sultana's pro-French Grand Wazier.

There were others with whom he had exchanged conversation across a fashionable dinner-table, or whispered a few words at a musical *soirée*. He recognized over the shoulders of the porters who were unloading portmanteaux and leather-strapped cabin trunks from a brougham several carriages ahead, Louisa, the German-born Duchess of Manchester. Beside her was the stout figure and weeping dundreary whiskers of her familiar companion, the Liberal Party Chairman, Lord Hartington. Now that an indulgent Providence had taken the Duke of Manchester to Himself, they no longer kept up the pretence of not being lovers; the Duchess took Hartington's arm as they ascended the steps. There was the purple-faced Lord Ranelagh, nicknamed in whispers round Whitehall, 'Lord Procurer of Wales', banished from all respectable houses for his blunt insistence that he should be permitted to have his will of any and every housemaid who took his fancy. The story was told how he and the Prince rode about Norfolk at harvest time seeking women field-workers; how, when they encountered one on the roadside or sheltering beneath a hedge, they would force her to lift her skirt up over her head, and would then place a five pound note in the orifice thus exposed, having laid wagers as to whether her pleasure at discovering such *largesse* would predominate over her sense of shame.

Beside Lord Ranelagh, with his hand tucked round his arm, was his associate in depravity, the blind Duke of Streltsau. It was said of him in the divans of Jermyn Street that he was so talented and potent a lover that any woman who submitted herself to him would, for the remainder of her days, be the victim of a desperate and febrile yearning for a similar satisfaction. A little way after them came Colonel Valentine Blake, and the clumsy, heavy-footed little woman - a tradesman's daughter - whom he had married when he had nothing left to sell to pay debts incurred at the card-tables, and whose unhappiness was written on her swarthy little face. Blake was commanding officer of the Prince's own regiment, the Tenth Hussars, as well as being an *habitué* of Villiers Manyon's establishment; he was known for his penchant for deflowering clergymen's daughters and young and inexperienced governesses, so that Mycroft's clubland associates were accustomed to referring to those street-women who claimed to be clergymen's daughters as 'Val Blake's gels'.

The procession of carriages lurched forward a few yards then ground to a standstill once more. Still with his head half out of the window, Mycroft looked past the carriage immediately in front of his cab, from whose bucket a couple of porters were removing two large valises and a gun-case, to the gleaming brougham beyond. A bowing, Assistant Stationmaster in satin-trimmed frock-coat, a ribbon of gold and a gold rosette about his silk hat, had lowered the steps with his own hand. He was now assisting the stooped, immensely tall, emaciated figure of Lord Lingard to descend to the pavement. Lord Lingard, black as an undertaker, stood leaning on his stick, staring about him from sunken eyes as if he scarcely knew where he was. He had once been a distinguished First Lord of the Admiralty, a close and trusted colleague of Lord Palmerston, but disease and a tendency for his mind to wander when it should have been at its most attentive had kept him from office for the past decade and a half.

While Lord Lingard stood waiting, the brougham heaved and rocked on its springs. Through its door, with the obstetric aid of the Assistant Stationmaster, twisted and squeezed the monstrously buxom Lady Lingard, holding out her tiny, frilly edged parasol before her like an absurd wand. As 'Babs' Kellegher, she had been proprietress and presiding genius of a night-house in Well Street favoured by military gentlemen and members of the nobility. Friends of the notoriously humourless Lord Lingard had provoked him into marrying her in the hope that her physical opulence would breath a glow in the dying embers of his spirit while providing her with financial security during her later years. Despite her elevation into the peerage, she continued to plaster her face with powder as if dusting a loaf of unrisen dough with flour, to rouge her cheeks and to ring her eyes as thickly with kohl as an Indian nautch-girl. Gossip had it that there was not one of the more raffish noblemen and gentry who formed His Royal Highness's unofficial court who had not enjoyed intimacy with 'Babs' Lingard - with the exception, of course, of Lord Rosebery, whose tastes, so it was reported, lay in altogether another direction.

Mycroft slumped back into his seat. He wished he could have instructed his jarvey to drive him back to Pall Mall; he wished he were at his obscure desk at the Treasury. There were two courts about the Prince of Wales, two guest lists to Marlborough House or Sandringham: very few of those who belonged to one appeared in the other. Those whom he had seen trailing up the carpeted steps to tile station entrance were like a procession of lost souls. What, he asked himself, was the significance of his being invited to join them? Who could possibly have suggested that he had anything in common with them? He was overcome by a leaden sense of unease. Even the cramped, straw-smelling interior of the growler seemed to have become darker.

At last the porters reached his cab; the driver leant over the back of his seat to help them unstrap the bags from the roof. Mycroft took coins from his purse: two half-crowns for his driver and a shilling for the porters to divide between them.

He reached the top of the steps and entered the vaulted, echoing, coke-smelling gloom of the station concourse. A regimental string band was playing a musical pot-pourri from *Patience*; Mycroft could scarcely make out the melody of 'When I go out of door' above the din of steam and the rattling of trollies. He followed his immediate predecessors, Lord and Lady Lingard, to the freshly gilded, beflagged gate leading to the side bay where the special train was waiting. The Stationmaster himself, silk-hatted and wearing a silk-lapelled frock coat, was waiting there with one of the directors of the Great Eastern Railway to bid His Royal Highness's guests a pleasant journey into Norfolk. With them, as the Prince's personal representative, was the massive, erect figure of Sir William Gordon Cumming. The thought occurred to Mycroft as he approached the gate that he had approximately twenty yards in which to feign a heart attack or a mild seizure. Sir William stroked his sandy moustache with the edge of his finger as Mycroft passed him. As he went on to the platform, Mycroft heard him say to the Railway Company director, "Common interest I suppose. Even a Royal can't always choose his acquaintances when there's a common interest at stake, eh?"

He continued up the platform. Nothing could have been more different from the usual two-and-sixpence-a-mile special with its tank engine and single carriage. There were six carriages of the style of first-class carriages forty years previously, when each compartment had been constructed on the model of a gentleman's enclosed family barouche. But though they were old-fashioned the paintwork was fresh and shone with varnish. The engine with the royal standards fixed on either side of the boiler, was as clean and burnished as if it had never devoured a shovelful of coals. The carriage immediately behind the tender was occupied by the valets and lady's maids who were accompanying their employers, and the Sandringham House servants who had come to serve refreshments on the journey. Mycroft noticed that the compartment immediately behind the first carriage was unoccupied. It represented the chance of spending several uninterrupted hours of solitude. Perceiving him hesitating close to the door, one of the railway's bowler-hatted attendants rushed to open it for him. Just at that moment, a voice called, "Ach! Mr Holmes!"

The caller had got down from a compartment only a few yards further down the carriage. A rush of steam from between the wheels caused him to appear through it like a pantomime demon king. He was a good-looking, youngish man; his head was bared, displaying a close-cropped widow's peak, and he wore his moustache trimmed and waxed. Although he was in civilian clothes, his bearing proclaimed him a soldier.

"Mr Holmes, if I am not mistaken!" he said. "Mr Mycroft Holmes!... Oh, I know! You will say I am having the advantage over you..." He interrupted himself by laughing.

"Not at all, sir," Mycroft replied. "It is I have the advantage over you. Although we have not previously met, I know without fear of contradiction that I have the pleasure of addressing Colonel-Major Baron von Goeben."

"Aha!" Baron von Goeben waved an admonitory finger. "It is the clever Mr Holmes!"

"Not in the least clever, I fear," Mycroft replied. "Perhaps the observant Mr Holmes. You are the holder of a commission in the Imperial Pomeranian Grenadiers. That is evident both from your stance - your natural height is a fraction below the regulation one metre eighty-five, I believe, so that you have had to strain a little when holding yourself erect - and from the way you hold the palm of your left hand against the side of your trousers instead of your thumb. And your English, though like your stature, well-nigh perfect, has just a trace of Hanoverian in it. Now, Baron, you may tell me how many of your Emperor's subjects there are in London who are Prussian Grenadiers, who are native to the Kingdom of Hanover, and who are likely to be invited to the home of His Royal Highness?"

Von Goeben clapped his hands. "Bravo, Mr Holmes!" he cried. "But I must tell you that I have also heard a great deal about you!"

"From Colonel-General Graf von Varzin, I daresay," Mycroft suggested.

"You are acquainted with His Excellency?" von Goeben asked. The hesitation had lasted only a moment, but it had been long enough to betray his unease. "I did not know," he added.

"I have learned over the years to respect Colonel-General Graf von Varzin," said Mycroft. "He is a man of considerable ingenuity."

He gave a little bow and climbed into the empty compartment. He felt satisfaction at having provoked the tell-tale twitch of awkwardness in the baron.

The engine got up steam. Smoke billowed across the platform. There was a sound of coughing further up the train. The tall, burly figure of Sir William Gordon Cumming emerged through the smoke. Then the guard of the train appeared in gold-braided cap and black-frogged coat, with his flag tucked under his arm. He slammed shut the compartment door to follow Sir William into the smoke once more. Now there was no escape, thought Mycroft. Two more figures emerged through the swirling cloud: the tall, emaciated, death's head figure of Lord Lingard was being guided down the train by his triple chinned, grossly buxom wife. Lingard turned his head and caught Mycroft's eye. His face was filled with the arid despair of a damned soul whose only chance of ease lies in the recognition of another soul damned to a suffering as great as or greater than his own.

Lady Lingard drew him past with a scowl. Mycroft heard the door of the next compartment being slammed. The guard's whistle shrilled. With a belch of smoke, the train moved forward.

CHAPTER TWENTY-ONE

The guests were driven, in a procession of shining barouches, from the tiny wind-blustered forecourt of Wolferton Station across two miles of coastal flatland to Sandringham House. It would have been difficult to contrive a scene more calculated to depress Mycroft's feelings than the landscape which stretched away on either side. Although the sea was nowhere visible, yet there seeped round the carriage windows the scent of salt flats, fish and decaying timber to remind him of his loathing of the desolation of the Norfolk shores. Though the visible bleakness was broken by coverts of bramble and low scrubs, the only trees to be seen were tortured, twisted relics of a gentler age from which even the bark had been plucked by the incessant winds. The land itself was under cultivation: broad turnip fields were divided by ditches filled with green scummy water, while the occasional collapsed and sodden remains of one of last year's haystacks stood against the vast grey sky.

Above the grim expanse wheeled a flock of gulls, noisily crying out their wretchedness. A long curtain of young fir trees behind an iron fence told him that they were approaching their destination. The causeway become an avenue with young oaks staked out on either side. The procession passed through a small village of clean, newly built cottages with neat garden plots around them, all sheltered by trees from the north-east wind off the Wash. Smartly dressed estate men in green bowler hats stood at the huge wrought-iron gates by the front lodge, and saluted with raised dog-whips each carriage as it bowled past onto the drive. Between the trees and on a succession of neatly trimmed and rolled lawns were spread an extraordinary assortment of dogs: sprawling French bulldogs, their tongues lolling over heavy dewlaps, lean borzois, alert and still, their effetely sensitive faces raised in watchfulness, fluffy chows trotting aimlessly, yapping spaniels, Eskimo sledge-dogs, their features concealed in the density of their own fur, Alsatians trotting menacingly like an appointed canine police.

The procession ground to a halt, allowing each carriage its turn to unload its burden of visitors. The pause allowed Mycroft to examine the outside of the house from the carriage window. Originally the modest country seat of Lord Palmerston's Parliamentary Secretary, the Hon. Charles Spencer, who had fled abroad after marrying his disreputable mistress, its new owner, the

Prince of Wales, had had its roof raised and a new façade constructed in the Elizabethan style. Spacious casemented bow windows rose from the ground to the newly ornamented and painted eaves, while twisted, ornate Jacobean chimneys rose above the very ordinary sloping roof-tops. The effect, decided Mycroft, was one of discomfort similar to that of seeing a naturally plain, modest young woman of the middle sort of society, who has been constrained to put on the whalebone and basque, the hoops and cage, the *posticherie* of one of the more flamboyant *demimondaines*.

Mycroft's carriage rolled forward; a shadow fell over it as it pulled up before the entrance. The carriage door was opened and the step lowered by a Scotch ghillie in full Highland gear. Mycroft heaved himself up to squeeze through the door as the carriage listed under his weight. The ghillie, taking his elbow, lowered him to the ground with such an exercise of restrained strength that he felt as if he were afloat. As he entered the surprisingly modest entrance *salon*, two dun-coated, unpowdered footmen took his hat and his coat and handed them back to the waiting hall-porters. In the gloom inside, Mycroft saw a gilded birdcage with a large white cockatoo which hopped along its swaying perch from one side to side. Other beasts, stuffed, stood against the panelled walls, including a monstrous baboon holding a small lacquered *papier-maché* tray between its paws.

A tall, fresh-complexioned page in dark-blue uniform jacket and black trousers approached Mycroft and asked him to place his visiting card in the tray. No sooner had he done so than a second page picked it up and examined it. The first page, in the meantime, informed Mycroft with the quiet discretion of one who has been commissioned to arrange a secret assignation, "It is Her Royal Highness's wish, sir, that you shall take tea with Her Royal Highness at five o'clock, in the Dairy Tea room."

Behind the first page, the second page, having read the visiting card, was discreetly communicating Mycroft's identity to the short, bearded, balding, stout gentleman who was standing a few yards in front of the foot of the main staircase; the latter nodded with the emphasis of the slightly deaf as he received the information. He advanced to greet Mycroft. Mycroft bowed stiffly from the neck as the Prince of Wales took his hand.

"Good of you to come, Mr Holmes," said the Prince. "Well done, eh?" Then to Mycroft's surprise he said, "Brought your own man, have you?"

"No, sir," Mycroft replied.

"Very good," said the Prince. "Much better to have a fellow who knows the ways of the place, what?"

There was the trace of a North German accent in the manner in which he pronounced his Rs.

"You'll see to it, Palliser." He turned to the first page.

"Sir," the page replied.

The Prince pointed across the *salon* to the caged cockatoo swinging furiously on its perch. "That chappie there," he announced, "he's called Mycroft. Deuced rum thing, eh? Not what you'd call a common name. He was given to me by a friend of the Imperial German Chancellor, Colonel-General the Graf von Varzin."

The cockatoo let out a deafening screech.

"Knows we're talking about him, eh, Mr Holmes?" said the Prince.

The second page was standing at Mycroft's elbow. Mycroft realised that he had been dismissed and allowed himself to be led by the page into the inner hall behind the stairs. What message had Guttmann intended to convey by so naming the cockatoo, he wondered? Throughout the ten years he had sought to thwart the schemes and machinations of Prince von Bismarck's confidential agent, he had never known Guttmann indulge in gratuitous insult. On the other hand, he had good cause to know that Guttmann regarded their relationship as that of duellists, and that there could be no true duel unless the antagonists were both aware that a duel was occurring. The cockatoo represented a formal challenge; the encounter was to take place in one form or another here, at Sandringham.

"And who may this gentleman be?" called out Colonel Valentine Blake. "You must be weighed, sir! It is the custom of the house!"

In the midst of a thicket of stuffed bears, wolverines, and giant tusked wild boar, under the mask of a massively antlered elk mounted on a broad shield, stood a cast-iron weighing machine. Around it was gathered a group of the guests who had just arrived.

"Fifty guineas says he's eighteen stone and a half!" called the Duchess of Manchester who was standing by the machine holding the burnished weights in her slim hand. Her accent was similar to, if slightly more pronounced than that of the Prince of Wales.

"You are unkind, Duchess!" protested Sir Allen Young. "My lords, ladies, gentlemen; this is my old friend, Mr Mycroft Holmes."

Mycroft inclined his head to the company.

"And not an ounce over seventeen stone," added Sir Allen. "I cover the Duchess's wager with fifty guineas of my own."

"I've heard it said Mr Holmes is a deuced clever fellow," Lord Hartington remarked from behind the Duchess of Manchester. "At least, that was poor old Dizzy's opinion. So assumin' Alleno is correct - and I've seen him judge a freshly-caught salmon to the last half ounce - one must make allowance for his brain, what d'you say? I'll add two pounds to Alleno's estimate - two pounds of grey matter, eh? Thirty-five gold sovereigns say that Mr Holmes is seventeen stone two pounds! D'you know your own weight, Mr Holmes?"

"I'm afraid not, sir," Mycroft replied.

"Related to that detective chap Holmes?" called out a gentleman he did not recognize. He continued without waiting for a reply, "Found my Aunt Marjoribanks's emerald tiara, don't you know? - it was in a pigsty near Pangbourne. Amazing fellow!"

"Have a flutter on your own avoirdupois, eh?" asked Lord Hartington.

Mycroft shook his head.

"Not a gambling man, eh, Holmes?" Colonel Blake sounded disapproving.

"But you'll not disappoint us by refusing to step up on to the scales, will you, Mr Holmes?" The Duchess of Manchester's smile reminded Mycroft of what an astounding beauty she had once been.

"Certainly not, Your Grace!" he heard himself reply as ingratiatingly as any courtier. He stood on the platform; the bar rang against the upper guard.

"Place your bets, everybody!" the Duchess called out gaily. "Your Royal Highness? Will you not place a bet on Mr Holmes's weight?"

The Prince had come round the bottom of the stairs. He was accompanied by Baron von Goeben. He eyed Mycroft up and down then cleared his throat.

"Very well, my dear Duchess," he announced. "I've forty guineas tell me Mr Holmes is seventeen stone seven ounces. How's that, eh?"

"As Your Royal Highness pleases," the Duchess replied.

She placed one weight onto the bar. The bar sank slightly before returning to the guard. The company remained silent as she placed and replaced various combinations of weights. She was standing so close to Mycroft that the curve of her bosom touched his arm and he shrank from the contact. The bar sank and then floated freely.

"By Jove! Eighteen and a half exactly!" Sir William Gordon Cumming was leaning across Lord Hartington's shoulder. "Louise has it, by God!" He turned to Lord Hartington. "Going to make an honest women of her, Hartle-Tartle? Now she's lucky as well as a widow?"

There was a gasp of shocked laughter in which Lord Hartington joined. The Duchess was smiling, uncertain whether to laugh or not. She was looking towards the Prince who was not laughing.

"I expect you wish to go up to your room, Mr Holmes," said the Prince, with a solicitude which sounded like a rescue. "To change, before joining my wife for tea, eh?" He placed his hand lightly on Mycroft's shoulder.

"Most kind of you, sir," Mycroft replied.

The Prince steered him to where a footman was waiting. As he followed the footman up the stairs from the gloom of the *salon* to the relative lightness of the landing, Mycroft was aware of being observed from a landing further above. As he glanced up he heard and caught sight of a flutter of maids' cap-strings and flounced, starched aprons, as their owners darted away into obscurity.

A quarter of an hour later, when he had changed into a less formal suit than that in which he had travelled, he stood at the window of the rather poky little room and looked out across the lawns and over the curtain of newly planted firs to the vast expanse of flat-land which stretched across three of the four quarters of the compass to the sea. His newly appointed valet had completed his very limited unpacking, refraining from giving voice to his evident distaste for the sparsely bristled shaving-brush which Mycroft had used since it had been given to him by his father so many years ago; rather than sentiment, inertia had prevented him from replacing it. The valet now withdrew, taking with him Mycroft's tails, evening shirt and dickey, to starch, press and return them before Mycroft should change for dinner.

There came a tap at the door so gentle that Mycroft was still wondering whether he had actually heard it when the latch turned and the Prince of Wales put his head round it.

"Ah, Mr Holmes! May I come in?"

"Of course, sir," Mycroft replied. "As Your Royal Highness pleases."

"First time at Sandringham, eh?" asked the Prince. "Our fellow lookin' after you properly, is he? Everythin' to your satisfaction?"

"Thank you, sir. I know I shall be very comfortable."

"Bit intimidatin', the first time, eh?" asked the Prince.

"It would be difficult to feel intimidated for long, sir, given the warmth and consideration Your Royal Highness has extended to me," Mycroft replied with complete sincerity.

"Good fellow!" the Prince exclaimed. "Most gratifyin'. Enjoyin' our view, were you? Plenty of sky, d'you see? M'wife likes plenty of sky. Danish, y'know. Plenty of sky in Denmark."

He glanced at Mycroft's gun-case on the stretcher at the foot of the bed. "Holland and Holland I see," he remarked. "First-rate."

"I can't take credit for them myself, sir," Mycroft replied. "Inherited them from my father."

He had rarely used them, and then only because social duty demanded it of him.

"Have mine made for me by Purdey's - by the young James Purdey. So good, they say, they aim themselves, eh what? Have to, d'you see? I'm such a devilish bad shot! Deuced rum thing - I shoot best back over my left shoulder..." He swivelled about to demonstrate what he meant. "Now why should that be, d'you suppose?"

For a moment, Mycroft hesitated, wondering whether the Prince was genuinely seeking an answer. He decided to take the risk. "I daresay Your Royal Highness has heard about the Japanese masters," he said. "When they teach their young Samurai knights to use the bow they teach 'em to aim, and then to think about something else entirely before loosing the arrow. They say that too great a concern about hitting the target spoils the aim - you must leave something to Almighty Providence. Now you, sir, when you turn to shoot behind you, are less concerned with your exact aim, and more concerned with taking your shot before the bird has passed over you."

The Prince stared at him in severe concentration. After a moment or two's thought he said, "Clever that. Leave somethin' to Almighty Providence, eh? Perfectly right when you come to think of it."

Again, he clapped Mycroft on the shoulder. "Deuced clever!" he repeated. "Never does to care too much, eh? Spoils things, what? They say you're a clever fellow. That Prussian fellow - friend of von Bismarck's - recommended you to me. Said you were just the fellow to throw light on the Pfalzel-Buckelburg Succession, and the whole question of the Rhineland. Can't discuss it now, of course. Have to go and take tea with my wife! Tomorrow evenin' - after a good day's shootin', eh? We can match your Hollands against my Purdeys - then we'll have a quiet word together."

"As Your Royal Highness pleases," Mycroft replied.

He gave the Prince a minute before going out after him into the passage. He hoped that by following other guests he would find his way down to the Dairy Tea-room. At the far end of the gallery, at the head of the stairs, he saw the spectrally tall, emaciated figure of Lord Lingard walking alone. A moment or two later, the ample shape of Lady Lingard emerged through the door of one of the guest rooms. A babble of masculine laughter followed her, and the scent of cigar smoke. Mycroft waited until she too had turned to go down the stairs. As she disappeared, he saw, across the gallery, a door leading to the domestic quarters. Framed in it were two neatly uniformed chamber-maids waiting like actresses in the wings to make their entrance. The glance of one of the girls directly caught his so that their eyes met for a second before she averted her gaze. Suddenly, he was on his guard. At first, he thought she must have recognized him; but he could not recall her. She was seventeen or eighteen, with a slender, well-formed figure; pretty, with pale, blue green, somewhat expressionless eyes, and a full head of straw-blonde hair piled up under her cap and streamers. There had been nothing coquettish in her look; forwardness in a junior domestic would not have been encouraged at Sandringham. But a properly-trained upstairs maid would surely have kept her eyes lowered at all times in the presence of her betters. The possibility occurred to him that she had not been recognizing him but identifying him. He was not given to being fanciful. There had been the business at Caburn Towers, five years previously, and the death of young Louis Ponsonby, and the affair at Vanderlys in Warwickshire the following year. On both occasions there had been female domestics involved, placed there through the malign agency of Carl Philipp Emmanuel Guttmann. But at Sandringham...?

The gentle tread of a footstep behind him caused him to turn. It was Sir Allen Young.

"Trying to plot a course to Her Royal Highness's tea-room, are you, Holmes? Need the services of an experienced pilot again, eh?"

"Thank you, Sir Allen. I'm much obliged."

CHAPTER TWENTY-TWO

Most of the ladies had withdrawn, with the Princess of Wales, from the dinner table when Sir Napier Soames M.P. - 'Fatty' Soames to his intimates - made his appearance. Like Mycroft, whom he resembled in shape, he had difficulty in making a low bow.

"Pray forgive me, Your Royal Highness," he wheezed. "Business of the House. The First Lord insisted I stay on after prayers."

"Of course! Of course, my dear fellow!" the Prince replied, waving an unlit cigar with an air of bonhomie. "As long as you ain't offended by the smell of tobacco when you take your meat, eh?

Sir William Gordon Cumming, who had been responsible for assisting the guests to their proper places at table, rose and led 'Fatty' Soames to the empty place on the opposite side to Mycroft. Soames nodded to the company in general, most of whom he already knew. Then he saw Mycroft. His rosy plump cheeks creased into a grin.

"Holmes, my dear old chap!" he exclaimed. "Hadn't heard you was to be here."

"How-de-do, Sir Napier," Mycroft replied with a shade less enthusiasm.

'Fatty' Soames was three and a half years older than he. When they had been boys together at Fernyhurst - which Mycroft recalled as an academic Dartmoor on the very summit of the North Yorkshire moors, with a Spartan regimen and a ready assumption of guilt not dissimilar from that of the most notorious of Her Majesty's penal establishments - he had been Soames's fag. Homesick, lonely, and perpetually hungry, he had proved far from assiduous in his menial duties toward his fag-master. 'Fatty' Soames had thus thrashed him with a battledore twice a week, telling him frequently, and with unctuous piety, "It's only for your own good, you know, old chap!"

Mycroft had been reminded of those days only a few weeks previously, when, sitting in the Civil Servants' gallery in the House of Commons, he had heard 'Fatty' Soames opposing, in the first debate in committee, the section of the Criminal Law Amendment Bill which proposed the raising of the legal age of consent in females from twelve years to sixteen. With that same unctuous piety of tone, which inspired in the depths of Mycroft's normally equable being a quite atavistic lust for revenge, Soames had argued that while it was regrettable that young females of twelve or thirteen years of age, of the labouring classes, should seek to seduce gentlemen for gain and the satisfaction of their female vanity, the Good Lord had endowed the Human Race with that gift which, above all, distinguished it from the animal kingdom - freedom of moral choice - and that it was not the business of government to circumscribe that freedom.

That same unworthy desire for revenge was compounded when, almost immediately afterwards, Soames, having put up for membership of the Diogenes Club, insisted on greeting him when they met as if they had shared the happiest days of their lives in a companionship of equals; there was nothing so infuriating, Mycroft decided, as the torturer who insists on letting bygones be bygones.

Cigars were lit, including those of the ladies who, like the Duchess of Devonshire and Lady Lingard, had remained; and the port circulated. Mycroft drew on his cigar. It was a *Corona-corona*, in perfect condition. A sense of content crept through him as if the ichor of the Ancients was seeping through his veins, which even the foolish-amiable features of 'Fatty' Soames across the table could not dispel.

"Lingard, m'dear fellow!" The Prince of Wales lolled back in his chair, beaming benevolently. He put his cigar into the space between his moustache and his beard, and pulled on it till the tip glowed visibly before removing it. He beckoned Lord Lingard to leave his place and to come to him.

Lord Lingard drew his length out of his chair. He looked like an eel standing on its tail, Mycroft decided.

"Your Royal Highness?" Lord Lingard asked, in the tones of an undertaker enquiring into the health of the widow.

"Oh, Lingard!" Lady Lingard called, removing the cigar from her moist lips. "You ain't 'alf a po-face an' that's the honest truth, so it is. Ain't 'e a po-face, Colonel Val?"

She turned her bulk round to Colonel Valentine Blake, sitting next to her. The Prince ignored her intervention. To Lord Lingard, he growled solemnly, "Scientific fellow, ain't you, Lingard? Read a paper to the Royal Society, couple of weeks ago, eh?"

"If it please Your Royal Highness," Lord Lingard inclined his head.

There was some stifled sniggering round the table. Lady Lingard repeated, "Old Po-face!" in a very audible whisper.

"What was the subject of your paper, Lingard?" the Prince asked with an air of grave interest.

"Skuas, Your Royal Highness," Lord Lingard replied.

"Skuas, eh!" said the Prince. "Can't say I know much about

skuas. What aspect of the life of the skua did your paper deal with?"

The sniggering round the table threatened to burst into open laughter.

"The courtship ritual and the nesting habits of the skua, may it please Your Highness..." Lord Lingard intoned.

The sniggering turned to helpless spluttering. The attitude of the Prince remained one of grave and courteous interest.

"Tell me, Lingard," he asked. "The skuas - do they build their nests flat?" He held out his hand with his fingers outstretched.

"No, Your Royal Highness," Lord Lingard replied. "They construct their nests in the cliffs above the ocean, do you see?"

He appeared to be entirely unaware of the crescendo of hilarity around him. The Prince nodded, "They would need to be deep, I daresay," he suggested. "To provide decent shelter, eh?"

"Precisely, Your Royal Highness," replied Lord Lingard. "They are thickly walled with a tightly woven thatch."

"Show me?" asked the Prince. "Show me with your hand, how deep?"

The laughter ceased. The guests around the table leaned forward to watch. Even the footmen against the panelled walls were watching intently. The Prince put his cigar to his lips and drew on it. Lord Lingard held out his hand and cupped his fingers into as deep a saucer-shape as he could manage.

"Like this, Your Royal Highness?" he asked.

He managed a ghost of a smile. But only for a moment: the Prince tapped the ash from his cigar into the cupped hand, then thrust the burning end into the centre of the palm. Lord Lingard let out a yelp of astonished pain which he stifled immediately. As he blinked back the tears which welled in his eyes, he managed to murmur, "As Your Royal Highness pleases," while everybody about the table except Mycroft happily parroted after him, "As Your Royal Highness pleases!" and collapsed at last into open merriment.

Lord Lingard tried to join in the laughter; the effect was one of hideously distorted mask, that of the broken-hearted clown. He stared about him, looking for somewhere to deposit the grey cylinders of cigar ash which still lay in his palm.

"It's no good pretendin', Lingard!" shrieked Lady Lingard. "Everybody knows you ain't got no sense of humour!"

A footman stepped forward with an ashtray. Lord Lingard dusted the ash from his hand. He resumed his place at the table as Lady

Lingard, noticing that Mycroft was the only person not so overcome with mirth as to be unable to hear what she had to say, leaned even further across toward, him, her enormous bosoms pouched like corseted blancmanges on the empty fruit plates.

"Lingard ain't never been able to see the funny side of things'" she bawled. "Ain't in 'is nature, d'ye see?"

Under the sharp edges of his starched collar Mycroft had begun to sweat. Practical jokes, particularly when accompanied with a callousness which appeared to suspend the Prince's normal good-natured courtesy, could very easily turn lethal.

The port, which had remained in front of Lord Ranelagh during the tormenting of Lord Lingard, was circulating once more. A pall of richly scented cigar smoke formed over the rest of the dinner table. Pretty young Lady Lechslade, who had been placed next to Sir William Gordon Cumming, added to it the scent of her Turkish sobranie cigarette, which she smoked in an ivory holder. She was describing a cruise she and her husband, junior secretary at Dublin Castle, had made up the Rhine, the previous autumn.

"So peaceful!" she declared. "Particularly after Dublin, don't you know? He needs to be quiet and carefree after a few months with the Irish!"

"That fellow Parnell!" 'Fatty' Soames intervened, placing his knife and fork down on his emptied plate. He wiped his lips with his napkin. "Manners of a gentleman," he continued. "Speaks like a gentleman. Decent property, I'm told. Went to a good school; 'varsity man - Cambridge. Doin' his best to destroy the constitution! Bring down the Throne - in Dublin, at any rate! Kill us all in our beds...!"

"Eat babies!" Sir Allen Young suggested.

"Wouldn't put it past the rogue," Soames agreed in the midst of the laughter. He put down his napkin.

"No jokin' matter - Parnell and his Irish Nationalists!" said the Prince. "They say Dilke's one of his cabal."

The laughter died on the instant. But the Prince turned the conversation. "You found Baron von Goeben's compatriots to your likin', did you, Amelie?" he asked Lady Lechslade.

"The Irish," she replied, "are so charming, and so - well - treacherous. And the Germans are so..." She hesitated, and giggled a little. "...so - polite? - and so trustworthy," she went on.

"Mr Holmes is an authority on the Rhineland," the Prince told her.

He smiled down the table at Mycroft without a hint of guile.

"It is true," Baron von Goeben confirmed. "Mr Holmes's views on the western marches of the German Empire are taken as seriously by our Chancellery in Berlin as by Whitehall."

"Have you seen the new Victory memorial overlooking the Rhine, Mr Holmes?" asked Lady Lechslade.

Mycroft shook his head. "I have heard of it, of course," he replied. "Germania - the Watch on the Rhine."

"Oh, it is quite magnificent!" Lady Lechslade enthused. "She stands on a hilltop overlooking the Rhine, a league or two below Mainz - sixty feet tall, in bronze, a laurel wreath on her head, and her sword drawn towards France."

"I believe Mr Holmes would like to take the sword from us," smiled Baron von Goeben.

"But why?" exclaimed the little Baroness, looking down the table at Mycroft. "France has always been England's enemy as well. My Papa told me it was always the French caused the trouble in history."

"I fear my knowledge of Germany is almost entirely theoretical, Lady Lechslade," Mycroft said. "My brother studied with Joachim in Leipzig, but I have only visited Trier and the Hunsruck."

"May I ask what made you visit the Hunsruck, Mr Holmes?" said Baron von Goeben.

"Certainly," Mycroft replied. "Wild boar. In the Hunsruck they know how to grill boar over charcoal as nowhere else in the world."

There was more laughter. Sir Allen Young said, "We now know where Holmes's heart is to be found, eh what?"

"I believe it is time we joined my wife and the rest of the ladies," the Prince declared, pushing himself up from his chair.

As they left the dining-room, he waited for Mycroft. "Well done, Mr Holmes," he said in a low voice, "always a problem when the ladies start talking about politics and such. Can't be severe on 'em, hey? Not like men, d'ye see? Don't know where to draw the line. Grateful to ye."

They passed through into the entrance. To Mycroft's displeasure, he found himself accompanying Sir Napier Soames.

"I say, Holmes," said 'Fatty' Soames. "Deuced awkward business. Held up by the PM. He wanted to sound me out; possibility of Dobson leaving the Board of Local Government, don't you know?"

He left Mycroft to draw the appropriate inference. "As a result, I forgot to tell my man to pack my plus-fours. Nothing to wear for the *battu* tomorrow. Don't know what the devil to do about it! Fellow might put a bullet through his head for less, what do you say?"

Mycroft resisted the temptation to agree to the point of actual encouragement.

The party spent only a short time with the Princess of Wales and the ladies in the drawing-room. There was music: Helen Gurney, the daughter of a neighbouring landed proprietor, who had studied the piano in Bonn, accompanied several of the ladies in songs by Mendelssohn. After four songs, however, and a short instrumental piece by Tosti, the Prince grew restless. He suggested the carpet should be rolled back for dancing. His former French tutor was brought in to play four hands with Miss Gurney. The Prince with the Duchess of Manchester led the company in an opening *galop*; Sir Allen Young, who spoke Danish among half a dozen foreign languages, escorted the Princess. In keeping with the lack of form or ceremony at Sandringham of which he was becoming increasingly aware, Mycroft was dragged onto the floor by Lady Lingard, "Ample people must stick to one another, eh, Mr 'Olmes?" She forced him to caper with her, her huge bosoms bouncing up and down in the whalebone cups of her low-cut gown, sending out an acid-sweet cloud of patchouli as they did so, while the Prince called across the floor, "Nothin' like dancing to a thumpin' good tune, eh, Mr Holmes?"

Mycroft hadn't the breath to reply, Lord Lingard-like, "As Your Royal Highness pleases."

At midnight the Prince announced that those ladies who wished to retire should do so. The remainder of the company proceeded through to one of the billiard-rooms, where the tables were laid for *baccarat* for the actual players and with paper and pencils for those who would wager on them.

Conspicuous were the tall screens lacquered with photographs of the great and good - Matthew Arnold, Lord Chief Justice Coleridge, Charles Dickens, Bishop Wilberforce, T H Huxley, Cardinal Newman, and Alfred, Lord Tennyson, conspicuous among them - in the company of generously proportioned young females, naked and semi-draped, in coy or provocative poses.

The Prince turned one of the chairs so that its back was against the *baccarat* table. He beckoned to Lady Lingard to sit in it, putting his finger to his lips as he did so.

"Streltsau," he called. "They say you're a connoisseur of the ladies, what?"

Again there was the furtive sniggering there had been round the dining table over Lord Lingard. Lord Ranelagh, grinning like an ape, led the blind Duke forward.

"Tell me, Streltsau," said the Prince. "Have you ever had your hands on Lady Lingard's bum, eh what?"

Lady Lingard leaned forward, thrusting out her bosoms. The Prince took the Duke of Streltsau by the wrists and placed his hands on the exposed upper hemispheres of Lady Lingard's decolletage. As the Duke stooped, Mycroft could observe behind the rectangular frames of his dark glasses, the milky blankness of the unseeing eyes.

"*Gott in Himmel!*" exclaimed the Duke. "Her Ladyship has bared herself before Royalty, *ja?*"

There was an uproar of mirth it almost drowned Lady Lingard's remark, "Only for you, my lord Duke, 'cause I've 'eard 'ow down-right wicked y'are with the ladies."

The Duke joined in the laughter as he realised the truth. In his broken English he tried to persuade Lady Lingard to allow him to compare the genuine article with the pretence.

It was well after two o'clock when the Prince declared it to be bed-time. Mycroft, whose idea of a late night was retiring at half-past ten after one of Mrs Turner's hearty suppers taken at his own fire-side, scarcely knew how he had managed to keep his eyes open. Even less could he understand how, when, under the Prince's strict rule, the bank was limited to a hundred pounds a game, he had managed to win six hundred.

The Prince congratulated him as they went upstairs. "Lookin' forward to our little conference tomorrow evenin', Holmes."

Mycroft noted the affability with which His Royal Highness had dropped the 'Mr' before his name. Despite his disapproval of the Prince's idea of a practical joke, he could not believe the warmth and consideration he had shown toward him to be anything but genuine.

"You're a shrewd fellow - I can see that for myself, already," the Prince continued. "Lord Granville said as much when he was here, a fortnight ago. I remember poor old Beaconsfield speaking highly of you: said you were a brave chap as well as a devilish clever one."

"I would hate to think I might prove a disappointment to Your Royal Highness," Mycroft told him, smiling through his fatigue. "I fear you might find out that I'm an abject coward."

"Dizzy didn't think so," the Prince replied, "and I don't suppose there were many more shrewd judges of character than he."

But Mycroft was afraid. As he had grown more and more tired, so the notion had increased in his brain that he was surrounded by grotesques, and that amongst them were those who were preparing to destroy him.

The valet who had been appointed to look after him was waiting for him. "I took the liberty of pressing your shooting jacket and plus-fours for tomorrow, sir," he told Mycroft, pointing to where they were hanging on the Crombie press. "A most individual herring-bone, if I may say so, sir. Very pleasing."

"Glad it meets with your approval," Mycroft growled. His irony was lost on the valet.

"It does indeed, sir. It does indeed!" he replied.

Mycroft, who never employed a manservant except when, as a house guest, it was expected of him - and then he normally borrowed Cyril from Princess Sophie - dismissed the man and undressed himself. He heard a certain whispering and rustling from the passage outside; he assumed it was the usual same, prevalent in house parties among the upper classes, of 'choose your partner', and thought nothing of it.

He had, of course, other matters to consider: the sort of matters a weary brain seizes upon to deny its possessor sleep until daybreak. Guttmann had recommend the Prince of Wales to seek his advice regarding the Rhineland and the Pfalzel-Buckelburg Succession - the very thing from which his master, Prince von Bismarck would surely have wished to distract his attention. Why?

Von Goeben was a friend of His Royal Highness - a frequent visitor to Sandringham House. He was acquainted with His Royal Highness's invariable timetable. He would certainly know, and would have advised Guttmann, that there would be no meaningful conference between the Prince and himself until the second evening - until after a day's shooting.

And there was the way the young housemaid had examined him. Her stare had lasted only a moment, but her look was imprinted in finest detail on his mind.

He climbed into bed. As he turned to extinguish the lamp, he found that his feet were obstructed from reaching the bottom of the sheets; not only that, his toes crunched through a dry, brittle surface into a shallow gooey mess.

"Devil take it!" he exclaimed aloud in the exasperation born of utter exhaustion.

Tugging at the bell-pull beside the headboard, he threw back the sheets. Not only was the bed made into an apple pie, but a real apple pie had been placed in the foreshortened fold of the sheets; his foot was placed in it.

He extracted his foot, swivelled round, and sat on the side of the bed with his foot, covered in stewed apples and cloves, dangling over the carpet. The valet entered. Behind him and fully dressed were Sir George and Lady Lechslade, Sir Allen Young, Colonel Blake with Lady Lingard, Lord Hartington with the Duchess of Manchester, and the Prince himself.

"Apple-pie bed!" guffawed the Prince.

"Apple-pie bed!" shouted the assembled company, laughing as if it were impossible to conceive of a riper joke.

The valet poured water from a pitcher into the wash bowl. Servants and guests - all had been prepared for this jape, Mycroft observed. The valet crouched down and washed the apple off his foot.

"Apple-pie bed, eh?''

The massive figure of Sir William Gordon Cumming pushed his way through the small throng by the door.

"Just makin' sure you'll be comfortable for the rest of the night, Holmes," he said.

Aside from being a thoroughly objectionable character, Mycroft had to remind himself, Sir William was also the Prince's equerry. Behind him came two chambermaids: one of them was the slender, pretty one who had eyed him across the gallery. She was carrying a freshly laundered pair of sheets under her arm; she kept her eyes lowered as she with her companion remade his bed.

His foot having been washed and dried, Mycroft went and sat by the fire.

"Takin' it in good part, is he?" called Colonel Blake.

"Of course he is!" Mycroft heard Sir Allen Young reply. "First rate fellow, my friend Holmes. Sound as a bell. Square abacus man!"

Mycroft struggled to assume a facial expression which would communicate his taking it in good part. Even as he did so, his attention was drawn to Sir William Gordon Cumming. Sir William was examining his shooting jacket and plus-fours with an acute gaze. But he was not doing so directly; he was inspecting them in reflection, in the full-length pier-glass by the chest of drawers.

"Everythin' all right, Holmes?"

The Prince had come into the centre of the room. Mycroft pulled himself to his feet.

"No, no, old chap! No formality, eh?" said the Prince. "I wasn't responsible for this one," he added. "Don't know who it was. Ain't goin' to inquire too deeply, eh? We all know how to take a joke!"

There was the possibility, Mycroft told himself, that Sir William shared the valet's admiration for his taste in herring bone tweed.

The maids completed their task, bobbed low in the direction of the Prince, and scuttered away. The Prince heartily wished him good-night once more, and the jovial company followed him away down the passage outside. Sir Napier Soames alone remained behind.

"Damn' good jape, eh, Holmes?" he said. "A real apple-pie bed, eh? Not bad, what? Just like the old days!"

It was the wistfulness in his voice which told Mycroft that if 'Fatty' Soames had been party to the jest, he had certainly not initiated it. Someone else was responsible for the scheme.

"Just like the old days," he agreed. Fortunately, 'Fatty' Soames did not notice the edge in his voice. A device occurred to him which would not have been unworthy of a Borgia: "Tell you what, Sir Napier," he said. "Borrow my togs tomorrow, what d'you say? There ain't much to choose between our fittings, don't you know?"

"I say! That's jolly kind of you, Holmes old chap! But I could never do that! I mean - what would you wear?"

But he could not conceal the look of surprised pleasure on his face. Mycroft patted him on the shoulder.

"I'm here on business, not pleasure, I don't mind telling you," he said. "HRH wishes to consult me on a matter of foreign policy; need to brief myself, so I'd be glad to give the old *battu* a miss tomorrow... But keep it under your hat, eh?"

"Rather!" said 'Fatty' Soames. "Mum's the word! Jolly decent of you, though."

His face shone with a sort of greed. Mycroft removed the suit from the Crombie and placed it over 'Fatty' Soames's arm.

"I suppose you have a pair of guns, have you, Sir Napier?"

"Oh yes!" 'Fatty' Soames replied, as happy as a schoolboy with two mince pies. "Wouldn't forget m'guns, eh? Not such a blitherin' idiot as that!" Oh I don't know, thought Mycroft as he closed his bed-room door after him. In the words of Gilbert's delightful ballad, he thought, *And who never would be missed, who never would be missed.*

CHAPTER TWENTY-THREE

"Mr Smedley ain't in yet, Miss," the office boy said. "He ain't all up with the lark an' that!" he added impudently.

He was unlocking the door of Smedley and Ditchling, Estate Agents (est. 1786, branches in Highgate and Belsize Village). Sophie glanced somewhat apprehensively at Cyril, whose temper had not quite recovered from her having rudely woken him before dawn as he had lain beside her, with an order to get up, rouse the coachman and tell him to bring round the carriage to take them to Hampstead at once.

"Why?" he had demanded.

"Because I wish to see the house - the one on Squire's Mount," she replied. "Lady Adolphus Murray sent to me yesterday to say it was still vacant. I may wish to buy it for myself. I have a fancy to be a neighbour of hers. I want nobody to get to it before I do."

Cyril yawned. "There's been horrible murders there," he said, as if that put the idea out of question. "You wouldn't like it."

"My poor dear boy," Sophie replied, had I refused to live in St Petersburg in any house where there had been a horrible murder, I wouldn't have had a home at all!"

And she had pushed him out of bed with her foot.

"It is early," Sophie admitted to the office boy. "There is a property in which I am interested. My eagerness..."

"To buy, Miss?" the office boy interrupted her. "Or sell? You see, sellin', you're much too early. Buyin' - well, you're just a little bit too early, if you sees what I means." He took a toothpick from his waistcoat pocket and started to prod at one of his back molars with it.

"Her Highness," said Cyril, "is h-interested in viewin' the Meadowthorpe property on Squire's Mount."

The boy took the toothpick from his mouth. "The Meadowthorpe property!" he exclaimed.

Without more ado he turned about, went down the narrow hallway, and disappeared into an office at the end. A few seconds later he re-appeared, followed by a red-faced, bespectacled little man in his shirt-sleeves, attempting to fasten paper cuffs about his wrists.

"Forgive me, madam!" he exclaimed. "Smedley, at your service. As you see, you have taken me somewhat at a disadvantage." He laughed self-deprecatingly. "You are interested in the Meadowthorpe property, the boy tells me," he continued in the rapid manner of one who is anxious. "It is remarkably well situated - the view across the Vale of Health to the Heath; the air, so clean; a very good class of neighbour..."

"That is one of the reasons for my interest, Mr Smedley," Sophie replied. "I have dear friends living nearby."

"Ah!" said Mr Smedley, taken by surprise. Tentatively, he asked, "May I ask whom I have the honour of addressing."

"I am Princess Sophia Trubetskoy," she replied.

"Your Highness!" cried Mr Smedley. "Pray forgive me for any rudeness, in my manner or appearance. It was quite inadvertent, I do assure you." He had stooped into a low bow. The impression he gave was of somebody suddenly seized by an attack of lumbago. Nevertheless, as he drew himself erect, he managed to turn his head sufficiently to give the office boy a look as if he would kill him when next he was afforded the opportunity.

"Let me assure you, however," said Sophie, "that I am perfectly acquainted with the recent history of the house. There is no need to avoid the subject on my behalf."

"No, Your Highness. Of course not! Your Highness is most kind!" He had to rescue his spectacles from falling off his nose.

"I would be obliged if you would assist me in viewing the property, Mr Smedley," Sophie told him before he could fall into an excess of obsequiousness. "I have my carriage at the top of the hill, by the new horsepond."

As she walked up to the pond, condescendingly permitting him to support her arm, she said, The other day, I was obliged to pay a visit up there, as now, at quite an early hour..."

She laughed as if in self-deprecation. "I'm afraid a most reprehensible curiosity drove me to take a look at Squire's Mount," she continued. "Curiosity is a woman's chief failing, as I'm sure I don't have to tell you, Mr Smedley. I was so surprised by its pleasant prospect," she went on, "because of its reputation, I suppose. I had expected it to look Gothic and horrid, like one of those houses in your sensational novels. And then I saw your sign at the gate, and I thought to myself, I would like a house here, close to London, and near my friends..."

They put down at Squire's Mount within a few minutes of reaching the carriage. As Mr Smedley took the keys from his pocket, he remarked, "Your Highness, there are some say this is the most beautiful prospect over London."

Sophie had to agree. The sun was just breaking through the morning mist. Beyond the rolling woodland and falling meadows, turrets, spires and pinnacles were gradually unveiling to gleam in the diffused light as if coal dust and smoke had never existed.

"My friends tell me it will be spoiled," she said. "They tell me that Mr Manyon will build villas over there to spoil the view."

Mr Smedley looked embarrassed.

"We shall have to try to stop him," said Sophie, as if that might prove a condition of her buying the property.

"If we are able," mumbled Mr Smedley sheepishly.

Sophie glanced at Cyril. He looked distinctly bored. "Keep your eyes open!" she commanded him. "Wide open!"

"Yes, Your Highness," he replied very deliberately.

He followed Sophie and Mr Smedley into the house. There was the dry, sterile smell of a place which has been kept secure from damp and decay but which has not been used for many months. What furniture there was was covered in grey dust sheets.

"We must give credit where credit is due, I'm sure Your Highness will agree," said Mr Smedley as he ushered them into what had once been Captain Meadowthorpe's sanctum. "There's no denying Tuttle was a most conscientious housekeeper, whatever may be proved against her." There was nothing left in the room with which to characterize its last occupant. Sophie contented herself with admiring the prospect from the window-bay. Below, lay the surface of the lake at the bottom of the Vale of Health shimmering through the green fuzz on the sunlit trees.

"You would give Mrs Tuttle a character, would you, Mr Smedley," asked Sophie.

"Oh, I would not go so far as to say that, Your Highness," he replied with an embarrassed little smirk.

There was a piece of furniture set against the wall beside the bay. Slipping her reticule up her sleeve out of the way, Sophie lifted the dust-sheet. Under it was a mid-eighteenth century bureau in walnut, with an escritoire top. Cyril's interest was suddenly woken. With his mistress still holding back the sheet, he started examining the drawers and searching behind them. Mr Smedley moved to take the dust-sheet from her, but Sophie shook her head. Nodding in Cyril's direction, she murmured indulgently, "They are just like children, you know."

"So I have heard, Your Highness," Mr Smedley agreed.

He had probably heard also, she thought, that Russians, even

Russian princesses, even Trubetskoys, smell of sweat and don't pare their fingernails.

Cyril opened one of the smaller drawers in the escritoire top. "Thought as much!" he announced.

He inserted his hand and tapped the roof of the drawer. A narrow double panel with a gap between the sides capable of containing documents, slid out from between the side of the drawer and that of the desk. "Never had no h-imagination, the blokes what designed these," he explained.

He felt between the thin panels with his finger-tips. "Hallo, hallo!" he said, drawing out a sheet of foolscap. "What have we got here?"

The paper was already beginning to yellow with age. He unfolded it. "A h-apothecary's handiwork if you asks me," he said.

"Let me see it," said Sophie.

Cyril gave it to her. As he did so, she shook her head very slightly to warn him to give nothing away. She saw that it was a printed schedule. Although there were no dates recorded, the doses - of a compound consisting of a powder and a liquid - were clearly stated, together with the intervals at which they should be administered. After the final dose there were the words, 'These should prove sufficient for the purpose.'

As she examined the lettering more carefully, she noticed the inequalities of type.

"A type-writing machine?" she asked Mr Smedley.

"Yes indeed, Your Highness," he confirmed. "They are employed more and more in places of business these days, I fear. They are an enemy to industry among clerks and office juniors, I'm afraid, and do nothing to further a proper courtesy in business dealings."

But Sophie was not in a mood to listen to his views on the deleterious effect of the new type-writing machines. In the amounts prescribed she found a dreadful sense of recognition, a recalling of the wretched end of Kathy, her beloved elder sister - a self-slaughter engineered twelve years previously by the machinations of Carl Philip Emmanuel Guttmann.

"A schedule for the administration of rat-poison, would you say, Mr Smedley?" she asked, calmly enough.

Mr Smedley blinked, and retreated a couple of paces. "I don't know, I'm sure, Your Highness," he said.

"You have not heard that there are rats in this house?" she asked.

Mr Smedley shook his head wretchedly. Sophie decided to put him at his ease.

"Even the best of houses are sometimes plagued with them," she said. Mr Smedley visibly relaxed. She folded the schedule and laced it in the reticule attached to her wrist. "Who knows?" she said, smiling. "It may prove useful one day."

She went to the bureau and stroked the escritoire top. "A very nice piece," she said. "It is to be sold with the house?"

"Yes, indeed," Smedley agreed. "If Your Highness so wishes."

"It was the late Captain Meadowthorpe's personal bureau?"

"So I have been told, Your Highness."

"Then I do wish," she smiled. "It will be *un souvenir - une chantillon pour conversation avec mes amis.*"

+ + +

"I hope you do not regard my coming here an intrusion, Mr Holmes," Sophie told Sherlock. "But as your brother is down in Norfolk, I could think of nobody else to whom I might speak in confidence."

She had come straight to Baker Street from Squire's Mount. Dr Watson was still at his breakfast, his *Times* folded in front of him. He had risen from his chair when Mrs Hudson showed Sophie in.

"Indeed!" Sherlock remarked. "So you, madam, are my brother's Snow Princess!"

He had emerged from his room, tying his necktie, his waistcoat unbuttoned.

"My home, so far as I have one," Sophie replied, "is in Nice."

"Snow does fall on Nice from time to time, I believe," Sherlock commented slightly petulantly

Sophie resisted the urge to point out how rarely snow fell on the French Riviera. She opened her reticule and drew out the typewritten sheet of paper.

"Mr Mycroft Holmes has spoken to you about the Tuttle case, I believe," she said. "My servant found this in the late Captain Meadowthorpe's bureau at his home on Squire's Mount. It was in one of the *soi-disant* secret compartments. I believe it to be a prescription for arsenic and chloral."

Sherlock took it and glanced at it. "It would so appear," he confirmed. "It is more within the province of my medical colleague here, I believe. See what you make of it, Watson."

He passed it across the table to Dr Watson.

"So you have been visiting the victim's home, have you,

Princess?" he asked as he completed buttoning his waistcoat. He made no apology for his appearance. He reached for his coat, examined it cursorily, and put it on. Sophie was not used to gentlemen paying so little visual attention to her.

"I have just come from Hampstead," she explained. "I have been viewing the property. I may purchase it. It is pleasant enough."

"You do not suppose it might be considered somewhat morbid of you?" asked Sherlock.

"That is for others to decide," she replied. "It is nothing to me."

Dr Watson cleared his throat. Sophie turned to him. "It looks as though the schedule refers to repeated doses of arsenic suspended in chloral," he said. "But I cannot imagine what it is intended for. The compound is used therapeutically as an emetic, and the dosage would indicate such a purpose - but I have never heard of it being prescribed to be taken at regular intervals. The final dose, however, is stronger than the rest. Were they all taken by the same person, I believe the final dose would prove lethal. It would be unlikely to prove lethal in itself - but in conjunction with the others..."

He shook his head. Sherlock secured the waist buttons of his coat, and went round the table to look over his shoulder.

"It would not be taken like that," Sophie asked, "Why somebody who wished to..." She searched for the word. "...*faire quelque chose en emulation*? - imitate Mithridates of Pontus?" she concluded.

Sherlock paid not the least attention. He was staring fixedly at the document.

"Good gracious, no!" Dr Watson replied. "Arsenic is unlike other toxic matter. It lingers in the intestine. Far from inoculating from poison the person who took it in such a way as is prescribed here, it would lower his resistance to its toxic effect."

"Could you tell me how long the person who took the final dose would have to live?" asked Sophie.

"An hour," Dr Watson replied. "An hour and a half at most."

Sherlock had taken a magnifying-glass from his coat pocket and was examining the document. "Absolutely fascinating!" he exclaimed.

He looked up and across at Sophie with a new interest. "We may take this to be," he continued, examining the document once more through the magnifying-glass, "at least if brother Mycroft's account of the case is correct, the schedule by which the fellow Meadowthorpe administered poison gradually to his wife... It is written on an Elliot Fisher type-writing machine," he continued. "The firm, Elliot Fisher, is in a small way of business in Cincinatti, in the United States of America. They manufacture a very unusual example of machine - one designed for use on the pages of office ledgers and account books. The stiff right-hand cover of the book is placed on a metal plate, and the lock-bar mechanism may be adjusted to suit the size of the volume..." He raised his head once more, to speak directly to Sophie.

"I have written a brief monograph on the subject of type-writing machines - *Variations and distinctive features to be observed in the letter press of type-writing keys, and their use in the detection of Crime; with special reference to crimes of fraud.* It is the first publication in the field, I believe. The letter-press of any two machines, do you see? - can never be exactly the same. And the Elliot Fisher machine is rarely to be found in these islands..."

"Do I understand," said Sophie, "that what you are telling me is that if we were to find a communication printed on the same type-writing machine as that, we could identify its source?"

"That is precisely what I am telling you, dear lady," Sherlock replied. "It would inform us as to the origin of the schedule. It might also explain why Meadowthorpe chose to undertake the risk of keeping such an incriminating piece of evidence."

"I am not clever like you and your brother, Mr Holmes," she told him. "But, if I am correct in supposing that the machine belongs to Mr Villiers Manyon, then Mr Meadowthorpe would have two purposes in keeping it. By being proof that Mr Manyon was - how do you say? - *complice* in the crime it would protect him against treachery on the part of Manyon. And he would be able to administer poison to himself in order to throw suspicion on Mrs Tuttle if she should become a *une gêne dangereuse*. He would not, of course, have taken the final dose..."

Her face puckered in thought. Sherlock was watching her with an indulgent patience which was almost kindly.

"Yes!" she exclaimed, after a moment or two. "Because he had been provided with the schedule to poison Mrs Meadowthorpe!...he did not really know about the effect of the poison. He did not know that it...accumulated - yes?...in the intestine!"

Sherlock came back to her, round the table to where she was seated. He took her hand and bowed over it.

"I now understand quite clearly, Princess," he said, "why my brother so much admires you."

CHAPTER TWENTY-FOUR

The Prince of Wales insisted that everybody be present at breakfast by eight o'clock so that they would be ready to leave for the butts by a quarter to ten. Having had less than five hours sleep, Mycroft went to the dining room feeling utterly weary. Fortunately the royal notion of a light breakfast was similar to his own - porridge, kedgeree, Cumberland sausage soused in a Cumberland sauce, kidneys, bacon, and scrambled egg, with cold cuts of ham to fill up the gaps.

The guests returned to their rooms after breakfast to collect their guns and change their boots. Mycroft followed the others upstairs, having been engaged briefly in conversation with Lord Hartington, chairman of the party of government, regarding the subject he would be discussing with the Prince that evening. He was about to go along the gallery to his room when he saw the man appointed as his valet leaving it. With a fleetness which would have surprised his acquaintances, he ducked into one of the water-closets with which Sandringham, unlike most country houses of similar size, was amply provided. The other guests would assume that he had come upstairs to change into his shooting togs. The valet, on the other hand, not finding them in his room, would assume that he had already put them on; he must not be permitted to see anything to contrary.

Mycroft sat down on the velvet-padded seat. He attempted to catch his breath. He remained utterly immobile when the door-knob was turned and even, on occasion, rattled impatiently. It was exactly as if he were back at Fernyhurst attempting to dodge a winter's afternoon of compulsory football despite the retribution which would certainly be exacted from him. He did, not move until he had heard the shouting, the cracking of whip, and the creak and clatter of dog carts leaving the yard below the frosted glass window.

There was a small squad of housemaids on the gallery, polishing the long casement windows, and rubbing the linenfold panelling, the air filled with the smell of beeswax. They looked at him curiously as he made off down the passage to his room. There, a window had been left slightly open; the air was cool and fresh. The basin and pail on his washstand had been emptied and cleaned, and the water in his glass carafe was clear, a scattering of tiny bubbles drifting gradually to the surface. The bed-linen had been changed. The room was clean and precisely ordered as only an uninhabited room - a room which does not expect to be inhabited in daylight hours - can be.

He left the door ajar and stepped behind it, adjusting it so that he could observe the passage immediately outside through the jamb between the hinges. There he waited. He told himself that it could not be long before word passed among the upstairs maids that he was there, alone of all the guests, his understanding of the practices of house parties of a certain class of society caused him to suppose it likely that the maids would keep it to themselves, in the belief that he had an assignation with one of their number.

After a quarter of an hour, the quiet chatter and rustling from the gallery ceased, and a complete stillness descended. It was broken some short time later by a single shot - a dull loud crack across the silence of the fen - followed instantly by another: the sound of two barrels being loosed off at a stray passing bird. After a brief interval, there came a sporadic 'crack-crack' of shots, and the abrupt yowl of a retriever unable to locate the bird brought down by its master. Rooks rose cawing from the trees immediately outside the house, their noise intermingling with the screaming of gulls.

Ragged volleys followed one on another, then silence, the shouting of beaters afar off and the barking of gun-dogs, then another series of ragged volleys. Mycroft's attention strayed; his eyes began to follow the particles of dust which hovered on the still air of the bedroom. It was only when the guns fell silent once again, and he heard the movement of starched linen close to him, that he quickly returned his gaze to the door jamb.

She was standing there, not three feet from him, her pale blue-green eyes as alert as any gun-dog's. Her blonde prettiness was slightly disfigured by a coarseness of the skin below her eyes, suggesting that she had seen and learnt more than was proper in a girl of her age. She showed signs of anxiety as she peered past him through the door, her fingers twitching and plucking at her apron.

He held his breath to the point of suffocation, remaining motionless and so silent that he was afraid that, in the silence between the volleys rattling across the muddy acres of turnip field, she would detect the sound of his silver hunter ticking in his waistcoat pocket. There was also the appalling embarrassment of her discovering him only to reveal that her purpose was entirely innocent. But that, he told himself with all the vanity he could muster, was quite impossible; Mycroft Holmes could never be so mistaken.

She tiptoed forward very cautiously, so that her head and shoulders, as she peered further into the room, disappeared behind the door panels. Finally she came into the room, to stand at the very edge of the door, the striped ticking of her leg-of-mutton sleeve almost touching his arm. When she had crept in so that there was half an inch to spare between the bow of her apron-strings and the mortice, he closed the door silently. She was unaware of his presence until the click of the latch. He turned the key in the lock and removed it.

"'Will you come into my parlour? said the spider to the fly'," he quoted. "But which of us, my dear, is supposed to be the spider, and which the fly?"

She had jumped. There was no deceit in her being startled. "Beg your pardon, sir!" she exclaimed. "You give me such a turn! I thought all the gentlemen was gone, sir!"

She stared at the key in his hand. She clutched at her apron, then, remembering herself she bobbed a curtsy. "If you don't mind, sir, I come to see your bed-linen was changed proper."

"What is your name, girl?"

She looked down at his feet. "If you please, sir. Bessie Martin."

"Very well, Bessie Martin. If I were to ring for the housekeeper, she would confirm that you had come here to ensure the bed-linen had been changed?" He put the key in his pocket and went to the bell-pull.

"Oh sir!" she said. "There's no need for that, sir. Please."

"I thought not. I'll tell you why you are here. You learnt from the other maids that I had not gone shooting. You came up here to confirm that was indeed the case."

"Don't know what you mean!" the girl protested. She had not moved away from the door, but stood staring down at the buckles on her stoutly made shoes. Gunfire tore raggedly through the stillness.

"Who set you to spy on me, Bessie Martin?" he asked.

She did not reply.

"Very well. If I were to let you go, whom would you inform that I was indeed still here?"

"Don't know what you mean, sir!" She raised her hand to the starched vizor of her mob cap. She pushed back a straggling lock of blonde hair to secure it behind her ears.

"How did you come to be employed here?" he asked. "Tell me that, and I might let you go before you find yourself in trouble."

"Don't know, sir." Her voice dropped almost to a whisper. "'Cause I give satisfaction in my last situation, I suppose."

"And you do give satisfaction, I daresay!" he told her.

"Hope so, sir," she whispered.

Another ragged volley sounded across the fields.

"Where was your last situation?" he asked.

She did not reply.

"Let me guess, Bessie Martin," he said. "Let me have one guess. A hotel, was it?"

"Mrs Moorcroft says as a good hotel is the best school for girls as'd like a situation here," she answered.

"And is the Vale of Health Lakeside Spa Hotel, in Hampstead, a good hotel?" asked Mycroft.

He was drawing his bow at a venture. She did not reply but remained frozen in immobility.

"Of course," he went on, "you had no need to fear the same fate as that suffered by poor Annie Gibbs."

He had been about to add, 'because you gave satisfaction,' when she sprang at him with a wild-eyed ferocity for which he was unprepared. He saw an expression of savage hate a moment before he noticed the silver pin which she must have taken out when she reached under her mob cap; its sharpened point thrust four clear inches out of her clenched fist. By the time he had managed to grab her by the wrists, the force of her leap had sent him stumbling back with a heavy thump against the door. Her hair, tumbled from under her cap was across his face; he struggled to clear his vision, to find the tip of the long pin caught in a fold in his shirt-front. It had all but grazed his skin; he had little doubt but that it was lethally poisoned.

He forced her down on to her knees. He pushed back her wrist until she dropped the pin; he would have broken her arm without a moment's remorse if she had not let it fall. He marked where it lay. She crouched, gasping. He let go her wrists and moved his foot to cover the pin.

She managed to convert her gasping into a wild sobbing. "I'm sorry, sir! I didn't mean no harm, sir!" she cried. "I were scared, sir! I though you was going to take advantage of a poor girl, sir!"

He looked down at her with something like admiration.

"I never done nothing like it before, sir! I swear it!" She threw her arms round his ankles; one movement of his feet and she would have the pin again, and, if he was right, wherever she managed to graze his skin, the effect would be the same.

"Don't tell Mrs Moorcroft! Please sir, don't! I'll be a good girl - promise I will! Only please let me off this time!"

He looked at the dishevelled head against his knees.

"Leave a poor girl her character!" she implored. "It's all I got!"

He pushed her away with sufficient violence to send her sprawling across the floor. He stooped down and picked up the pin. She watched him as he took out his handkerchief and folded it before replacing it in his pocket. She sat up. He realized that there had been no sound of shooting from across the fen for some minutes. But there were men's voices calling across the fields, and they were coming nearer. Suddenly, and with a gesture as abrupt in its change of mood as when she had attacked him, the girl clutched at her skirts under her apron, shook her head so that her cap fell awry and her hair tumbled onto her shoulders. She drew her skirts up above her ankles, exposing the black woollen stockings about her calves and the clumsily stitched lace edging of her drawers just below her knees.

"Please don't, sir!" she began to cry. "I always been a good girl, sir! Don't take my reputation. Oh please! It's all a poor girl's got!"

He ignored her. Taking the key from his pocket and put it in the lock.

"I'll do anything," she screamed, "but not that. Please not that!"

"You will remain in here until I have spoken to His Royal Highness," he told her quietly.

He was on the point of leaving the room when there was the sound of boots on the gravel below the window. Voices were calling across the terraced lawns. "There's been an accident!... Terrible accident!... Ride over and fetch Sir William Gull from White Lodge. Gentleman's been shot! Over by Seagrim's Coppice! And fetch proper bandages!"

There was a pause, then the same voice explained to somebody in a more ordinary tone, "'Tis that Mr Holmes - the fat gentleman in the herring bone. Walked right out in front of the guns, he did! You'd think a gentleman'd have more sense."

The girl's face showed unfeigned surprise mingled with dismay.

"Perhaps, my dear," Mycroft told her, "you have made an even more dreadful mistake than you think. And Mr Guttmann does not readily forgive carelessness in his minions, does he?"

He opened the door and left her still sitting on the floor in a state of dishevelment. He locked the door after him and dropped the key into his pocket. There was no sound from inside the room as he set off downstairs; he could only suppose that Bessie Martin, if that were indeed her name, had exhausted her repertoire.

CHAPTER TWENTY-FIVE

The Prince of Wales was already in the *salon* when Mycroft came down the stairs. He was surrounded by others who had hurried in from the butts, their gaiters, or the stockings over the bottoms of their plus-fours, splashed with mud. Mycroft noticed that the Duchess of Manchester was wearing a man's pair of plaid trews under her Hunting Stewart tartan skirt. Breath steamed on the cold air coming through the open doors. Outside, on the drive, the loaders were setting off to clean the guns they were holding on either arm. Everybody stared up at Mycroft. The Prince exclaimed, "Deuce take it, Holmes! Thought you was supposed to be hurt!"

His tone suggested that Mycroft's robust health was a breach of manners. He looked Mycroft up and down and asked the question the others were thinking. "Who the devil are they carrying in?"

Mycroft noticed the aghast expression on Sir William Gordon Cumming's face - quite different from the amazement and curiosity on the faces of the others. It made him wonder what sums at cards Sir William must have owed Colonel-General the Graf von Varzin or Baron von Goeben that he should have succumbed to becoming their agent. At the same time, he could be quite certain that neither Sir William nor the Imperial German Ambassador would have fired the would-be fatal shot. He wondered who had.

"I might offer a suggestion, if Your Royal Highness permits," he said. He was still standing four treads up the stairs, where everybody could see him. "Your Royal Highness," he continued without waiting for permission, "I suggest that, not for the first time, the appearance has been taken for the reality. Sir Napier Soames borrowed my clothes for this morning's sport. Moreover his name, when called in the open air and at the distance separating the butts, would sound very similar to mine."

The Prince advanced to the foot of the stairs. He was short in stature, and Mycroft, standing four steps up, towered over him.

"Why were you not with us, sir?" the Prince demanded. "I cannot recall your excusing yourself!"

The large cockatoo named Mycroft, sensing the anger in his master's voice, screeched in fright and bounced up and down on its perch, battering its pinions on the bars of its cage. The Prince's anger was famous: the entire company in the *salon* had frozen into immobility. Mycroft, however, who had felt so apprehensive the previous day, now felt himself firmly on his own ground.

"Your Royal Highness will not have forgotten," he said, "that you were gracious enough to command my presence at a private audience, this evening. It so happened that Sir Napier Soames, an old school companion of mine, confided in me last night his acute chagrin at his man's having neglected to pack his shooting clothes. It occurred to me that I could best serve Your Royal Highness by spending at least a part of the morning in quiet consideration of the matters Your Royal Highness might wish to discuss with me. I therefore offered to lend my gear to Sir Napier for this morning. I realise that I owe Your Royal Highness a profound apology for what must appear a gross dereliction of duty on my part, only adding that it was because no opportunity to excuse myself presented itself which would have avoided saving my school friend from the most acute embarrassment."

There were murmurs of "Hear, hear!" from the gentlemen for whom, as Mycroft had calculated, the obligations of public school loyalty, like the code of the Samurai, overrode all other considerations. Mycroft was saved from the Prince's immediate verdict by the sudden appearance of Sir Allen Young. He came in from the direction of the billiard-rooms; failing to notice the Prince among the others standing in the *salon*, he exclaimed loudly, "I say! It ain't Holmes they've brought in! It's 'Fatty'!"

It would perhaps have been better, thought Mycroft, if he had kept the relief out of his voice - particularly when he noticed him standing on the stairs, waved to him, and called out cheerfully, "Devil take it, Holmes old chap! There you are!"

Then he spotted the Prince and came to attention. "Your Royal Highness, forgive me. I didn't see..."

"Is Gull with him?" the Prince asked. "How is the poor fellow?"

"Sir William has him on one of the billiard tables, sir," Sir Allen replied. "He's extractin' the shot from the fellow's backside. But it's a deuced rum thing, sir. Sir William says it's Eley number seven."

"Can't be!" the Prince exclaimed. "Don't shoot birds with number seven! Don't keep number seven here at Sandringham - no damn' use for it! Gull's a fool!"

There was a murmur among the others. Sir Allen said, "If Your Royal Highness pleases, Sir William showed me one of the shot. There was no mistaking it."

"With Your Royal Highness's permission," Mycroft intervened, "Might I be permitted a private word with Your Royal Highness?"

Sir William Gordon Cumming had pushed his way to the Prince's shoulder. "Do you not imagine, Holmes, that His Royal Highness has more pressin' matters to attend to at a time like this, than yourself?"

Mycroft ignored him. "With all due deference to Your Royal Highness, might I point out that Eley number seven is a calibre of shot so lethal that there may be those who would consider this unfortunate accident a matter for the Norfolk Constabulary?"

"You will come to the library, sir!" said the Prince. He sounded like a headmaster summoning a boy to his study. Mycroft stepped down from the stairs and dutifully followed the short, burly figure through the small crowd and into the hush of an empty and rarely used room.

The Prince closed the door behind him. Banks of signed photographs, in silver and tortoise-shell frames, black and white, sepia, hand-coloured, and fading to yellow, stared at Mycroft from every surface. He recognized the royalty of Germany, Russia, Greece, and Bulgaria, and had no doubt there were a full dozen other sovereign powers represented who would have been at one another's throats but for the extraordinary awe in which they held their mutual relative, the Prince's ageing mother, the Widow of Windsor. The peace of Europe, the Concert of Powers, depended so completely, thought Mycroft, on the *virtu* (in its Italian, Renaissance sense) perceived by lesser breeds in the English branch of the House of Hanover: a *virtu* which no breath of corruption must be allowed to tarnish.

"I hope, Holmes," the Prince began, "you do not suggest that one of my guests is the perpetrator of a deliberate and criminal act."

"I cannot say so, sir," Mycroft replied.

"I should certainly hope not!" said the Prince. He was obviously very close to losing his temper.

"Not with any degree of certainty," Mycroft went on.

"What on earth do you mean by that, sir?" The Prince's voice shook with scarcely controlled rage.

"Your Royal Highness, I will tell you with absolute certainty that a crime has been committed - and a far worse one proposed," Mycroft continued calmly.

"Do you know, sir, who fired the shot which has hurt poor Soames?" the Prince roared.

"The shot which was intended for me - no, sir," Mycroft replied.

"It was a blind man, sir! A blind man who had never heard of your existence before last night?" The Prince swallowed. "It was the

Duke of Streltsau, sir!"

Mycroft was silenced, if only for a moment.

"There, sir! What do you say to that?" demanded the Prince.

"Does His Grace usually go shooting, sir?" Mycroft asked.

The Prince spluttered.

"Without the ability to see?" Mycroft added.

"Unlike some men," said the Prince, "loafers, idle stay-at-homes, the Duke is a true sportsman! Cards! Women! Shootin'! He's never let a little thing like his blindness stand in his way! He has the spirit of his blind ancestor, the old King of Bohemia who fought at the Battle of Crécy and whose coat I am proud to show as my own!"

He had drifted from his purpose. He returned to his anger. "You're a clever man, Mr Holmes. That's your trouble. Everybody tells me what a clever man you are! I hate clever men! They're so busy bein' clever they can't see in front of their own faces!"

"I take it, sir, that His Grace's loader directs his aim," Mycroft pressed on, "height, direction of flight, bearing by the clock, and so on. And that he would be responsible for loading His Grace's guns with the correct shot."

"Of course! Of course, damn it! What the devil d'you think you're drivin' at?" demanded the Prince.

"His Grace's loader - was he a local man, sir?" asked Mycroft. "One of Your Highness's people?"

"No! He came with the Duke. He's a forester from Bohemia."

"May I take it Your Royal Highness has him held under restraint?" asked Mycroft. "Pending inquiries into this unfortunate accident?"

"Certainly not, sir! The Duke will deal with his own man!" But the indignation in the Prince's voice was slackening; already he could see the force of what Mycroft was saying.

"Forgive me, sir," Mycroft continued. "But neither you nor the Duke of Streltsau will be able to deal with the fellow. You will find that he is already on his way to London or, if he is not, then to one of the eastern ports. I daresay we shall also find that already in the servants' hall they are saying that he has eloped with one of the chambermaids - the maid who calls herself Bessie Martin."

"How the devil can you say that!" exclaimed the Prince.

"I don't imagine for a moment that it is her true name. We may discover it soon enough. I have the young person under lock and key upstairs in my room."

"You had the audacity to...!"

"If Your Royal Highness would have the goodness to hear me out," Mycroft interrupted him. "This Bessie Martin person came to my room after the other maids had left it. When I questioned her purpose in so doing, she attacked me with this..." He drew from his pocket his large red handkerchief, unfolded it, and displayed the long pin with its sharpened, silver point. "...If Your Royal Highness would care to have it examined and tested by any medical man or chemist, you shall find that poison has been applied to the point. Your Royal Highness may notice for yourself the tiny flecks of a dark, gummy substance on the exposed portion at the end... No, sir! Do not touch it! The slightest break in Your Royal Highness's skin and the poison will take its effect! It is strychnine; once in the body it will produce the convulsions and severe muscular contractions which in turn produce the *risus sardonicus* which makes it so readily identifiable."

The Prince took a step back. He stared at Mycroft. "I believe, sir, you are as mad as a hatter!" he said. "One of our junior domestics! A murderess!"

"If Your Royal Highness were to inquire of Sir Philip Doughty at New Scotland Yard, Sir Philip would confirm that there have been several occasions when guests at great houses have died unaccountably, and one of the junior servants has, at the same time, disappeared without trace. There was the tragic end of Lord Cormorant's younger son, Evelyn Rookwood, at Vanderlys in Warwickshire..."

"Absurd!" the Prince shook his head fiercely. "Absurd!"

"The matter may easily be put to the test, sir," Mycroft suggested. "We have only to go upstairs to my room and suggest that Bessie Martin allows herself to be pricked slightly with this."

He folded the pin back into his handkerchief. Still staring at him, the Prince nodded. "Very well, Mr Holmes. Let us put it to the test. And then, perhaps, you may find yourself in time to take the afternoon train back to Town."

Mycroft followed him out of the library and across the *salon*. The other guests had mostly dispersed. Sir William Gordon Cumming was keeping the stuffed baboon company, while the white cockatoo, Mycroft, was scuffling up and down on its perch, occasionally launching its beak savagely at a strip of dried cuttlefish wired to the bottom of the bars.

"Sir William," ordered the Prince, "you will please attend the Duke of Streltsau, present him with my compliments, and ask him to be so obligin' as to send his loader to await me in the library. Immediately, you understand!"

"If Your Royal Highness permits," Mycroft said, "I would advise Your Royal Highness most strongly to send at once to Wolferton station to telegraph down the line to all stations to Liverpool Street and the East Anglian harbours, to command the holding of any passenger answering to the description of the Duke's loader."

"You have said quite enough for the time being!" the Prince snapped back at him.

They went upstairs, Mycroft following immediately after the Prince, Sir Allen Young bringing up the rear although he had not been invited. When they reached the gallery, both the Prince and Mycroft were out of breath. Indignation at the way events were turning out lent the Prince a certain stamina.

Mycroft fell back a few paces as they tramped toward the guest room passage. Sir Allen placed his hand on Mycroft's shoulder.

"Deuce take it, Holmes!" he murmured. "I hope you know what you're up to!"

Mycroft was too short of breath to reply.

CHAPTER TWENTY-SIX

The bedroom door was open. Mycroft could see the light from it. "Our birds have flown," he said, at last catching his breath.

The Prince was not impressed. He strode to the room and looked inside. All was as clean, empty, and still as it had been when Mycroft had come up to it after breakfast. There was not the least sign of the bed-cover having been disturbed where the maid had sat on it.

"Well, Mr Holmes?" said the Prince. "Perhaps you will now explain yourself!"

"She has escaped!" said Mycroft. "Sir, I beg you to send word to Wolferton this instant! See! I have the key to the door on my person!"

He pulled it from his pocket.

"But no lock with which to use it!" Sir Allen pointed out.

He drew the Prince's attention to the back of the open door inside the room. The handle, the mortice, the lock itself, and the section of the wood in which they had been set - all had been removed with such skill that there was only the least sign of recent splintering on the carpet at their feet.

"This is the work of a skilled man!" said the Prince. "The young female gave the alarm to one of her colleagues, and Mrs Moorcraft sent for a man from the carpenter's shop."

Mycroft sighed. He left it to Sir Allen draw the Prince's attention to the obvious. "If Your Royal Highness don't mind me sayin': the lock was removed from the inside."

Mycroft went over to the chest of drawers. Lying on the top were several broken pieces of stained wood, screws with tiny wood chippings still clinging to the threads, one door handle and the lock intact. He turned to see that the Prince was out in the passage once more. He and Sir Allen were forced into a trot as they followed the Prince across the gallery and down the stairs.

Sir William Gordon Cumming was waiting below in the *salon*. "Your Royal Highness, His Grace's man was not with His Grace. They say downstairs that he has not been seen since we returned from the butts. I have sent to look for him..."

"Be so good, Sir William," the Prince said immediately, "as to take a hunter from the stables. Ride over to Wolferton quick as you can. Have a description of the Duke of Streltsau's man telegraphed down every line to London and the coastal harbours."

"As Your Royal Highness commands!"

Then the Prince said, stepping across to the library, "We had better go back in here, Holmes - and you, Alleno. You're said to be acquainted with Holmes. You may as well join us."

Mycroft and Sir Allen followed the Prince into the library. The Prince closed the door. He sighed heavily. "By God, Holmes!" he said. "They suggested we had to have you here to keep you out of trouble. It seems you've brought the trouble with you!"

"May I know, Your Royal Highness, the nature of the trouble from which I am being preserved?" asked Mycroft. His tone of voice suggested that it could scarcely have been as grave as the trouble into which 'Fatty' Soames had stumbled in his place.

"From makin' a damn' fool of yourself by interferin' in a case of domestic crime," the Prince replied. "You have friends, sir! Friends in high places - particularly in the Foreign Office - who have a high regard for your brain when it concerns itself with questions of government policy abroad. They are anxious you should not wreck your reputation by interferin' in matters which are no concern of yours and are of no general consequence in the affairs of the Nation, sir!"

"I was given to understand, sir," said Mycroft, "that you were advised to invite me here to question me about the Pfalzel-Buckelburg Succession."

"There had to be a reason, sir!" snapped the Prince impatiently. "Your name does not appear on the pages of my wife's guest-book!"

"And the reason was most considerately provided by the man who insinuated himself into Your Royal Highness's presence under the assumed rank of Colonel-General Graf von Varzin?" Mycroft asked.

The Prince hesitated. "What do you mean, sir," he demanded. "I will have you know the Count von Varzin was sent here by His Imperial Majesty, the Kaiser, to invest me with a very signal honour."

"It gives me no satisfaction whatever," said Mycroft, "to suggest that if Your Royal Highness would care to examine the Prussian Army List for the past few years, you will find no mention of a Graf von Varzin holding the Kaiser's commission in the Prussian army. If Your Royal Highness would care to examine the *Almanach de Gotha*, you will find no reference to a *Graf* von Varzin. There is indeed a title attached to the Forest and Manors of Varzin. It is that of *Freiherr von Varzin*, and is held by Prince Otto von Bismarck himself."

"Do you realise what you are saying, sir!" the Prince asked in a tone of silky anger.

"Perfectly, sir," replied Mycroft.

"With Your Royal Highness's permission," Sir Allen Young intervened, "and with some acquaintance with Mr Holmes's past career, I venture to suggest that he would not make such a statement without having personally verified it."

"Precisely so," said Mycroft.

"I am not aware of having asked for your advice, Alleno," said the Prince. But use of Sir Allen's nickname demonstrated the half-heartedness of his rebuke. He lapsed into something like a sullen silence. At last, he said, addressing Mycroft, "Who are you suggesting the fellow was?"

"With tolerable certainty, sir, I can say it was Carl Philip Emmanuel Guttmann, once valet to the Prince von Bismarck."

"Valet!" exclaimed the Prince.

"For the past fifteen years," Mycroft explained, "he has been the Imperial German Chancellor's confidential agent. He is the organising genius and prime mover of a network of spies and secret agents. I may say without exaggeration, Your Royal Highness, that C P E Guttmann, though he may have started his career as a mere valet, is the most subtle, the most dangerous politician the continent of Europe has known since Machiavelli." He paused.

The Prince glared at him, but said nothing. Undeterred Mycroft continued: "It would have been bad enough had Guttmann, and his creatures in this country, succeeded in engineering the conviction of Mrs Diana Tuttle for the murder of the late Captain Meadowthorpe, in such a way as to suggest - quite falsely, I hasten to add - that Your Royal Highness or Your Royal Highness's immediate friends and *aides* had procured such a conviction by interference with the true course of Justice. I would put to Your Royal Highness the extent to which a resulting scandal would be compounded if it were believed that, because I had interested myself in Mrs Tuttle's defence, I had been brought here, to Sandringham House, and had been hurt - or killed - in what was given out to be a shooting accident involving the use of Eley number seven cartridges."

"You understand the gravity of what you are saying?"

"Of course, Your Royal Highness," Mycroft replied.

"You are suggesting that my own cousin in Potsdam, my mother's nephew, is implicated in a diabolic plot to interfere in a case being heard by our own High Court, not to mention an assassination here at Sandringham."

"No, sir," Mycroft replied immediately, with a conviction he did not feel. "I would suggest no more than that the man Guttmann has, as a good confidential agent, anticipated his master's aspirations, and has worked independently of his master to bring them to fulfilment."

The Prince showed evident relief. "What do you suppose those aspirations to be, Mr Holmes?" he asked.

"That is the matter I intended to put to Your Royal Highness this evening," Mycroft replied. "Guttmann, of course, had planned that I should not survive long enough to do so. Prince von Bismarck's aim is to extend the Prussian hegemony to include the Grand Duchy of Pfalzel-Buckelburg. Your Royal Highness will be aware already that the Grand Duchy, though small, possesses strategically the most important railway junction on the west bank of the Rhine. It is of no value to the defence of the German Empire. Its offensive strategic value to Berlin, however, is immeasurable."

Silence descended, Mycroft was aware of Sir Allen standing behind him, as still as himself. This, he decided, as he heard the melancholy cry of a gull circling above the elms outside, must be how a prisoner in the dock must feel as he awaits the jury's verdict.

"I suppose you regard me as having played into the hands of this Guttmann fellow," said the Prince quietly.

"I would not presume to pass judgement on Your Royal Highness," Mycroft replied. "I would only ask Your Royal Highness to consider what I have put before you, and to test the extent to which it conforms to what Your Royal Highness already knows?"

The Prince nodded. There was an interval of silence. Suddenly, he reached for a silver cigar-box which stood on a walnut table by his left hand. He took a cigar, then almost in an afterthought passed the box to Sir Allen and to Mycroft. "What of this Mrs Tuttle?" he asked.

"Mrs Tuttle's defence," said Mycroft, "has been placed in the hands of a young, inexperienced barrister by solicitors who clearly believed that Your Royal Highness's best interests would be served by her being convicted with the least possible fuss. Fortunately for Mrs Tuttle, not only is Mr Marshall Hall, her counsel, convinced of her innocence, but, despite certain pressures being exerted he is determined to defend her to the best of his ability. I believe that, by the time she comes to trial, he will be provided with material evidence in her favour sufficient to convince any jury. Your Royal Highness may rest assured that the defence requires no mention of Your Royal Highness whatever, either directly or by inference. In fact, I will go so far as to say that the interest taken in the case by myself and my immediate associates is precisely to ensure that that remains so."

The Prince nodded. "You will wish to return immediately to London, I suppose?" he asked.

"If Your Royal Highness will permit," Mycroft replied.

"You'd best not be seen smoking as you go upstairs to your room," said the Prince.

"Of course not, Your Royal Highness," Mycroft replied. "I'm obliged to Your Royal Highness."

He stubbed out the cigar. It was a fine *Corona corona* and he had scarcely begun to smoke it. He thought for a fraction of a second then placed it carefully in his waistcoat pocket.

CHAPTER TWENTY-SEVEN

"Dr Bickleigh, with the assistance of two colleagues, you performed the autopsy on the body of Captain Septimus Meadowthorpe?" Marshall Hall asked.

"I did," Dr Bickleigh replied.

"And you would not say that, in retrospect, you have any doubts as to the conclusion the three of you came to?"

"None whatever."

"Dr Bickleigh made that perfectly clear, this morning, in his reply to Mr Cathcart!" Mr Justice Muckleburn intervened, his fat, empurpled face leaning across the open ledger in which he had been taking notes. "I fear you propose to continue wasting the court's time with unnecessary questions, Mr Marshall Hall," he said, affecting a weary fatalism.

Mycroft, seated on the solicitors' bench behind Marshall Hall, could sense in the young man's posture and the ivory white knuckles of the hand with which he was gripping the narrow lectern in front of him, his tenseness and anger. For two days now he had endured the caustic irritability of Mr Justice Muckleburn, not to mention the sneering condescension of the Attorney General, Sir Richard Webster, and his junior, Mr James Cathcart, QC.

"M'lord, if Your Lordship will bear patiently with me," Marshall Hall replied, "I trust the purpose of my line of questioning will become perfectly clear to your Lordship."

"I will bear patiently with you, Mr Marshall Hall," said Mr Justice Muckleburn. "I am a patient man... none more so," he snarled. "It is the gentlemen of the jury whom you have to consider. You may find them less indulgent than myself; it is they, after all, who are being kept from earning their livelihoods!"

He turned and smiled sympathetically in the direction of the jury-box; it was occupied by twelve middle-aged men in sober broadcloth Sunday suits, wearing serious, attentive expressions on their faces.

Mycroft wondered if persisting in retaining Marshall Hall as Mrs Tuttle's counsel had not been a mistake. Even Mr Archibald Russell, his junior, was staring up at him with an expression of apprehension. Grouped around the table in the well of the court, the scribblers for the public prints were smirking across at one another. Over in the dining-room of The Wig and Pen, during the luncheon adjournment, they had been laying bets as if the real adversaries in Number Three

Court at the Old Bailey were young Mr Marshall Hall and Mr Justice Muckleburn, rather than the Attorney General and Mr Marshall Hall.

There were worse signs and portents than these. A little way along the solicitors' bench from Mycroft, Mr Augustine Bullfinger reclined in an attitude of post-prandial slumber, his face relaxed into a state of cherubic calm. Beyond him, Josiah Hartz was smiling as he perused his finger-nails. At the further end of the bench in front, the Attorney General's junior, Mr James Cathcart QC, was lounging in an attitude of easeful boredom. Sir Richard Webster had absented himself for the afternoon, intimating that he was engaged in important government business; Mycroft suspected that he was enjoying an afternoon nap in the Reform Club.

"Dr Bickleigh - you were, I believe, medical adviser to Captain Meadowthorpe's wife during the period of that lady's last sickness and death, some four years ago?" asked Marshall Hall.

"I was."

"You signed Mrs Meadowthorpe's death certificate?"

"I did."

"Would you be so kind as to tell the jury the cause of Mrs Meadowthorpe's death?"

"Enteric fever," Dr Bickleigh replied, "contracted by her drinking water from a public fountain in Italy."

"And the duration of that last illness?"

"Five or six weeks, I recall."

"Thank you, Dr Bickleigh." Marshall Hall paused momentarily. "Perhaps you would remind us of the duration of Captain Meadowthorpe's last illness?" he asked.

It was Bickleigh's turn to hesitate. "Five weeks," he said finally.

"Five weeks and four days, to be precise?"

"If you say so, Mr Marshall Hall."

"I do say so. I suppose five weeks and four days could be expressed loosely as five or six weeks, could they not?"

"I daresay," Dr Bickleigh replied.

"Very well. Now, the symptoms of enteric fever are similar, are they not - exactly the same, indeed - as the symptoms resulting from the taking of arsenic suspended in chloral, in a certain dosage and over a similar period of time?"

"Mr Marshall Hall," Mr Justice Muckleburn intervened yet again, his voice shrill with sarcasm, "I must remind you that the charge against the prisoner is of procuring the death by poison of Captain

Meadowthorpe. Do you propose to add the murder of the victim's wife to the charge? If so, I have to tell you that it is the first time in my experience of the criminal courts that I have heard learned counsel in a capital case seek to add to the indictment against his client."

Once again, he turned to smile in sympathy at the jury. He turned back to Marshall Hall. "Mr Hall, I must remind you that not the least of my duties here is to ensure that the accused's case is properly represented."

"M'lord! I beg Your Lordship to hear out my questioning of this witness!"

The rise in Marshall Hall's voice, together with the hectic pallor of his lean, sensitive face, struck the gravest anxiety in Mycroft.

Mr Justice Muckleburn nodded. "A few more moments, Mr Hall!" he replied.

"I am grateful to Your Lordship," Marshall Hall replied.

"The answer to your question, Mr Marshall Hall," said Dr Bickleigh without waiting for the question to be put, "is, yes. The symptoms of death from enteric fever - or typhoid, to give it its vulgar name - are similar to those of arsenical poisoning, subject to certain conditions, of course." He sounded positively anxious to help.

"You have informed us that Mrs Meadowthorpe contracted enteric fever from drinking infected water from an Italian public fountain."

"Yes, Mr Hall. She did!" snapped Mr Justice Muckleburn.

Marshall Hall managed to ignore the interruption. "Travellers in Italy are, of course, well advised not to drink from public fountains," he said. "In the knowledge that she had been foolish enough to do so, I suppose you would have had no doubts about your diagnosis of her sickness?"

"None whatever."

"Can you tell us in which city she committed this act of folly?"

"In Florence. From the fountain in the Piazza Santissima Annunziata." He smiled ruefully.

"You have visited Florence, Doctor?"

"No, never."

"But I am sure you are aware that, unlike in other cities of Italy, the water from the principal public fountains in Florence is renowned for its exceptional purity - that the incidence of enteric fever in the municipality of Florence over the past two decades is actually lower than in your own practice in Hampstead?"

"I was not so aware."

"Then I am enlightening you, Doctor... Doctor - I would like to draw your attention to an event which occurred shortly after the interment of Captain Meadowthorpe's wife. I refer to the visit paid to you one evening by the accused. Perhaps you will inform us what she told you on that occasion?"

Mycroft glanced up where Mrs Diana Tuttle sat, high up in the dock, as if within the ramparts of a wooden tower. On either side of her sat a wardress, a stout matron with her grey hair drawn severely back under her regulation black police bonnet, and a lean, craggy faced female with a wispy black moustache. Mrs Tuttle herself, as far as he could see her features over the sharpened points of the iron *chevaux de frise* designed to prevent her from leaping over the front of the dock and assaulting His Lordship, was a strikingly attractive woman whose eyes were remarkable for their long lashes, with a neat, dimpled chin, and with dark hair in luxuriant ringlets on which was set a red, military, pill-box cap with a black lace veil. The lines about her eyes and mouth, and the sunken pallor of cheeks untouched by any cosmetic blush, testified to what she had endured in Millbank gaol and what she was continuing to endure.

"Mrs Tuttle came to tell me," Dr Bickleigh was replying, "that she - the accused - believed that she had seen Captain Meadowthorpe, in the conservatory of his house, and at a moment when he supposed himself to be unobserved, remove a bottle from where it had been buried in the earth of a plant pot, and place it in his pocket."

"Did the accused describe the bottle to you?"

"Yes. She described a small bottle coloured purple and ribbed perpendicularly."

"In fact, the sort of bottle into which apothecaries dispense poisons, for easy recognition?"

"Yes."

"And why do you suppose the accused wished to impart this information to you?"

"She was uneasy regarding the cause of her mistress's death."

"Let us be entirely certain as to what you are saying, Dr Bickleigh," Marshall Hall said. "You are telling us that Mrs Tuttle harboured a suspicion that Captain Meadowthorpe poisoned his wife?"

Dr Bickleigh, Mycroft noticed with considerable relief, was eager enough to reply so as to ignore the gasps of astonishment around Number Three Court.

"Yes, sir. She said she had seen the bottle once before when she had gone into Mrs Meadowthorpe's sickroom to remove a tray, and Captain Meadowthorpe had been with his wife. Mrs Tuttle said that she had noticed the bottle on the marble of the wash-stand, behind and under the rim of the basin."

"In effect, half-concealed?"

"Mr Marshall Hall, I cannot devote my entire time in this case to rebuking you," snarled Mr Justice Muckleburn. "Young and inexperienced you may be in your profession, but not so young that you are not perfectly aware of the inadmissibility of hearsay evidence."

"I beg Your Lordship's pardon," Marshall Hall inclined his head meekly.

The boy would make a barrister yet, thought Mycroft; he had accepted the rebuke with becoming humility, secure in the knowledge that he had made his point with the Jury.

"You saw no reason, Dr Bickleigh, why you yourself should entertain any unease regarding your opinion of the cause of Mrs Meadowthorpe's death?"

For a moment Dr Bickleigh stood in silence, his gloved hand twitching, where it had been resting on the ledge before him. He glanced owlishly but rapidly about him. Finally, he came out with, "None, Mr Marshall Hall. And I endeavoured to put Mrs Tuttle's mind at ease over the matter."

His perspiring look of embarrassment was so obvious to Mycroft that he could scarcely believe that it was not equally obvious to judge and jury. Mr Justice Muckleburn allowed the jury no time to consider the implications of Dr Bickleigh's awkwardness.

"With success, it would appear," he intervened immediately, "given the prisoner's later attitude toward the unfortunate victim in this case." He laughed, and the twelve sober, solemn tradesmen in the jury-box laughed with him.

Marshall Hall ignored the interruption. "Would you say, Dr Bickleigh, that the bottle discovered in the accused's bedroom by the officers of the Hampstead police answered exactly to the accused's earlier description of the bottle she believed to be in Captain Meadowthorpe's possession?"

"Yes."

"But you drew no inference from that similarity?"

Mr Justice Muckleburn leaned forward over his ledger. "Why should he have done, Mr Hall?" he demanded. "And why should we draw any inference from it either? Are poison bottles so very uncommon?"

"I believe we may have the answer to your question here, if it please your Lordship," Marshall Hall replied.

He beckoned to one of the court ushers, and spoke to him in a low voice. The usher took a sheet of paper over to the witness-box.

"Document entered into evidence as article fourteen (b), My Lord," said Marshall Hall. "A schedule for the administration of a pharmaceutical compound - a dosage to be administered, it would appear, over a period of five and a half weeks. We shall be calling as witness the lady, a foreign lady of the highest rank and title in society, who has purchased for her own residence the home on Squire's Mount of the late Captain Meadowthorpe. She will testify to the court that, in her presence, the document was discovered by one of her servants in a secret compartment of a bureau belonging to the late Captain Meadowthorpe... With Your Lordship's permission..."

He turned to Dr Bickleigh. "The elements of this compound are not specified on the schedule. Perhaps you would recognize of what it might be composed?"

Dr Bickleigh looked quite shocked. He turned to the judge. "I take it to be the receipt for the most common of emetics, Your Lordship," he said, his voice shaking slightly. "Common, but to be taken only under the supervision of a qualified medical practitioner."

"And what, Dr Bickleigh, would be the ingredients of this common emetic?" asked Marshall Hall.

"Arsenic, sir. Arsenic suspended in chloral."

"We know that you were medical adviser to both Captain and Mrs Meadowthorpe. Tell us, Dr Bickleigh: do you recollect ever prescribing arsenic suspended in chloral to anybody in the household on Squire's Mount?"

"No, sir!" Dr Bickleigh shook his head emphatically. "And certainly not in those dosages."

"Why, Dr Bickleigh? What is remarkable about the schedule?"

"If taken in the amounts described, over the period described..." He paused for a moment. "I have little doubt but that the final dose would prove lethal."

"Thank you, Dr Bickleigh... Perhaps you would tell us this: if you had known of the existence of this schedule in the Meadowthorpe home when the accused came to you to confide in you her unease - I will rate it no higher - at Mrs Meadowthorpe's death, would you have dismissed it quite so readily?"

Dr Bickleigh was still in a state of shock, Mycroft noticed. "No, sir. I would not!" he replied.

"Thank you, Dr Bickleigh... I have done with the witness," he said to the judge.

He scooped the sleeves of his gown over his arms and sat down. Mr James Cathcart, QC, half rose.

"No further questions at this point, M'lord," he said.

Villiers Manyon came into the witness-box the following afternoon, and took the oath. There was no somnolence about Number Three Court; there were no sneers on anybody's lips when Marshall Hall rose to examine the witness. Even Mr Augustine Bullfinger and Mr Josiah Hartz sat alert, though their faces remained impassive. And the Attorney General was in his place.

Only Villiers Manyon seemed entirely at his ease. He was a large man, burly as a race-course tipster; but there was not the least hint of vulgarity in his tailoring or general appearance save for the single, enormous ruby pin with which his necktie was secured. He gave the impression, as Princess Sophie had not when she had appeared immediately before the luncheon adjournment, that he was conferring some sort of favour on the court by having descended from Hampstead Hill to appear before it.

Marshall Hall asked that the schedule should be put before him. "Do you recognize this document, Mr Manyon?"

Villiers Manyon examined it. He held it out to return it to the court usher. "I do not think so," he replied dismissively.

"Perhaps you will do us the favour of examining the contents of the document, Mr Manyon?" Marshall Hall asked.

Manyon pretended to glance down it. "It appears to be an apothecary's schedule," he replied.

"A schedule referring to what, exactly?" asked Marshall Hall.

Manyon gave him a smile, as if to suggest that he was not tricked so easily. "I suggest you enquire of an apothecary, Mr Hall."

"Marshall Hall, if you please, Mr Manyon."

"Mr Marshall Hall," Manyon repeated with the air of avuncular benevolence of one who is accustomed to the behaviour of the wayward young. There was, the faintest titter of amusement from the jury-box. "You do possess a type-writing machine, Mr Manyon?" asked Marshall Hall. He sounded sullen, bad-tempered, as if he had been put off his stride.

"Not personally, Mr Marshall Hall. No."

"Of course he doesn't!" Mr Justice Muckleburn intervened in a manner even more choleric than usual. "He is a gentleman! I hope we shall find there is some method, Mr Marshall Hall..." His emphasis on 'Marshall' deliberately echoed Manyon. "...in the apparent madness of your line of questioning. I hope you do not intend suggesting..." He let out a rasping bark of a laugh, as it momentarily overcome by the sheer wit in the remark he was about to utter, "...that there are experts in type-writing as there are in hand-writing!"

He looked across at the jury, inviting them to share his merriment. They did.

"I hope Your Lordship will bear with me for a moment," said Marshall Hall. "Mr Manyon, I daresay that there is, in your private office at the Lakeside Spa Hotel a type-writing machine."

"Yes, sir," beamed Manyon, secure in the judge's joke about experts in type-writing, "and I employ a lady type-writer to use it - on the principle..." He turned, smiling, to the judge, "...of keeping a dog so that one does not need to bark oneself."

Mr Justice Muckleburn returned the smile. Mycroft noticed that Marshall Hall also permitted himself a smile.

"Of course, Mr Manyon," he said. "You have a number of ladies in your employ, I believe," he went on, as if to add his own contribution to the banter. "I mean, in addition to your domestic staff."

The faintest possibility began to occur to Mycroft that Marshall Hall's questioning from the very beginning had been designed to prevent Manyon from realising he was being drawn into the mire. Now, he was suggesting that 'we are all men of the world here'.

"I can see I shall have to plead guilty to that, Mr Marshall Hall," Manyon replied amiably. "I fear it is all too well known"

Still smiling, Marshall Hall nodded. "I expect some of the ladies - in your employ - resort to the use of preparations to enhance their complexions, the skin-surface of their arms and shoulders when exposed in the evenings. In a word or two, cosmetic preparations."

"Personal vanity is the chiefest failing of the fair sex, Mr Marshall Hall," smiled Manyon, "and what is a mere man to do?"

"What indeed?" Marshall Hall agreed. "I expect that as an hotelier, engaged in the provision of comestibles for your guests, you will need to have recourse to a considerable quantity; of fly-papers... I do not mean you, personally, you understand, Mr Manyon, but your lieutenants."

"Mr Marshall Hall, throughout the hearing I have borne patiently with you," intervened Mr Justice Muckleburn. "I really cannot see where this is leading us!"

"If Your Lordship pleases," Marshall Hall replied. "I am sure Mr Manyon can. Mr Manyon will be aware that cosmetic preparations for the skin and the preparation of fly-papers have a common basis - in arsenic. Your Lordship will have heard and noted testimony that the schedule presently in the witness hand is for the administration of a compound based on arsenic... Mr Manyon," he continued without waiting for Mr Justice Muckleburn to comment further, "this type-writing machine which is not yours, precisely speaking, but which is in your private office, in the Lakeside Spa Hotel - is a machine made by the firm Elliot Fisher, of Cincinnati in the United States of America, is it not?"

"My dear Mr Marshall Hall..." Manyon no longer emphasised the first barrel of his interrogator's name, Mycroft noted. "I have not the faintest idea where it comes from! Birmingham, I expect. That is where most mechanical hardware is manufactured, I believe."

This time, there was no laughter from the jury-box.

"It is made by Elliot Fisher," said Marshall Hall. "I can tell you that. I have several examples of invoices here, issued by your private office at the Lakeside Spa Hotel - the letter-press, not to mention the action of the locking-bar mechanisms are immediately recognizable as those peculiar to the Elliot Fisher machine. Would it interest you to know, Mr Manyon, that the schedule which is present in your hand was also type-written on an Elliot Fisher machine?"

Mr Justice Muckleburn leaned forward across the open volume in which he had been scribbling notes. "Mr Marshall Hall," he snarled, "I put it to you that in an age when young men..." He did not actually add, 'like yourself', "...cannot be bothered to learn to write legibly, or even to make the effort to move a pen across paper, there is an increasing resort to manufactured type-writing machines. One may suggest that our cities are flooded with them - to the detriment of literacy, I daresay."

"But not, if Your Lordship pleases," Marshall Hall replied, "with those manufactured by Elliot Fisher of Cincinnati. They are designed for a special purpose - for use with ledgers and office account books. And I believe if Your Lordship would make enquiries, you would find that they have not generally been adopted in this country. Indeed, there are something of a rarity."

"The fact they are a rarity, Mr Marshall Hall," retorted Mr Justice Muckleburn, "does not make any one of them unique."

"Your Lordship is, as always, quite right," Marshall Hall replied, "and I am sure that the gentlemen of the jury will take due note of what Your Lordship has said... Mr Manyon, I wonder if I might draw your attention to the type-written letter 'r' in the document you have in your hand - the letter 'r' is what I believe printers describe as 'lower case'. You will observe that the curlicue on the upper right of the top of the upright is faint. Are you aware that the letters 'r' in lower case in these invoices is faint in precisely the same manner? and the letters 'o' in lower case - would you care to examine them, Mr Manyon? - there is a point on the mid left-hand side where - fractionally, I admit, they are faint almost to invisibility, where they become the image in little of a broken ring. The same will be found in these invoices. And the numeral seven?... My Lord," he turned to the judge, "I could go on demonstrating a number of such similarities, in the print on the schedule and on invoice, issued by the witness's private office. It is for Your Lordship to decide at what point the rarity of the make of type-writing machine combined with the similarities in the quality of the print begin to approach uniqueness."

Villiers Manyon did not wait for any conclusion to be drawn. Mycroft noticed that though he was still smiling, as if to give the impression that he was positively enjoying the experience of being in the witness-box, he had begun to sweat below his receding hairline, and that his neck had reddened round his collar. "I do not believe I have positively stated that this document was not printed on a machine in my office," he said.

He reached out to grip the side of the witness-box. "The Court must be well aware by this time of the connection between myself and the late Captain Meadowthorpe's household which existed over some years. I may have failed to recall an occasion - indeed, may never have known of it at all - when a member of Captain Meadowthorpe's staff - Mrs Tuttle perhaps - sought advice on the destruction of rats."

"Would you say, Mr Manyon," asked Marshall Hall, "that the suspension of arsenic in chloral is an effective way of administering it to rats? I have never heard that rats are predisposed to consume draughts of chloral."

"I know nothing of such things, Mr Marshall Hall."

"And the amounts mentioned in the schedule, Mr Manyon?" asked Marshall Hall. "They are surely somewhat copious for the elimination of rats - unless, of course, you have rats up in Hampstead the size of bull terriers...?"

"I know nothing of such things," Manyon repeated, clutching and releasing and clutching again at the rim of the witness-box.

There was a desperation in the way he tried to save himself by reaching for something Mr Justice Muckleburn had said earlier: "I am a gentleman, sir! I leave such matters to those whom I employ to look after such things."

"Of course, Mr Manyon," the judge assured him. "I am certain that is perfectly understood." And he smiled briefly in the direction of the jury. "Mr Marshall Hall. Do you have any further questions to put to the witness?"

"I have, M'lord. If Your Lordship pleases, there are a number of important aspects of the case on which I wish to seek elucidation from this witness."

"I daresay! I daresay!" Mr Justice Muckleburn's normally irascible voice - irascible, at least, when addressing Marshall Hall - had now sunk to a mumble. He seemed unsure of himself, and glanced down at his ledger as if seeking guidance from it. Then he raised his head and cleared his throat. "This would be a suitable time to adjourn for today," he announced. "We would have to break off the business of the court in any case, to allow the ushers to light the gas. The gentlemen of the jury have had to pay the closest attention to our proceedings all day..."

"My Lord!" Marshall Hall was about to protest. Mycroft tugged at the tail of his gown. Marshall Hall glanced round, and Mycroft shook his head, only barely perceptibly. The barrister was taken by surprise, but by this time he knew better than to ignore the older man's advice.

"Mr Attorney?" Mr Justice Muckleburn asked.

Sir Richard Webster half-rose. "As Your Lordship pleases."

Marshall Hall nodded his assent.

"Very well," said Mr Justice Muckleburn. "We shall resume at ten o'clock tomorrow morning."

The Clerk called, "The Court will rise!"

During the hubbub which followed, Marshall Hall turned to Mycroft. reassuringly, Mycroft told him, "You are making your point perfectly well, my dear boy. What is emerging, will be perfectly apparent, even to an English jury. We do not wish to stir up the hornet's nest any more than is good for the public weal."

"Do you mean that His Lordship...?" Marshall Hall began.

"No, no, my dear fellow! Not necessarily! But I daresay that a number of his colleagues on the Queen's Bench have had recourse to the entertainments provided at the Vale of Health Spa Hotel."

And he shook his head and tutted at the fallibility of the great men of this world.

The following morning, fresh, rain-washed sunlight cast a shaft through the lantern windows in the ceiling of Number Three Court. As Mr Justice Muckleburn took his place on the judicial throne, and advocates, solicitors, clerks, jurymen, visitors, all resumed their seats, one place, Mycroft observed through the motes of dust drifting in the unaccustomed brightness of the light, was conspicuously vacant. There was nobody in the witness-box. For a few moments, there was subdued talking from bench to bench. An usher left the courtroom, doors swinging behind him. He returned a moment later, and handed up a piece of paper to Mr Justice Muckleburn, who unfolded it.

He cleared his throat. "Mr Marshall Hall? It seems that your witness does not propose to appear this morning."

Marshall Hall was on his feet.

"It seems," the judge continued, "that yesterday evening, an urgent matter of business required that Mr Villiers Manyon, accompanied by his daughter, take the overnight steam-packet from Dover to Calais. Mr Manyon had the temerity..." His voice wobbled. He paused to recover himself; he held up the sheet of paper. "...to leave a letter of apology with one of the police constables at the main entrance."

CHAPTER TWENTY-EIGHT

Marshall Hall was enjoying himself, that was evident to Mycroft. The young man was leaning back against the book-rail of the solicitors' bench behind him. He had thrown his gown back to leave his arms clear to gesture or wave papers in the direction of the jury. There was a look of elegant disdain on his classically regular features wholly different from the nervous tensions he had evidenced during the early days of the trial.

Mr Augustine Bullfinger and Josiah Hartz were no longer seated at the other end of the bench. They had resigned their place to a Mr Hillmore, a nephew of Mr Stote's, who had only recently joined the firm of Marcus, Bullfinger, Stote and Marcus as its youngest partner.

Somewhere in the public gallery, escorted by Colonel Barnaby, but out of sight of the lawyers' benches, was Princess Sophie. The previous evening, Mycroft had driven back with her to Mayfair. They had been descending Ludgate Hill when Sophie had announced, "I believe your Mr Marshall Hall to be *un preux chevalier, sans peur et sans reproche*. Your Poet Laureate describes him perfectly: *his strength is as the strength of ten because his heart is pure.*"

Mycroft had felt instantly that he would become very suspicious if he were ever to discover that she had invited Marshall Hall to dinner.

"...Gentlemen, you may not be aware..." Marshall Hall was addressing the twelve stolid, middle-aged men, with their serious, attentive expressions and their decent sabbatarian suits "...and I hope you will forgive me if you are already aware, that it is the privilege of my distinguished and learned friend, Mr Attorney General, when he leads a prosecution, to have the last word. I know that His Lordship, with that impeccable regard for even-handed justice and fair play for which he is renowned, will advise you in his summing up that it is no business of defending counsel to present a case on behalf of the accused. It is the affair of those responsible for the prosecution of the accused to bring a case and to prove it beyond a shadow of a doubt. In a situation in which my distinguished and learned friend exercises his privilege of making his final address to you, the jury, after the defence has summed up on behalf of the accused, it is only natural - it is the inevitable effect of human psychology that it will appear as though defending counsel has presented an argument which it is Mr Attorney General's duty to put to the test. For this reason, I cannot stress too strongly to you that it is the obligation placed on the prosecution - particularly grave where the charge against the accused is a hanging matter - to prove positively and absolutely the guilt of the accused, and not merely to demonstrate a lack of skill in forensic debate, and lack of learning in the law, in one like myself who is so much less experienced than Mr Attorney General and the eminent counsel who sit with him in this courtroom.

"I hope you will bear with me, gentlemen, if I put another general point to you for your careful consideration. I wonder how many of you will recall with me those telling lines from the play *Othello*. They occur at that point when the Duke and his grandees are sending Othello and Desdemona, newly wed, to Cyprus. As Othello leaves the Ducal palace, Desdemona's father draws him aside and utters the dreadful words:

> *Look to her, Moor, if you have eyes to see.*
> *She has deceived her father, and may thee...*

"It is on the basis of that brief remark - that single imputation on Desdemona's character - that the entire tragedy rests: the brute slaying of one who had committed no offence. You may ask what Shakespeare's tale has to do with the charge which the accused has to answer. It is this. It is the suggestion that because a woman may be perceived to be delinquent in one instance, a quite different accusation which has been brought against her may be deemed already half-proven. The fact that my client - a young, lonely, penniless widow, accustomed within the bounds of matrimony to the warmth and comforting reassurance of a physical relationship - should succumb, despite her earlier suspicions regarding his actions, to the advances of an employer who displayed toward her a certain tender solicitude does not necessarily mean that she is predisposed toward committing a peculiarly calculated and callous murder.

"You heard Mr Attorney General quote Congreve's lines - and I confess I could hardly believe my own ears, for it is not mere etiquette or the customary usages of the Bar which cause me to speak of him as 'distinguished' and 'learned', but a most sincere respect for his reputation - the lines, I say,

> *Heaven has no rage like love to hatred turned,*
> *Nor Hell a fury, like a woman scorned.*

"I put it to you, gentlemen, that this is my distinguished and learned friend's equivalent of Brabantio's

> *She has deceived her father, and may thee.*

"Before God, gentlemen! Is it seriously to be supposed that you are to retire to the room set aside for you deliberation over my client's fate, and that you will say to yourselves, 'Well, Mr Attorney General told us that Hell has no fury like a woman scorned, so Mrs Diana Tuttle must hang? Of course it is not, and my distinguished and learned friend would be as appalled as myself if he thought that was the way you would set about the matter. No... what might be expected of you is that you will say, Mrs Diana Tuttle did this, and she knew that, and that she was at this place, and she had the opportunity if she so wished to do that, and since Hell has no fury like a woman scorned, she must be guilty as charged.

"But is not that an equal absurdity? Because, gentlemen, and I make no apology for saying it again, it is a sacred obligation placed upon the prosecution to prove its case beyond a shadow of a doubt, and upon you according to your oath to try it solely upon the basis of that proof - evidential proof! There has not been the least shred of evidence placed before you that Mrs Tuttle had any expectation whatever of Captain Meadowthorpe marrying her. The only argument Mr Attorney General has advanced to lead you to such a supposition is that because she weakened so far as to allow her employer to take advantage of her vulnerability (and perhaps it was the effect of misguided gratitude rather than base, animal passion), she must inevitably have hoped that he intended to marry her - and that when she discovered that he had no such intention, she fell into so deadly a fit of jealousy that she procured his death be slow poisoning. Now I put it to you, gentlemen, is that an example of proof positive? Could any of you endorse such an argument with the schoolboy's time-honoured tag *Quod erat demonstrandum*? Could you condemn any woman to be hanged by the neck on such evidence? I think not.

"Let me put to you the possibility that there may have been another motive for the killing of Captain Meadowthorpe. By his marriage and, it must be said, by the death of his wife, Captain Meadowthorpe had become a rich man. The motive to which I refer is, of course, not passion or fury, but cold financial greed. There has been no suggestion that I have heard - or you - that the accused was going to benefit materially from his death. There were those who did, but Mrs Tuttle was not one of them. You are not here as a coroner's jury, and we are not here to examine the circumstances of the death of Captain Meadowthorpe's wife. Your attention has been drawn, however, to the remarkably similar symptoms of Helena

Meadowthorpe's fatal illness and that of her husband. Perhaps I may be permitted to point out to you that nobody has suggested that the accused was in any way responsible for Mrs Meadowthorpe's death. It would scarcely have been possible, since Mrs Meadowthorpe fell ill in Florence, when Mrs Tuttle was in Hampstead.

"So here we have two examples of a person dying of a lingering sickness whose symptoms are - one might say, classically - those resulting from the administration of arsenic over a period lasting some weeks. Two, I repeat, gentlemen: those of a wife, and then her husband. The effects of these two deaths bear a remarkable similarity: both result in the transfer in ownership of a great deal of property."

The jurors in their sober, nonconformist suits, the members of the Bar in their rusting gowns and grimy, ill-fitting wigs, the members of the public in the gallery, silk-lapelled gentlemen and fashionable beauties in enormous feathered hats, and even Mr Justice Muckleburn himself, who had ceased hawking into a large spotted handkerchief - all sat motionless. Even the shorthand writers and the gentlemen of the press had stopped writing in anticipation of Marshall Hall offering an alternative accusation in court to that against his client.

"I say this, Gentlemen of the Jury," declared Marshall Hall, "only to emphasize the fact that the accused benefitted from neither of these deaths to any degree whatever. Not a sixpence - not a farthing - came her way. Indeed, were she not in the unfortunate situation in which you now see her, the only result she could have expected from her employer's death was to find herself without means, occupation, or shelter. Nor has there been any evidence to suggest that she had deluded herself into the belief that she might be a testatory beneficiary of the deaths of either Mrs or Captain Meadowthorpe. I expect, gentlemen, it will now have crossed your minds as to why my distinguished and learned friend, Mr Attorney General, employed that aphorism which - if I may quote Shakespeare again - *hath grown somewhat worn i'the use*. I refer, of course, to his remarks about Hell knowing no fury like a woman scorned. It is the sole possible motive left for him to ascribe to my poor client.

"But is it possible to hold with any degree of certainty that this was *un crime passionel*, as the French call it; a crime impelled by the sort of motive Mr Attorney General would have you believe drove Mrs Tuttle to murder her employer? Evidence has been placed before you for your careful consideration which may lead you to the conclusion that the poisoning of Captain Meadowthorpe was the result of a most carefully laid plan, schemed over many months. I need hardly remind you of the appearance before this court of the Princess Trubetskoy, a member of the highest nobility in her own, far distant country, with no interest in this case save the interest of any Christian lady in the cause of Truth and Justice. I need hardly suggest to you, gentlemen, the very natural reluctance that must have been experienced by a lady of the Princess's blood and birth at the thought of appearing before a criminal court in order to give evidence in a case which has excited, not to say gratified, the taste for sensationalism which informs our more popular newspapers. You will recall, I am sure, the delicacy of feeling demonstrated by His Lordship when he invited the Princess to take a seat beside him, under the symbol of royal authority, rather than she should have to expose herself by standing in the witness box.

"But do not let your memory of a beautiful and gracious noble-woman, and the unforced courtesy and consideration of His Lordship, cause you to put from your minds the significance of the evidence the Princess Trubetskoy caused to be placed before you, and to which she testified. She was inspecting the property of the late Captain Meadow-thorpe on Squire's Mount in Hampstead, with a view to purchasing it as a *pied-à-terre* for her visits to London. In the so-called 'secret' compartment of the late Captain Meadowthorpe's private bureau, her servant discovered a sheet of paper. It was a schedule for the personal administration of some liquid compound, undated to be sure, but with the intervals and times of day when the compound should be administered, together with the precise dosage.

"It was never my purpose to ask you to draw any conclusion from my examination of Mr Villiers Manyon regarding his culpability in this sorry business. If the dictum that this is not a court of morals is to be applied to the accused, it must stand even more strongly where a witness on oath is concerned. It may have occurred to you that Mr Manyon is little better than the keeper of a disorderly house within the meaning of the law - albeit one so expensive that it would be unlikely to tempt you or I from the path of virtue..."

An excellent point, thought Mycroft. There was nothing more calculated to arouse the prejudices of your chapel-going tradesman than a whiff of vice among the wealthy.

"...Nevertheless, in the absence of any proof to the contrary, his word upon his solemn oath must be taken to be as reliable as that of any man of the cloth. My sole concern was to draw your attention, gentlemen of the jury, to the fact - for fact it is, and beyond dispute - that my client, had never as far as has been proved purchased or acquired arsenic. There was a schedule drawn up of advice on the employment of arsenic suspended in chloral in order to procure the death of a human being; but it was a schedule which my client neither drew up nor read (you would hardly suppose she would have left it in her victim's desk for anybody to find if it had been hers).

"We have, on the other hand, a house not a quarter of a mile away where arsenic is in general and daily use; where there is an example, the very rare example, an almost unique example you might suppose, of the type-writing machine which was used to print the schedule; and where there is also, or so you might think, abundant motive for the crime, namely the acquisition by Mr Villiers Manyon's young daughter, Parthenope, of that wealth which apparently - I will go no further than that - had been lost to the Manyon family when Manyon's ward, Helena, had married Captain Meadowthorpe.

"As we have made clear, we are not here to point any finger in accusation, or even to suggest the identity of somebody who should be standing there..."

He did point his finger - directly up at the small pale face of Mrs Tuttle.

"...where that poor, guiltless lady sits under the shadow of the noose. I seek only to demonstrate to you that there are other individuals walking free, perhaps several, against whom the evidence regarding their possible implication in this case points more strongly than that presented against my client. I must repeat - I make no accusation. I remind myself even as I remind you of those words uttered by His Lordship upon another occasion, which should be framed and hung in every court of law in the land:

Strange are the coincidences of Truth.

"But if we are to bear in mind these words of a wise judge when we are thinking of the proprietor of the Vale of Health Lakeside Spa Hotel, how much more so should we bear them in mind when we are thinking of this poor lady! Already we have heard Mr Attorney General suggest that, because she was capable of a single moral lapse - I do not deny that it was a grievous one, and grievously has the unfortunate lady answered for it! She is therefore capable of ever more dreadful offenses. I beg you to remember that in the sphere of sexual morals women are, for the most part, what men make them. There is no reason to suppose that because a woman is the lowest and most degraded of her kind - and I am thinking not of my client, but of those that haunt the garish thoroughfares of the metropolis at night - even if she trades her body shamelessly in the market-place, she will necessarily be disposed to kill a fellow human being. Gentlemen, on the evidence before you I dare you to find a verdict of wilful murder - dare you to find it in the face of so much doubt, such implausibility. Gentlemen, have you been given the least iota of a reason to suppose that this poor woman is capable of the crime with which she is charged? Do you know that it is the practice in this land that when there is a charge of fatal poisoning against a prisoner the task of prosecuting that prisoner is laid upon the most distinguished trial lawyer in the land - I mean, of course, my distinguished and learned friend, Mr Attorney General? And do you know why, gentlemen? It is because murder by poisoning is regarded as the most heinous, the blackest, the most evil of all such crimes. Murder by poisoning must be premeditated. There is no other way. And you, gentlemen, are being asked to take an oath before the throne of Almighty God that you believe this poor woman, this pitiful creature, to be a Messalina, a Lucrezia Borgia! Gentlemen, I defy you to do it! And when you have done it, to have to live with that picture before you..."

He held his outstretched palm towards Mrs Tuttle. He let his voice fall into a whisper:

"...for the rest of your days!"

The excellent Mrs Turner, thought Mycroft to himself, would have called it 'egging the pudding'; there was too much at stake here for even a young man's self-indulgent display of histrionics. But then he heard a strange, frog-like croak from the jury-box. He looked, and saw that one of the jurors, a square-shouldered, waxed-moustached fellow who might well have been a retired army warrant officer, had broken down and was sobbing noisily into a large handkerchief. He turned to look at Mr Justice Muckleburn; the ancient, purple-faced, scarlet robed figure was slumped back in his judicial throne, his wig awry, and was dabbing the corners of his eyes with his ceremonial gloves. Suddenly the entire courtroom was filled with the sound of applause, applause which nobody seemed incline to try to silence. To his astonishment, Mycroft beheld Sir Richard Webster, the Attorney General himself, lean forward to reach across the bench to where Marshall Hall had sat down in a theatrical attitude of exhaustion, and to shake his hand in manly approval. Relieved though he was that the case had been won in all respects save the necessary legal formalities,

Mycroft could not entirely overcome his distaste over such an intemperate, modern display of public emotion.

Marshall Hall, for his part, had indeed been enjoying himself, and now he was basking in the approval that was being displayed toward him on all sides. But he too felt a core of unease in the centre of his satisfaction. He had not thought of it when he was on his feet; now that he was finished he was forced to remind himself that, however great his success, it would not make Ethel love him, or save him from the carping, febrile misery she displayed almost perpetually in his company.

He felt as if, when he had been standing up addressing the jury, he had been taking a holiday from his domestic unhappiness.

Epilogue

"I shall go to my family's home in Petersburg," Princess Sophie announced. "It is on Stone Island. It looks quite like that!"

She was walking in St James's Park in the low afternoon sunlight, her hand resting on Mycroft's arm. She pointed her parasol across the lake to the Horseguards.

"From a certain angle, of course," she added. "In a certain light."

"As grand as that, Princess?" Mycroft asked.

"Oh yes!" she replied lightly. "It is quite peaceful there, you know," she went on. "And the white nights in Peter are magical. Will you come with me, Mr Holmes? Cyril is coming; he wishes to see the apartment on Moika where our great Pushkin lived. So you won't be lonely for your beloved London..." Her voice trailed away; she knew that any attempt to seduce Mycroft away from the immediate vicinity of the Diogenes Club was futile.

Mycroft raised his hat to a couple with a small dog, who appeared to claim his acquaintance. They smiled and nodded back, while the dog, straining at its leash, yapped at ducks sailing on the lake.

"You are most kind, Princess," Mycroft told her. "But my government duties, you know... There will be trouble in Ireland shortly. Mr Parnell is as accomplished a political strategist as any in the House, but many of his followers believe in conspiracy and armed revolt. There are also the Musselmen of the Upper Nile. Already they are at war; it is only a question of time before their leaders declare *Jihad* - a holy war against the infidel - which in our case means against Her Majesty's representatives in the Sudan."

"*Bozhe moy!*" Sophie laughed. "How can you tell me things with so much certainty?"

"It is my *métier*," he replied simply.

They continued strolling in the evening calm.

"I shall be returning to London earlier than usual," Sophie told him. "In the middle of August. I am to be the doyenne of the ladies-of-honour - is that the right expression? - at Grand Duchess Jolande's wedding on the seventeenth of September. I shall have to pay a visit to Worth, in Paris - and it is so much easier to travel to Paris from London than from my mother's home in Nice."

"Who is to look after your new home on Squire's Mount in your absence?" asked Mycroft.

"Diana Tuttle, of course," said Sophie.

"You are taking Mrs Tuttle into your employ?" Mycroft asked.

"I have taken her into my employ, dear friend," Sophie replied. "Who better to look after Squire's Mount for me than somebody already familiar with the place?"

"And somebody familiar with the secret compartments of your bureau?" Mycroft asked.

She took her hand from his arm. "Mr Holmes! You are not suggesting...?"

"That she was guilty of poisoning her lover? No," he replied. "But a sort of accessory - an accessory who may not have been entirely conscious of being an accessory. I mean no more than that."

"You must explain exactly what you do mean, Mr Holmes," she warned him.

"Princess!" he said in a chiding tone of voice, as if surprised by her obtuseness over the matter. "The woman had her suspicions regarding the death of Mrs Meadowthorpe; now her beloved Captain starts sickening in exactly the same way! She has no idea as to what the fellow is up to - though you may depend upon it, she suspects that he is up to something. It doesn't occur to her, of course, that his intention is to incriminate her. But he is about to desert her in favour of Parthenope Manyon, if he has not done so already. So she lets him carry on having his bouts of sickness... I am not suggesting that she intended he should die. Perhaps she wished only to punish him by letting him suffer a little. Perhaps, even, she hoped to gain a stronger place in his affections by her devotion in nursing him - men have been known to marry their nurses, don't you know..."

"But Meadowthorpe killed himself," said Sophie.

"Only according to a Gradgrind notion of fact," Mycroft replied. "He was murdered - murdered - by Villiers Manyon, who persuaded Meadowthorpe to follow the course he did so that he might remove the least vestige of suspicion regarding himself over the death of his wife and incriminate Mrs Tuttle. It was Manyon, I dare say, who fixed on that last fateful night, who set the precise time at which Meadowthorpe should take the final dose and when he should send Mrs Tuttle for Dr Bickleigh. I am entirely certain that he reassured the wretched man that he would be present that evening in Dr Bickleigh's house to ensure that, whatever occurred, Bickleigh would arrive at Squire's Mount not so soon that Meadowthorpe could not hide the poison bottle in Mrs Tuttle's room, but soon enough to preserve him from the worst effects of the dose, and to be witness to his accusation against her.

"I need hardly point out to you, my dear Princess, that his actual motive for being at Dr Bickleigh's was the precise opposite: that he wished to make sure Bickleigh did not reach his patient before the poison had taken its desired effect... Well! The fellow was an intolerable bounder. He deserved to be allowed to die; as a confirmed gambler, he had left his marker with Death since his disgraceful behaviour at the Rorke's Drift Mission... In any case, I'm sure Mrs Tuttle will prove an excellent housekeeper."

A fragment of breadcrumb was on the path at his feet. With the ferule of his stick, he flicked it over the grass verge into the lake, and watched as one of the ducks paddled across to snatch it.